ELEANOR WASSERBERG is a graduate of the Creative Writing Programme at the University of East Anglia. Originally from Staffordshire, she now lives in Norwich. Her first novel, *Foxlowe*, was longlisted for the Authors' Club Best First Novel Award and shortlisted for the 2016 East Anglian Book Awards and the Shirley Jackson Novel Prize.

Praise for *The Light at the End of the Day*:

'A masterpiece of storytelling. Eleanor Wasserberg is a skilled portrait artist of the human instinct, and her characters are perfectly balanced in their intricate colours, beauty and flaws. This book broke my heart'

NICK BRADLEY, author of *The Cat and the City*

'Haunting, magnificent and deeply personal. It will stay with you' RACHEL EDWARDS, author of *Darling*

'Psychologically acute and emotionally absorbing, this distinctive tale of a privileged Polish-Jewish family overcome by the horrors of war is full of unforgettable characters. The Oderfeldts' refusal to believe what is happening to them at every turn has something urgent to say to us now'

RACHEL HORE, author of *Last Letter Home*

'A beautiful and tragic story of love, cruelty and loss. Wasserberg is a natural storyteller with hypnotic descriptive powers. In her company you feel completely held, as if in the palm of a hand'

MEGAN BRADBURY, author of *Everyone is Watching*

'Among so many other books set in this period, I found this story to have something new to share. The Oderfeldts are the sort of family you would usually love to hate, flawed and spoiled by their privilege, but watching them lose everything felt like a tragedy. This is a story that highlights the strength that can exist within all of us and the importance of friendship when there is nothing else left'

LOUISE HARE, author of *This Lovely City*

'Superb – the terrifying chaos of the Second World War is brilliantly realised by Wasserberg, whose very fine writing ensures that even minor characters are brought compellingly to life. Rich in evocative detail, and heartrending'

FRANCES LIARDET, author of *We Must Be Brave*

Also by Eleanor Wasserberg:

Foxlowe

The Light at the End of the Day

ELEANOR WASSERBERG

4th Estate • London

This book is dedicated to Ignace,
to Jerzy (George) and to Mark Stefan

4th Estate
An imprint of HarperCollins*Publishers*
1 London Bridge Street
London SE1 9GF

www.4thEstate.co.uk

HarperCollins*Publishers*
1st Floor, Watermarque Building, Ringsend Road
Dublin 4, Ireland

First published in Great Britain in 2020 by 4th Estate
This 4th Estate paperback edition published in 2021

1

Set in Adobe Garamond Pro

Printed and bound in CPI Group (UK) Ltd, Croydon

MIX
Paper from
responsible sources
FSC™ C007454

This book is produced from independently certified FSC™ paper
to ensure responsible forest management

Find out more about HarperCollins and the environment at
www.harpercollins.co.uk/green

There is a gold light in certain old paintings
That represents a diffusion of sunlight.
It is like happiness, when we are happy.
It comes from everywhere and from nowhere at once,
   this light . . .

The world is very dusty, uncle. Let us work.
One day the sickness shall pass from the earth for good.
The orchard will bloom; someone will play the guitar.
Our work will be seen as strong and clean and good.
   And all that we suffered through having existed
   Shall be forgotten as though it had never existed.

'There is a gold light in certain old paintings'

DONALD JUSTICE

Kraków, 1939

I

THE ODERFELDT APARTMENT was the last building on the grand Ulica Bernardyńska, its final, corner jewel. One side looked out over the river, but it was the sight from the dining room the neighbours envied: a perfect view of Wawel Castle. The red brick walls of the Wawel jutted out into the street, as though reaching for their neighbour, and a turret sat exactly opposite the window of the main drawing room, as though they had been designed to mirror each other. Dining in that drawing room under the gaze of portrait faces in golden frames, many imagined they were at the Wawel itself, some state occasion, looking out over the terraces and turrets, the flash of green lawn. Adam Oderfeldt liked to smoke his pipe on the apartment terrace with his artist friends, and watch the sky darken over the green-tinged tower tops. On summer evenings the family threw open the windows and invited neighbours and friends for parties in the shadow of the heart of Poland.

Janina Kardas was navigating her way towards the Oderfeldt apartment, in the strangely cheerful sunshine of early afternoon. She wore her best clothes: a fur hat and a heavy winter coat, beautifully tailored with a matching ermine trim. The coat and hat were too warm for early September in the city, but she wished to display herself today as a woman of obvious good breeding. She remembered snatches of German

3

refugee tales, how people were stopped in the street. She imagined herself seized, accosted, jostled, until the attacker, in some kind of uniform, noticed her coat, her hat, and looked then into her delicately lined face, not young or pretty enough to be in danger, she comforted herself, but somehow authoritative. He would step back, uneasy, for surely she knew people, surely her husband was someone of importance? And Janina's imaginary self sneered a little, tugged her clothing back into place, patted her hat back onto its perch, and strode away.

Janina passed the shuttered bakery. Two weeks ago the baker had been holding forth yet again, lectures that war was coming. It had been the same for weeks, pastries and doom, and she was irritated by it. The shelves and displays had all been empty that day, and upstairs, heavy footsteps had dragged heavier furniture.

'You're leaving?'

'It will happen soon,' he'd said, chewing the thin lips on his lean face, so wrong for a baker, who really ought to be fat, adding, 'I'm going to Lwów, I'm not sticking around.'

'But my rolls and doughnuts,' she had replied.

The baker had rolled his thin lips in and out then leaned in so she could smell the ginger on his breath. 'You are crazy,' he whispered. '*You* should get out of Kraków. You and all your . . . set.' He nodded slowly as though passing on a secret code.

'What a lot of hysteria!' she said. She lowered her voice. 'I'm not some poor Jew in Germany. And so what about my pastries? Am I to starve because of your paranoia?' The baker shrugged, dismissing her, and she swept out past a group of poorer women who had caught the idea 'war' in the room and were worrying about it. Only a week or so later, Janina thought the word 'war' had become so familiar it had lost its sting, until the radio spoke it, and she could have folded in on herself like an earwig in terror.

Now she tried to ignore the crowd, who were muttering phrases that frightened her. A woman holding a boy's hand, wearing an ugly green shawl, was saying to an old man, 'But we have surrendered, haven't we? The radio . . .' and as she passed a couple pulling suitcases, the woman's hair all in disarray, pins sticking out like a sewing cushion doll, Janina heard the man muttering, 'They say the army is decimated, just utterly decimated.' As she hurried down Bernardyńska, Janina yelped as people brushed against her, even jostled her without apology, crushing the fur on the edge of her coat. She heard snatches of conversations that made her head pound. They became a rhythm with her feet on the pavement: *no, it is a matter of days, it is a matter of hours, it is now, we must leave, we must leave.*

By the time she reached the Oderfeldt apartment, shameful sweat coated her lower back and her temples. Janina rang three times, holding the bell longer than was polite, before a servant finally came. It wasn't one she remembered, but the girl did an awkward little bob, flustered, and said, 'Oh, another one, are you come to see from the windows too? They are all upstairs—' and then she ran off before Janina could reply.

She was left to walk up the stairs alone, and the strangeness of it made her feel shy: no servant to announce her, no invitation, but then nothing was as it should be these days. She was reassured by the gleam of the banister and the thickness of the rug she could feel through her boots. From the main drawing room came muffled sounds of voices, sounding quite relaxed; she determined to dismiss the servant's alarm, and find comfort in her kind of sensible people.

Entering the room, Janina noticed first the elegant buttoned back of Anna Oderfeldt's dress. She smoothed down her own coat, feeling dowdy as always in comparison to Anna. Along the windows, a row of backs: scarves obscuring hair and faces, hats on inside, people craning and on tiptoe. A drone of low, shaking voices. The Oderfeldt daughters were there, Alicia with her face pressed to the glass, her hands splayed out, smudging the pane. She always behaved like a baby, this one; she must be thirteen or so now, but indulged into endless infancy. Her older sister Karolina paced, wearing boots inside. She looked purposeful, grown up, as though she were to announce a plan soon. Perhaps they were about to leave. Janina tried to catch Karolina's eye, but she was unseeing, moving her lips a little as though rehearsing a speech, or praying. Unsure what to do, Janina cleared her throat quietly, then loudly. Adam Oderfeldt turned and gave her a tight-lipped smile.

'Ah! Another neighbour come for the view. Come, Mrs Kardas. Janina.'

She smiled her approval. At least Adam was behaving like a gentleman, observing the formalities.

'Would you like a drink?' Adam offered. He gestured to the sideboard, where vodka and *nalewki* sat in shining decanters. Anna turned too, pale as milk, but her gaze slid to Karolina, still walking behind Janina, before she was drawn back to the window.

'No, thank you, Mr Oderfeldt. I just wanted to . . . I wondered if . . .'

Others turned then, just for a moment. The same pale faces, pinched with confusion. She recognised acquaintances from her son's school, lawyers and their wives who had come to dinner, doctors like her husband, Adam's friend Stefan from the university, the Hartmanns, David Schultz and his ugly bride of only a year, or was it two? Janina and her husband Laurie had gone to the wedding, before he died, and given them a generous gift of Meissen china. Had they ever received a thank-you note? Janina didn't think so, and returned the wife's weak smile with a cold blankness.

'Yes, come and see. There's nothing clear, but come look at her if you like,' Adam replied.

She joined the others, craning and peering. The castle looked empty and serene – immovable. It seemed to promise that everything would be all, all right. The red brick glowed in the early autumn sunlight, cheerful against the bright blue sky. Janina remembered telling her son Aleks the story of a dragon who lived in a cave beneath the castle, fire-breathing and strong, its heart beating for the city. He'd listened and then solemnly lectured her that this was just a story, and that real dragons were called dinosaurs. That was when Laurie was still alive; she'd gone straight to tell him, that already their baby said no more stories, and she'd cried on his shoulder like a fool. It's all right, he said to her. It's all, all right.

For a stomach-dropping moment, Janina thought she saw a soldier on the lawns around the castle, a man running, but then he was gone; perhaps she'd imagined it. Below them, in the street, the pool of people she had waded through had become a flood.

'Are you leaving?' she murmured to Anna, at her side.

'It seems so calm,' Anna whispered.

'You know the Friels already left? Two days ago. They've left everything behind. It's all just sitting in their house,' Janina said, unsure if she was soothed or alarmed by Anna's show of nonchalance.

'They've probably just gone to visit family,' Anna replied, in the same low tone, but on quickening breath that told her irritation, or perhaps her fear.

Down the line of watchers, the same murmur rose, *maybe we should leave too, just for a while . . .*

'Ben Friel wore a *kippah* every day, not just for special occasions,' Anna added.

'Yes, and they had a mezuzah on their doorframe,' Janina readily added, before dropping her gaze to the street once more. She remembered her mother's marble mezuzah, packed up in the attic along with all her things from the old house. She had meant to nail it outside their own apartment door, imagined the comfort in passing the old talisman as she came and went, a relic of childhood. Instead it had remained in its box all these years. It was the first time she had thought of it for so long. Would someone search the house, find it? She wanted to ask Anna, but was stalled by her neighbour's slow movements, her cool sipping of the glass in her hands. It was childish to worry. It was vulgar to panic.

Janina caught sight of a group of Polish soldiers, heading away from the city, heads bowed, leaving their mothers behind. *You should be ashamed*, she thought. She wondered if her boy was safe.

'Do you think if you did decide to leave, I could come with you?' she murmured again to Anna, feeling a hot blush across her neck and chest.

But Anna had moved away, hadn't heard her; she was kissing the cheeks of the Hartmanns, first the wife and then the husband. The wife, Miriam, had an old spat with Janina that went back to the girl wearing too much make-up, and walking out with Aleks when they were too young. Janina had called the girl a slut. The optician, Miriam's father, had refused to treat Janina after that, and she had to travel across the city into the old district, back to her childhood doctor. Now, Miriam's heavy mascara streamed down her cheeks, collected in ugly clumps in the creases of her eyes. Her eyes slipped over Janina, who wanted, suddenly, to apologise to her, to take her hand, but instead she stood mute. She turned back to the window to hide her awkwardness there.

'There must have been another radio announcement,' she said. 'Look how many people there are out in the streets now.'

'They can't be in the Wawel already, you don't think?' Stefan Lis said, his voice muffled by glass as he pressed his face once more against the window.

'No new flag there, as you see,' Adam replied, pouring another vodka. His hand played a tune between decanter and glass. 'It will be all right,' he added.

It will all be all, all right. Janina caught herself in the windows, nodding as though to ritual prayer or radio music.

'Look at them all leaving,' Miriam said to her husband, and he raised his voice in return, breaking the hush of the room: 'But where will they all go? Why make ourselves homeless, stateless, when we don't even know—'

'They'll go to the border, Tomas, and then see from there,' Miriam replied, her voice suddenly full of disdain. Everyone smiled and nodded *goodbyes* and *good lucks* at them even as Tomas continued to insist, 'We're not going to leave, at least not just yet . . . Adam, we'll be here for dinner tomorrow . . .' and the discussion continued out of the room and down the stairs.

'And Mrs Kardas, where are you going?' Adam called.

'Oh! Home. Such a lot of nonsense and hysteria.'

2

ANNA ODERFELDT watched her widowed neighbour disappear down the stairs in her old-fashioned hat and coat. A mean relief rose in her; if Adam had overheard Janina, it would have been hopeless, but he was too distracted, enjoying, as always, the way their home was the hub of the street. She had hoped Janina would be too embarrassed to ask again to join them, had banked on her stuffy ways. If Anna were to dwell on it, past the gaping fear, she would find how guilty she felt, how wrong it was to let the old woman drift away like that. How vulnerable and small old Janina had seemed, almost tiptoeing down the stairs. Instead she stood as still as possible, tensed her muscles, deepened her breathing. *Harden yourself*, she thought, *be wood, be ice, be steel. Are you going to let an old woman slow you down, while you get your daughters to safety, their smooth, pale skin, their soft bodies that a bullet will tear through like silk?*

Soon the drawing room was quiet, emptied of its guests. Karolina had slipped away, probably to use the telephone, or send a final letter, Anna thought, and she found space among the tides of her thoughts to pity her heartbroken daughter, even as she envied her the simple distraction of such a clean, sharp emotion. Alicia had slipped behind the drawing-room curtains, still fixed on the view of the city below. Those curtains had been a wedding gift from her brother-in-law: thick pink damask lined with silk.

'I'll tell Janie to take down the curtains,' Anna said.

'They have curtains in Lwów,' Adam replied, with a smile.

'We could . . . sell them, or use them for something else. I've heard refugees can—'

'Aneczka, we are not refugees! We are going to stay with family until things calm down.'

Alicia unwrapped herself from the curtain, her face flushed and hot, just as Janie, her face also blotched red, came into the drawing room without knocking.

'Madam,' she said, 'please select which clothes you would like us to pack in the girls' rooms.'

'I want my painting, Janie,' Alicia instructed.

'Are you going to wear your painting?' Anna snapped. 'Are you going to eat it?'

'Are we going to eat and wear the curtains?' Alicia replied.

'Now, now,' Adam said, as though hushing a baby. 'Of course we should take the things we love, just in case.'

Janie and Dorothea rolled and pressed, clicked shut trunks of fabric and books. In Karolina's room, Alicia and Karolina pulled on layer upon layer, buttoned into fur coats so they sweated as they pulled on their boots.

'What else do you want to take?' Karolina asked, cupping her sister's face in her hands.

'My sketches. Are you taking your poems?'

'Some of the books, but I can't take all of them . . . and my letters . . .'

Alicia studied her sister's face. 'How many are there?'

'Lots. He writes every day.'

'Too many to take.'

'Probably,' Karolina said, her voice breaking.

Alicia silently took her by the hand and led her to her own room, full of piles of unpacked clothes and shoes. She crouched down at a corner under a never-used desk.

'What are you doing?'

Alicia ignored her. She felt along the skirting board for the loose panel, pressing on it until it gave way. She held out a hand from beneath the desk.

'What's in there?'

'Just sketches and things.' She felt into the dusty space, where diaries, translations and sketch after sketch were hidden.

Karolina ran to her bookshelf and returned with a stash of letters, which she kissed before handing them to Alicia to tuck behind the walls.

As the hour ticked by, Karolina went down again and again to check for messages, to ask if the telephone had rung. Each time Janie shook her head, kissed Karolina on her hand or her cheek, and each time Karolina said, 'Well, there's still time,' and Janie replied, 'Perhaps he is on his way, in person.'

By early evening, the house had taken on the strange echo of a stripped building. In the main hallway, their Persian rugs had been rolled into thick, red sausages, lumped where diamonds were sewn into the backs. Silk dresses, fur coats, pairs of Parisian gloves with pearl edging, books, papers: they were all layered against the walls, some in leather cases, others in boxes and even baskets from the kitchen. The radio drifted between static and news of the new, almost bloodless occupation, in Polish and German words. Adam rushed back to the dining-room window, but the Wawel looked just the same. Across the city, people did the same thing, expecting the sky, the colour of buildings, even their own faces reflected in the windows, to have changed. Rushing to gather together their possessions, to keep the servants and their daughters calm, Adam and Anna passed on the stairs, stopped, held hands, pressed their foreheads together.

'I can't believe it,' Anna whispered.

'Perhaps it isn't true.'

'The radio.'

'Yes, all right. We're leaving soon.'

Janie, and even the cook, Dorothea, began to load up the beeswax-scented cars.

'Where is Robert?' asked Adam. 'I want to talk to him about the route.'

'Robert left early, sir,' Dorothea called to him as she leaned all her weight into a pile of material that would not fit into a case. Adam recognised the drawing-room curtains.

'Leave those, Dorota,' he said. 'Left where?'

'Well, out of the city of course, sir.'

The family stood in mute shock at this.

'Robert's gone?' Karolina said.

'But he was supposed to drive us – that can't be right,' Anna said, strangely close to laughing. 'Has he really gone?'

The servant women were frowning, whether at Robert's sedition or the family's response, it was impossible to tell.

'He has family,' Dorothea said, as though this explained everything. Adam stared at her. 'He's a Jew,' she added, in a tone close to snapping.

'Hysteria, just hysteria,' Adam muttered, but he himself began to stack random objects in the hallway, and the family followed him, began to help packing. To Alicia it was like playing upstairs when she was small, carrying piles of laundry and sighing in an imitation of Janie. She used to imagine how strong and capable she looked, and how the flush of exercise might make her cheeks glow in a pretty way.

Adam carried his paintings, slid in like secrets among the layers in the cars: Adam's own face in paint with his red hair and smiling eyes. Alicia's wild four-year-old face with her fringe, unfinished in its beautiful frame. Alicia's pretty brown-eyed stare, her red dress billowing confidence in its rich, lush folds.

In the hallway, the family stood in the new echoing space, with so many rugs and paintings gone. Both servants were sweating, and Janie was crying.

'Well,' Anna said, 'we'll be back before long.'

Janie pulled Karolina and then Alicia into her, kissing their heads. Alicia was stiff and shocked but Karolina clung to Janie's neck. They shook hands and Dorothea even kissed Anna's cheek.

'Good luck,' Janie said, and then she melted back into the house, wiping her face.

'We will be leaving too, sir, very soon, so we'll lock up the house,' Dorothea said.

'Papa, what about Mimi and Cece?' Alicia asked. 'Will they come with us or with the servants?'

Adam didn't answer.

'I'll leave the dogs some water and food,' Dorothea said, smiling down at Alicia.

Then she too was gone, her shoes sounding loud and hurried on the naked stairs down to the kitchen.

'Go and use the toilet,' Karolina instructed her sister. Alicia blushed and stared: only Janie spoke to her of such things.

'Yes, go,' Anna joined in. 'Who knows when we will stop.'

As Alicia obeyed, her sister turned to her parents.

'Papa. Mama. I—'

'Darling Karolcia, I know what you're going to say and it's impossible,' Adam said.

Karolina shifted her feet. 'I can't leave him. I won't.'

Anna could have shaken her, made her teeth rattle. She tried to keep her voice level. 'Karolina, the whole country is under attack. They're saying Kraków is Germany now. Do you understand? We have to leave.' Karolina met her with dreamy silence, her eyes brimming. 'You're enjoying this,' Anna snapped, as Adam tutted at her harsh tone. 'This isn't some romantic drama.'

But Karolina wouldn't pick up Anna's bait, instead looked to her father.

Her parents shared a glance, in which a long-practised battle of wills was settled in Adam's favour. Anna sighed out her frustration. As she left she considered holding Karolina's face in hers, in apologetic admiration of the stubborn set of her daughter's jaw. Instead she vented at Janie as she went down the stairs, 'Perhaps you might move a little more slowly? I'm not sure the entire German army will have time to come and steal quite *all* of our things!' Her voice faded as she stepped out into the street, lit a cigarette, her hands shaking a little.

Father and daughter faced each other. Karolina began. 'I know you think I'm asking permission but I'm not. I'm just informing you that I'm staying. You can write to me at his address, if you stay out of Kraków for a long while.'

This wrong-footed Adam, who had been braced for a stormy passionate speech, not this calm informative one. He aimed to set Karolina off-balance in turn.

'I see. Are you in trouble?'

Karolina's cheeks flooded red and she stammered out a *No*. Adam pushed his guilt away.

'Then there is simply no need to be reckless.'

'I can't leave him here.'

'You've told him we're leaving?'

'Yes.'

'He's written?'

'No.'

'Telephoned, spoken to your mother, spoken to me?'

Karolina glared at him. 'It's chaos,' she said. 'The message might not have got through.'

Adam took Karolina's hands in his. His own elegant, soft fingers folded over her chewed nails and torn cuticles. He saw in them his daughter's hours of innocent fretting over her lover, while her parents felt the very ground lurch under their feet.

'May I suggest a compromise, my Karolcia?'

She nodded.

'His apartment is on our way out of the city. We'll stop there, and you can speak to him. Tell him he must come with us, because, no, listen—' for Karolina had begun to withdraw her hands, shaking her head. 'Because it is as impossible for us to leave you behind as it is for you to leave him. If he loves you as he says, he will come, we'll take him. And you can marry in Lwów if you like, from your uncle's house. If he will not, his love is not enough and so you must make your farewells and recover.'

'He will come,' Karolina said.

'Well then, everyone is happy.' He kissed her hands, one and then the other, feeling the rough edge of her torn skin under his lip.

Without Robert they had only one driver, so everything had been moved into the larger car, and the sisters perched on top of their possessions, their necks twisted against the roof. As the car pulled away, Alicia imagined the dogs scampering around the empty rooms, enjoying freedom, scratching the walls, sleeping in Papa's bed, on the satin sheets. She imagined them greeting the soldiers as they came in with excited whines and yelps, and being shot between their watery brown eyes.

Karolina buried her elation as deep as she could. She knew it was indecent to be so happy. The war had decided things for them after waiting for so long. Within a month they could be married. She felt a surge of joy and squashed it by focusing on the familiar street, telling herself she might never see it again; she found she could not care.

Sun glinted on shop front windows. It was as though they were leaving for a late summer holiday in the mountains or to meet a train with a visitor from Berlin or Paris, Anna thought. As they continued onto the main roads out of the city, she saw lives carried in baskets and on backs, pushed in carts and prams.

Alicia saw a boy with a half-eaten apple, his mouth full, cheeks puffed out like a mouse, as though he must eat all of the food at once, before it was too late.

'Papa,' Alicia said, 'we didn't bring any food or anything to drink.'

A long silence, in which the crowd they crawled through called out to itself: *Let me through, for God's sake, let me through. Did you hear that?* Their own panicked stupidity hung over the car, and Anna felt the terrible impulse to laugh again.

'We'll hold on until Lwów,' Adam replied. 'Your uncle will have a whole table of treats for us. You are going to have to learn,' Adam said, raising his voice, 'to be hungry and to be patient.'

His knuckles on the steering wheel were pushing against the skin, a ripple running through his hands. Alicia shifted, the hidden rug-diamonds pushing at her muscles.

An hour later they were still in the city. The roads were clogged. Waves of panic struck the crowd when rumours of planes began, though the sky was clear and silent. Some cowered next to the car, which shivered with the weight of their bodies pressed against it. A man gripped the door handle on Anna's side, sheltering under his jacket. She shrieked, kicked out as though to shoo the man away.

'Just drive, Adam,' she pleaded. 'They will move.'

But the carts and the throng and the horses made an impassable ocean. Adam nudged and blew the car horn and each time the car shuddered to a halt the mounds of beautiful things tottered. Little thuds in the earth, against the car, among the crowd, turned Karolina's mind to her book, forgotten on her bed. The god Poseidon shaking his trident, whipping up the winds, the earth, the oceans. The thuds grew: a fight had broken out. Shouts of wordless rage. The crowd surged one way, then another. The car rocked and Karolina let out a squeal. Alicia clamped her hand over her own mouth as she saw the source of the disturbance: two German soldiers, their rifles gleaming, walked towards the car. *They are here.* The crowd parted around them as a shoal of fish.

Adam's knuckles working, their grind and roll, was the only movement in the car. Breaths held, the family became a painting, locked in place. Alicia wanted to look at her mother but instead she saw only the bright white fur of her collar from the corner of her eye, the very tip of her mother's chin, and the slow pace of the soldiers, one bending down, graceful as he touched the side of the car. He turned to his colleague and gave a low whistle of appreciation.

The first soldier rapped politely on Papa's car window. *Tap-tap-tap.* Quick, businesslike. His companion shielded his eyes and peered into the car, nodding at Anna when he caught her eye, and at this courtesy Anna allowed her lungs to empty, slowly, without any kind of release, but it was something. The first soldier stood back, waiting.

'Adam,' Anna said.

Adam opened the door and the soldier pulled him out, without malice, without any moment of eyeball-to-eyeball triumph, and he didn't throw him to the ground, and there were no gunshots or heavy blows to Adam's head, he was not pushed to his knees, nor his coat dragged from him, he was not spat at. All of the horrors of Adam's humiliation, all of the imaginary moments of terror Alicia had dreamed awake for a long time: they did not happen. There was no blood. And yet Alicia screamed all the same, because her Papa was touched by a German soldier, and he was out of the car, and they were inside it.

'Stop, Alicia,' her mother whispered. The white panic of her eyes killed Alicia's scream in her throat.

Adam's head was bowed, his fists clenched but his face turned to the floor like a servant. They were demanding something, and Adam opened his hands. He flicked his gaze to Anna, and as she met his eyes she saw urgent terror. Anna could only nod and show her husband a second of raw horror of her own, a look of love and apology and anger all at once. She threw open her passenger door, and rushed to the back of the car, pulling out first Alicia, and then Karolina, with skin-breaking force, dragging them over the piles of their possessions. They tumbled out on a layer of detritus, instantly dusted and muddied by the fall, scrambled up and away from the car, away from Adam. The crowd swallowed them, hid them, Anna clutching her children to her hips.

'Mama, our things,' Alicia gasped. 'All our things. Mama, my painting.'

Kraków, 1937–1938

3

ALICIA'S FATHER led her by the hand through the damp, misty streets towards the Glowny. Her breath billowed like smoke. Warm lights were beginning to glow in the windows of the bakeries; their cinnamon sugar doughnuts sat fluffy, piping out scent and heat. She slowed, pulling Adam back, to look at a tower of pastries. She shook his wrist, meaning *Papa, I want.* It was usually enough. But Adam had other plans, and pulled her mittened hand back into a stroll. She trotted along, confused, but a bloom of excitement tempered her instinct to stamp and pout.

Mama had said it would be a surprise. 'I'm not coming,' she'd said, 'only your Papa and you. A special birthday treat.' Her mother had smiled and smoothed down the red satin of Alicia's new dress; it had been too thin for the wintry air but the seamstress had lined it for warmth that week. When Alicia and Papa left, her sister Karolina hadn't said goodbye.

Alicia pulled the fur closer around her, used the edge of it to stroke her cheek. It smelled of her mother's heady perfume: lilies and something like cake. The Glowny rose before them, the horses clopping around the cobblestones, the Cloth Hall standing in the centre, warm and inviting. Alicia wasn't allowed to wander in there, where cheap curios were sold: her places were the boutiques and sweet shops of the boulevards off the square, like the Ulica Floriańska, the street Mama said could be Paris. It was coming to the hour, and so the bugler would be playing his thin wail soon. Adam slowed, stamped his booted feet in the cold, and enveloped Alicia in his arms to listen. He was always respectful of the bugler.

'Think how cold he is up there, Alicia,' he said. 'Lucky us in our coats and furs.'

A small crowd gathered under the church spire to listen. Alicia admired their velvet capes and fur-lined hats, some in mink like hers. The women wore pearls over their coats and the men's boots were shiny like Papa's. Some of the men wore their small *kippah* at the back of their heads, white cotton or silk and decorated with coloured threads. Adam's was slightly different, in a dark blue, with a white threaded design. It looked like a drawing of an ocean, with his red hair around it the sand of a volcanic beach. Alicia looked around at the gathered people and wondered what their servants were like, and if they were as ugly and kind as her Janie. Adam grinned down at her and danced with her clumsily to the tune as others around them hummed softly and applauded when the glint of gold from the bugle disappeared.

'Happy Birthday, my Ala,' he said. Was that it? A trip to Glowny to see the bugler? For her last birthday she had received a music box and a doll, handmade in Prague and dressed in silk. She'd felt too old for the doll, but propped it against the sill with the others.

'Come,' her father said, 'I am taking you to dinner like a proper little princess!'

'Dinner? Not at home?'

She thought of the silver platters, and her new puppy on her lap, Karolina ignoring her.

Her Papa beamed at her. 'You shall sit and dine and you shall even drink wine. You are going to the best restaurant in town, as is fitting for a lady such as yourself. You are twelve now, no longer my little one.'

He made a little bow, stiff in his thick coat, and Alicia laughed as he darted a kiss onto her nose as he came close.

'Come.'

Adam led her across the square, past couples laughing and leaning their way to restaurants, and past the horses, the man playing a violin with a hat for change, the last shoppers with their arms full of boxes.

The Wentzl stood proudly at the edge of the Glowny, its windows aglow. Piano notes and the tinkle of cutlery and conversation floated across the square. Adam stepped back to let Alicia go in pride of place. The waiter, a penguin with a full beard like her father's, beamed down at Alicia in her satin and fur. She stood up straighter, and gave an imperious nod copied from her mother, eyes sliding away, neck turned just so.

They were ushered upstairs with an air of hurry, but Alicia moved slowly, her hand on the polished banister, feeling truly like a lady of a huge house, feeling like Mama, and enjoying the power of making everyone wait. Adam indulged her, and a waiter hovered with Adam's great overcoat, heavy and slipping in his hands.

The room was as grand as home. The walls were buttercup yellow, so the wintry weather dissolved into a summer light, as though they had stumbled into a fairy land in a snowy wood. The Glowny stretched below, framed by plush golden curtains that Alicia itched to roll up in. The table was set with flowers and shining silver. The waiter danced with elaborate precision to place her napkin around her throat. Adam kissed her hand as she sat. 'Happy Birthday,' he said.

Alicia was in heaven: her father all to herself, her sister at home, an adult treat just for her, and to be admired by Adam and the room, who she felt certain was gazing at her pretty face and curled hair. This was perhaps all she ever wanted, as well as the occasional treat and sweet and pretty dress. The deep wells in her, the unsatisfied untapped springs of her heart, stilled and were silent.

Adam ordered for her while she pulled at her white under-gloves, noticed with horror a hangnail, and slipped them back on, glancing around to check no one had noticed. She caught the eye of a lady in an old-fashioned dress who seemed to be looking at her with disgust. The woman sniffed, an ugly look distorting her face. She must have noticed the hangnail, Alicia realised, and flushed. She put her hands into her lap as the woman turned away.

Alicia was distracted from this by the arrival of cheese and bread, plates of butter, pickles, glistening beef in a sticky glaze. It was not so different from the food at home, but pret-tily arranged on gold-edged plates, and with sweet red wine that she sipped as elegantly as she could. Adam tested her on German and French verbs, asked what she was reading; she told him about the swallowed, stolen ruby of Agrapur, cut from the thief's belly by the Maharajah.

'Your sister shouldn't give you such things to read,' he said, but smiling and, she thought, impressed.

'Thank you, Papa,' she said, when she remembered to.

'You are welcome, my little Ala,' he replied. 'But this is not all,' he said, leaning back in his chair and opening his arms wide. 'There is another gift, but, really, it's for me so you must indulge your Papa.'

'Not a doll, Papa, please, I have so many . . . I'd like . . .' she cast about, caught off guard by the unexpected opportunity; she rarely ever had to ask for anything at all, 'a fur like this one of Mama's, or for her to give this one to me, will you ask her?'

She stroked the fur against her cheek again. That wasn't right, it wasn't what she wanted at all, but since she didn't know *what* she wanted, the white fur would do as well.

Adam laughed. 'I'm sure you can have it, but what else? Let's see if we thought the same.' He smiled, seeming delighted with this idea.

Alicia tried again. 'Lessons.'

'Lessons? In what? You want your governess back? Poor Miss Paula, I'm not sure she would have *us* again!'

She faltered. 'I don't know.'

'Piano? Riding?'

'Yes, riding,' she said, swallowing something.

'All right, we'll arrange it tomorrow.' Adam drained his glass. 'But you haven't guessed! Because it's a trick! It is something wonderful but also something that you will *not* like.'

His mouth twitched and Alicia understood. She slumped in her chair.

'This is something for your Mama and me. So we have something to remember how pretty you are. It is a treat for us. You will do it for us? And you will not . . . *sabotage?*'

Now she laughed. She'd been five years old, already the favourite. The young genius her Papa had paid to paint her was irritated by her fidgeting. He made her stand for long, silent, still minutes in the natural light, and she wanted to play with her sister. That night she grabbed a pair of scissors from the sewing kit in Janie's room and chopped off her hair in a jagged, spiteful line. Her parents had almost laughed themselves sick over her stubbornness, and paid the artist double when he said he would abandon the painting. Still it was left unfinished, her wild hair in wisps around a ghost-like chalky face. It hung in Papa's study, where he often liked to point it out to visitors and tell the story.

And now he wanted another.

'Is it the same man?' she asked.

Adam laughed again. 'No, darling Ala. I want to ask my friend Jozef Pienta. You'll like him! He is a great artist, and you know, quite poor.'

Alicia wrinkled her nose.

'He will then have the money to make even more beautiful things, and I will have another picture with your hair all shiny and long.'

Sweets arrived, pastries glazed with sugar syrup, creamy gelatinous pudding, ginger biscuits. Alicia tried to finish her wine, but its sharpness hurt her throat.

'Here,' Papa said. He came around to her side and dunked a biscuit into the wine, ate it.

'Papa!' she shrieked, deliciously outraged. 'Manners!' He laughed deeply, held out his arms to encompass the golden shining room, so people turned to look. Alicia's awareness of the woman in the corner, the hangnail, came back to her, and she wished he would sit down again.

'Why, isn't this my city, my table? My biscuit, my wine?' He laughed again, deep and mellow, and Alicia poured her wine over her dessert like a syrup, ate until her stomach swelled and her head swam.

Later, she'd return again and again to this night. The sharp sweetness of the wine and cream. The waiters crowding plates among the candles so the food caught some of the golden flame, and the whole room in gold, as the sun went down, so all was warm and full and her father laughing and laughing. Sometimes she'd hear again that woman's angry sniff, try to remember the set of the woman's mouth, and whether it was in fact the whole room that turned away after her father's joking speech, or if that was only her mind playing tricks.

Stepping out, rewrapped like a present, Alicia was grateful for the warm fullness of her belly and glanced back at the gleaming rooms.

'When can we come back?' But Adam didn't hear, stamping and re-knotting his scarf around his throat. The wind had dropped, an icy stillness descended, and glittering ice crystals had grown on the stones of the square. As they came further away from the Wentzl, the dark and cold seemed to leach away Alicia's pleasure. Adam held out his hand for a cab, but none stopped. Pinched faces hurried past.

'Let's walk home, then,' Adam said. 'It will be fun.'

A couple were sitting on the steps of the old town hall, leaning against one of the lazy stone lions. The woman's legs were bare, Alicia noticed with a small thrill of shock. Her Papa hurried her along, then dropped her hand to rub his own together inside his gloves, and in the moments he stopped, Alicia took greedy sips of the strange sight on the steps, the urgency of the man's hands, the small sounds of distress of the woman. The back of the man's head was pressing, pressing, and the woman was shrinking back. When the man shot his hand up the woman's skirt, exposing a shock of white flesh, Alicia gasped, and tugged Adam's hand. Her Papa looked at her in indulgent expectation, before catching sight of the couple behind her.

He took an instinctive step forward, then stopped, his head slightly cocked, as though trying to see clearly.

'Hello,' he called. To Alicia his voice sounded soft, almost comforting. She had stopped watching the couple, and saw only her father's form, striding forwards.

'Hello, hello, stop,' he said, much more strongly now, his familiar voice. Alicia felt her blood quicken, watching him pace, his long coat billowing behind him, towards the man with the urgent hands. Adam flicked his gaze back to her. 'Stay here,' he barked, and she ignored him, trotting after him just as the couple responded to the approach.

The man had stopped crushing the woman against the stone lion, and was smiling, biting his thumb and looking down. Alicia recognised the look as one of her own, when she was disciplined by someone she didn't respect. He had long girlish eyelashes and he seemed small, much smaller than Papa. But the hands, his thumb in his teeth, were large and dirty. He wasn't wearing gloves in the cold, which made Alicia think he must be very poor. She sneered, emboldened by this realisation, and the bulk of Papa beside her. The woman shrank even further into the stone, pulling down her skirt, her face blank. *You should say thank you*, Alicia thought savagely. Her mother's voice came to her, the cadence of overheard gossip in the house, unguarded chatter in the kitchen. *Having your legs out like that.* Instead the woman looked at her shoes.

'Hello,' Adam repeated. He hesitated, glanced back at Alicia. 'It's cold and late. Is everything well?'

Alicia glared at the woman, who still hadn't said thank you or taken the chance to run away. She had a sudden, unbidden image of the woman from the restaurant, her pursed lips and stony face, the angry straightness of her back.

The man continued to nod and bite his thumb, smiling, on the cusp of laughter even. Perhaps he isn't poor at all, but mad, Alicia thought, and that's why he doesn't feel the cold. Perhaps he will be taken to the mountains to lie in a room painted white and with starched clean bedsheets. The man, slow and unsteady, lurching to hold onto a lion's mane, pulled himself to stand. The woman at his feet hissed something. Adam settled into his feet, crossed his arms as the man belched smoke into the cold air between them, brought his face level to Adam. He had to get on tiptoe to do it, and swayed dangerously.

'Go fuck yourself,' he said.

Alicia's shock made a laugh fall from her mouth before she could cram it back into her chest. The man narrowed his eyes at her, and Adam began to back away.

'Come,' he said to her, soft. When he took her hand, she felt his fingers inside his mittens were trembling. Then they were wrenched from her, there was the dull sound of something hard on flesh, and her Papa was on the ground. The stranger kicked him as he lay there, silent and only curled up with his hands around his face. Once, twice. Adam was silent. Alicia cried out, an animal sound. The man looked her up and down, taking in her rich clothes, the glint of red silk.

'What's that, little bitch?'

'Don't,' Adam said, pulling himself up.

A small crowd had formed, almost a circle. Alicia looked around at them. 'He kicked my Papa.' She tried to scream it, but it came out very small. Some were shaking their heads, others were sneering. Disorientated, Alicia watched Adam slowly pull himself to his feet, a bloom of red near his temple. His hands shook as he removed his *kippah*, knocked askew, and put it in his pocket. He faced the man, so much taller and stronger. *Kill him, Papa. Throw him to the ground, make his blood splash across the ice.* Adam followed Alicia's gaze and looked out at the gathering crowd too.

The woman on the steps called out. 'It's cold. I want to go home.' The man ignored her, staring at Adam with a disgusting look of triumph on his face. Adam's fists were clenched and he'd moved in front of Alicia.

'I want to go home,' the woman said again. The man gave

a mock bow to Alicia, blew her a kiss, and strutted back to the steps.

'We're going home,' Adam said. As he pulled her to him, the small crowd began sliding away. Alicia heard the woman on the steps hiss something again. Some in the crowd laughed.

As they retraced their steps down Bernardyńska, Adam's grip firm and his stride quick, they didn't speak. Alicia was lost in fantasies in which she murdered the couple on the steps. The man she scalped, making him kneel and apologise first, or had him hung from a lamppost. The woman's face she ripped off with her nails. She kept at the edge of her thoughts her burning shame at her father's humiliation, unable to look at its full white heat. Instead she imagined slipping out of bed later, returning to the steps with a gun. She tried scraps of different dialogue, indulged in the man gibbering at her feet, panicked spit trailing from his mouth, his hopeless, pink, squirming sobs.

As they reached the comforting block of home, Adam stopped and crouched down so that his long coat trailed on the pavement. He put his hands on Alicia's shoulders and she began to pitch forward into the comfort of his arms, but he held her stiffly away from him, shook her a little.

'Say nothing to Mama and Karolina. Or Janie or to anyone. Do you understand?'

She nodded, but her eyes were fixed on the bright red, striking as a midsummer flower, plastered across his temple and down his cheeks.

'They'll see,' she said, in answer to his questioning gaze, and pointed at the wound.

'Well, I slipped on the ice. Yes?'

She nodded.

'It will be difficult for you to lie because you are a good girl, but it is because I ask you to. Yes?'

She didn't reply that lying came to her as naturally as breathing.

Never had home seemed so solid and warm. Alicia wanted to scream at Robert to close the door, lock it, to shout that there were bad people all around, but instead she let him take her gloves as he asked, 'And how is the birthday princess? Did you enjoy your dinner?' Then, when he caught sight of Adam, he melted into silence. Alicia saw her father bow his head briefly; close his eyes as though in standing sleep.

Robert shut the huge double front doors, locking them in place.

'Papa slipped on the ice,' Alicia said. Robert nodded at her.

Some of the cold, set faces from outside, their harshness, had crept into the house with them. The pinched look of the woman in the restaurant, the woman on the steps, the crow of the man as he weaved back to her.

'Karolina was sent to bed a few hours ago, and Mrs Oderfeldt is in the drawing room, with the radio,' Robert said, in answer to a silent question.

Karolina slept with a book in her hand, another rising and falling with her belly's breath, a journal filled with her scrawl. Alicia tried to make out the words, looked for her name, but the room was too gloomy. Karolina's brown hair was bushy like Alicia's but unlike her sister she had always resisted Janie's attempts to tame it with oil and irons, and so it grew rather wild. Alicia studied her for a moment, wondering if she would look like Karolina in five long years, when she was seventeen too, or if she might be prettier. She jerked Karolina by the foot.

Karolina jumped and her book smacked on the floorboards. 'If you had a nightmare get in with Janie, for God's sake,' she mumbled.

Alicia crawled over her sister's body and sat cross-legged beside her.

'Come to crow? Go on,' Karolina said, sitting up. 'You know Papa never took me to dinner at the Wentzl. Was it very beautiful?'

'Yes. It was like a painting. Yellow. It glowed.'

Karolina nodded and dozed again as Alicia described the room, the food, the wine and their Papa's rumbling laughter, the square behind the windows dipping into night. In her mind's eye, she erased the sour-faced woman at the nearby table like a bad sketch, and then lightly said, 'But it was icy on the way home and I slipped, and Papa slipped too trying to catch me and cut his temple and bled a little.' As she said it she realised she would need to give this extra detail to Papa. 'Oh, and he said he will take you to the Wentzl too, for your next birthday.' In the weak window light Karolina snorted and rubbed her eyes.

'Really.'

'Yes, and also another painter is coming.'

'Oh! Another portrait of Princess Alicia! The last one makes you look like an ugly ghost.' Karolina followed this with a gentle push of dismissal.

Alicia settled on the stairs for a while before going back to bed. From the study, the radio rose and fell, punctuated with static. Only the odd word floated up, muffled by the thick carpets. She heard her name, and her Mama's voice calm and steady. So, the lie was holding.

That night she dreamed of being drowned and trapped in paint like an unlucky fly. At her back, the canvas was cold and through the gloop of the sharp-smelling paint she saw her parents and Karolina, huddled in a cold place like the woman on the steps, watching her.

4

THE GIRLS ATE SEPARATELY from their parents, in the smaller room that had been their nursery, now piled with books and clothes, a desk for Karolina in the corner. Janie and Dotty came in and out with platters, the glint of sunlight on silver. Karolina was at her most animated at breakfast, telling Alicia of a new poem or story she had dreamed or sketched out that morning. The dogs, Mimi and Cece, both Alicia's, weaved between everyone's legs, causing Janie to shriek and curse on the stairs when she thought she was out of earshot.

Alicia, weary after her broken sleep, almost feverish still with rage, had slept late. She came in blind to the unexpected stillness, so consumed by the earthquake in her little life that it took minutes for her to identify that the squirming tension was not inside her own body, but in the room.

'Karolcia?'

Her sister looked only confused, half shrugged with a nod to the two servant women. Janie stood at the windows, her hands clasped, head slightly bowed. As Alicia looked at her, she gave her a watery smile. Dorothea was serving up fruit, but gone was her chatter: *I hope you like this, this is your favourite, I saw these at the market yesterday, look at that lovely colour in it, look at that shine!* Instead the clink of china made a tuneless song.

'Karolcia?' Alicia said again.

Papa had told, or had failed in the lie, and they all knew, saw, as she had, how they were all laid low, something had been ripped away from them.

'I don't know,' Karolina mouthed. 'They've been like this all morning.'

'Janie, is it about Papa?' Alicia felt she should cry too, match Dorothea's blotched cheeks, but felt only the deep stirrings of anger again.

Alicia moved to sit by her sister's side. She started to say, 'It was a man, with huge hands, and a boy's face, and he was only so short, but somehow he hit Papa.' She only got as far as 'It was . . .' and Karolina began whispering over her, 'Someone is dead, I know it, it must be Papa or Mama, one of them has died in the night.'

Alicia chewed some fruit, let the juice drip onto the tablecloth. The other words, pressured in her throat like a blocked pipe, she swallowed too, trying to explain: it wasn't just the blood and the strike and the shock of their tall, solid Papa on the ground, it was the way the air changed, the laughter of the crowd, the sneer on that woman's face, her hiss, and the woman back at the restaurant, something in the set of her lips, her scowl at Alicia as though she didn't belong. All this she swallowed, thinking on her secret, before she could allow Karolina's words in. Karolina though was pressing on, her continued whispering, asking, 'But which? It must be one of them, no one else is so close, it can't be Uncle Schmuel or a cousin or something like that, who would they weep for?' And Alicia found the question facing her easy to the point of shame. *It must be Mama*, she thought. *It must be Mama, because if it is Papa I won't live anymore.* Karolina kept on whispering, until Dorothea banged a serving spoon on the table, 'Enough!' and they all jumped.

'Go up to your Mama and Papa now. Karolina, your hysteria is ridiculous.'

Alicia's mouth was full, and she burst some of the peach on her tongue, feeling its sticky juice as an outpouring of relief.

The dogs were in the upstairs dining room, lying in the weak sunbeams. Alicia scooped Mimi up as they approached their parents, who sat, formal, as though posing for portraits, in the high-backed chairs under the bookcase. Her Mama had her hands folded in her lap as they entered, but now held out her arms. There was an awkward moment as both girls hesitated, Alicia with Mimi squirming against her chest, Karolina looking at her mother in abject surprise.

'Come,' Anna said, an edge of annoyance in her voice.

Karolina went to her. Too tall for a full embrace, she felt her mother's shoulder dig into the flesh around her own collarbone. Alicia put down the dog.

'Girls, we are changing some plans. Karolina, you won't be going to Zakopane with the Hartmanns. You'll stay here for the season. Alicia, you're also to stay inside over the winter, so there will be no riding lessons.'

'Papa!' Alicia cried; though she didn't care about the riding lessons, she was unused to things promised to her being taken away again.

'Is there an epidemic?' Karolina asked, who loved to read about gruesome plagues sweeping through cities.

'Yes,' Anna answered Karolina, after a quiet had descended, and Adam had gone to move newspapers around on his desk. 'Your father was reading about a disease in the morning papers, and we'd like you to stay inside as much as possible. We'll take some walks together, of course,' she said, softening at the sight of her elder daughter's dismay.

'There may be some difficulties, but we are surrounded by friends and our city, and all will be well.' Their Papa spoke slowly, as though giving a ceremonial speech, or a toast at one of their long, late dinner parties.

'I thought it must be,' Alicia caught her Papa's eye and he reddened further, shifted in his chair. 'We thought it must be family who had died,' she went on, 'or something terrible.'

'Well,' their Mama said. She seemed at a loss and looked at her husband. 'Go, go to your rooms.'

They stayed in their own sets of rooms for the rest of the day. Karolina wanted to go to the Jagiellonian, to visit their Uncle Stefan, but Adam, in a message from Janie, forbade it.

'Besides, the university will be closed, out of respect,' she added. 'Your Uncle and the others will all be at home, as we are.'

'Yes,' Karolina said. 'Of course,' in such a good impression of her mother's clipped tones that Janie gave her a tiny head tilt of deference. As she left Karolina made a face at Alicia, who buried her own in a throw rug, fearful of laughing.

'Out of respect for *who*?' Alicia almost whispered. She could feel the lie, the way it had got tangled between the servants and her parents, knotted into the wrong words.

Karolina shrugged, went to her desk and brought a small, leather-bound book to Alicia.

'Shall I tell you the next part of the story?'

'Have you translated the next part yet?'

'No, silly. I only translate little bits. I have the translation here in Polish. One of Uncle Stefan's friends did it.'

Alicia sat up, looked again at the pages. One side was full of the Greek symbols in beautiful shapes, their ink tails flicked like tiny tadpoles.

'Why don't you just learn the Polish off by heart, and then you can pretend to translate it, just changing a few words? Then you wouldn't need to study so much.'

'But I like the translation part. Besides, I think learning thousands of lines off by heart would be a little difficult, no?' Karolina laughed.

Alicia was silent. This was a rare day of warmth between them, and she wouldn't spoil it by saying how she didn't understand this; in fact, she had committed the poetry Karolina had read to her so far to memory with ease.

'I might study with Uncle Stefan too when I'm older,' she said instead.

Karolina gave her a small smile, which Alicia translated with disappointment. 'I think you will marry a nice rich man, Ala, and live with lots of beautiful things, like Mama.'

'But Uncle Stefan—'

'Remember how you tortured all your governesses, and Papa drew you out of school?'

Alicia laughed. 'But that's not the same! That wasn't . . . I don't need to learn all the names of the capital cities—'

'Exactly. That's not for you.' Karolina pulled her hair lightly, and Alicia saw her sister believed she was kind to her, like Janie when she flicked flies out of the window instead of crushing them against the window pane. Her secret swelled, *I know something, I know something true and real that changes everything, more important than your book. It isn't a disease at all, it's what happened to Papa last night.*

'Where were we up to?'

Alicia considered reciting the poetry. She'd become a new kind of ally to her sister then. But she felt instinctively that Karolina would be threatened, would feel something had been taken away from her, when Alicia had so much already.

'Odysseus has just been blown back, all the way back far from home,' she told Karolina. 'He could see the Ithacans tending their fires and he was nearly home but then they opened the bag of winds.'

Karolina took her stubby pencil and mimed driving it into her heart, making Alicia snort. It was just like Papa at the Wentzl. They were often the same, but only when her sister was alone with her did she seem like Papa.

'Ah!' she cried. 'How could I forget? It's so heartbreaking! Close enough to see the fires!'

Alicia shrugged. 'It was his own fault. He's always lying to his men. Easy to warn them and explain.'

'I thought you would like him, the liar,' Karolina said, without malice.

Alicia went still.

'I mean, he's slippery and clever. You can be like that.'

'Can I?' *Do you know I'm clever? Do you know the lie about last night?*

'Of course! You lied about that dress you stained. No one even guessed.'

'Yes.'

'Yes,' Karolina nodded, dragging out the word. 'All right, back to Odysseus.'

The afternoon was an unusual one: obeying their parents, they stayed in their part of the apartment, curled up on the small, soft nursery chairs, the sound of the doorbell and hushed voices, occasional louder voices, interrupting Karolina as she read. Alicia committed the translated poetry to memory, played its tune with her fingers along her dress, saw phrases in gold, how they looped back to each other, the same refrains. She saw the azure blue of the sea and the oil glistening in the hair of the heroes, and felt the heat of the sands as though on scorched bare feet. Since her father's fall, her whole body had been tense. Now, no adults to make her sit up or keep her fingers still or to pet her, she sank further and further into her chair, in the cool room, her sister's voice spinning the story for her, and felt that if this was a sad day, she wanted all days to be sad days, of stillness and quiet.

5

THE DAYS TURNED still colder and bleaker, so the apartment was full of the smell of tapers and burning kindle. The havenday of reading was long over; the sisters were summoned back to the family rooms, told to welcome and be polite to many guests. Neighbours drifted in and out, ate little, left teacups brimming. Adam began to gather up the newspapers and take them with him to his office, instead of leaving them around for Karolina to read. Anna stayed in more than usual, and Alicia could hear her pacing in the upstairs rooms, stopping at windows, turning, pacing again. The radio was always crackling through the house. One of these dull mornings Janie told them to be ready in the big dining room downstairs early: their Uncle Stefan was to visit.

Uncle Stefan wasn't their Papa's brother, who lived far away; he was his oldest friend, but Alicia always felt he looked like a brother to him. His face was an echo of Papa's in the way her own was an echo of Karolina's: the same thin, sharp bones, the crooked smile and a merriment in the brown eyes. He was tall and thin like Papa, even more so, and often had a bruise on his forehead, or his arm, from bumping into the low beams and narrow doorways of the university. He and Adam spoke in almost their own language when they were together, half-sentences which were caught up by the other, and left to drift into laughter or nostalgic silence. Unlike the rest of the house, Uncle Stefan seemed unchanged by the great plague, which made Alicia love him even more.

'Sad times,' Adam greeted him with a clutch on the arm.

Stefan peered into his friend's face. 'Yes, yes,' he said, as though acknowledging the existence of an academic argument he was about to dismantle. 'What happened to you?' he gestured to his own temple, mirroring the welt on Adam's face.

'He slipped on the ice,' Anna said.

'Ah, is that what we call it these days?'

'Call what?' Adam said sharply.

Stefan glanced at Anna, confused. 'Adam, I was only joking. I know you don't drink so much anymore.'

'I was with Alicia,' Adam muttered.

'Come on, I have books for Karolina, and here is Anna so beautiful . . .' – he kissed her hand and she laughed – 'and come on, Adam, it was far away. It won't happen here.'

'Not so far.'

'Far away? So I *can* go to Zakopane?' Karolina asked her mother.

'The Hartmanns wrote to say they've cancelled,' Anna replied. 'As a precaution. We told the girls about the epidemic,' she said to Stefan, who raised his eyebrows in response.

'Come on now,' he said, in such gentle rebuke that both Anna and Adam looked away for a moment. Taking their silence as permission, he gestured for Karolina and Alicia to come closer and began, "There isn't an epidemic, except of . . . unpleasantness.'

'There *is* a measles outbreak, it said so in the newspaper,' Anna said, flushing.

'Some windows were smashed in Germany and some people were hurt,' Adam picked up Stefan's thread, left Anna's

43

dangling. She retreated to her sofa, furious. It had been Adam's idea not to tell their daughters in the first place.

'It's far away and nothing to worry about here,' Stefan added, aiming what he hoped was a conciliatory smile at Anna, but her face was closed, and he would need to flatter her all evening.

'Why were people hurt?' Karolina asked, as Alicia thought about the man on the steps and the way his back curled as he kicked her Papa. Perhaps he had come from Germany to smash windows too.

'Well.' Stefan gave an elaborate shrug. 'This is the fate the gods have—'

'Don't!' Adam held up a hand, but laughing. 'Don't start quoting at us, it's ten o'clock in the morning and too early for epic!'

Stefan mirrored Adam's gesture, and matched his laughter too.

'Come, Karolina,' he called. Alicia watched as he pulled more of the green-covered books out of a leather satchel. The two of them stood slightly apart, Karolina smoothing her hands over the pages.

'Did you bring me anything?' Alicia called to him, as the family drifted towards the table where tea was being served. 'It was my birthday last month, and we haven't seen you since then.'

'Ah, and how was the Wentzl?' Stefan directed his question to both Alicia and Adam, who dropped his gaze for a moment. Alicia tried to summon the night again, its nauseating mix of the rich, warm room and the images of blood on the ice.

'It was wonderful,' she said. 'It was a lovely treat from Papa. Only I slipped on the ice on the way back.'

'Oh yes, getting cold now,' Stefan replied politely, with a small smile of amusement at her grown-up tone.

'We haven't been into the centre since,' Adam said. 'The news came through the next morning.'

'But you can't lock yourselves away,' Stefan said. He'd spoken mildly, but Adam reddened.

'You think we're afraid?'

Stefan sat back, his thin face becoming thoughtful. 'No, only . . . sad. Too sad, I think.'

'Don't you feel anything? Did you read the reports? They made people . . .'

He broke off, noticing how his daughters had become still.

'Of course, of course. It's terrible,' Stefan said, without fire. 'But remember '35. We all worried, and what happened? Nothing. Only you have more German Jews on your payroll, and I have more in my classes, and very welcome they are too.'

'I know,' Adam said, picking up his tea. 'I'm sorry,' he added. He eyed his friend, noted he was wearing, unusually, his *kippah*. Adam had put his own away after Alicia's birthday, folded it away with a twinge of regret at how it had been his father's, given to him with a rare emotion from the old man, his eyes moist. Adam had worn it not as a believer at all but as a mark of respect, love, even, for his father, for the memory of his proud face when Adam had first put it on. He wore it for weddings, holidays, days he wished to mark with respect, such as Alicia's birthday. Now it was gently pressed between handkerchiefs in his bedroom as though just another piece of cloth.

Stefan followed his friend's eyes. 'What? I'm going to my mother's for dinner.'

Adam lowered his voice. 'It hasn't given you any trouble?'

'None at all.' Stefan heard the untold things in Adam's question; saw how he held himself in his chair. An image of his friend being beaten made his stomach shrink, and he reached for Adam's arm even as he dismissed the idea: Adam would have told him.

A silence descended, the rattle of the tea things, the crack of a broken book spine from where Karolina sat.

Alicia leaned over to Stefan. 'My present,' she whispered, but it carried, and they all laughed at her.

'All right,' Stefan said. 'I confess my crime, I forgot the birthday girl.'

'Oh, Stefan! How could you? You held her in your arms when she was born!' Adam cried. 'You are no longer my brother!' and the two men collapsed in childish laughter. A look passed between Anna and Dorothea, who was pouring Stefan's tea, and Anna's anger ebbed away. She settled more comfortably on the sofa, her head tilted as though to hear better her husband's newly cheerful voice.

'All right,' Stefan said, wiping his eyes. He turned to Alicia. 'What would you like? Here, I'll give you a choice. A doll, or a globe.'

'A globe?'

'Yes, a globe of the world. You know, when I was your age, turning, what are you, eight?'

There was more laughter at this from the parents.

'She's twelve! A crocodile is a better Uncle than you are, Stefan. A snake would do a better job,' Adam said.

Stefan laughed, waved this away. 'When I was your age, I wanted a globe more than anything. So I could see the whole world, understand my place in it' – he started to make his teaching gestures, slicing the air – 'so I could travel to far-away places by tracing my finger over the surface. Do you remember that one my father had, Adam? In his office.'

'I never saw it, but you talked about it often enough.'

'Well, it's in *my* office now.'

'Did you ever get your own, when you were younger?' Karolina asked.

Adam started to shake his head.

'No!' Stefan threw up his hands dramatically, making them laugh again. 'I asked, and asked, and I was very patient, and then my parents bought me a book of maps, which wasn't what I wanted at all!'

'Well, Alicia will want the doll,' Anna said, smiling. 'She's not a twelve-year-old boy with an obsession.'

'I'll have a globe, Uncle Stefan, please.'

Adam laughed. 'Your uncle is only teasing you. He will buy you a doll or a pretty thing.'

'With the sea a dark blue colour,' Alicia said. 'And a star where we live, so I can see the whole world, understand my place in it.'

'Of course,' Stefan said. 'But you know, I was only telling a story about myself. Really you can have any pretty thing you like.'

'We're having a new portrait of her done,' Adam said. 'It's her birthday gift to ourselves.'

Her parents began talking about the painting, her Papa gesturing to the windows, where she'd probably have to stand. Karolina was busy with her books, reading some of the spines, looking up occasionally to shoot a look of puzzlement or thanks to her uncle.

Stefan turned to Alicia. 'Another portrait, Ala? So, you'll be famous!'

'Will I?'

'Oh, yes. Your parents, you know, they only hire the very best. You will be like the *Mona Lisa*.'

She looked blank, so he added, 'Maybe one day you will

47

hang in a gallery, and there will be a little card' – he held up his hands as though making a frame – 'that says, "Alicia Oderfeldt, famous."' He smiled down at her, then checked his smile at her solemn face. 'Ala?'

She took a moment to speak. 'Please, the globe. Won't you get me one?'

Stefan took her hand and kissed it, his face alight with amusement at her serious expression. 'As you wish.'

6

THE PAINTER STOMPED towards the huge apartment block, his precious canvas beginning to curl. Irritation bubbled in him, and he found that his breathing had become erratic and shallow. Back in his small studio, his project was pulling at him. He could feel its colours draining away, his vision becoming wispy and faint, so that when he was free to stand before it again, he would find only the ghost of a brilliant idea. Instead of capturing it he had been compelled to catch the tram across the city, his sketching tools in a leather case, his fresh canvas sheets in a roll over his shoulder. He had felt only annoyance at Adam Oderfeldt's letter. There was no satisfaction for Jozef in a portrait piece of a spoiled child, who had a reputation as a spiteful girl who had ruined another painter's work with a tantrum and a pair of scissors. Besides, being in the hushed exquisite apartment made him anxious and awkward. Something blocked his ears so that he had to ask the family and servants to repeat what they said, and his own voice sounded strange and muffled in his head. He felt watched and judged by everyone in the house, and an exhausting mix of irritation and guilt at Adam's aggressive friendliness, his patting him on the back, offering the him *nalewka*, expensive cigars, a coat.

'I was waiting in the rain,' he said, when the plain-faced servant finally opened the door, holding a sewing kit. She flushed.

'I'm so sorry, sir.' She had a slight stutter, which got worse as she gestured with the kit. 'I would normally come down right away, but I was sewing, upstairs I mean, so I didn't hear.'

'Oh, it's, please, it's all right, it doesn't matter.'

'Won't you come in right away?'

She avoided his eye as he came inside, and this made him so miserable with guilt and being always all *wrong* in this place, some invisible spell of *wrong* cast even as he stepped onto Bernardyńska, that he almost turned back to the door. Instead he stammered a little himself as he followed the girl up the stairs.

'It's only that my paints, and my canvas must be dry, you see.'

She nodded, without turning around, and so he cast around for ways to please her, and said, 'This house is always so clean and well kept. You must work hard on it.'

This was met with a glare. 'I do not clean, sir.'

He almost threw up his arms in defeat, and was silent.

In the drawing room, the youngest girl was playing with a small dog by the fire, teasing it as it rolled and wriggled on a thick rug that looked like sheepskin. Jozef was assailed by the familiar envy as he thought of the same scene in his own home, the threadbare, cold, hard nature of it. The grate empty except for some newspapers. The soot on the cheap mat before it, full of fleas that jumped like sparks in a fire and feasted on his ankles. The girl glanced up.

'Hello, Alicia,' he said, the muffled feeling thicker than ever in his ears and spreading to his throat. He liked children, but the necessity that he please this one made it difficult. The girl was dressed in a ridiculous way, in layers of bright silk and white stockings that were becoming peppered with dog hair. Her hair was curled like a doll's, and when she turned her face was blank like porcelain. She was plain, with nothing of the mixture of sharpness and softness that beauty required, that her mother had. Her nose had a small kink, the lips were thin, the skin rather sallow.

'You're the painter, I suppose,' she said, in a bored tone matching his thoughts, sounding eerily like her mother, who Jozef had always found cold.

'Where is your father?'

'Smoking on the terrace.'

'And your mother?'

'Upstairs with Karolina.'

Jozef felt the canvas slip a little in his newly warmed hands. He felt a vague panic about how to paint such a vacuum, before reminding himself that it was not to be one of his true pieces, only a family portrait. The girl watched as he laid the canvas down and placed the leather satchel next to it.

'Why have you brought those?' she asked. 'Papa has ordered everything in for us.'

On an upstairs terrace, Adam greeted the painter with his usual warmth.

'Ah, you are here! You have seen little Alicia? But she was so young the last time you saw her properly! Isn't she a little beauty? But why are you wearing this suit jacket? It's all sodden from the rain! Why didn't you bring a coat, or even better, you should telephone and we'll send a car! Honestly, why must you insist on living in this peasant way?' He laughed, flicking ash over the balcony edge, his beard and moustache quivering. In the course of this speech he had lit a cigar for Jozef, and man-oeuvred him into a beautiful wrought-iron chair. Jozef fought his bad temper and quelled the image of his abandoned piece back at home, smiled in what he hoped was a genuine way.

'So, you'd like a portrait of your youngest?'

'We'll talk of it later! You'll stay for dinner?'

'No! No, I must get back.'

'So, what do you think of Alicia? Isn't she bright and funny?'

'Yes, of course. A lovely child.'

Adam watched him, nodding.

Jozef shifted in his chair, breathed out on smoke, 'How are you, after Germany then? I read—'

'What a shock! It's all the neighbourhood's talked of for weeks. I cried, you know, I'm not ashamed to tell you. Such a terrible night, such a frightening thought. But . . .' Adam leaned forwards, 'it doesn't seem so bad as all that. I was worried, we all were, and there were rumours, you know, always these rumours. But nothing has changed. You know, we aren't poor. A poor Jew is in trouble. Perhaps, maybe, if we were poor . . . but we are not like that. It's just not the same for us, in this part of the city, you know, not the same at all.' He shrugged, looked out at the Wawel, gestured to it with his cigar, as though it confirmed his tumble of frightened words. He went on, 'I hope it is not disrespectful to ask that we go ahead with the painting? You don't mind?'

Jozef shrugged. He'd read the reports of the German pogrom with a distant disgust; saw the pictures of people beaten in the streets, glass glinting on the pavements, with a muted horror that he forgot when he turned the page. He noticed the name for it was *Kristallnacht*, which he liked for its crisp sound, wondered how the artists were responding to it, something about refracting, through mirrors and glass, perhaps, or the *Juden* in red paint, repeated like a chant. There would be lots of red. If he were German he'd do a piece himself, perhaps make a name for himself with it.

He watched his patron pace and smoke and gesticulate, now talking about what he wanted from the painting. Jozef barely needed to listen, it was always the same: regal, refined, pretty. Probably the wretched, pampered dog at her feet.

Adam blew out a plume of smoke, continued as though Jozef had replied to his earlier question. 'Yes, yes, it's certainly not a matter of disrespect. You'll come for our party? The view is perfect from here. We are having the whole neighbourhood over. To talk, drink, just be together, you know. Some people are bringing German families who are coming to stay until things are calmer. Can't blame them, I'd do the same, if there were the same dangers here.'

'Oh, well I—'

'But you'll be visiting so much for the portrait, you might as well. It's next week. Alicia's a princess, you know,' Adam went on, with no trace of irony that Jozef could discern. 'You should look at the Infanta portraits, for example, to give you an idea.'

'Yes, of course.' Jozef choked down laughter. 'We'll start right away.'

'Oh, we'll pretend there are some others to consider for the commission, just for appearances' sake.'

'Oh?' Oh God, Jozef thought, I *hate* this. The games of high society, and I don't know the rules. He'd lost commissions before, after Adam had promised them to him. Turned down other work, and failed rent.

'I promise, it's yours. You can start discussing after dinner,' Adam said, settling into the chair opposite him, and laughing as Jozef started to protest. 'After! Anna and my other daughter will be back home, and we've invited some friends. Then you can decide on some ideas, you know, look for the best place in the apartment, think about lighting, and so forth.'

'I really must get back.'

'To a sad little bowl of unsalted soup? You know, they say you cannot make art on an empty stomach!'

'Who says that?'

'They! Everyone! Come on. I think it's beef tonight.'

'I should go home and change.'

'Not at all, not at all. Please, Jozef. I want you to feel at home. Things have been so . . . what a dreadful time! You must stay and relax, have fun. We all should.'

As dinner guests began to arrive Jozef recognised a fellow painter, a rival from Warsaw. They shook hands wearily.

'Milo,' Jozef nodded. 'Enjoyed your piece for the Hartmanns.'

'And your last,' Milo murmured, seeming close to laughter. He'd made an effort, a good quality suit. Jozef smelled starch; Milo must be doing well. He felt the shabbiness of his own suit, the turpentine stains on his cuffs. He moved away to the windows, sipped his wine, watched. It was always the same people at these things: doctors, lawyers, businessmen and their wives. Tonight many of them carried the same edginess as their host: talking slightly too fast, in a determined way, gripping arms along with strong handshakes, as though to reassure themselves that they were all still real. Jozef felt the rare quickening, deep in his gut, of an idea: a scene, like this, in a beautiful room, with well-dressed men and women, posed in the elegant, relaxed way of pre-dinner drinks, but their faces distorted in raw terror.

Hopeless to try to sketch it out now: Adam caught his eye, gestured for him to join a circle. As hands were shaken, Jozef leaned in, pointedly turned his arm so the unpatched holes in his left sleeve were visible, said, 'I'm Jozef, the bohemian spectre at the feast.' This earned him many 'Of course, of course,' smiles, some vague compliments on his earlier work for the Oderfeldts, and hearty laughter from his patron.

'You remember Stefan, my dearest friend,' Adam said, leading Jozef to a new circle.

'Yes, of course,' Jozef lied, shaking another hand, but holding it a moment longer when he recognised him after all.

'Professor!'

'Ah, Jozef! How wonderful to see you here. Are you the one to paint Alicia? How wonderful for you!'

Jozef laughed. 'Well, I hope.'

'Do you? I imagine these commissions must bore you to death.'

Jozef only smiled. 'I wasn't aware you knew the family.'

'Knew? Adam and I are brothers in name. We grew up together! Well, are you doing well? What are you reading at the moment?'

'I don't read much now. I only draw and paint.'

Stefan tutted good-naturedly. 'A shame, when you had such a good scholarship, but art is a lofty aspiration.'

'I do miss the university,' Jozef said. 'Those beautiful painted ceilings and doors.'

'How like you to notice the colour of the paint, not the knowledge within.'

'I should have known,' Jozef laughed and shrugged. He felt so much better. A genuine friend, someone he liked and trusted. He didn't have to impress Stefan, or study his face or speech to know which step to take next. The commission was certainly his, if Stefan and Adam were such friends.

As they took their places for dinner, the wine and candle-light relaxed Jozef further. He'd hoped to be sitting next to Stefan but instead was at the end of the table, next to an older woman, plump in grey satin, her thin hair artfully arranged over what Jozef suspected was a balding patch. He held out his hand for her.

'Mrs Kardas, isn't it?' he said. 'We met last summer.'

She looked a little shocked; when she took his hand, nodding along to the introduction, her hand had all the paper limpness of a dead moth.

'I know your son quite well,' Jozef pressed on, a little dismayed. 'We had some classes together at the Jagiellonian.'

Mollified, she simpered as though he had given her the most extravagant compliment.

'Aleks is such a clever boy,' she said. 'He simply sailed through his classes. Professor Lis over there says he's still held as a shining example at the university. *Shining*, that was his exact word. You know he graduated over six months early? He's left for France now, to continue his studies. But of course you must have heard.'

Jozef drained his glass. He imagined his long dead father, aped his voice in his mind, his advice, which would be to view these excursions into high society as a holiday: *Enjoy the rich food*. He had no advice for a dull dining companion. A smaller voice, his mother's, whispered, *They're only Jews, after all*.

Talk around the table was the confident debate of old friends, looping from personal anecdotes and memories, laughter at old well-worn jokes, gentle competition over the looks and intelligence of their children. No one mentioned Germany, the stack of newspapers on Adam's desk, until Milo, the painter from Warsaw, cut through the currents of conversation.

'How do you all feel about this latest attack on the Jews? Didn't you say,' he said, waving his fork at a doctor to his right, 'your family has fled? Why didn't they come tonight? You're German, aren't you?'

'They would have been welcome,' Anna said, sounding more fevered than she meant to.

The doctor, Karl Weiss, took a while to reply, nodded at Milo, as though absorbing a complicated patient history.

'I'm Polish. So is my wife,' he said.

'It's Laura's family, isn't it, come from Berlin?' Janina pressed. 'What did they say?'

'Yes, her sister's family,' Karl replied. 'They were grateful for the invitation,' he said to Anna, breaking into a warm smile at her, which she returned, 'but they want to rest.'

Into the waiting quiet, Janina asked, 'Are they hurt?'

'No.'

'What did they see?'

Karl sat back in his chair, pressed his lips together. 'Nothing you haven't already read.'

This was enough to open the space for the conversations they truly wanted: details from the radio and the newspapers, the newsreels, were shared and picked over, offered up to Karl for him to only nod at, or say, 'No, they didn't see that, but they were lucky, perhaps . . .' Occasionally someone would hear something new, a detail they hadn't seen before: the old men kneeling in the glass, the cutting of hair, the people pulled from their beds, a fire in a family shop, a beautiful painting slashed to ribbons; they each found a detail to focus on, one story, a person or a family, and let the others – the whole houses emptied, the disappearances – lie untouched somewhere in the spaces of the unsaid things.

Adam said again and again, 'I cried, I'm not ashamed to tell you.'

'It may well turn out to be a good thing,' Stefan said, raising his hands to quell the *Oh Stefans* this prompted. 'It's one thing for them to go along with the things they say, the pictures, the . . . it's another to see their neighbours beaten up, see the windows smashed in a street they know.'

'Laura's husband thinks the same,' Karl returned. 'It was their German neighbours who drove them to the border, in their own car. Some of the boys stood about, he said, refusing to hurt anyone.'

'They didn't stop anything either,' Adam said.

'But it's not been so bad as the rumours promised. Some of the neighbourhood was practically hysterical,' Janina said. She leaned in to Jozef to add, 'I was quite alarmed, I thought maybe Aleks should leave earlier, or maybe not leave at all, but my husband would have wanted him to go.'

A wave of similar sentiments were rolling around the table: *It's not so bad, things will be calm, Kraków has always been a safe and pleasant kind of city, especially this neighbourhood.*

'I've seen a few signs,' Milo called out, which quelled these voices. Jozef felt a small thrill at Milo's reddening face as everyone turned to look at him. He'd been seated towards the top of the table, near their hosts. Perhaps Anna liked him better, with his more elegant clothes and his swagger. 'The same as in Berlin,' he said, as he picked up a shoot of asparagus, dipped it, put it in his mouth, as the table watched and waited.

'What signs? I haven't seen any signs,' Jozef said after this pause. Milo shot him a look, swallowed.

'Yes, you have.' He directed his gaze to the rest of the table. 'They were pasted all over the old Jewish quarter. Someone put one on the doors of the temple.'

'You mean the Remuh? No, we would have heard,' Stefan said.

'What did they say exactly?' Tomas Hartmann said. He was a lawyer, and used the tone of a lawful investigation, as though he might pull out a notepad and begin a case.

For a moment, Milo's face glinted a kind of triumph. 'Cartoons, Jews and dogs, you know, that kind of thing . . .'

A quiet bloomed, except for one man, another doctor – Jozef thought he'd said, something to do with the throat was his specialism – who clicked his cutlery against his wine glass, as though about to give a speech. But when everyone looked at him expectantly, he stopped and shrugged.

Adam spoke. 'I have noticed there is a little more . . . perhaps nastiness on the streets, but only late at night, among the rougher elements of the city, and they are drunkards and scoundrels, just looking for a fight. They are just . . . angry at everything because they're poor. What talk is there at the university?' he asked Stefan.

'Just as I've said,' Stefan replied in gentle tones. He shrugged. 'What can we do but stay calm and wait it out? There've been beatings in Germany for years now.'

'People are dead,' Karl said.

Several conversations broke out at once. 'Yes, that's what I heard,' 'Yes, we shouldn't be surprised,' came from some, though their tone was a return to the brittle forcefulness that had so struck Jozef earlier in the evening. Others were more shocked, saying, 'What, just killed in the streets, just in front of everyone like that?' and 'The law is still the law, they should complain, what are the police and lawyers doing?' There seemed a kind of grim satisfaction, Jozef thought, in the first group, showing off their worldly cynicism in their bland acceptance of the news, pitying their cosseted and blind peers.

Milo seemed to be enjoying his moment in the spotlight, called out again so that his words carried over these smaller groups, so heads turned back to him and there was even the scrape of chairs as people moved to hear him more clearly.

'There are rumours that soon Jews will be stripped of their businesses, professional licences, that sort of thing.' When the guests only nodded, tutted into their laps, he added, 'I mean, here in Poland too.'

He looked around expectantly, and Jozef felt there was a certain ugly hunger in his face, which turned bewildered as most around the table chuckled and seemed to relax.

'Well, that isn't possible,' Tomas Hartmann said, and sat back in his chair, as though at the end of a long meeting. 'These lower elements, youths without any direction, you know, and the odd fight, that's one thing, but a law like that could never be passed here. Even with Piłsudski gone, things can't get so bad.' Again the table fed these lines back to itself, a murmuring echo, *That isn't possible.* Jozef was sitting too far from Milo to do what he wished, which was to lean in and whisper, *Well, that didn't have your intended effect.*

'The books and beatings, they aren't always groups of angry young men,' Milo said. 'It's the government too.' But his spell was dissipating; shoulders had dropped a little, and the table turned to remembering their last scare, when Piłsudski had died, and they had stood at the funeral procession wondering what would happen now that the refrain ran hollow: *Piłsudski would never, Piłsudski is a friend to Jews.* 'Do you remember? All that nervous chatter! But it turned out to be nothing . . .' Soon determined conversation moved back to this new painting of Alicia, how much the family's other paintings were admired, how they would like to see them, *Oh, could we? They hang in one of the drawing rooms, I think? Shall we take* nalewka *in there?*

As they glided over the thick rugs, the house lit up for the party, the Wawel splendid from the windows, Adam touched Jozef's arm.

'Go find the girls, they are in my study, I think.'

'They aren't in bed?'

'We let them stay up; Alicia will never sleep when we have guests. And you should talk about your painting.'

Jozef was surprised by the rush of relief he felt on hearing he had the commission. He must have been more worried about money than he thought. The canvas at home, even the thrill of his strange new idea, had faded. He looked for Milo, hoped to savour his moment of triumph, but he was ahead with the others, and a servant was waiting to show him to the study.

The two sisters were sitting together by the fire, the youngest in the same silly frothy dress. Jozef lingered near a bookshelf, pretending to study the gold-leaf titles and thick leather bindings. The girls hadn't seen him. Alicia was reading, probably a studied pose, Jozef thought, she's been told to read and is gazing at the pages to please her sister. But on watching her for a few seconds he saw that she was truly engrossed, biting her lip a little, turning the pages greedily. The older one was dressed more like a servant than a lady of the house, in a dull brown dress, her hair un-styled. This one would be more at home, Jozef thought, in the tenements of his own neighbourhood, the smell of grease in the air, holding a baby or two. He approached them and smiled at Alicia.

'Shouldn't you be in bed?'

He winced. He sounded like an angry schoolteacher.

Alicia ignored him. The older one smiled at him. Jozef felt a mild panic, smothered by wine: he had forgotten this one's name.

'Mama told us to wait up, so you could talk about your portrait,' the older girl said. She gestured awkwardly for him to sit in the leather chair by the fire, and he gave her a grateful smile.

They sat for a while, watching the embers burn. Despite himself, and his acute awareness of the awkward silence, Jozef began watching the colours with a painter's eye, imagined the spark of that sunset orange on a canvas, wondered if that particular red could be captured. He felt a kind of hopeless shame at the silence that thickened around them, except for the fire and the stubborn turn of Alicia's pages. It should have been he who made the effort, but his old sullenness in this house had descended, his heavy dinner weighing him down into the chair.

'Alicia, would you like to ask Mr Pienta about his ideas?' the older girl asked, her face red.

Alicia placed her book aside with infuriating affectation, patting it in place like a prissy middle-aged woman. *My God*, Jozef thought. *I will have to find a way not to throw her off that damned balcony.* When she looked up at him, he tried to find some interest in the planes of her face in the firelight, some light he could use. She caught his eye, tilted her chin a little, and the effect was so akin to flirtation that he shrank back and folded his hands.

'Your father has asked for a portrait, something . . . pretty,' he said, feeling helpless at the flatness of his tone, but too irritated to rouse himself to false enthusiasm. She nodded.

'Would you like to hold your little dog perhaps, or maybe a book you like? It is good to have something to do with your hands, or they fall like this,' and he let his dangle like a broken puppet. The older girl laughed. Alicia caught it and gave a second-long smile that was so open and unstudied she instantly became a child again, free of poise. Then she closed her face again, straightened her back.

'The last time I was sitting down, and I had my hands in my lap like this.'

She showed him the way ladies folded their hands together.

'Yes, I've heard about the last time,' he made a vague attempt to tease her. 'Are you going to chop off all of your hair for me too?'

'I was just a child then,' she said, primly. Then she felt cross with herself; she always laughed when Papa mentioned it, and this was Papa's friend. 'And Papa really wants this one. He . . . I really want him to . . .' Frustrated, she looked into the flames. She couldn't explain her clawing need for her Papa to be confirmed in the eyes of Kraków as important, a patron, a rich man, not some dog in the street, without talking about the man who had attacked him. A now familiar flare of rage overcame her and she hid her face in Mimi's fur for a moment, imagined her little pet biting off that man's face, his huge hands thrown up to protect him ripped away by the dog's sharp teeth.

Jozef dug his toes into his shoes. *I'm trying, you spoiled brat,* he thought.

Alicia was looking into the fire now. 'I won't ruin this one,' she said. 'I want it to be beautiful.' *I want Papa to love it,* she thought. *I want it to be famous, I want that man to see it and to be afraid of us.*

On his way out, woozy with wine and *nalewka*, the oppressive heat of the study, the effort of playing his part, Jozef met Milo as they were being handed coats by two tired-looking young servants. Jozef had lost his impulse to crow at Milo and felt shy instead, and a vague panic about having to share a tram or even a long walk back to their part of the city together, labouring over conversation. He offered an awkward smile. 'I'll maybe get a cab,' he said.

'Won't they lend a car?' Milo replied, focused on the buttons of his coat. He spoke mildly, but when he glanced up there was a sharpness to the set of his lips. The servants retreated, probably hoping they could collapse into chairs or beds, drink their cheaper booze, gossip about them all.

'Well, I don't want to go back up and ask, you know,' Jozef said, set his face in a brief grimace, hoping to find common ground. *We are both outsiders here; I won, but it's awkward for me too.*

'Of course, of course.' Milo's voice dropped to a loud, drunken whisper, the effort of keeping his voice hushed straining the muscles on his throat and causing flecks of spit to form at the corners of his lips. 'You can't trust them to share their expensive things, they sit on piles of gold, they have money sewn into the curtains, there's gold in the fucking walls. In the walls, imagine, you could punch this through' – Milo struck the wall with his fist – 'and coins would spill out, but fucking wait to see if *you* get a penny of it over what you agreed in your contract, and they'll probably try to screw you out of that as well.'

Jozef began to stammer, 'Well, I don't . . .' and Milo waved his words away, lurched at the door. He fumbled with the large, heavy doorknob. 'Where're their servants? They can't even run a house properly, it's all smoke and mirrors you know, pretending to be upper class, they all come from shoe sellers and market stalls. Good luck with the portrait, but don't expect anything from these fucking dogs, you know.'

Jozef had unconsciously been nodding, a tic of his nerves, trying to scramble what to say, how to defend his friend, how to deal with the aggression spilling around him. *Please, please, just leave, just go*, he thought.

Milo took his silence and the nods to mean agreement and shook Jozef's hand before wrenching the door and stumbling down the steps. Jozef sank for a moment against the coats still hanging from the beautiful oak stand.

His mother had never had much time for Jews, but even she would have been ashamed of him just then, he knew. To allow such a breach of manners, to insult the host who has just fed you, to use such language in their very home: this would have appalled her, although she would have also – later, when he told her about it, in a letter or a visit – reminded him to check his contract and keep a tab on expenses.

Jozef counted seconds, feeling his cheeks warm with the embarrassment of this childish fear of Milo walking slowly, their paths crossing. He buttoned and unbuttoned his coat. He should have said goodnight to his hosts, but his reserves of social energy were used up, and he felt a desperate desire for his small, draughty room, his bed, the silence and the blank walls. He hesitated over a bell he suspected would summon a servant and allow him to pass on a message, or at least be subtly shown how to behave, but weariness from it all made him open the door himself and step into the night.

At the top of the stairs, in the spot his younger daughter took to overhear conversations between him and his wife, Adam Oderfeldt stared at a knot of wood. He'd thought it would amuse him to overhear the two painters and their impression of his daughter, the house, his friends, himself. Pienta in particular he had hoped to impress, liked to have the younger, poorer man around to be generous to, to ostentatiously not comment upon his stained cuffs. He felt a series of small collapses in the solid wood beneath him, as though it was not solidity beneath him at all but a thin crust which covered seething lava. The painter from Warsaw with his news from Berlin and his drunken bitterness, and the man who had struck him on Alicia's birthday joined many others, smaller, less clear, easy to dismiss, but considered together something began to take shape. Averted eyes. Contracts more carefully checked. Requests for other opinions. A certain gleam in the eyes when sharing news from across Europe, perhaps searching his face for fear. The trickle of news from Germany, someone's cousin, someone's schoolfriend, someone's brother-in-law, and now open attacks, in the streets there, and signs going up around Kraków.

Adam placed a palm on the step, tried to feel the massive weight of the house, how its foundations sent deep roots into the street. Tried to feel the comforting solidity of the Wawel, but found instead only a flimsy seal that could be punctured and peeled away like tissue paper. Adam sat for a while listening to his sleeping house, the only sound the far-away clinks of Dorothea and Janie working downstairs.

He sought out Anna. He wanted the steadiness of his wife's slim body next to him, her deep breaths. He found her in her room, already with her hair around her shoulders, always thinner than it seemed in its elaborate twists.

'Goodnight, dear,' she said. 'Did your guests leave? I'm afraid I might have abandoned them rather rudely.'

Adam sat on the edge of the bed, felt a dull ache in his back. He looked down at himself: the pristine shirt beginning to crumple, the soft belly beneath, the long, spidery limbs. He had broken his leg skating years before, and the splintering ease of it came to him then, how he had snapped like kindling. He wrapped his arms around his knees like a child.

'So we'll ask Jozef to paint Alicia for you. I didn't like his dirty cuffs tonight or how much wine he drank, but I liked the earlier one he did of us well enough, I suppose.' She was chattering insistently, the business of the house, their decisions, and he gratefully took the hint. He wanted only to lie down next to her.

'Don't invite Milo again,' Anna added.

Adam started, hung his head. So she had heard it. 'Of course not,' he said.

Anna pulled at the skin of her cheeks in the mirror, eyed the reflection of her husband on the bed. She wondered if she could try to describe the revulsion she'd felt earlier: how Milo seemed like rotten meat with perfume spilled across it; how somehow he had insulted her, something in the way he took her hand, some cast to his voice. Instead she only said, 'I didn't like his manners at the table, holding court like that.'

Adam watched her, rubbing some lotion into her hands and smoothing it across her forehead. She caught his eye in the mirror.

'Do you go to France this summer?'

This caught him off guard.

'I might. Let me know if there's something I can bring you.'

She made a small sound of assent, turned with a questioning look.

'May I stay?' he always asked, a formality he couldn't shake. 'To sleep.'

'I've upset you, but it was you who talked about France.'

'It doesn't matter.'

'Anna, dearest Aneczka. I'm . . . please be a friend tonight.'

He spread his hands in a hopeless gesture. For a terrible moment he felt he might cry in front of her, which had happened only once in their marriage, when her mother had died. Anna had cradled him like a baby and said nothing, her face only a little paler than usual.

'What is it?' she said now.

He laid back, the canopy of her pretty bedroom, birds and blue swirls in silk, swimming above him. He was drunk. *I'm afraid*, he thought. *A man attacked me, with Alicia there, her little hand wrenched from mine, and I lay sprawled on the ground like a child, and now she lies for me, and another man insulted me in my own house, and even Jozef who I thought loved me, said nothing, nothing, and across the border they are killing people right there in the streets, I can't wear my* kippah *now, I've hidden it away, and now even you are angry with me over this old problem of France, and I am all alone.*

'What do you think of this rumour, about businesses?' he asked, into the silks.

'What, are you worried?'

'No.'

'Then what?'

'Perhaps a little.'

He heard her feet on the carpet, felt her weight, cat-like, on the end of the bed. She put a hand on his shoulder. Adam began to lean into her, but then she shook him gently. 'Well, stop. It will upset the whole house. We've already kept the girls inside these weeks, and for what? So they can grow pale and bicker. Go into work. Work harder so you don't fixate on things like a boy.'

7

IN THE DAYLIGHT HOURS the apartment took on a different mood. Adam was presumably at his factory, lines of fabric and textiles, the crunch of sewing machines; or in some well-lit office with plants and the smell of leather. Anna welcomed Jozef when he arrived, ordered tea and pastries, but had since disappeared. Jozef had painted in Adam's study last time, his patron at the desk. Now, sitting in the small room Anna had led him to, the plate of pastries demolished, he felt nervous, unsure which rooms he was allowed in, unsure where the girl was, where her mother had gone, or who he was to ask. The pastry, some almond flaky thing, expensive, made a sticky paste at the back of his throat and the tea had run out. Outside the door all was quiet. Should he ring a bell? In the corridor he caught sight of a servant, but she bustled away before he could ask. Fighting the irritation that descended on him, Jozef pressed on, knocking on doors, finding beautifully furnished empty rooms, until he found his way back to the large room which overlooked the Wawel, the huge dining table from the previous night cleared and laid with a pressed new tablecloth. With relief he saw the older girl was curled in a window seat, reading.

'Good morning.'

'Oh! Excuse me, Mr Pienta.' She started to uncurl and closed her book.

'Please, Jozef, please. Don't, no, please don't let me disturb you, only—'

'I'm sorry, I was supposed to come and fetch you, Mama has gone out but then I lost track of time.'

She was wearing the same kind of simple clothes as the previous evening, her feet bare in a pool of winter sunlight. Her hair was pulled into a messy plait which left curls around her face. She arched her back, stretching out from her reading pose, and glanced at the Wawel with a smile. Jozef could see the composition. The play of light on the grey and brown, warming it like sun on autumn foliage. The strands of hair, the edge of the cheek.

'I should paint a portrait of you, Karolina.' He was pleased he remembered her name this time.

She turned from fetching her book. He'd expected a pleased blush, perhaps a smile. Instead, to his surprise, there was an unmistakeable frown for a moment, before her face went blank.

'I'm sorry if I offended you,' he stammered, feeling his face grow hot.

'I'm not offended.'

'What are you reading?'

'Some poems. I'll take you to wait for Alicia, she's choosing a dress.'

He walked with her, watching her bare feet sink into the carpets. Perhaps, he realised, with a rush of horror, she thought he had been flirting with her. She would tell her parents and there would be uproar. He stopped and she turned to look at him.

'I only meant, you were accidentally, in that pose reading by the Wawel, it was a good composition. I thought you might like a portrait like your sister's. That's all, I wasn't trying to flatter you,' he said, feeling like a little boy explaining some blunder, irritated still more by the rules and games of this world that Adam kept pulling him into.

Karolina bit the inside of her cheek. *She must be about sixteen, seventeen*, Jozef thought. *I should be more careful.*

'It's only that,' she faltered, her own face flushing. 'Thank you for the thought, but Papa and Mama would never think of it. It's only Alicia they'd want.'

'But,' he said, moving towards her and trying not to smile, 'I painted a portrait of you and your mother, years ago. Don't you remember?' As he asked her, he felt vertigo from trying to reach back to those days, trying to align the little child he had painted, all chubby arms and squirming, with this still, barefoot creature fixing him with a level gaze.

'That was before Alicia was born.' She spoke simply, without bitterness.

Jozef had been the favourite himself. He was the only boy, and his sisters had been lumped together and dismissed, while his voice was always heard, his work celebrated, his whims indulged. He considered comforting Karolina with denial, a claim that Adam had also asked for a portrait of her this time, and explaining to him afterwards. But he could see the sharpness in Karolina's eyes, and saw that she would resent the platitude.

'Parents love all of their children, but there is always a favourite. It's no one's fault,' he tried. She nodded. He went on, 'It's not always good to be the golden child, either. The pressure.'

'I don't think Alicia feels any pressure.'

He hadn't meant to get pulled into petty family politics.

'We should find your sister. I'd like to work in the morning light.'

His encounter with Karolina had made him even less interested in Alicia. They found her in her room with a pile of dresses, an obscene frothy pile of silk and frill and lace.

'I don't know which one,' she said as they came into the room. 'I should have asked Papa before he left for work.'

'Good morning,' Jozef said, unable to resist the rebuke to her manners. He wouldn't indulge her any more than he had to.

'Good morning,' she replied listlessly. She seemed genuinely worried about the dresses, and Jozef felt a flash of exasperation.

'It really doesn't matter about the dress,' he said, trying to keep his voice soft. 'It's just sketches today.'

'Alicia? Did you hear? Don't worry,' Karolina said, kneeling down to where her sister was rummaging, almost feverishly. She was sitting on a pile of fabric.

'You look like the Princess and the Pea, Ala,' Karolina teased her.

'It has to be perfect,' Alicia almost whispered.

'What you are wearing today is fine for now,' Jozef said.

They went back to the window where Karolina had been reading. The older girl found another window seat, with a dog curled in her lap, to watch them and sometimes make notes in a leather book. Jozef wondered if she was also sketching, but thought better of asking her. He asked Alicia to stand naturally by the window so the light found one side of her face.

It was like navigating in a snowstorm. There was nothing to catch the eye, to create a composition from. A blank of plain face and dull hair and the white smock he assumed was day wear in the house, a kind of rich girl uniform. To relax her, he asked Karolina to hand Alicia the dog, which lolled in her arms.

He'd expected laziness, distraction; he had a stock of wheedling phrases and false jollity stored up, expected long breaks and trifling chatter. Instead she was so focused as to be unnerving, stood almost too still, breathed in shallow sips as though afraid. Karolina was also puzzled, he could see, glancing up from her notebook and watching her sister with a small smile that told her surprise.

Jozef tried to relax her. He asked questions about her education, what she was reading, what her favourite game was. Who was her best friend? Alicia, her head and face turned slightly from him as directed, answered from a tiny opening at the side of her mouth in the shortest possible answers, until she crossed into rudeness.

'Alicia,' Karolina said. 'Mr Pienta asked you about Mimi, did you hear him?'

Alicia broke the pose and glared at him. She put down the dog, which trotted away primly, tinkling bells. 'She is three, I heard the question. Why don't you want to sketch?'

'Alicia!' her sister rebuked her.

Jozef smiled at her, repressing his dislike. 'I *am* sketching. Only you are a little . . . stiff. Try to relax a little. Try—'

'I'm standing how you *told* me to stand.'

Her face was reddening in a warning of tears. Jozef retreated to the sketch, pretended to be engrossed in the dull lines. His own petulance threatened to overspill and wash away his mask of deference; he allowed himself, half ashamed and half satisfied, to think vicious insults against Alicia as he sketched the same line again and again. By the time he got to *spoiled little bitch* he had exorcised some of his irritation. He glanced up again, to where Alicia was still standing in the odd puppet-like way, the muscles on her neck so taut they looked painful. Her arms in the white smock were bare and goose-bumped; he saw they were still carrying some puppy fat.

'Come, come,' he said, softening his voice and soothing his conscience a little. 'Let me show you what I'm doing, maybe that will help.'

He had only meant this for Alicia, but they both came, Karolina breaking the spine of her book as she laid it face down. They stood behind him and he tried to explain.

'For now I'm just trying to get an idea of the shape and the pose. See?' He ran his finger over the edge of the composition. 'At the moment it's too much of a block, like a square. Best is if there is some graceful line, here—' he broke off to curve the edge of the line where Alicia's arm and side could make an oval with his finger, smudging the pencil line. 'And on the other side, something different. See now you are like a stiff old photograph, like—' and he turned to them, made a rictus face, his arms pinned to his side, leaned onto his toes so his calves strained. It worked; the girls laughed. 'There is no interesting line in the shape to—'

'Yes, I see,' Alicia said. Karolina was also nodding, but her eye was wandering back to her book. Jozef smiled at Alicia but it was clear to him she had no idea what he was talking about. At least she might relax a little.

She went back to her position, curved her right arm into her side, placed her left arm on the edge of the windowsill, tilted her right shoulder slightly forward. Jozef laughed in surprise. Professional models in the big studios needed more coaching.

'That's it, just exactly as I said, absolutely perfect. You're quick.'

The girl flushed with pleasure. *That's how to handle her*, Jozef thought. *No one tells her she's clever.*

'See,' Jozef went on, 'now the light is catching you in interesting ways. Let me just . . .' He rummaged, found his chalk. 'Karolina, you see?' but she was reading now, looked up briefly, smiled and nodded, returned to her other world. Alicia made a movement when he said 'see' but he held up a hand, showing her his palm, and she stayed still with a smile.

He began to dart chalk over the sketch: here, the crook of that elbow, here, the left cheek, pushing the right further into shadow. A small crown of light here towards the fore-head: Adam would like that, but it also drew the eye up to the face. He felt specks of excitement, worked quickly to anchor the ideas. His own work, that wispy ghost back in his studio, evaporated. He fell into a rare state of focus, vaguely aware of the two girls and the turning of Karolina's pages, her occasional yawn and stretch, noting the movement of light, its creep across the carpet and angular growth along the curtains. A portrait like this would usually be punctuated with rests for the child, but after her brief lesson Alicia was perfectly still, moved just so when directed, her eyes fixed on some far-away point. The sunlight warmed the room, the low hum of the city outside was soothing in its monotony, the contrast between the hush inside and the bustle below; the three of them stayed as though under a spell. There was no awkwardness in the silence between them now, but a quickly strengthening thread of purpose.

8

Anna had worn the wrong shoes. They pinched around her toes, and a low throb of pain had begun in a ridge where the leather dug in. The sun had coaxed her into walking the short way from the apartment into the shopping district around the Ulica Floriańska.

She had been in the apartment too long, absorbing Adam's nerves, the crying of the servants, the quiet confusion of her daughters over their parents' lies and pronouncements. Restlessness tickled at her as she sat for hour after hour in the stiff-backed chair in her husband's study, listening to him read out sections of news reports, watching him fiddle with the radio, echoing the reports as though continuing a long debate, though she had said nothing, a half-read magazine in her lap.

When she'd said she was going shopping, Robert had gone to ready the car, and Janie began collecting her outdoor things: boots, coat, gloves. But then the doorbell had rung and the painter arrived, and there was tea to order and small talk to be made, and she would have been trapped with the man all day if she hadn't slipped out as he ate his pastries, giving instructions to Karolina to take care of him.

It was poor manners, she knew, but he was only a portrait painter. Besides, she thought, as she walked as slowly as she dared, hoping for a stately rather than hobbling effect, Karolina would soon need to learn how to host. She was seventeen

76

now, and couldn't curl up like a little beetle with her books much longer. Perhaps they would send her to university, all her beloved books and their musty smell; she would meet a husband there, or perhaps she might marry one of Adam's business associates. A society wedding, with a reception at the Wentzl or at a villa out near Zakopane, perhaps. The newly-weds would settle in Kraków, one of the nice apartments near the river. The ghosts of Anna's parents would say to each other, *Look at the way our little Aneczku's daughter lives. Look how our blood has trickled upwards.*

With the distraction of her daydreaming Anna had crossed the Glowny, barely registering the Cloth Hall and its crowds. She stopped now to look back at the square, pleased she had forgotten to feel anxious. So, the air tasted the same, people seemed friendly, even happy enough. She couldn't see any posters, any signs. Milo's face drifted across her mind, its satisfied sneer. A man stepped in her way, apologised, moved around her. A small group was gathering to hear the bugler on the hour. All was as it should be. Anna turned and tripped over a little as she did so. A man caught her arm.

'Oh! Thank you.'

'Watch your step, the cobbles are so uneven here.'

'Yes, I know, I—'

'Not from here, are you?'

'Excuse me?'

'I saw you, looking around. Waiting to hear the bugler?'

She set her mouth a little, annoyed with herself for falling, literally, into conversation with this overfamiliar man, who up close she saw was wearing a dirty coat and no gloves. She gave a tiny nod, started to move away.

'He'll be playing in a minute,' the man said, touching her arm again.

She should just keep walking, but instead she said, 'Yes, I know that.'

'Lived here all my life. Good time to visit.' He tapped his nose, and his eyes began wandering over her face.

This was too much. She turned sharply and walked, ignoring her screaming feet. With a jolt she saw that he was following her.

'Oh, don't want to hear him? I said it's a good time to visit.'

'Yes, I heard you.' She sped up.

'Don't you want to hear why?' He took hold of her arm.

She felt a heat rising, began to glance around for, what? Police? The Glowny was full of people, so why did she feel so afraid?

'I *live* here, and I'd appreciate if you left me alone.' She was dismayed that her voice had a tiny shake in it. He was too close, she could smell vodka on his breath, and he still had hold of her arm. He was studying her face.

'Kraków accent, is that?'

'Excuse me?'

'You're from across the river.'

What she had thought was aggressive flirtation, the vague threat of a strange man talking to her, a pretty woman, in the street, became something else. He was looking not with admiration or even with open, disgusting lust. She began to feel cold.

'I beg your pardon? I live right here in the centre.'

'Hmm.' He smiled, gripped still tighter. 'You hide it well, but I can hear it in the vowels.' He tapped his nose with his other hand, grinned at her. 'I know all the sounds of Kraków. I bet you speak Yiddish, don't you?'

'Let me go,' she hissed, and wrenched her arm away. 'How dare you touch me?' Her voice rose. 'Excuse me!' she called out to a group of men nearby. 'This man is—'

The man backed off as the men approached. He seemed amused. She waved the men away, feeling that her throat had closed and if she were to speak, her voice would betray her and get stuck.

Ignoring the pain in her feet, she almost stamped to the Ulica Floriańska, rehearsing how she should have spoken to the man, angry with herself for falling into such a young girl's trap, angry that Adam's fears had seeped through the apartment walls and followed her through the streets. In the old neighbourhood it was rare for strangers to approach you like that; everyone knew each other, but as she'd grown up and the family had got richer there had been more and more forays into the city, and she had had catcalls, looks, even a touch once or twice. It had been an annoyance, like flies in summer. Strange that in the middle of a crowd, older, in the day, she should feel so afraid. No. She was spooked by Milo and his needling, by Adam's childishness. She wouldn't look at it.

She stopped at the window of a favourite millinery shop, where the displays were always imaginative. The assistant was arranging ribbons, dangling silk butterflies around the jewel-coloured hats. She caught Anna's eye for a moment, gave a courteous nod. Anna indulged in a quick thought to her younger self: *You can just walk in and buy one, Aneczka, if you want*. Leaning a little against the glass to relieve the pressure on her feet, she looked like her childhood self, she thought. Her little fingers splayed, she moved so her nose was pressed against the glass for a second, felt its cold bite. It was so like the way Alicia stood against the windows at home that she felt a tiny tug of warmth for her. In the glass she studied her face, looking for Alicia and Karolina there, finding, with a jolt, her mother instead.

'Anna?'

She jumped. What did she look like, peering into the window like a street child? Worse, it was Janina Kardas, holding her hand up and squinting in an ugly way, a kind of twisted smile. *Oh, go away*, Anna thought, *of course it would be you who would catch me off my guard.*

'Mrs Kardas, hello,' Anna said, limping a little as she came to take her hand.

'Janina, please.'

'I was just . . . I came to see if any of the new season's clothes . . . I love these displays, don't you? Isn't it mild today? Aren't you hot in that thick dress?'

Janina frowned at the barb, which Anna instantly regretted. *I should just go home*, she thought.

'Oh Anna, your shoes!' Janina cried. 'What on earth? Is that blood?'

'No, of course not.'

'It is, it is!' Janina crowed. 'It's seeping right through your stockings! Won't you sit down?' Her grip on Anna's arm was strong, guiding her into the shop where the sweet smell of leather, the tick of an ornamental clock, soothed some of Anna's nerves. The shop girl from the window offered a chair, then tea, biscuits. *Would madam like some water?* As she bustled away, Janina, who had also accepted a chair, took Anna's hand with alarming tenderness.

'Are you all right, my dear? Are you . . . ?' Her face was open with glee. Anna almost laughed.

'Oh my goodness,' she said, shaking her head. 'I was just remembering . . . at the window. I used to shop here when I was younger,' she lied. Imagine, another baby, at her age! She felt a pang of affection for Adam, prone on the bed the night before, imploring her to be a friend to him. The idea that their neighbours took for granted that they were still lovers pleased her.

Janina gave her hand a squeeze. 'It's only that you looked so strange.' She kept her hand on Anna's. Her older soft skin made Anna think of her mother, who had loved her granddaughters so much. Neither of them could remember her, though Karolina had written poems about her that Anna had secretly read, sense memories that had clutched at her: the surprising strength of her grip, the smell of slightly burnt hair, her way of cupping the girls' faces in her hands. Anna released Janina's hand, picked up a hat, began turning it over in her hands, feeling a familiar terrifying hollowness gaping inside her. She could never imagine holding her children's hands, or cupping their faces in her mother's way.

'Anna?' Janina said.

'My feet do hurt, you're right. My own fault, I rushed out this morning without thinking.'

'Is everything all right?'

'I wonder if I shouldn't have come into town today.'

'But there's nothing to fear.'

'A man—' she broke off as the girl arrived with a tray of tea things. What would she say? *A man touched my arm, and told me this was a good time to visit, and then heard something in my accent?* The girl was very young, wore too much make-up. The tea was in good quality china, and Anna felt she would have to buy something.

'This is a beautiful style,' she said, gesturing behind her, as the girl clinked saucers around. 'I'll take three.'

The girl smiled. 'Of course, madam.'

Janina said, 'Yes, you must feel you should be at home, comforting the children.'

'To them it's just some broken windows in another country.'

Janina flushed. 'Well.'

'It's Adam who is so affected.'

'But you've come out? A wife should—'

'Yes, yes, but he's gone into work today.'

Janina was silenced by Anna's tone. They sipped their over-sweetened tea. Anna watched the people outside, strolling, linking arms, nannies with their charges. Some glanced inside, and she felt on display, but oddly grateful for the glass and ribbons, the girl's manners, even Janina.

'We should visit the German refugees arriving,' Janina said. 'Make them welcome.'

'Yes, I'm going to throw a party,' Anna said, irritated by what she heard as an education in manners.

'A *party*?'

'A gathering. To welcome them, and show solidarity.'

Janina made a small sound that Anna couldn't interpret.

'The painter arrived, from last night, you know. Did you speak to him?' Anna said at length.

Janina shifted in her seat. 'The one from Berlin? He seemed—'

'No, that's the other one, and neither are from Berlin. You're thinking of Milo something or other, but I mean Adam's friend, Jozef. He's going to paint Alicia.'

'I didn't listen to either of them much,' Janina said with a sniff.

'You seemed to, when Milo was talking about Berlin. You were interested then.'

Anna watched Janina as she angled a hat from side to side, far too ostentatious for her, deep in thought.

'Aleks writes to me about these things too,' Janina said. 'He reads about them in Paris, sends newspaper clippings. He gets nervous. It's natural for the young to overthink things, to get a little excited.'

Janina turned the hat over and over like an absorbed child. It was Anna's turn to touch the older woman's hand.

'I forgot he would be there already! You must miss him.' When Janina only nodded, Anna went on, 'You're right. We shouldn't be frightened. Kraków is safe, look,' she dropped to a whisper and nodded towards the shop girl, wrapping her hats in tissue, placing them into boxes, 'it's so calm and friendly.' She called to the girl, 'When you've finished, please call me a cab back to Bernardyńska.'

When the cab arrived, Anna offered her neighbour a lift.

'No thank you,' Janina replied. 'I'm going across the river.'

'To the old neighbourhood? Why?'

'Why not? I go all the time.'

'Is it . . .' Anna had meant to say safe, but that would crumble away the thin crust they had built between them. 'Is it *nice*?'

'I like to go to my old doctor and optician, and I have a favourite cobbler there as well.'

'I never go.' Anna suddenly felt ridiculous in this, as though the old quarter were another world, not streets away.

'Well,' the older woman seemed at a loss what to say. They stood in the street, the cab waiting, Anna's boxes piled in the back. Anna didn't know whether she wanted to be rid of this woman or to keep her close, talk, hold her hand. She felt they were in some kind of tiring dance, the two of them, always circling, never really speaking in any real way, but each sensing how the other was shaken, and wanting to prop the other up. Perhaps she would want to cling onto any face she knew, after the strangeness of the last few weeks and the changed air in the house, her own inexplicable fear in the Glowny.

'Come to my cobbler,' Janina gabbled, a little flushed, evidently mortified by the long silence that Anna had allowed to open up between them. 'You could come and have your shoes stretched. I used to go to the one two streets along,' Janina said in a confidential tone as though this were some great secret, taking Anna's arm and guiding her away from the cab. 'But I can't go there now.'

She stared into Anna's face, waiting.

'Oh,' Anna said.

'I just couldn't possibly.'

Anna was silent.

'The daughter, Mira, at the other shop, you know. I made a complaint about her at the school. It was years ago.'

'She went to school with Aleks?'

'No, no! She was his teacher.'

'A teacher and a cobbler's daughter?'

Janina made an impatient sound, clicking her tongue.

'She was the daughter-in-law. Very above herself. She didn't teach him properly. And she wore terrible clothes, a shorter skirt, in a school! I had a petition made up.' Janina sniffed. 'They wouldn't serve me after that, so I go to this other place.'

'Why don't you just use one of the smart shops in town?'

'They look good, but they don't use the proper old techniques.'

Anna felt this was unlikely, wondered if the real reason was the grudge against Aleks's hapless teacher, a hope that it would get back to the family, so many years later, that Janina Kardas was a customer of their near rival. She laughed inwardly at the pettiness of this; found she even admired it a little. She too played out her own petty grudges, tiny acts of peevishness which brought her a guilty joy: cancelling orders from certain places because of a look, a tone of voice she didn't like, even, on one occasion, because a girl was too pretty. Perhaps that's all it was with the painter, she realised. Perhaps Milo simply fell victim to this pettiness of hers. The thought soothed her.

'But of course Adam gets most of your shoes from France, I suppose?'

On an ordinary day this would rile her, but she was so distracted by the oddness of the whole day that Anna let it slide.

'Well, I should get home. You won't let the cab take you across the river?'

'No, I like the walk.'

The Floriańska was busy now, the cab driver beginning to clear his throat, and they said goodbye, each left with a strange discomfort of things unsaid, but not sure what they were, or why they felt a sudden impulse to confide in a woman they had never liked.

I'm sure she's expecting, Janina thought to herself as she negotiated the crowds, with a stab of envy. Anna's pale face, the tiny tremble when she'd taken her hand, even her throat was tense. *Probably another daughter, it tends to run that way.* She tried to laugh at Anna's obvious distaste for the old neighbourhood and Janina's habits of still shopping there, but felt instead only a vague embarrassment that she might be committing a *faux pas* that would be all over the Bernardyńska before long. *Did you hear, Janina Kardas buys her shoes from a cheap cobbler across the river? Imagine, perhaps Kardas didn't leave her as much as you'd think. Perhaps he was a swindler or a drinker—* she broke off, too furious at this imaginary gossiping neighbour to continue.

Anna lost Janina quickly in the crowds, and sat back. What a disaster her tiny adventure had been. She felt too hot in her layers, cross and tired. The ugly hats jostled around the back seat on the cobbled streets. Perhaps she ought to have gone to the old neighbourhood with Janina, but she felt so haunted today, she could almost imagine she would meet her mother in the street.

Leaning her head against the back of the seat, she tried to untangle the strands of her mood. Adam, the rude man on the Glowny, her daughters' coldness, their blank response to Adam's grief, too like her own. Janina's needling about turning her back on the streets of her childhood. None of it was the knot. Closing her eyes, she made herself look at it. It was the news from Germany. Adam had let it take root in him and perhaps she had done the same, but been unaware.

She had seen real violence once before, when she was small. Perhaps a story or a lie, it was hard to untangle sometimes in her mind. Perhaps decorated memory. Her hand was held tightly in her mother's hand. Gloveless. So it was summer, but they were poorer then, she checked herself, so that's no help. They were living in the old house: a dustier, darker, pokier sort of life, but loud with the chatter of Yiddish running in currents through the rooms. She remembered dinners, probably Friday nights, full of people. But this was outside of the house. In the street. There is the dim ghost of her mother by her side again, her hand. There were shouts and a rough pull on the pavements. There were ugly sounds, spat-out insults. Her mother had stumbled and pulled Anna, but in the wrong direction, and for a moment she saw through the legs of the crowd a man on the road, a beating in the street. Other men were surrounding him, kicking. He tried to get up, but fell again. The crowd had gone quiet. Anna saw the blood dripping from the man's eye and lip, the soft, peachy parts of his face split open.

The silence had been the thing that struck her. In playground fights there was a lot of noise, gleeful chants and whooping. Here everyone lost their voices: dull thuds rang out as the crowd became still and then drifted. Perhaps there was the crack of a broken bone too, a rib or a jaw, as they left. She had started to cry, she thought now, or perhaps her mother had only said, *Don't cry, don't cry*, as they walked back to the house. *These things flare up sometimes, but you are safe.*

You are safe, you are safe, she sang to herself in silence, as the cab approached home. She mouthed vowels to herself, certain the man had only been trying to spook her; she sounded perfect.

When she came into the dining room where the painter was working she found her voice again and chattered into the quiet.

'I saw Mrs Kardas,' she said. 'We'll be inviting her over for dinner more. And I'm going to have a gathering for the Germans who are arriving. Girls?'

She saw too late how she had disturbed a rare peace in the room. Karolina glanced up, distracted, and gave her mother a smile, then soon curled back over her pages. The painter had stopped to give her a small formal bow and nervous nod of acknowledgement when she arrived, but was now concentrating again.

Anna was caught by a clutch of affection for Alicia, her solemn little face, her carefully placed limbs. Her hair had been left loose this morning, and she was still wearing her housedress. Soon she would be grown and curled and buttoned, pinned into place. Adam's wish for an expensive portrait, meaning a near constant visitor and a battle of wills with Alicia, had exasperated her; now she felt she understood a little. Karolina's childhood mildness had gently drifted into the quiet young woman now catching the edge of a sun-beam that fell across Alicia. Karolina lived in the corners of the house, curled on chairs, found suntraps like a cat. Anna felt a vague, constant care for her, level and steady as breath. But Alicia, difficult, spoiled, prone to flashes of rage, and so adored by Adam, for her she felt a waxing and waning, a tidal pull of pride and dislike.

Your children are safe, she picked up her silent song. *They don't even look Jewish.*

9

THE DRAWING ROOM smelled of musky perfume and sweat; despite the cool day, people's heavy, dark coats, the layers of wool, were making pools under their arms and on their lower backs. Jozef imagined the bloom of dark patches creeping along silk and the drips among the tiny hairs at the backs of necks. It pleased him to think of the elegant guests this way, their fleshy under-selves, the sharp tang of their bodies: under breasts, underarms, the lines under the buttocks. It wasn't that he found it titillating, or even subversive, to strip them like this. He did it as a kind of guard against his nerves, certainly, but also as a kind of painter's exercise, tracing the body, enjoying peeling away layers of careful pinning and arranging, the theatrical absurdity, really, of money and its pretence at being better, because of a thicker, denser, softer fabric, a shinier pin.

He stood in his accustomed place at the edge of the room, near the windows, sipping the best quality Russian vodka. He'd come to know the view from this point in the room very well over the last few weeks, where his easel was set up, and the sketches of Alicia layered over one another, so he could flip through them like a child's game and watch her shape emerging, the lines becoming cleaner. As the afternoon progressed several of the guests had come over to peer at it, made practised noises of appreciation, turned away with barely concealed sniggers. They could only see charcoal and pencil, not the painting to come.

The vodka was too strong. Jozef would have liked it watered down, but when the servant, Robert, had offered the glass, he felt somehow it wouldn't be the thing to ask. He held the glass in both hands, trying to warm the ice. The cold against his skin was welcome: he too was wearing a too-thick suit, black, borrowed from his landlord. Watching more guests arrive, he realised he stood out. Some of the men wore the caps on the back of their heads, and it was only he and the servants who were in full black. The women wore smart dresses and scarves, high heels, as though attending a society wedding.

Anna was circulating and Jozef watched her with interest, how she made a complicated dance of the room, touching arms and guiding guests together, catching an eye here, a wave there, a whisper to someone that led to a smile and a squeeze. Jozef tried to imagine her body beneath the silk dress with its long, flowing jacket that trailed behind her, as with the others, but found he couldn't do so easily; instead she seemed made of fabric and pins, like a clothespin doll. He followed her as she navigated the invisible currents of the room with supreme confidence until she came to Jozef's side.

'And Jozef,' she said, as though continuing a conversation from earlier, 'you must be lonely, standing here by your easel. Come, I'll introduce you to some of Adam's friends.'

'I prefer to be here, Mrs Oderfeldt.'

'Anna, please. But you look rather odd standing here alone.'

He shrugged, a little stung. 'I am a little odd, I suppose.'

She gave him a vague smile, but stayed still.

'I like to watch people,' he added.

'Artists do that, I suppose.'

'Yes, I imagine most of us do.'

'I don't really.'

'You don't find people interesting?'

'I hope you aren't going to paint us all, drinking in the middle of the day.' She looked over his shoulder, where the easel stood. 'Alicia and Karolina are enjoying your company, I think.'

She was still looking over his shoulder as they spoke. The effect was unnerving and somehow belittling. He felt like a small child being reprimanded.

'Karolina must find it a little boring, sitting with us all the time,' he said.

Anna shrugged, took a glass from a circulating waiter, sipped. Jozef realised she was a little drunk. 'I'm not sure I know what Karolina thinks about anything,' she said, and let out a laugh, the controlled merriment of rich ladies who must flirt and be charming.

Jozef wondered where Karolina was, spotted her in conversation with Stefan on the other side of the room. Even in that second-long glimpse he noted the supple bend of her spine as she perched on the arm of a chair, leaning in to whatever Stefan was saying, nodding. It struck him that she was perfectly relaxed; he had never seen her that way before, so languid and happy. It made her mother's tension, the set of her neck and back, the tightness in her shoulders, still more noticeable.

Anna continued, 'But I think as long as she has one of Stefan's books—' she broke off as Alicia approached. Jozef noticed how the younger daughter ghosted Anna's movements, the confidence of her stride, the slightly arrogant cast of the neck, even though she was shorter than everyone in the room. She threw indulgent smiles at the guests as a film star might: Jozef half expected her to give a regal wave. Anna made a tiny pulse-like movement towards her daughter, but seemed to catch herself, placed a hand on her hip.

'I don't like your hair this way, Alicia,' she said. 'It's rather too grown up.'

The girl's hair was pinned up, very much like Anna's and the other older women's, in a French chignon.

'Papa likes it,' Alicia said, in a neutral way that could be defiant, but was hard to read. 'He said I look like Pola Negri.'

Anna laughed. 'Stay here with Mr Pienta while I talk to the other guests.'

'Yes, Mama.'

Anna gave him a nod and swept away, was soon embedded in a circle of women, joining their choruses of *Did you hears* and *Well I nevers*.

Jozef sank down onto the sill and Alicia joined him, her back to the Wawel.

'Are you sad?' she asked.

'No, why?'

'About Germany.'

'Oh! Well, I know your Papa was upset. But I, I think . . .' he dropped his voice, and she smiled slightly, moved her head closer, 'I think, well, that—'

'I don't care,' she interrupted him. 'I don't know why we should all be here being upset about dead men we don't know. If it was Papa or you I would be sad or Uncle Stefan a bit but I don't really care about anyone else.'

He was surprised by the strength of the warmth he felt on her casual dropping in his name next to Adam's, and suppressed a grin.

'What about poor Karolina and your Mama?'

She looked shocked. 'I meant men of course!' but she covered her mouth in delight at her *faux pas*. 'If Karolina died I would cry for days.'

Should he ask again about Anna? He decided not to. Alicia seemed to fall into thought, and they sat for a moment in comfortable silence. This felt the most natural state for them after these weeks, the only sound the scratch of his work and the occasional murmur if he wished her to move, but she was so instinctive in her understanding of the shape that he only needed to raise a hand, nudge the air, and she would find it perfectly. It was like conducting the world's most talented orchestra.

'Is the painting going to be good?' she asked, after a while. She asked this often; in the beginning he had read in it the whine of a child, and dismissed it with a shrug; now he weighed the question.

'Yes, Alicia. I think it is going to be good.'

'The shape is right,' she said.

'Yes.'

'And soon we'll be painting?'

He laughed. 'Soon *I'll* be painting.'

A hush fell over the buzzing room. Karolina's laugh was the last voice to die, a clear ringing laugh that was beautiful, Jozef thought, in its difference to Anna's earlier studied one. He wondered what her Uncle Stefan had said to make her laugh like that. She was usually so solemn, even sad, with him, but then he was practically a stranger to her. Adam's silver spoon against crystal glass silenced them all.

'A moment for our friends in Germany,' he said.

A collective hanging of heads then. Some people looked into their glasses, others shifted their stance. A general air of uncertainty hovered: was a party the right thing? Were they playing this all wrong? Glances shifted to the Weiss family and their German visitors. A couple, thin and tired-looking. They were both blond, with the kind of pale freckled skin that made a person look always on the brink of illness. They could have easily passed, Jozef thought, and wondered briefly why they didn't simply pretend; then he remembered they must have had to register. That's when they should have come, he thought, not waited around for things to get worse. The couple blinked around, seeming to shrink back as the room looked at them, raised glasses, nodded with comforting smiles. Through the minds of the neighbourhood ran currents of thought not unlike Jozef's. People imagined their own family, and their own streets, their own offices and surgeries, lecture halls; they imagined the thugs coming, the glass glinting in the streets like jewels, but then came the thought, *Except we would have left sooner, imagine staying, when things were already so bad; wearing stars on their sleeves like in some kind of children's game, imagine being so reckless, careless with your safety, your children's safety, so foolish.* And even though the smiles stayed fixed in place, the gentle nods, the kind eyes, the German couple felt a change in the air, dropped a hand each from their own glasses, found each other's. The quiet stayed a little too long, and the husband, Friedrich, found his voice, spoke in Polish.

'Thank you. We are so lucky to have family here in Kraków, and the comfort of the community here.'

This was too banal for the neighbourhood, who waited, watching.

'Thank you,' Friedrich repeated.

His wife, glancing at her sister, added, in worse Polish but with a better understanding of the audience, 'It feels so very different here. It is such a joy to feel safe again. Our son was – was beaten. He's only fourteen,' she faltered. She had a whole store of angry descriptions, in German anyway, an urgent desire to explain how he'd been dragged from Friedrich's grasp, before the neighbours had intervened, and the look of nightmarish terror that had crossed his confident features, as though the years had fallen away and he was a little child again. Instead, she burst into tears.

This satisfied them for now. The tears were infectious: soon the room was wiping cheeks with the backs of hands, producing silk handkerchiefs that flapped around like tiny processional flags. A huddling began, a shifting together. Jozef couldn't keep his usual position as watching outsider from here, all of them bunched up together like this, and it made him feel anxious. Adam, his eyes red-rimmed whether from tears or the daytime drinking, shot him a hard kind of look. Behind him, Jozef felt the Hartmanns shift closer together, and to the side of him, the movement caught his eye as Anna and Janina Kardas held hands. The older woman was whispering something, and he wondered if they were supposed to be praying, felt a sudden embarrassed horror at the idea: would he ignore it, pretend he knew the words, say the Lord's Prayer instead? He caught some of Janina's voiceless words and found it was only the soothing whisper to a nightmare-woken child: *It's all right, it's all right, it's going to be all, all right.*

10

ALICIA FOUND THE POSITION by the window now came as naturally as breathing or lying. At first she thought it was that her muscles remembered their place, but when she tried to recreate the pose in her room, without the light and the easel, she couldn't find it so easily. Instead if she closed her eyes and imagined her painting, the flow of lines Jozef had described to her, the way the shape needed to curl like the edge of a shell, she could see the way the charcoal lines on the page would need to come together.

Today the light was good, rich and slightly pinked by the late winter sunset. Alicia could trace in her mind's eye how the shadow on her left side would make the glow where her hand was placed on the sill seem to bloom more richly, and how the smock she wore would absorb the golden pink light like a delicate thin petal. But he was still working with the sketches. She sighed.

'Alicia? Shall we take a break?'

She had prided herself these weeks on how disciplined she'd been, read the surprise in her family's faces with delight.

'No, keep going.'

She watched him sink back into the place that seemed like a kind of waking dream, the strain in his face when he had to talk to them all gone. Karolina was watching him too, Alicia noticed, sitting just to one side, her head tilted.

'How does it look, Karolcia?'

Jozef stopped again, bowed his head briefly. He gave Alicia a polite smile, but she knew when she had irritated an adult, and felt annoyed at herself.

'It's beautiful,' Karolina smiled.

Alicia frowned. 'Beautiful? It's still just a sketch.'

There was a tiny rattle as Jozef laid down his pencils.

'But does it look good? Is it going to be good, do you think, Jozef?'

Karolina's eyebrows shot up just as Jozef looked at her.

'Alicia! Please address Papa's friend as Mr Pienta. Where are your manners?'

Alicia broke the pose now, since he'd stopped working. She swallowed, feeling the secret of the man on the steps pulsing in her guts. She came to Jozef's side.

'I'm sorry to be rude.'

'You are—' Karolina said.

'—Only Papa calls you Jozef, and you aren't even working together. But we're working together, aren't we?'

'I don't mind, really,' Jozef said, seeming amused. 'Jozef it is.'

'Can't we begin the painting? The pink light today,' she stood and leaned against the window, letting her forehead rest against the glass, 'don't you want to use it?'

'The pink light?'

'It's making the white on my smock seem warm, and we could have roses, or something else, that same kind of shade, on the other side, to balance.'

He looked at her. 'You see the light that way?'

'What other way is there to see it?'

Jozef leaned over to catch Karolina's eye. 'Do you hear your sister talk about this light?'

She had a book in one hand, another hand stroking the dog's ears. 'I'm sorry, I wasn't listening,' she laughed.

Jozef edged along the ledge towards her. 'Tell me what *you* see in this light,' he said to Karolina.

'It's lovely sunset light. Homer calls it rosy-fingered.'

'That's dawn,' Alicia said. They ignored her.

She turned again to the window, where the precious light was now deepening into more sunset hues, splintering into golds, reds, purples. *What a waste*, Alicia thought.

'Shall we continue, are you tired?' Jozef asked.

'No, I mean, yes, I'm not tired. But the light is going.'

'We need to go up for dinner soon,' Karolina reminded her.

'I'm sorry we lost your pink light. Tomorrow we'll try earlier,' Jozef said.

They began the slow stretching out after their sessions, Karolina unfurling, Jozef rifling through the sketches, selecting which ones to keep from the day, Alicia breaking the spell of her fixed pose. Jozef fetched his battered leather satchel and laid the sketches into a larger book. Alicia followed, enjoying the images of herself slide into place. Her face was getting more detailed.

'I don't really look like that,' she said. 'That's not really my face, is it?'

Jozef laughed. 'Everyone says that.'

'Won't it really look like me?'

Jozef hesitated. He'd softened and sharpened Alicia's features: straightened the nose, widened the eyes, made the cheeks fuller. It was the Alicia Adam wanted, his little Ala. Not even that, it was the Alicia he really saw, and it was Jozef's job to reflect that back to him, to filter the world as Adam saw it.

'It's an artist's impression of you.'

'My nose is smaller.'

'Yes,' he admitted.

'Will my hair be down like this?'

Jozef looked at the empty space where the portrait Alicia would be standing, saw her painted figure there in the reddening light.

'Yes, I think so. We'll need the colour. We'll need to make your hair more golden, I think.'

Alicia pulled some strands of hair around to look at them pinched between her fingers.

'Yes, brown wouldn't be right.'

He laughed. 'I'm glad you agree.'

'And the rest, what colours?'

Karolina gave him a shy smile and an awkward good-bye bob, drifted away with her books clutched to her chest. 'Come, Ala,' she said, but so gently that the force of it fell short of pulling Alicia away from the briefcase and talk of colours. She stayed, hovering near the sketches. Jozef had run out of things to pack away, run out of buttons on his jacket, and looked at her.

'Well, white is quite traditional for the portrait of a young girl, but—'

'It won't look right.'

He found he felt less surprise at her confident exclamations now, and noticed she no longer couched them in fake uncertainty.

'Yes, white wouldn't be right. It would make everything too flat.'

'Flat?'

'Like the shape, you know, there need to be things to draw the eye.'

'So a deep colour.'

'Yes. Something bright. See what you have among your dresses. We'll start painting tomorrow.'

II

IT WAS A WHISPER of a knock, fingers rather than a fist, as though lightly drummed on a table. Anna turned over, still half in a dream of swimming. She often had the same dream: dropped into an ocean, a cold one, but turquoise like a summer shore. She knew somehow that her children were with her, but she could never find them among the waves. She'd drop her head below the surface of the water, trying to see their legs kicking. She would realise that she had to swim home. In her dream, home was always her father's house, never her own. Anna turned over a silk-covered pillow, heard the rain outside. The fingers rapped again. She opened her eyes, watched the door without urgency. It was the dead of night. The servants wouldn't wake her unless for some drama, and this was a polite, hesitant sound. Adam opened the door, skulked through with the slow, deliberate movements of one awake in a sleeping room. He was always considerate. She watched him through the fringes of her eyelashes. He was looking for something on her writing desk by the window. In the dim light from the lamps outside, she saw that he was fully dressed.

'You're not going into the office at this time of night?' she murmured, her voice gravelled by sleep.

He turned and peered at her; bent over and thin, he looked like the gaunt figure of a spectre. 'I'm sorry to wake you,' he whispered. Do you have our identity papers and passports in here? They aren't in the study.'

She sat up. 'What? Where are you going?'

'Do you have them?'

'No, why would I? They should be with Robert.'

Adam turned and went to her dresser, his face flashing white in the mirror. He began rifling through the objects on it, and opening and closing drawers.

'Adam! I said I don't have them. Come here.'

Anna switched on a light, wincing at the loss of the dark. She rubbed her eyes, still under the lull of sleep and its disordered thoughts. It took her a moment to look at him, obediently sitting on her bed, and reach out her hand.

'What is this? I told you not to be afraid. What, are we all going to run away, like in a children's book?'

He wasn't looking at her. She saw that he had taken the time to wax his beard and moustache, and smelled aftershave on him.

'Come on, take your shoes off.' She lay back, ready to have him lie in her arms, stroke his hair like a small child. It had been like this one or two nights a week since Kristallnacht. But he had always come to her straightaway, and not dressed or distracted like this, not talking about leaving. His weakness infuriated her but she would stay calm to keep peace in the house, and besides, he looked so sad and small.

Adam stayed still, looking at the space where her offered hand had been.

'*Adam.*' She spoke sternly, from fear that he was becoming, as her mother would say, soft in the head. 'You didn't come in here to look for papers. You want me to calm you down, and I will, but then you must stop this nonsense. It isn't manly or right. Do you understand?'

He took a breath, and then addressed the wall. 'I'm going to France. Edie has had a baby. She sent a telegram.'

Anna sat up then, fully awake. She fiddled with a loose thread on the coverlet, snapped it off. She visited the tiny space she allowed Edie in her mind for a moment, where the French girl slept cramped and small.

'You must go to her then. She's very young and it's her first. She's probably afraid.'

'Anna, you're too good.' He ignored the jab about Edie's age.

'Yes. Didn't you know?'

'I knew I didn't deserve you.' He took her hand as though to kiss it.

'You impossibly stupid man,' she said, not unkindly. 'Didn't you know she was expecting?'

He looked stung. 'I did. I think he's early.'

This broke through the thin layer of calm she had swiftly constructed. 'We agreed you would tell me,' she said, snatching her hand away as he reached for her.

'I know. Only when I'm here, it all seems . . .' he was getting into danger now, so he opted for a boyish shrug. 'I know it isn't ideal,' he continued. 'I would rather not leave you all here.'

'And it's a boy?'

He gave a tiny smile, again to the wall. 'Yes.'

'I see,' she said, and the bitterness in her voice made his stomach shrink with fear. This could be too far. He could lose everything.

'There's no question of it changing anything for Alicia, you understand. I mean in terms of inheritance, or . . . I would never—'

'Nor Karolina?'

'Nor Karolina, though I always think she'll take care of herself, she's so clever. I think Stefan imagines her as president of the university one day. Well,' he went on after a pause, 'I'll ask Robert about the papers.'

He kissed her hand, and she felt a coolness in her heart, imagining the girl in bed like this, sitting up, her baby on display in her arms, her baby son, waiting to be kissed. When Adam moved to kiss her lips, she turned away.

'How long will you be gone?'

'A few weeks.'

He kissed her arm where she had turned slightly from him.

'Aneczka, I love you. There's no question of me leaving you, ever, ever. You know that.' She gave a tiny nod, her humiliation seeming like a buzzing in her head.

He paused at the door. 'Will you indulge me, and not take the girls into the city while I'm gone? Just visits from Jozef and Stefan.'

She stared at him, a small smile on her face. 'Well that will certainly indulge Karolina, who likes to imagine she's living in a novel. Perhaps I should lock them in a dungeon?'

'Be reasonable. I don't want you all walking around Kraków. Remember what Milo—'

'We all agreed he's a bitter little nobody,' she said. 'Adam, for goodness sake, please find some bones in your spine. I know I didn't marry this jellyfish of a person. Off you go to France and we'll be fine. Robert is with us, and we live in the best neighbourhood in the city. I won't be shut away.'

It was late, the house asleep. Even the servants' chatter and rush had calmed. Alicia's dresses were wrapped in tissue paper and packed into large trunks, ready for Janie to pick out, air and press the ones for wearing that week. Inside each tissue fold was a cloth bag stuffed with lavender or cloves. When she opened the first trunk she'd thought to tear at them all, ripping the tissue and laying the dresses on her bed, like Mama in preparation for a trip. Instead she found pleasure in holding each package up to the lamplight, trying to see what colour lay inside, and carefully unfolding the envelope-like ends to reveal the fabric inside if it seemed, as Jozef had said, bright.

Alicia felt by instinct that the fabric also mattered, though Jozef hadn't mentioned it. The texture of these things must matter too, even the imagined texture, as a way to absorb or reflect the light, but also to make layers of weight. She sat back on her heels, on the floor next to the trunk, thinking. She closed her eyes. The heavy curtains would be behind her, the window to her left. There her hand would rest on the window ledge, cool and smooth to the touch, the white paint. But Jozef had said these things would melt away to leave only the light and her figure. So it wouldn't be the view of the Wawel at all, but a kind of blank backdrop. She opened her eyes. It would need to be a rich, heavy fabric too, rich and deep like the colour. Otherwise the whole image would be too weightless, fly away from the canvas, be a failure.

Around her, there were small stirrings in the house, the creak of feet on floorboards. Alicia glanced at the windows, where the darkness was still absolute, too early for the servants to wake again. Since her birthday she had imagined intruders, mobs, violence in the rooms full of their pretty furniture and glass ornaments. Blood on the carpets. The intruders wore the face of the man on the steps. Her door opened.

'Oh dear, what's this, a midnight tantrum?'

Her Papa leaned against the doorway, his arms folded, slightly bowed in his usual way, always cramped by the scale of rooms. He was gesturing to the floor, where despite her careful unwrapping, layers of tissue and abandoned clothes lay in piles, as though thrown there in rage. He wasn't dressed for sleep – the dressing gown he sometimes wore on days of no visitors was not flung around his shoulders – but as though for the office: suit trousers, a jacket, a scarf.

She steadied her breathing. 'No, Papa.'

'Now Janie will have to clear this up.'

'No, Papa, I'll do it.'

She moved to sit on the edge of her bed as he came into the room.

'And why are you up so late?'

'I need to find—'

He waved away her words. 'I'm glad. I came to give you a kiss as you slept, but now we can say goodbye properly. I'm going away for a few weeks. What present would you like me to bring back?' He sat next to her on the bed.

'Why?'

'Oh, business. France again. Do you want a dress or a new coat? Gloves?'

'Why are you leaving in the middle of the night?'

'Oh, and why is my Ala unpacking all of her dresses in the middle of the night? Are you running away too?' He laughed.

Alicia looked around at the dresses. 'I will tidy them away.'

Adam gestured at the piles of fabric all around them. 'Poor little Ala, with nothing to wear! You're like your Mama, she never has enough clothes.'

'I need something for the painting, Papa.' She looked at him. 'It's important.'

'Well, all right, I'll bring you a French dress, something pretty. But you know I won't be home for a few weeks, and I was hoping to be hanging up your new portrait by then.'

Her eyes slid away. 'Oh, no, that's too long.'

'Yes?'

'Gloves are fine.' She was eyeing the dresses again, trying to see the glint of something, like a bird seeking out silver fish in a river.

Adam watched her for a few seconds. 'Are you cross that I'm going away again?'

'No, I don't mind.' She slid off the bed and began picking through the dresses.

'Oh!' he clutched at his heart, laughing. 'Your poor Papa!'

Alicia laughed, but only for a moment. 'Papa, I want the painting to be very good. It's important.'

'*Córeczka*, it really *isn't*. I only want a pretty picture of you. It's not for you to be . . . worried about! Don't you know you should never worry about anything at all?' He pulled her gently from her listless picking at the fabrics, into an embrace. Alicia breathed in his smell of cigars and the rich buttery cream he put into his red beard, which tickled the side of her neck as she clung to him. 'Don't you know that?' he repeated, holding her back again, by the arms, and searching her face.

'Do you worry?' she asked, instead of answering.

He shrugged. 'No.'

'Never?'

'Alicia, what is there to worry about? Everything is all right.'

'But my birthday.'

He stood up, releasing her. 'That was nothing, Ala. Please, we shouldn't talk about it.' He looked at her again. 'Is there something else?'

She shook her head. What else was there, but the blood on the ice, that man's sneering face?

'Then I'll say goodbye. Be a good girl.' He kissed the top of her head, gave her nose a squeeze. 'I'll see the painting when

I'm back. Be good for Jozef and for your Mama and Janie. Jozef tells me you've been very good.'

'Yes, Papa.'

'Alicia.'

'Yes?'

'I mean it, no more of this sulkiness. Be happy and light-hearted. It's no good, this worrying. You are *not* to worry, understand?'

She looked at him blankly. He was stooping to look into her face, his hands in his pockets. His face looked thinner than usual in the low light. Alicia said, 'I understand, Papa, of course I won't worry. *Bon voyage en France.*' She found a face to match the lie: open, wide eyes, an easy smile.

'Your accent's getting better,' he said, relaxing and smiling at her. '*Merci. À bientôt, ma chérie.*'

He blew her a kiss, and pulled the door closed behind him gently. Alicia listened to his footsteps on the stairs, heard the low murmur of Robert's voice, the heavy front door opening and closing. She glanced around her room, its familiar contours and shapes, the dresser with its mirror, the dolls, the boxes of hats and shoes, a few books on a small, painted shelf. Everything was the same as always, and her Papa said she was not to worry, that he wasn't worried. But she'd felt the grip of his hands on her shoulders that night, crouching in the ice, and heard the way his voice had sharpened in the weeks after-wards, and too many parties, always gathering, drinking. He was worried, and now he was gone.

12

THE NEXT MORNING Alicia needled her sister with her late-night goodbye with Papa, reshaped the details: he woke only her, to say goodbye, to ask what gift she would like. Karolina's face was serene, nodding along as she ate her eggs, one eye on the door. Janie and Dorothea chattered in low voices to each other and to the girls: 'There will be a thaw today, maybe a walk, you've been indoors too long, see what your Mama thinks.'

Alicia pressed further, like picking at a painful scab. 'He said he would miss me the most, of course.'

'Of course.'

'But he will bring you some gloves.'

'I like your hair that way, Karolina,' Dorothea said, as she placed a jug of water on the table.

Karolina gave her a distracted smile, touched her hair, braided into plaits and knotted at the nape of her neck. The thick curls were escaping already, reaching out like tiny ivy tendrils.

'You look pretty,' Alicia said, both to soften her crowing over Papa and to get her sister's attention.

Karolina became still, her head slightly cocked to one side, a forkful of egg balanced in her hand. She put down her fork as footsteps approached the door, seemed to hesitate outside.

'That won't be Papa coming back, he said he will be gone for a few weeks at least.'

'That's good, my old ones are too thin.'

'Karolcia?'

'The gloves,' she murmured. Janie approached the door as though to open it, and stepped back as Anna came in, rushing, almost hitting her.

'Oh! Sorry, Janie, I didn't mean to—'

'Mrs Oderfeldt, excuse me—'

They all seemed stuck for a moment, the girls sitting at the table, the servants hovering, Dorothea casting glances around the room as though searching for details that might be wrong, and Anna standing like a debutante announced at a ball, her hands clasped together, looking at her children, a little flushed.

'Do you need something, Mrs Oderfeldt?' Janie ventured.

'Mama, what's wrong?' Karolina asked.

Anna frowned, and then gave a strangled kind of laugh.

'Nothing's wrong, Karolina! I only thought,' she said, approaching the table and putting up a hand to Dorothea, who immediately brought her a napkin and set her a teacup and saucer down, 'since your Papa is away, I would come and see you this morning instead of sitting upstairs by myself. Isn't this cosy?' She laughed again. 'Perhaps while your Papa is away we should do this every morning.'

'Did Papa say goodbye to you last night, Mama?' Alicia asked. 'He came to see me especially.'

'Yes, of course,' Anna said, her voice higher than usual. 'He'll be in France for—'

'He already told me,' Alicia said.

'Alicia, do not interrupt me.'

'Is Mr Pienta coming today?' Janie asked as she brought a jug of milk. 'Should we prepare a lunch for him?'

'No, I think we'll have a break from the painting today,'

Anna said, though she hadn't planned to until Alicia's smugness had riled her. It had the intended effect.

'But Mama—' said Karolina, as Alicia slumped in her chair.

'I'll send a note.'

'But Mama, we were going to begin painting today, it's already late, and Papa wanted it finished when he came back,' said Alicia.

'Did he? I don't suppose one day will make much difference.'

'He won't get the note in time,' Alicia said. 'We agreed to start early today, because the light—'

'Then I'll ask Robert to telephone to his building,' Anna said, in a fit of pique, raising her eyebrows at Dorothea, who left to relay this instruction.

'But what is poor Jozef going to do today? He will have been expecting to come,' Karolina said. 'Mr Pienta,' she added, to her mother's glare.

'I expect Jozef will be glad of a break from the company of two silly young girls for today,' Anna said, looking levelly back at Karolina, who blushed and pushed her plate away.

Anna disappeared for the rest of the day, into her own rooms, with vague instructions to her daughters to do something useful like sew or read some French. After stripping and washing in delicious hot water, they devoted themselves instead to exactly what they wanted to do: Karolina began writing, trying to compose a poem; Alicia sent Janie to her Papa's study for good quality paper and pencils, and began sketching.

She tried first to draw Mimi, trotting about and whining, but she wouldn't stay still for long enough. Then she sat in the doorway of Karolina's room, and sketched her as she wrote, but the perspective was off, the shape wrong, and Karolina shooed her away, 'I can't think straight with you huffing and puffing over there.'

That afternoon Alicia went down to the kitchens, forgetting to tread softly so as to eavesdrop; her clatter on the steps made the servants go silent, and greet her with too-wide smiles. Janie was sewing something, a yellow silk with blue trim, with a pile of mending on the table. Dorothea was rolling sugar paste, clouds of white puffing from the table as though from a magic potion.

'Hello, little one. Here,' Dorothea said, throwing her the body of a sugar mouse. Alicia held it up to the light from the windows, still sluggish through the rain. It was mint green, shading into blue along the narrow neck. When she bit into it, the paste inside was flecked with white. The sugar was too sweet and grainy.

'Can't we have shop-bought ones?'

'Don't you like it?'

'Yes, it's delicious, only I like the ones from Karlmann's with the little eyes.'

'And what are you doing?' Dorothea asked.

'I'm looking for something to sketch.'

'Sketch?' parroted Janie, as Robert came in, and she sat up.

'Alicia, miss,' he nodded at her. Robert was shorter than her Papa, but stockier, with a wide chest and thick arms. He always moved slowly, almost delicately, as now when he picked up a mouse, and dangled it into his mouth like a cat, swallowing it whole.

'Robert!' Dorothea protested, laughing. 'These are for guests later.'

'Who is coming?' Alicia asked.

'The painter, of course, and the Friels. Perhaps only Mrs Friel and her daughter.'

Alicia rolled her eyes. She hated Rebecca Friel and her narrow face and scraggy body.

'Can I have another mouse?'

Robert weighed one in his hand, and gaped his mouth, fish-like, for Alicia to copy. She laughed and put down her sketching things, put her hands behind her back and tried to catch the mouse in her mouth, missing it as it fell to the floor.

'Stop wasting my sugar!' Dorothea cried. 'What are you going to sketch? You haven't drawn in a long time.'

'No,' Alicia lied, 'my painting is making me want to.'

'Well? Shall we pose for you?' Dorothea put her sugared hands behind her head, and posed with a grin on her face, making Janie and Robert explode into laughter.

'Yes, draw me at my work,' Janie said, and bent over her sewing like an old woman.

'There are already lots of paintings like that,' Alicia said, thinking of the ones Jozef had shown her, golden ringlets bent over sewing, a basket of work at the feet, jugs of water on stands next to windows. All of it about the light and the shape.

But they weren't listening to her now, tossing the joke from one to the other, until Robert picked Dorothea up, making her shriek so loudly that they all glanced up, and quietened.

'Go on,' Dorothea said, laughter still in her face, 'take one up to your sister too,' and put two mice into Alicia's hand.

On the way back up the stairs Alicia mashed the mice together, one green, one yellow, and ate them as a sugary mush. Anna, changed into a beautiful green satin dress, but with an old cardigan thrown over it, opened the door to the dining room as she passed.

'Alicia, won't you stop creeping about the house like a criminal?'

Anna crossed to a large mirror that hung on the landing, checked her earrings.

'Can I sketch you, Mama?'

'What?'

'I want to practise.'

'No, I'm going out.'

'But there are guests coming. Dorothea is making sugar mice.'

Anna stopped encouraging her hair to curl under her fingers, muttering something under her breath. She looked at Alicia in the mirror.

'I'd forgotten. Do you mind very much if we cancel? You can see your friend another time.'

Rebecca Friel was the only Bernardyńska neighbour around Alicia's age, and so they had shared language tutors, dancing tutors, and sat together, morose and bored, at a thousand parties, concerts, or winter outings to skate on the frozen river. Alicia felt certain that time became different when Rebecca was there, and flowed as slowly as treacle.

She sighed. 'That's not very nice of you, Mama. I was looking forward to seeing my friend Rebecca.'

'I know, darling, only I've made arrangements now—' She patted her daughter awkwardly on the shoulder. 'Another time. I know your Papa would prefer it.'

Anna ran down towards the kitchen to pass on the instruction. Now there would be talk: two cancelled arrangements in one day, with Adam gone, too.

On her way out, after brazening out the obvious disgust of the servants at the late change of plans, she swapped her cardigan for her mink and checked her lipstick in the hallway mirror again. She caught sight of Alicia there, sitting on the staircase, looking young, with her hair falling around her face.

'Goodnight, Ala,' she called.

'Mama, who are you visiting?'

'No one, darling, it's a concert. Goodnight, now.'

'If I stay up, can I sketch you when I get back? I like the green of your dress.'

'Well, green will hardly come out in a pencil sketch, will it? And I'll be late.'

Alicia didn't bother to explain that the sketch could carry colour in it, a promise.

'I'll wait up anyway.'

'Alicia, go up for your supper and then to bed.'

Alicia stayed still.

'Dorota has some sugar mice for you,' Anna added. 'Go.'

It was like walking into a memory. Some slant of the light, the gentle lilt of the voices, Polish and Yiddish layering each other like instruments in a duet. Anna felt all wrong in her silk dress and furs. She was struck, as she walked along the Ulica Josepha, by the colourful murals above the shops: peacocks and fruit, which she'd forgotten about but now remembered. In the street there were conservatives, women with covered hair and men in long black coats, their hair in *peyas*, heading for home as the sun set. Anna felt a rush of warmth for them, these echoes of her grandfather and uncles. Her father had worn a *kippah* to *shul* on holy days but that was all; her mother insisted on Friday night dinner, and left the rest. Her mother used to stride along this street, with the practised grace of an insider, weaving between pavement and street, nodding to acquaintances, her purposeful gait making her skirt swing.

The address was crumpled in Anna's coat pocket, taken from Adam's desk.

She passed a dumpy woman with a cold smile. Anna heard her name, turned to see the woman looking her up and down frankly. Anna pulled her coat around her.

'Blanka's daughter? You are Blanka's daughter? I remember them, all of you, you lived just three or four streets down.'

Anna nodded. She didn't recognise the woman at all.

'Blanka was a friend of mine,' the woman smiled, coming back towards her. 'But you look very well,' she said, pausing just enough to make sure Anna heard what she should, which was, *You look very rich.* 'Did the whole family move?'

'I live nearer the centre now,' Anna said. 'My parents—'

'Yes, of course, I remember, very sad, only a few days apart.'

'Yes.'

'I live on the Ulica Bernardyńska,' Anna said, unable to help herself, as though this would seep into the cobbles of the old neighbourhood, down through the soil to the cemetery, and reach her mother's ears.

'How lucky,' the woman said flatly. 'What brings you to this part of the city?'

'I'm visiting a friend. In fact,' Anna said, taking out the piece of paper, 'I'm not sure of the street, do you know where this is?'

The woman glanced at the paper, sniffed. 'Further back, a fair walk from the Remuh. Past our neighbourhood. I wouldn't be going there as it gets late.' She looked Anna up and down again, and Anna felt herself blush.

'I'm visiting my friend who is unwell.'

'How kind.'

Anna glared at her.

'Will you be visiting your mother and father's plot? I notice it doesn't get many stones.'

'Do you?' Anna snapped.

'Oh, yes. I visit regularly; they're buried next to my dear Frank.'

'Well, I'll stop by another time. It's getting late, Mrs . . .'

The woman met her gaze, set her mouth in a line. Anna almost laughed: she had forgotten the bluntness of people in this part of the city. It was refreshing after her tiresome dance with Janina.

'Thank you for the directions,' she said, and swept past her.

Back at the Oderfeldt apartment, the evening passed in a storm of bad temper. Karolina read and would speak to no one, except for whispering furiously as she wrote notes in some of the margins. Alicia, without Jozef to speak to or any progress with the painting made all day, became fixated again on finding a dress, prodding her sister with questions about which she thought she should choose, until Karolina shocked them all when she exploded, called her a brat, and left to go to bed early, slamming doors through the house as she went. Dorothea was in a rage, her cooking for the evening all wasted, and she and Janie had quarrelled about nothing, all the light-heartedness of the afternoon forgotten. Only Robert was calm, methodically cleaning the cars, singing showtunes. Finally the household, without Anna and Adam to float through it, asking for more drinks and more heat and making telephone calls, darkened, turned cold, and went to sleep.

Alicia woke to thunder and the satisfying sound of rain against her windows, burrowed deeper under the covers, thinking of Papa in France and wondering if it was raining or warm like the Italian coast they had visited the previous summer. She was sure it was by the coast, where he was, because once he'd sent a postcard with a turquoise ocean on it.

In her mind, all of France was by the sea, fields of lavender where sand should be. She stayed with this image for a while, enjoying what painting it might make, the purple against the blue, but a flicker of lightning pulled her back to the room, slicing across her ceiling and showing up the faces of her dolls. She got up to watch from her windowsill, broad enough to sit on. Lightning was playing behind the Wawel, behind its turrets and walls, like huge cameras taking photograph after photograph. There would be a better view from the dining room, she realised, and she pulled on her housecoat.

Downstairs the thunder sounded louder, as though the cavern of the house was echoing the sound and magnifying it, and Alicia froze on the stairs when the lightning came again, tinged with blue from the small window near the back stairs. She wished she had Mimi or Cece in her arms, but the dogs always found their way under the kitchen table in storms. She pushed on to the dining room. There, framed by the huge windows, was her Mama, kneeling on the windowsill where Alicia had spent hours posing for her portrait, her green dress bright against the dark glass and the shock of white mink at her feet. Her hands were pressed against the glass, and her neck arched to better see the sky behind the Wawel.

'Mama?'

Anna turned, squinting into the dark room, just as a huge lightning fork flew across the sky, making Alicia gasp and point. 'Oh! Look!'

'Oh, I missed it! Well, come on, come and watch.'

Alicia, who had already turned expecting to be sent back to bed immediately, raced to the window before her mother could change her mind. She stood next to her in the same pose, watching the sky. Her mother smelled of perfume and cigarettes. She nudged Alicia with her shoulder.

'It's been fantastic,' she whispered. 'There was just— oh!'

They gasped together as the white gash spread wide across the sky, lighting up the room, their faces, the street below. Anna giggled, bobbed in place for a moment. Alicia caught the giggle, copied the movement.

'There's more thunder,' Alicia whispered.

'Count now until the lightning comes back,' her mother replied. She did on her fingers, 'One, two—'

'There!'

'So it's very close.'

'Is that how you know?' Alicia whispered.

'That's how you know.'

'Why are we whispering?' Alicia asked, giggling again.

Her mother shrugged and smiled across at her. Her red lipstick seemed to shine in her white face. Alicia inched closer to her, cold. She leaned against Anna's arm, as she did with Papa, a language he understood; he would let her burrow under his jacket or coat, warm her fingers on his belly. But her Mama only rested her head against hers for a moment then stood on her tiptoes again to catch another fork of lightning.

'Did you see that one?' Anna murmured. She looked down at Alicia again. 'Should we wake your sister up? Wouldn't she like this? Something to write about.'

Alicia shook her head. A lie came to her, blossoming naturally from the stem truth of wanting this moment to herself: Karolina was afraid of lightning; once she'd come to share Alicia's bed during a storm, and had shaken all night, the tremble of the covers keeping Alicia awake. She knew the lie would hold; their mother never liked to admit she didn't know things about her children, and would say, *Of course, I forgot.* Alicia let the lie unfold and drop, kept silent. Her mother seemed content with her shake of the head, and perhaps she, too, didn't want anyone else to come in, to puncture the strange closeness between them.

'When I was younger, storms would put out all the lights in the old neighbourhood,' she whispered. 'We used to light one candle and put it in the kitchen, and we'd all gather round it, your grandmother, grandfather and me. Sometimes the neighbours came from next door too.'

Alicia stayed still, caught sight of her mother's reflection in the glass, nodded, *Go on*. She daren't speak in case it broke the spell. Her mother rarely spoke about being younger, and when she did, it would be in snatches to Adam or Stefan, or tiny things at dinner parties, never, never just to her like this.

Anna nodded back, looked up at the sky again to catch another strike. 'Oh! Look at that one,' she whispered. 'Your grandfather hated it, would be muttering prayers under his breath. That was one of the only times he prayed. He said he thought the lightning would strike the house, burn it down. But my Matenka, my mama, she was like me and you. Oh, she loved it. She'd count the seconds between thunder and light, and when it got low she'd go to the door and open it to watch the storm, letting all the wind and rain in. Your grandfather would tut but let her do it. I used to stay at the table, because I didn't want my papa to be angry with me, but when I was Karolcia's age I used to go and watch with her. We'd jump, and— oh! Did you see that one?' she laughed, and Alicia did too. 'Just like that! We'd jump and laugh. I used to wish I could buy her a picture of lightning across the sky, you know, a photograph.'

'Did you?'

Anna was quiet for a while as three forks spread across the sky in silver tinged with blue. More flickered behind the Wawel. 'No,' she said, no longer whispering.

'I remember her a little,' Alicia said.

'No, you don't. She died when you were very little.'

'I do. She visited the house and she sat with her coat on. She had very strong hands.'

'Karolina or I have told you that, and you think you remember.'

Alicia kept quiet. She wanted to steer her mother back to whispering, to bouncing on her toes like a little girl, smiling at her in the silver light.

'She did have strong hands. She was a seamstress. She made clothes.'

'I know what a seamstress is, Mama.'

'Well.'

'So, she made clothes like ours?'

'No, simpler ones. She sold them in the market at home, I mean in the old neighbourhood.'

The old neighbourhood held a special glamour in Alicia's imagination. It was across the river, you could even see parts of its rooftops from her bedroom window, but she'd never been. It was still Kraków, but might as well have been another country. Her mother very rarely talked about it, but almost all of Bernardyńska used to live there, and reminisced about its cobbled streets, and market stalls selling the best borscht in the city, and shortcuts down back alleys, past rickety cafes full of old men playing board games. All this they discussed as though it was a place lost to them forever, not streets away, across the river, and only when the dinner parties were of the later, louder type, when she could easily listen from the staircase without being caught out of bed.

'Will you take me? To the old neighbourhood?'

'There isn't much to see, and you don't belong there.'

13

THERE WAS NO ONE in the world Jozef expected to see less than Anna Oderfeldt at his door. He had received a message cancelling his invitation to the Bernardyńska apartment that evening, and looked forward to the blank peace of time alone with his thoughts and work. Anna stood in the grey evening light, her dress bright against the stone of his building, flashing him a smile. He was in a half-buttoned shirt, unshaven, holding a paintbrush. He'd been working on Alicia's piece, from the sketches, worried he'd lose the thread of it. He looked down at himself, lost for words.

Anna laughed in her awful affected way. 'I'm sorry, I'm disturbing you.' When he still didn't invite her in, she took out and lit a cigarette. He glanced behind him at the chaos of his damp-smelling room, wondering what would be more insulting to his patron's wife: to send her away, take her to a bar, or let her in, make her sit among his laundry and piles of canvas and the stink of turpentine.

Anna laughed again, but she had turned red. 'Oh dear,' she said. 'I appear to have shocked you.'

'I – please, come in. Was I supposed to – I had a message from Robert, from your – I'm sorry if I misunderstood,' he said, backing into his room, casting about for detritus to pick up and throw into a corner, clearing a place for her to sit. Anna glanced at his bed, the crumpled sheets, unmade, as she sat on his one chair next to the small kitchen table. Seeing this, it was his turn to blush, and stammer, 'I wasn't expecting company. I'm a slob when I'm working, you see.' This was better: take refuge in the artistic excuse, part of his narrative with the Oderfeldts.

Anna rested her chin on one hand, passing her cigarette to the other. She gestured with the cigarette, a question in her eyes, and Jozef took one, if only to have something to do with his hands.

'I'm sorry it's so cold in here. Would you like something to drink? I have some vodka, but it isn't very good.'

She nodded, and he busied himself pouring some out. He swallowed his swiftly at the sink, feeling his annoyance rise. He wanted to work, she had pushed in here but seemed to have nothing to say, she was bringing all of the awkwardness of his visits to Bernardyńska here, to his own home, and he didn't have Karolina or Alicia, or even Adam, to cushion his distress. When he turned to hand Anna the vodka, he saw she was looking around the room in a kind of dream.

'I grew up in a room like this,' she said.

He laughed in surprise. 'I don't think so.'

'It's true. I just met a woman who knew my mother. She was chastising me for not paying my respects at her grave. She's buried a few blocks away.'

Anna drained her glass.

'What are you working on?'

'Your husband's commission, of course.'

'But everything is at our apartment.'

'I have lots of versions and sketches coming. That's how I work. We have the shape now, and I'm starting to think about the colour in the composition . . .' He stopped as her eyes slid past him and around the room again, clearly bored.

'Even the colour of the walls is the same,' she said. She put her chin in her hand again, drummed her red nails against her cheek, meeting his eye. 'My daughters enjoy your company, I think.'

'They're a credit to you.'

She raised her eyebrows. 'How polite you always are.' She held out her glass, and he refilled it. 'Go on.'

'Mrs Oderfeldt?'

'Anna, for God's sake. Go on, ask me what on earth I'm doing here.'

He took a sip. 'To what do I owe the pleasure?' he asked, using the old-fashioned greeting. She laughed, and he made her laugh blossom by adding a little bow with a flourish of his hand.

'Adam has left.'

This shocked him. 'Left? He's left you?' The red lipstick, the evening visit started to make some sense. He felt a twitch of lust, but it was quickly taken over by a twinge of regret over his painting, which would now never be finished, and, strangely, by the end of his visits to the apartment across the river, the long hours in the dining room, Alicia's attentive face. Karolina's calm presence. He sighed, put out his cigarette in the sink. Would Adam still pay him? Anna was laughing. Was she already drunk?

'Don't be ridiculous,' she finally said. 'He's gone to France for a while. On business,' she added.

'And that's why you're here?'

'So it's fallen to me to talk to you about my daughter.'

Anna was watching him. He kept his face very still as his heart sped up. He had done nothing, nothing to disgrace himself. He admired her, the quiet space she built around herself, and yes, the supple grace of her body, the kind warmth of her brown eyes, the way she became lost in her own world, as he could. But he had never spoken of it, never touched her. He hadn't even drawn her, except in his head.

'She's . . .' Anna frowned. 'I've never seen her so obsessed by something before. She's never seemed all that interested in anything, to be honest. If you ask Adam she's fascinating but I've always found her rather bland.' Anna lit another cigarette. 'She's driving me to distraction hunting for this dress you asked her to find, and talking about colours.'

Jozef breathed in and out, his relief making him break into a rare smile. 'She's clever. She's got a natural understanding of—'

'Well, stop . . . *involving* her. I'll just tell her what dress to wear. She only needs to stand there, just let her stand there.'

'Yes, Mrs Oderfeldt.'

'*Anna.* Don't be angry.'

'I'm not.'

'Can I have another drink?'

He poured her one, as distant thunder sounded.

'Shall we go to bed?' she said.

'You're very beautiful, but—' he said, too quickly.

'Yes,' she said. She smiled and stood up, putting her cigarette out in the vodka glass. 'Don't worry, I'm sure you have lots of lovers. Models, other artists, that sort of thing. Don't you all live hedonistic lives, like Parisians?' She laughed.

He blushed. 'Yes,' she answered herself. He felt she was laughing at him, and his little life in his little room. He crossed to the door, opened it just as more thunder rang out, sounding closer. He lost his nerve at this. 'Perhaps you should stay until the storm—'

'I have my reputation to think of,' she whispered in mock-scandalised tones. 'Perhaps I could borrow an umbrella?'

'I don't have one,' he admitted. 'Well, I did, but it's broken,' he added lamely.

'What a pity. My mink will get ruined. Goodnight!' she trilled, and walked out into the night. In a shop window in the fading light, the electricity of the gathering storm pressing on her, Anna touched her face, straining in the dark to see her features more clearly. She knew there were small lines around her eyes and mouth. She looked at her hands, still young-looking enough, and small. Adam loved her small hands, liked to lace her delicate fingers through his own, elegant long ones. She looked into the window again, but the night was too dark to see, and anyway her tears would be swelling and reddening her pale skin. She glanced up at the sky where thick drops had begun to fall. She wanted to be curled up in a clean bed, chaste in silk nightclothes, listening to the storm. She sent a tendril of thought to Adam in his other life, then withdrew it as she set off across the cobbles, slippery in the rain.

14

A PACKAGE ARRIVED from France, expensively wrapped in cloth and sealed with wax, layers of scented tissue paper. Adam's beautiful handwriting, almost like calligraphy, on cream letter paper, *Darling Ala, I hope this is right. My fashionable friend informs me it's just the thing.* Alicia held up the dress, heavy and thick, against the light. It was a dress for a younger girl, a party dress, with billowing sleeves and a high neck. She had lots of dresses like this, the same folds of fabric, the same buttons along the back. But this was what she'd asked for: a deep, rich colour, the colour of spring flowers and fresh blood. The fabric, too, was just right: heavy and thick, velvet. 'It's perfect,' she informed her mother, who was reading the note with a blank expression. It was only later that she remembered it was the same colour she'd been wearing that night, so the man from the steps would recognise her more easily. So perhaps her Papa understood the secret importance of Jozef's painting: the thought warmed her.

Later, she wore the dress for Jozef's visit, watched him for his reaction. He was quiet and absorbed in setting up by the window, fussing over pencils and sheets. Karolina was watching him too, running her pen over her lip, before going into her secret written world. Alicia stood in position, letting the red announce itself into the image, pleased with the weak sunlight hitting her arm and the side of her face so that the red seemed richer. She thought of the blood on the ice for a moment, its awful beauty. Finally Jozef looked up and took in the image, meeting her eye. He nodded. 'Perfect,' he said. 'The richness—'

'That's what I thought,' she replied.

He gave a low laugh, glanced at Karolina, who was laughing too.

'Really, Ala, you are an arrogant little madam,' she said.

'She's right, though,' Jozef whispered, and they laughed again.

'Now can we start painting?'

'Yes. Now we'll begin painting,' Jozef said. 'You'll be famous soon,' he added, as Anna came into the room. She came to stand by Karolina.

'Karolcia, I do think you need to occupy yourself while your sister is busy with the painting.'

'I am, Mama.'

Anna leaned over to read from Karolina's notebook, but she snapped it shut.

The days without Adam slipped by, the routine of the apartment barely affected. Jozef would arrive just after breakfast, Alicia would change, and she, Karolina and the dogs would set up camp for the day in the dining room with him. Jozef would eat pastries they'd saved from breakfast or if Anna remembered, she'd send Dorothea with fruit and coffee. Anna herself would wander in and out, fuss the dogs, exclaim over Karolina's daydreaming in a fond enough way, and sometimes even doze on the chaise longue, sometimes with a book, sometimes half-read letters.

'Is that from Papa?' Alicia called one afternoon, seeing his handwriting.

'Yes.'

Alicia stayed in position, her hair pulled to one side, catching and sticking on the heavy velvet of her dress.

'What does he say?'

'It's a private letter.'

'Is he coming back soon?'

'He doesn't say.'

'We should go to France to visit him, once the painting is finished.'

'I don't think so. It's summer soon, and we'll be going out to the Zakopane house.'

Anna trailed off as the others sank into their now customary concentration, into a rhythm all their own. She watched Karolina carefully. She watched her watching Jozef, in small snatches at first, then in a longer gaze at Jozef's profile, his broad cheeks, his shaved face. *I suppose she's not used to seeing a shaved face*, Anna thought. Maybe something so simple had been the start of it.

Anna wasn't a fool. Something would have to be done, but somehow she'd been unable to say what she'd planned when she went to Jozef a few evenings before. She supposed it was simply too much to bring up the growing attraction between her eldest and the young man, when she was also there hoping to find comfort and distraction in his bed. She searched for the right word. *Schmutzig*. Grubby. It would have been grubby of her. The heat of injured pride stirred in her skin as she studied Karolina's figure, escaping wisps of her daughter's hair alight in the late afternoon sun. *I won't be jealous of my own child*, Anna thought. *I won't sink so low.* That other child, the French girl, Edie, was quite enough.

Adam's letter was the usual tone of just before a return from Edie: respectful, unsure, that of an old friend who was no longer certain they had any claim to your time. He mentioned Edie and his new son in the lightest way, as though acquaintances of Anna's she might be vaguely interested in. *She's doing quite well, he is healthy and has red hair. We spoke of them moving closer, to Poland, but she doesn't want to leave her mother.* Towards the end of the letter his anxieties seeped through. *I hope you haven't been taking the girls into Kraków. The newspapers in France are reporting this law has been passed in Germany after all. I trust you are being sensible, dearest Aneczka.* Anna sighed, realising she would soon have to manage Adam's fear all over again, and worse, the fear of a new parent, a thousand new ways for the world to hurt you.

She glanced at her eldest daughter again, felt the echo of her young infatuation, the buzz along the skin, the butterflies, the racing pulse. A confusion of envy and protective love enveloped her. Karolina would have to have her heart broken, and cry, and no doubt write some poems about it. It was a shame that once the painting was finished they would have to gently remove Jozef from their lives. Anna liked his quiet, thoughtful face. She liked his honesty. Should she be angry with him? She was quite certain he hadn't taken advantage of Karolina. Besides, he also exuded a kind of youthful awkwardness that made her hope he, too, would not suffer too much when they were separated.

Anna brought the letter to her face, stroked its edge along her cheek, smelled it, imagining she could catch a trace of Adam's scent in it, moustache wax and coffee. Imagined it was a love letter, and she an unmarried, restless daughter; imagined trailing excitement and lust around the house, leaking so strong they could smell it down in the street. She felt instead the steady pulse of her heart, the calm affection for

Adam that was a mixture of loving friendship, fond exasperation and a kind of reflected pride in her position. She still, after all these years, enjoyed being Adam Oderfeldt's wife. Besides, he could be sweet and funny and when they were lovers it wasn't unpleasant. Still, she'd missed something, she felt, watching Karolina. She'd cut passion out of her life like a brown piece of apple. The thought made her feel irredeemably old.

'I'm going upstairs,' she called over. 'This room is too warm. Karolcia, open a window.'

The girls were pulled out of their strange spell. Jozef's paintbrush clattered on the sill, probably staining it, as he went to help Karolina with the window, stiff in its frame. Alicia was looking at her mother with unconcealed annoyance.

'Why should we let in all the cold air, and the noise from the street? Now we won't be able to concentrate.'

'Alicia, please,' Anna said, suddenly exhausted.

'Papa always likes the air,' Karolina reminded her, now kneeling on the sill, one arm uselessly supporting the window as Jozef struggled to lift it.

'He goes out on the terrace,' Alicia replied, breaking her pose and stretching. There was a crack as she rotated her neck.

'Fine, do what you want with the *kurwa* window,' Anna snapped, and snatched up her letter, slipping on her shoes. Her daughters exchanged a shocked look, and Jozef's back was still turned. Anna saw he had flushed with embarrassment as she left the room, feeling her own face blush.

'Well,' Jozef said. 'The *kurwa* window is open now.' Karolina laughed. They were still close, her kneeling on the sill, his sleeves rolled up, and she let the laugh carry her to lean into him for a moment, her arm against his. If he lifted his arm, she would be nestled against the whole side of his body. But he only pressed, slightly, his arm to hers, and she could be imagining it all.

Alicia had been looking down into the street below, but now she came over to look at the canvas, and Jozef moved away. Her little shoulders fell a little when she saw it, and Karolina felt a rush of love for her and her persistent openness, her lack of mask, even after all her lessons.

'I know, I know, it still doesn't look like much,' Jozef said to Alicia's silent disappointment. There was a smile in his voice. Karolina found his kindness to Alicia almost unbearably attractive. Alicia only kept looking, her head moving slightly to catch the light on it in different ways.

'See,' Jozef went on. 'I'm layering up the background. It looks like brown sludge now, but look here,' he pointed at something on the canvas, 'here is your little paint-ghost. See her shape?'

'Yes,' Alicia smiled.

'Now imagine her in red, with the gold of the hair. See this splash of white here?'

Alicia nodded.

'That's where the sunlight hits the top of your head.'

Karolina would have expected a bigger smile here, more chatter, but instead Alicia gave a deep breath and a nod again, just like Jozef did when he was pleased with the mix of colours or with the curve of a sketched shape.

'Yes.' Alicia gave him a small smile then. 'Well, let's keep going. It sounds like Papa will be home soon and I need it to be finished by then.'

Now it was Jozef and Karolina who exchanged a look: a practised exchange of apology, swiftly accepted with indulgence, then deepened for a moment into something else, before breaking off. Alicia fell back into her concentrated space; Jozef, despite himself, affected by her impatience, began to mix the reds. Karolina stayed on the sill, enjoying the contrast of warm air at her feet and cool air against the back of her neck, enjoying how she could gaze at Jozef in plain sight under the guise of watching an artist at work.

In her room, Anna lay on the bed, all the windows wide open, freezing air washing over her stripped body. She thought of Adam and Edie. She thought of Jozef and Karolina. She thought of Jozef.

Across Europe, her husband was carefully holding his mind still. He found this stillness in a memory of himself and Stefan as children, camping in the forests outside the city. City boys, they'd marvelled at the layers of stars, and challenged each other to find the dark spaces, the emptiness between them, that they were used to in their city night skies. That was what Adam did now, in front of the guard. He pushed all the pinpricks of light away, tried to think of blankness, to make his face blank too. The man had been holding Adam's papers for a long time. He had smoothed the documents over with his palm, like an archaeologist discovering some precious artefact, and his large, girlish eyes, long eyelashes like the baby Adam had just left, flicked between the old picture and Adam's face.

When the train had chugged across the border and into Germany, Adam felt his usual boyish disappointment at the lack of otherness, foreignness: the fields were just the same, the glimpse of cars and farms and bridges, all the same as France, or home. The passengers continued their murmur of pleasantries and complaints about the weather and the rattle of the windows and the quality of the pastries from the first-class coffee cart, how perhaps it was the same as the standard class after all, and perhaps they had wasted their money. Adam read a newspaper in French, trying to stretch his vocabulary, exercise his linguistic muscle, but he found his heart quickening at the headlines alone, and placed it to one side as the train pulled into Offenburg. Again the same wooden platforms, pots of flowers, women in winter coats and hats, only the German signs to make any difference. One man got onto their carriage, nodded politely as he moved down to a booth.

But then the air in the carriage changed, a collective fumble, a break in the easy conversations. Three guards stood in the doorway, looking every inch the soldiers in their dark grey suits and military-style caps. One of them called out 'Border control' in German, then another translated into French. Despite the destination of the train, there was no translation into Polish. The second guard's voice though was surprisingly gentle, and Adam sipped his coffee, knowing his papers were in his inside pocket. He looked out of the window, unable to account for how the carriage seemed to be charged with anxiety, unable to tell if it was coming from his own traitor heart, which betrayed his new-found fear at every turn. On his night train to France during the earlier journey, Germany had passed in a blur of darkness and glimpses of low-lit stations, the lulling rock of the sleeper carriage, where Adam drifted in and out of sleep, dreaming of his children. The silent, sleepy train guard had collected their papers at one stop, and returned them stamped.

One guard moved to the end of the carriage, a slow walk with his arms behind his back, like an officer. *Perhaps it is the army*, Adam thought, *a show of strength, more posturing, as the newspapers say. The whole country is like the new boy at school swaggering about.* He came to a stop at the door, and the second guard began to move, this time gesturing for papers, leaving the third guarding the other door. The arrangement caused an irrational surge of panic in Adam, and he took out his passport and papers, arranged them carefully on the table. A woman was arguing with the guard in French, with a northern accent too strong for Adam to easily follow, but he caught the gist, which was that part of her identity papers were missing, and she would be fined. The woman's voice fell into a deeper and deeper hiss, until the guard, worn down or bored or in search of something else, abruptly walked away, shocking the woman into silence. His footsteps grew louder as he approached Adam.

'Papers,' the man said in German, although they were right there, on the table, and Adam gestured to them. The guard held his eye, and Adam gathered them up, handed them to him, feeling like a boy who has misunderstood the school rules, with the whole class watching.

Then began the long period of blankness, Adam searching again for darkness between stars. The carriage noticed the length of time, became quiet, some craning to look, others carefully looking out of the window, listening. The rustle of the papers as the guard sifted through them again and again, held them up, as though against the light, to match picture to picture, stared openly at Adam.

'Remove your hat,' the guard said, in perfect Polish.

Adam did so, held it in on his lap like a cat.

'Part of your papers are missing.'

'Excuse me?'

'Part of your papers.'

'I don't understand. Everything is here.'

The guard gave a small patient sigh, as though Adam was a very slow child or employee. He pointed to a blank space in Adam's border card.

'Religion.'

Now the carriage moved again: a rustling, as even the politest turned to look.

'There is no requirement for such a thing in Poland.'

'But we are in Germany.'

'But I am Polish, and passing through on my way to Kraków.'

'In Germany you must obey German laws.'

'But I am not subject to this law,' Adam said, keeping his voice slow and steady, as though at a dinner party, arguing for fun, counting points on his fingers, relaxed, watching Stefan's face as he marshalled his counter arguments. 'It surely does not apply to other nationals.'

'Fill it in,' the man said, thrusting the papers back to Adam. He folded his arms, as Adam smoothed the paper back down on the table. Adam took a pen from his inside pocket, a beautiful gold-plated thing that he used to sign the biggest contracts. He held it for a moment, hoping the guard would feel discomfited by the sight, by the fact that he, Adam, was clearly an important man, but the guard only stayed rooted to the spot, oblivious.

Adam's mind raced. All the newspapers he'd read. All the radio broadcasts, late-night conversations. He thought about writing *Catholic*. There was a low hum of impatience from the guard at the furthest door, a check of a watch. The guard standing over him though was calm, impassive, as though there were all the time in the world. Adam wrote, wafted his hand to dry the ink, handed the paper back. When the guard read it he seemed pleased, nodded. He exchanged a nod with the guard at the door. 'But this is a crime, to conceal your Jewish identity. There is a big fine. Luckily for you, you are rich,' he gestured at Adam's pen.

'But I wasn't concealing anything. I told you, this is a German law—'

'And you are in Germany,' the man said.

'It's two thousand Reichsmark, payable immediately,' the man from the door called.

'That is ridiculous.'

'If you can't pay, we take you off the train, and to a police station.'

Adam's breath quickened. He took out his wallet, pressing down the rage to somewhere beneath his ribs.

'I can write a cheque.'

'Cash.'

Adam was ashamed to feel his blood rising. 'Who carries so much?'

'The pen will do,' the guard said. 'Gold?'

'Yes.'

The guard gave a low whistle, exchanged a look with the guard by the door.

'You know there are people without enough to eat?' the guard said. He spoke in everyday Polish, but his accent was pronounced. Perhaps he'd spent time there, or studied over the border. In Kraków, he could even be one of Adam's employees, a nod of respect as he walked through the door.

It had been an extravagance, it was true. He'd bought it in the early days, before buying the apartment and after the first big order had come through, and he'd asked Anna to marry him, all in the same week. He liked the coolness of it against his fingers, the weight. At first he'd displayed it on his desk, as it reminded him of his father's things. Somewhere in the apartment were his father's pens, some also in gold and silver. Over time he'd stopped displaying it, carried it around like any pen, dropped into briefcases, shoved into suit pockets. Once he'd let Alicia use it to draw with.

'You know this?' the guard pressed.

Adam nodded. The guard took the pen, turned it over in his hands. He spun it like a baton and handed it to the other guard. Adam looked out of the window, feeling it was desperately important to seem as though this encounter had ended exactly as he had wished. He had escaped a fine, and it was only a pen. In the time he moved his eyes to look at the now empty platform, the guards had slipped off the train. There was a piercing whistle, and the train began to move. Adam wanted to ask someone if it would stop in Germany again, or continue straight over the border, but the low murmur in the carriage had not returned. For a few minutes, it seemed that no one even moved, and then people began to slowly unfold papers, open bags, painstakingly, wincing if they made too much noise, as though trying not to wake a sleeping beloved. Adam felt eyes on him, even heard the inrush of breath more than once, as though people were preparing to speak, but kept his face turned, angry at the carriage and its pity. Or perhaps they were silent because they hadn't known he was a Jew – how could they? And now *they* were angry. Both incensed him, and he turned the anger inwards, nursed it, carefully avoided re-imagining how he would laugh in the guard's face, and the carriage would laugh too, throw the guards off, make a complaint to the driver or the police or the government, someone, and the guards would stand humiliated on the platform, unable to meet his eye as he watched through the window. He searched and found again his memory of Stefan, the cold of deep night as they camped under the stars, their young eyes hunting darkness.

15

ADAM BROUGHT HIS SECRETS trailing after him into Kraków: the way his new son's fingers had curled around his thumb and squeezed with a surprising strength that made him laugh aloud; the way in the days after he arrived he had slept at Edie's side, like a husband, her in the crook of his arm, listening to her moaning softly when the creaks of the floorboards meant the nurse he had hired was up with the baby, the thin cries sinking through the ceiling. How he had promised Edie he would stay, that the girls were old enough now, Anna was his beloved friend, everyone would understand. Whispering this into Edie's dark hair, her slim neck, his hands wandering over her still soft belly and thighs, until she made a sound to make him stop, still bleeding and sore as she was. How when Edie developed a fever, sweat soaking through the sheets and her eyes wild with fear, he'd spent a fortune on bringing a private doctor from Nice, and stayed up all night praying, promising God as carelessly as a new lover, and then whispered still more fervent promises to Edie as she slipped in and out of awareness, barely able to recognise him, asking for her mother. How the doctor had spoken sharply to him, *Where is the girl's mother? You must bring her here, she is asking for her. Don't you know how ill she is? Women die from this.* How when Edie's mother had arrived, sent for by train, she had been cold to him and accused him of ruining her daughter's

139

life, in such rustic French he could barely understand her, but he promised her, too, that he would be moving here just as soon as everything was settled in his marriage, that he loved Edie, that he would die too if she did not recover. How when the doctor came downstairs with a relieved look, said it was not as bad as he had feared, as it could be, that her body would fight it off. And yet he took Adam aside, *Best if she doesn't get pregnant again, you understand.* How when Adam, leaving the baby in his grandmother's arms, went to see his lover, asleep but breathing steadily, the smell of sickness leaving her, he was already wondering if there was a train to Kraków that afternoon.

All this Adam filed away in his mind, making Edie, and even the perfect baby son, so heart-bursting in the flesh, faint impressions on the back of his mind. When he was out of France they were like shadow puppets. His life with Anna and his daughters came back into focus, switched places from where they, too, had been dancing shadows on the walls. This he found easy, a long-practised sleight of focus, the twist of a kaleidoscope. More difficult was the in-between world of the train, his returning sense of dread, which at the house in France had been held apart, cocooned in the villa as they were, few newspapers, no radio. This he also tried to file away as the train pulled into Kraków, his fellow passengers avoiding his eyes, finding instead that he fell into thinking of Alicia's birthday all those months ago, and that his fear was again taking root.

He hadn't telephoned ahead, or sent a letter with more than vague promises to be home soon. So when the cab pulled up in front of his apartment, he could stand in the bustle of the street, just then warming and waking to the day, and watch the apartment for a moment. He loved this building: its pride of place on the street, its companionable stance next to the Wawel. The curtains were still drawn in the upper rooms, but he was surprised to see, as it was only seven o'clock, that the large dining-room window curtains had been pulled back to the light, and figures moved back and forth, in the silent shadow way of people glimpsed from afar. It must be the painting, he realised: the painting was still being created. The thought gave him a jolt of energy, and something like relief: here life had carried on just as before, his wife and daughters had been busy, and Jozef had been here to keep them company, distract them. It meant, too, he thought, searching for his key, that there would be a wait until he could relax with Anna, since a guest would be there, but perhaps that was a good thing, a sort of interval (he smiled to himself now, finding in the rhythm and sound of the unlocked latch and the swing of the heavy door that he was slipping back into his Kraków life with ease), a palate cleanser between courses, he thought, before feeling a twinge of guilt and blushing at his own coarseness. *So what*, he thought, *it's only in my own head*.

He was pleased that there was no Robert, no Dorothea, no Janie to accost him in the hallway or on the stairs, so he could slip into his house, absorb the sounds of home before announcing himself. He could hear the clatter and low voices of the kitchen, and somewhere a radio murmuring. One of the dogs was yapping on the top floor. But outside the dining room, where he'd seen the figures, as he listened at the door all was quiet. When he opened it, he was struck with an explosion of affection for Alicia, who was sitting cross-legged by the fire, her hair loose as she pored over some papers. He started towards her, exclaiming, 'Ala, your Papa is home!' and as he did so caught Karolina and Jozef in the corner of his eye, waved to them too, blew a kiss to Karolina.

'Welcome home, Papa,' Karolina said, her voice sounding lower and calmer than it had before, more like her mother's.

'Mama didn't tell us, oh she never tells us anything—' Alicia said, gripping the back of Adam's jacket as he embraced her.

'I'll fetch her,' Karolina said, and raced out of the room, before Adam had time to hug her too.

She knows, he thought. *Anna has told her; perhaps she thinks she's old enough to know.* But in the moments it took to disentangle Alicia, kiss her forehead, and obey her pull towards the painting, he had already soothed Karolina in his mind, explained, smoothed over the fact of Edie and little Marc Stefan, made a fantasy story of meeting a baby brother.

Alicia clung to his side as he moved to where Jozef stood next to his canvas, and Adam tutted, rolled his eyes in mock irritation, but was delighted. He shook hands with Jozef, who was without a jacket, his shirtsleeves rolled up in the over-heated room. An ashtray on the windowsill held the dregs of some cheap rolled cigarettes, and the floor was draped with cotton sheets to catch the drips of paint and some strong-smelling spirit. Adam returned Jozef's warm and nervous smile.

'Adam. You've been missed. How was France?'

'Busy, busy. And here, too, I see! It's very early for painting.'

'No, Papa,' Alicia said. 'Morning or evening light is best.'

Adam laughed. 'Is it, Ala?'

She nodded, didn't catch his laugh.

'Do you want to see it, it isn't quite finished—' Jozef began, but just then Karolina and Anna came into the room. Anna came straight to Adam, gave his hand a squeeze and held onto it as she turned towards the others.

'You missed your deadline,' she said to Jozef, with a laugh: her real, low laugh, not the performance Adam knew she could make. It eased his guilt a little that they had become friends, he had not left her all alone.

'It's very nearly finished, Mrs Oderfeldt.'

'Well, can I see?' Adam asked.

Anna released his fingers, and Alicia found them.

There was no sheet to theatrically pull away, so Alicia only steered him around to face her own image, and he caught the colour first, along with an impulse of excited recognition of a loved face.

'You wore the dress I sent.'

'Of course, Papa.'

There was a silence as Adam moved closer, then further away from the painting, stood slightly to an angle, looking. He felt nervous, as though being tested for something. The anxious anticipation in the way Alicia had gripped his hand and the way they all stood, quiet, watching him, confused him and made him unsure what to say. So it was that it took him a few moments to truly look, and stop seeming to look. He noticed the lush folds of the dress first; saw Edie's young hands unrolling the fabric for him, smoothing it over, its richness. It was all there in the paint, the bloom of fabric at Alicia's shoulder. Her face was a rare, still expression he recognised, the very beginnings of a smile, just emerging on one side of her mouth. She'd been made prettier: her eyes larger, darker, her pale cheeks given some blood. The sunlight was hitting the edge of her hair, making it seem almost blonde. He stepped closer, to see the paint mix that made that sunlight illusion seem real.

'So, Adam, tell poor Jozef it's good, won't you?' Anna laughed again, but this time in her performance way, a warning he was straying into a *faux pas*.

'Oh, Jozef, I'm sorry! It's so good, so very, very good. You've outdone yourself! Bravo indeed,' Adam said, shaking Jozef's hand again, who had turned pink. 'We should celebrate, shall we have something special for lunch?'

'It's not quite finished yet,' mumbled Jozef.

Adam looked again. 'But surely it is? I can't see anything—'

'We need to add something in the background,' Alicia said. 'Just something else to deepen it, it's too shallow.'

'Oh?' Adam beamed down at her. 'How sophisticated an art critic you've become!'

'What does your eye go to first?' Alicia replied.

'Alicia,' Karolina said, 'Papa is probably tired from his journey.'

'It's all right,' Adam said, while Anna went to call for coffee. 'Um, I think . . . the dress, I suppose. I noticed the lovely colour of the dress.'

Alicia shared a look with Jozef, who nodded at her in the way of a teacher, like Stefan would, and Adam felt a rush of warmth for him, who had come to like his Alicia so much.

'Well,' Alicia said, 'that's good, but do you see, Papa, how the background needs something deeper, perhaps a little flash of red too?'

'How wonderful that you've been learning.'

'I started drawing, too—'

'She's very good,' said Jozef, simply.

Later, Adam came to Anna as she was falling asleep.

'I'm sorry, I thought you'd still be undressing, and we'd have time to talk.'

He lay beside her, on top of the covers. She kept her eyes closed, but reached and found his hand.

'Welcome home. I'm glad.'

'Did you think I wouldn't come back?'

'Of course not, never. How was everything?'

'They are both well.'

'Marc is a good name. What will the surname be?'

'Payant, like Edie.'

Anna gave a tired smile. 'Does she mind?'

'Not that she mentioned.'

'How was she when you left?'

'Her mother is with her.'

'That's best. I'd have loved mine with me, those first months.'

Adam was silent. This was a terrible habit of Anna's, to bring up old grievances from years ago, instead of current ones. He hadn't felt it was seemly to have the grandmother here, instead of a team of night and day nurses. His mother-in-law visited, but Anna had wanted her practically sewn inside her own skin, sharing her bed as she tried to recover, especially after Karolina.

'Well,' he said eventually. 'I'm sorry.' Then, 'Aneczka.'

'Hmm?' She opened her eyes and saw how close his face was, breathed in the smell of him. She shifted her hips and came closer.

'You missed me,' she said.

'Of course.'

He felt his body relax, sink a little further into the mattress. The threads of what he had planned to say were already disappearing. He could already hear the conversation, well-worn like grooves in a wooden floor, *And so? It doesn't sound so bad . . . Well, and what do you mean? A look? He looked at you? Are you a child? It's only a pen . . . Move to France? Why? Is that truly the reason? If you want to move there, then go, but don't think we'll come too. There are limits, Adam, to my patience. This* he heard in her half-awake voice, softened by sleep, perhaps also a stroke on his arm, his cheek, so that the harshness of the words would be soothed even as he heard them. He replied, too, in his head, and fell into the beginnings of sleep, a place where he was unsure if the conversation was real. He always slept well next to Anna, her surety, her lack of fear.

'May I stay,' he murmured. 'My room feels far away.'

'To sleep?'

He opened his eyes, saw she had turned, to face the ceiling. In the twilight she could be Edie. They had the same small, sharp features, the same high cheekbones, but Edie was dark, and Anna fair. He saw that there was a new softness around her neck in the weeks he'd been gone, or perhaps he was only used to Edie's younger, tauter skin. He fixated on it, the beginnings of their older selves (he, too, was noticing his own belly rounding a little, the hairs he asked the barber to pluck from his nose, thinking of his father and grandfather and the uncles, how as a boy he had stared, disgusted, at the wiry black sprouts) and feeling a little deepening of his love for Anna, an opening beneath a floor he had thought already as deep as it would reach. He looked over the rest of her face and body, its familiar contours and freckles in place, its gently rounding, slowly wrinkling beauty. He stifled a smile: how she would smother him with this very pillow, if she could hear his thoughts. Or perhaps it would be that she could discern the admiration in them: that he loved her fading beauty in a deeper way than Edie's. Perhaps he should leave Edie, stop being so greedy, stop giving Anna a reason to take lovers herself, as she surely did. He stroked the satin sheet between his fingers. Had she brought anyone into this bed? Of course not. The girls, the servants: it would be impossible. The thought made him rub his feet together in boyish contentment, a feeling of security, as though they were adrift on this warm bed on a stormy sea, and he could burrow into these blankets with his wife and remain safe.

Anna was aware of his gaze, held her face still in the way of one used to being admired, a slight raise of her eyebrows. She held her poise as he reached for her, but then exploded into a snorting laugh as he unexpectedly touched her neck, making her snap her chin down on his fingers and squeal.

'Adam!'

He laughed too, pulled her to him, and she lay on his chest, tucked her head under his chin, still shaking from the shock of laughter. They breathed each other in, slowed, became still, let quiet blanket the room. Adam drifted into a memory from the early days of their marriage: they'd been sitting in this quiet way, he reading a sales report, she writing thank-you notes for wedding gifts. The curl of paper and the scratch of pen, the hum of the street, made him aware that their silence together was no longer charged, thinking of what to say, aware of how to seem. Instead it was steady, calm, and he had thought aloud, *I'm comfortable with you.* She'd laughed, surprised; it was a more emotional statement from him than she was used to. 'How romantic,' she'd replied, in a new tone, laced with a sarcasm he was also unused to, and she pretended to swoon in her chair, making him laugh. When the silence came back, the edges of the laugh remained hanging in the air, and the charge had somehow returned. So it was in their marriage, comfort and edge, and he liked that, loved Anna simply and as an adored friend, but accepted and even enjoyed her occasional disdain for him, a kind of flirtation.

'Silly boy,' she murmured now, as though the memory of his new wife had reached out and found this older version of her.

He reached for her, and they made love in their lazy, uncomplicated way, with the relief on both sides that he had, in fact, chosen to return to her, and not upset everything in any vulgar way, that the island bed stayed steady, that they still knew one another.

16

WHILE ADAM AND ANNA made love, Anna's imagination flitted through fantasies, some from years back, some more recent, alighting on Jozef, his figure in the doorway that night in the storm, the softness of his expression as he rejected her changing, in her mind's eye, to sharp desire. At the same moment, the real Jozef sat on an uncomfortable stool in a neighbourhood bar. He was three drinks deep into conversation with some old university friends. All of them saw themselves as artists: poets, translators, filmmakers; but only Jozef and Milo had no other income, which the others admired and envied while enjoying their warm rooms and thick coats. They liked to meet, these artists, to see themselves reflected in their old friends' faces, to be able to say, *I met with my friend, the painter, the filmmaker, I am one of the luminaries, this is my identity, not that man in the office, not that man who hasn't read a book properly in years.*

When Jozef had arrived, late because he had stayed for dinner at the Oderfeldts', he scanned for Milo as he kissed cheeks and clasped arms, and felt both relief and disappointment that he was missing. Their friendship, already meagre and marked by competition, now had a blank space in its centre, like a moth-eaten hole in wool picked at over time. So why did he feel disappointed, he wondered, as he settled into small talk with Ben, a teacher and writer who hadn't written a creative word in two years, that Milo wasn't here? It was the painting. He wanted to tell Milo about the painting. How good it was. How proud of it he was.

'Jozef! We miss you,' Ben opened the conversation. 'You never see us now, always moving in more elevated circles!'

'How is life as a pet painter?' teased the filmmaker, a short, tense man, from across the table. 'Do you have a warm spot by the fire and plenty of tidbits to eat?'

Jozef waved away the teasing, lit a cigarette. 'It's good. They're paying well, and the work is good.'

'A portrait, is it?' a man asked as he joined the table. Jozef glanced around, a little perplexed.

'This is Maurice, perhaps you've met? Another painter,' Ben said, as the two painters shook heads and hands. Maurice had a strong grip and an open, friendly face.

'So, a portrait? I saw your . . . the Oderfeldts, right? I saw your, what was it, the mother and the eldest, years back, I heard it was good.'

'You saw it or you heard about it?'

Maurice laughed. 'All right, I heard about it. From my friend Milo.'

Jozef gulped down more beer, wiped at his mouth. There it was, the hopeless irritation that could blight whole evenings. He glanced around at his friends. How he wanted to relax, to not feel that bleakness come over him. What was it? So he knew Milo too? Everyone knew Milo, the consummate connection maker, the schmoozer. The silence stretched a little too long, and Maurice's smile flickered. Jozef made what felt like a monumental effort to be friendly.

'Ah, a friend in common,' he said, and the smile came back in full force, a good smile, expensive teeth. The others relaxed into new conversations, all variations of *what are you working on* and lying replies. Jozef felt the effects of the beer begin to hum in his head, felt lighter. 'We go way back. We were in competition for the commission.'

'So, it's a portrait?'

'That's right. Of Alicia.'

'A beauty?'

'She's a child,' Jozef replied, irritation rising in him again. 'What about your work?'

'Is it finished?' Maurice pressed, ignoring the question. He covered his rudeness a little with a swig of his drink, another crinkle-eyed smile. His moustache was coated in beer foam.

Jozef felt the twinge of anxiety between his ribs. This stage of a painting was like the beginning of a love affair: an obsessive desire to be close to it, keep touching it, constantly worrying that if you are away too long it will forget you, and refuse to take shape. He felt it was good, knew it was good, in some hard kernel buried deep, but it could all fall apart in these last days. That must be it, he thought. He looked away from the currents of fear he knew ran deep: an image of that thick front door closing on him a last time, no commission for some years perhaps, in which Karolina would fade from him, in which those long afternoons in the dining room, in that golden light, would be lost.

'You know how it is, the last . . . the end of a project,' he tried.

'I don't think my work is like yours. I'm in a slightly different field.'

'Oh.' He was being rude, he knew it. Was it that Maurice had called Anna just *the mother*, that Jozef knew how she would hate it? Or that Karolina was just *the elder*, like part of a list, like calling a star a speck, like reducing her to just one of the boring, rich patrons, not the . . . what *was* Karolina to him? He took another gulp, wished he was home.

Ben nudged him as he went for another drink. 'You should work together,' he called over his shoulder.

'So. It's finished?' Maurice tried again. He seemed amused by Jozef's coldness.

'Yes, almost,' he conceded as he put his glass down. 'I just have to make sure I get it right.'

'Milo said—'

'Please, I don't want to hear what that prick had to say.'

This was louder than he intended and the whole group recoiled, delighted, shocked whoops, hands to mouths, laughter. Jozef, grumpy but mild, rarely swore. The others delighted in the idea of an artists' feud in their midst.

'Oh dear . . . you've fallen out over the commission?' Ben laughed, settling back into his seat.

'He insulted—'

'Your work?'

'The family.'

'Yours?' The filmmaker was surprised. Jozef's mother had been well liked among the university set, and her death had saddened them. Milo had sent flowers to her funeral.

'No.' Jozef took a hasty swig of beer, angry with himself; he hadn't wanted to discuss Milo at all. 'The Oderfeldts.'

'Oh, but that's just sourness at the lost money,' Ben said.

'Yes, perhaps.'

Yes, he was relieved Milo wasn't there. He felt now how his discomfort with Milo's hatred for the Oderfeldts had sharpened into disgust. Karolina, glowing Karolcia, the richness of her inner life, the way she watched, thought, sealed things away in her heart; how could anyone insult her? And Alicia, so clever, so much cleverer than anyone realised, a true talent. Adam and Anna with their complicated dance, always a kind of charge between them that was bewitching to watch. He could paint them together, he thought: ask for a new commission. He'd try to capture that charge somehow.

'Milo can be a prick,' Maurice said, laughing.

Jozef raised his glass to him.

'So. You said you're in a slightly different . . . not a painter? Or are you more of an honest artist, making modern pieces, not my stuffy portraits?'

Maurice watched him calmly. 'I do some modern pieces, yes. But portraits can be very . . . lucrative.'

'Ah, you think I'm a sell-out.'

'I think there's a lot of money to be made, and why not make it?'

'Would I know any of your work?'

'Oh yes, but you wouldn't know it was mine.'

Jozef raised his eyebrows and sipped again, feeling stupid and slow. 'Um, you're . . . you work under a different name, you mean?'

Maurice laughed. 'Oh yes, lots of different names.' Jozef felt his stupidity rebound on him again as he understood. A forger. Maurice leaned in, so Jozef could smell the beer on his breath. Up close, he noticed the sheen of wealth, so well-rehearsed was he in spotting money: that shirt was thick and warm, the coat looked lined and from the kind of tailor Adam might use. 'I have one hanging in your patron's apartment,' he whispered, and then gave a wheezing kind of giggle. '*Thousands* I got for that.'

Jozef wanted to smile, match the man's conspiratorial air. It was rare for him to make a new friend. But instead he felt a reflected embarrassment for Adam, thought of his pride in his pieces, how he showed them to guests.

'Which one?'

'As if I would tell you! See if you can spot it.'

Maurice laughed again, clapped Jozef on the back. 'If your piece is good, maybe I'll paint it one day,' he said, and broke into drunken laughter at Jozef's face. 'Now don't be precious, you'd be lucky to have the compliment,' he added, before heading back to the bar.

The evening got colder outside and the windows began to mist up; Jozef was seized by his usual childish impulse to draw in the cloudy glass canvas it made. They were all reluctant to go home, and stayed until past midnight, huddling into their coats whenever the doors opened and let in an icy blast of air. They fell into old tracks of conversation about university days and their plans for the future, politics and complaining about wives and girlfriends who didn't support them enough, before a few more drinks tipped them into tearful confessions of how much they loved those wives and girlfriends, how guilty they felt at their betrayals, that other lover, that kiss, that fumble at that party. Always these led to good-natured baiting of Jozef, always with his empty bed. They'd all long ago come to separate, never-discussed conclusions that their friend loved men, and protected him and themselves from any embarrassment by building a wall of aggressive jokes about his secret women, his affairs with married ladies, or his sad and lonely love affair with the blank canvas: Jozef, a caresser of paintbrushes, a seducer of dust sheets, a fucker of paint.

'I know at least three girls off the top of my head who would have your clothes off you so quickly your head would spin,' the filmmaker cried.

'Come on,' Ben and the others, the poet, the playwright, the translator, added, smiling at the familiar taunts, awaiting Jozef's usual lines in return: *I'm too busy, I don't like city girls.*

When his mother was dying, they'd put all this to one side, but now it seemed Jozef had recovered a little, they returned to it with gratitude.

Jozef smiled, sat back, let his head hang. He blushed a little, felt the familiar mixture of envy and comfort in old friends and the fixedness of their view of him: even if he felt he might fly apart, their Jozef was immovable. Taking a deep drink, he imagined telling them of Anna appearing at his door that night in the storm, the way the whites of her eyes had glowed in the lightning flickers, and weaving in a lie that led them to bed together, changing the narrative of both that night and the one of Jozef they thought they all knew so well. He grimaced into his glass at the thought of how the gossip would spread like water and lap right up to the apartment walls on Bernardyńska, hurting Anna and all the rest. He tried to assemble the nebulous wisps of feeling he had for Karolina instead, but that was even more unthinkable, to present her to them in this dirty bar, to their innuendo, to the questions: *How big are her tits? I hear those rich girls are filthy in bed, the well-read ones will do the best dirty talk, ha ha . . .* even if behind all the play-acting there was a genuine happiness for him, he couldn't do it; he wouldn't be able to explain what she was to him, since he didn't know, and it would all end in a row. By the time he put his glass down, Jozef's face was the smiling, blushing mask they all knew from the thousand versions of this conversation they had had before. They circled around the conversational track again as he nodded, smiled, laughed along, and they were no closer to knowing their friend's insides than before.

Jozef wondered if Ben was aware his friend was a crook, then felt provincial and stupid for worrying about it. What did it matter if Maurice made money selling the odd knock off? A tiny voice from within answered: *It matters*. He might capture that same light, that same shape, the brushstrokes that made Alicia's face, but it would be just an echo. Maurice was never in that room, with Karolina behind him, watching and pulling at the invisible thread between them, and he'd never met Alicia, slowly understood how she was half-hidden from the world, even from her own family, watching and thinking from behind a doll-mask.

He watched as Maurice returned to the bar again and again, free with his money, while Jozef was already feeling a familiar anxiety about how he would eat the next morning: he'd spent his coins on this last drink, and Adam hadn't yet paid him. He swallowed down a tiny echo of Milo's attack with the warm dregs of beer: *Money in the walls, you think they'll pay you what you're owed?*

The next day Jozef went early to Bernardyńska, breathing into his hands on the tram to check there was no lingering beer on his breath; it was sour, laced with the cheap coffee he made weak and with too much sugar, but there was no beer in it and he was relieved. An image of himself as a blundering drunk pawing over the girls made him close his eyes. At the apartment there would be good tea and hot rolls at this time in the morning, and maybe a chance to catch the family in its sleepy morning state, the papers spread out at the adults' table, the girls sharing elaborate dream-stories downstairs, asking him what he thought they meant for their futures. Jozef's stomach grasped at itself, complaining, a mixture of hunger and an old anxiety. Soon the painting would be finished and there would be money, for a while, but no more of those rooms, those mornings and evenings with the Wawel watching over him as he worked. And then the money would run out and he would wait, cold in his own little apartment, for Stefan or Adam to pluck him out again, send him to one of their friends' houses, perhaps, or if he was lucky, think up something else for him to do at Bernardyńska.

The tram was full of the first wave of workers: early shifts, or perhaps fearful of losing jobs. There were the cheap poorly fitting suits and scuffed shoes of the younger clerks and shop assistants, the hurried, wispy hairstyles of women who worked in the department stores perhaps, and at least one teacher or governess, clutching a cloth bag full of files and books. Jozef liked groupings like this: the way the inside casing of the tram made a frame, the way the travellers entered into an unconscious swaying dance together. A grey palette would work, with flashes of yellow and white for the overhead lights, struggling against the morning gloom. In fact there was lots of red on the women, skirts and scarves, it was apparently in fashion, but in grey he would be telling the truth better: early morning in the city, the damp dullness of it, the wishing for the warm blankets again. He scanned for an interesting angle of limbs, a shape that could be drawn out in paint to make the whole fit into a kind of invisible pattern. Most faces were lowered into newspapers, and something about the collective hunch could work on a canvas. The newspapers were full of rumblings and mutterings about Germany, the echoes of a fight between giants.

On approaching the apartment he saw he had misjudged the time; he liked to be early, to work in the morning light, but the windows were still dark, the curtains drawn. Jozef ambled up and down Bernardyńska for a few minutes, relieved it was a mild morning, if grey, stopping at the bakery to watch the loaves being laid out in the window and to catch the delicious smell. He surprised himself by not feeling foolish but enjoying what felt like stolen time, in the mild air, watching the city rouse itself. When he returned to the apartment door, Robert's hesitation was smoothly submerged as he welcomed Jozef in.

'The family aren't yet up, please let me show you upstairs—'

'It's all right, Robert, I'm sure there's plenty to—'

Robert nodded at the bottom of the stairs, gestured to the dining room, where Jozef had been working these last months, assured him tea and rolls would be sent up for him, and melted away. Jozef play-acted as he walked up the stairs, letting his hand rest on the banister. *My house, my family, my money, my paintings on these walls.* He paused before entering the dining room, let a fantasy that he had left a wife sleeping catch hold of him for a moment. She was turned with her back to him, sleeping in satin sheets, so he did not have to define her face, some queasy cocktail of Anna and Karolina. The room had a fire lit and the lights dimly on and there was his painting, as he'd left it yesterday afternoon, waiting to be finished. He approached it, but then the others on the walls caught his eye, and he remembered Maurice's comment: *See if you can guess which one.*

He'd said he'd made thousands. Could be an empty boast, of course. The paintings were arranged too stiffly in rows, not left the necessary space to breathe as they would in a gallery. It made the colours bleed a little into each other so that this dark one cast a shadow over this blue one. They were all framed in the same elegant way, by a framer in Warsaw to whom Adam sent all the family work; he used gold leaf on simple, clean lines and a very thin glass. Jozef caught his reflection in his own portrait of Anna and Karolina, which he'd avoided looking at, he now realised: why had he not returned to it like an old friend, a reassurance that he could do it? Karolina was so young in it, and his memories of her from that time refused to settle on the girl he knew now; how he had ignored her, dismissed her, barely noticed her at all. The whole painting had been rushed, between lessons at the Jagiellonian and caring for his mother and meeting his friends. He couldn't believe it was the same rooms and the same people. He studied his brushstrokes now, Anna's younger face, rounder, softer, and Karolina at her feet, a blankness to the expression. People had praised it at the time; Adam had adored it, he said. He saw now it was empty, a student's exercise.

Next to his own failure was another modern piece, one of Milo's? Jozef searched for the signature, found it. Not Milo but a name he recognised from a slightly older set, also from the university circles. A still life, rather dull. Some fruit and flowers, autumn light.

He scanned along the others, more family pieces and a painting of the apartment itself, interspersed with photographs. Some well-known Poles, a few locals like himself, mostly well regarded and expensive, but not of the calibre to attract a forger, not worth thousands. Nothing seemed out of place or obviously a fake. Maurice's beer-sodden swagger began to seem like any other drunkard's boast in a crowded bar, and Jozef's vaguely formed daydream of finding a new route to support himself faded. He was surprised by the weight he felt settle back onto him, unaware of how much he had secretly invested in this idea, and why.

He turned to Alicia-in-paint again, started to mix some final colours. He could work without Alicia there now. Really he should have the whole canvas transferred to a rented studio space, or his own rooms, and finish alone. No one ever mentioned it. He tried to settle into the world of Alicia's image, to let it reveal what it needed. He stared at the blank sludgy space behind her shoulder.

The air changed somehow, a tiny shift, some scent on it perhaps, soap and starch, paper, and beneath those the scent of her skin. She moved in quietly, noticing how he was working. Hearing how she carefully, carefully pulled out a chair, the tiny creak as she settled into it, made his chest give a little clutch of gratitude and something deeper that he wasn't ready to name. He kept dabbing mindlessly at the paint mix, eyeing the space where he knew something was missing. He wanted to turn and speak but it was sweet to feel her there, knowing she watched him work, perhaps unaware he knew she had entered the room. He knew her legs would be tucked beneath her, her hand scrunched in her hair, head cocked to one side, watching him with that air of calm. His hand hovered with the paintbrush. He was aware of his untucked shirt and that he hadn't combed his hair. He heard the flick of a notebook and the scratch of her pen. A rush overtook him to think she might be writing about him. He turned to watch her in turn now, her hair falling over her concentrating face. She raised her eyes to him, touched gazes.

'Sorry,' she whispered. 'I didn't want to stop you working.'

'I haven't started yet,' he replied, louder than he'd meant to. Somehow it broke the spell, and she began to move from the table.

'Karolina, don't go, it's fine—'

She put her notebook back on the table, pivoted so her hand stayed touching it; a childlike pose as she leaned into her hand and let her other limbs dangle awkwardly. She cast her eyes around the room, a slow blush covering her cheeks.

'I . . . wrote you something,' she said, her blush deepening.

Warmth rushed through him, and an anxious drumming in his ears, too. 'Will you let me read it?'

'I'm too embarrassed. I'll leave it here for you.'

She moved to the door. 'It's finished, isn't it?' She nodded towards the painting, Alicia's eyes on them both.

'No, still some touches.'

When she opened the door, the sounds of the house flooded in, now awake. Alicia was shouting Mimi's name, who was yipping in return, her tiny paw falls skittering on upstairs floorboards. Doors opened and closed, heavy curtains were swept back. Warmth was spreading through the rooms and the smell of breakfast drifted up from the kitchens. Karolina stayed in the doorway, twisted her hair.

'Do you want to stay while I read it?'

She nodded, closed the door.

He was startled by the force of her kiss. He'd imagined (for he had imagined it) a shyness to her, her inexperience making her still and sweetly hesitant; instead she kissed him with hunger and confidence, pressed her body to him in a way that made him almost laugh in surprise. At first he was aware of the family noise, trying to notice sounds approaching even as he lost his hands in her hair and broke the kiss to bury his face in her neck, but it didn't take long for the world to contract, for both of them, as though the apartment and the household didn't exist. By the time Alicia came flying through the door, holding roses ('These are the ones we should use, for the background, they're from Mama's bedroom and the perfect colour, come on!'), Jozef had promised Karolina his whole life, shocked himself with how easy and simple it was. 'I know how to make money,' he said, 'and I'll marry you just as soon as I can afford to.' She had only kissed him and smiled, and removed her hands from his as Alicia threw open the door.

Jozef finished the painting that day. He didn't need to delay any more, now that he knew the painting and his connection to Karolina would not end together. Into the roses, just behind Alicia's painted hair, curling in the background like wallpaper come to life, he put Karolina, always curled up behind the work, watching, beautiful, waiting to be seen.

Kraków, 1939

17

ANNA LOOKED BACK to where her husband and the car and
all their possessions had been. The crowd was surging again,
and she felt she would break her hands, so tight was her grip
on the slippery coats of the girls. A man with a sack on his
back, a storybook robber, knocked her almost off her feet. The
ground was mulch beneath them, with the almost sweet smell
of churned mud. Anna had no idea what to do.

'Come,' she said, and pulled the girls, pliant and in shock,
in the wake of the sack robber-man, trying to match his path
as people were forcibly removed from his way. Someone
caught her arm and her very lungs seemed to leap out of her
chest. She turned to find Janina Kardas gibbering something
about a horse and cart.

'We must get to that cart . . . but where is Adam? Where is
your car? Anna, what is happening? This is awful!' Anna could
only nod at her.

'Where is Adam?'

Alicia began sobbing, her tears riding on the name of her
Papa.

'I see,' Janina said. She straightened herself, shoving a man
who fell into her right in the chest.

'Listen,' she said. 'There is a horse and cart not far, which
is taking people for money and things. What do you have
with you?'

'I – everything was in the car. But we should go back, Adam is—'

'Absolutely not. What do you have? Fur? Jewels?'

'I, yes. And . . . there are pearls sewn in here.' Anna gestured to the back of her coat. 'But we need them for . . . oh maybe we should just go back to the apartment, and Adam can find us there?'

Janina pulled her by the elbow, the girls trailing, now mute with astonishment. The horse and cart was standing a little way off the road, with a man clambering over what Anna thought must be sacks of grain, or material; when they got closer, she saw it was people.

Alicia was pulling her roughly. 'Mama, we can't, Papa, and all our things. Mama, my painting is just left there in the dirt!'

Karolina pulled her sister's hair. 'Be quiet,' she hissed.

Anna turned to Janina, whose face was tight and ugly in its concentration.

'We can't possibly,' she said helplessly.

'What, are you going to walk to Lwów?'

'Adam will come with the car, I suppose,' Anna said in desperation.

'Oh! The Germans will give it back, I'm sure,' Janina replied acidly.

All four of them were holding each other's arms now, like treading water in a sea current. Anna had a sudden image of Adam, twisted in the dirt, his head bleeding. She was silent. Janina helped her to undo the buttons on her coat when she found her own fingers were not able to grip them. Then Janina pulled the buttons off, one by one, leaving their threads dangling, making Anna think of plucked-out eyes. The older woman held the mother-of-pearl buttons in her palm, sorting through them like a fisherwoman looking for cockles.

'You could try these,' she said. 'And then you have your fur as well.' She had to shout as the murmur of the crowd became louder nearer to the cart, pushing and calling out offers. Somewhere below them, car engines purred. The sky was still clear, and the screaming noise of an invasion strangely absent. *Shouldn't there be,* Anna thought, *the whistle and thud of bombs, like the fields in France in the last war?* She wondered if her beautiful apartment would be bombed, the front all ripped open for the world to see. Her new *chinoiserie* wallpaper would be ruined and covered in soot. Where was her husband?

Janina patted the shoulders and hair of Anna's daughters, padded like swaddled babies. Alicia scowled at her, while Karolina's face was alert, her breathing heavy.

'Well, come, no time now.' Janina heard the briskness and coldness of her own voice.

'Mama, I can't,' Karolina said.

Anna glared at her. 'You can and you will.' She began to pull Karolina through the throng, but her daughter retaliated with strength. 'No. Papa said we'd go to Jozef's apartment on the way—'

'Karolcia, please!'

'—I want to be with him—'

'The city is *being invaded*—'

'I can't leave without him, Mama, please, I—'

'Your father has been arrested or God knows what, and you want us to go traipsing through the streets wailing for your lover?'

As they argued Anna was pulling Karolina, aided by Alicia and Janina, towards the horse and cart. The driver stood balanced on his seat, facing back towards the city, pointing. People in the cart were saying, 'Go, go, please can we go?'

'No free journeys,' the driver called down. 'We go straight to Lwów but you must pay.'

'Please, Karolcia,' her mother and sister said in unison. Alicia clung to her waist and Karolina sagged where she stood, defeated. Janina was holding out the mother-of-pearl buttons and caught hold of Anna's fur stole.

'Here,' Janina said. 'For all of us.'

The man appeared to click his tongue, though the sound was lost.

'My daughters, at least,' Anna said.

Janina began scrabbling at Anna's coat, the shock of her strong, old fingers making Anna cry out. 'She has pearls sewn in here,' Janina was saying, pulling and prodding Anna in the back with her free hand. Anna shook Janina off, and quickly removed the whole coat, throwing it at the driver, who caught it deftly, and pulled her onto the cart. She hauled up Karolina, ignoring her tears, and then Alicia. From up here, Anna could see the extent of the crowd. It seemed the whole population of Kraków was flooding out of the city. Janina was holding out the buttons to the driver, arguing. The calls to go were getting louder now, and Anna realised she was adding to them, a rising wail, to leave her neighbour behind in the mud, leave her possessions and car and Adam somewhere next to the road, have the horse lumber on, move, move. The cart made a sudden lurch as the crowd pressed against it, and Anna heard screams, some from her girls. The driver made a settling motion with his hands, as though they were dogs, and sat on the stool, his reins in hand. One of her coat buttons dropped into the mud from his hand as he took the reins.

'Help me up, help me up,' Janina was screaming, but Anna couldn't release her grip on her children. As the cart began to move Janina gave such a howl of rage that one of the other women pulled her up, and she sat heavily opposite Anna, her face contorted with fury. Anna looked away, finding it unbearable.

As the cart jolted, the crowd around seemed to press against it, and Anna felt again just as in the car how she could mow them all down if she was driving, crush them under her wheels, just to get away, before begging God to forgive her. Hands pulled at their clothes and limbs, trying to climb up. The horse stumbled and whinnied in fright as the driver braced and cajoled, his pockets full of jewels and beneath him a pile of furs, coats and money.

Anna carefully held the fact of her husband's loss away from her, finding she could make her thoughts flow around it. Her eldest daughter's face was slack with grief at leaving Jozef behind, and so she watched Alicia instead: poised now, quiet, a little pale, her hat still in place. Anna was proud of her. She should have left her to care for Karolina in her love-struck hysterics, even Janina, who would help, while she went to look for Adam like a good wife. But he was gone and she was glad to be on the lurching cart making its sickening dips and wrenches through the mud, glad to be elevated from the throng, with her children safe before her.

'Unbelievable, that you would leave me there on the ground, after I helped you,' Janina said.

A rush of unexpected tenderness for the old woman assaulted Anna. She threw her arms around her and buried her face into the space between her neck and shoulder. Janina's dress smelled of sweat and lavender.

'Thank you, thank you, Mrs Kardas,' Anna said. 'I don't know why I— oh!' They clutched at each other as the cart lurched again. 'I'm so sorry, I'm sorry, I was so afraid and I just want to get away, but Adam . . .'

'Janina,' the older woman replied stiffly, 'please, for God's sake, Anna, call me Janina.'

'Janina, I'm so sorry.'

Around an hour out of the city, the old horse was getting tired. The crowd didn't seem to thin but swell, as though they were rushing together to some powerful rapids. All around them the trundle of other carts and the trudge of feet against road, wooden wheels against tracks, praying, the calling of names. The Oderfeldts called silently for their lost ones, like a heartbeat pulse: *Adam, Adam, Adam*, and *Papa, Papa, Papa*, then Karolina's *Jozef*, added to the thousands of silent calls bursting into the air.

Alicia had left her gloves in the car, along with their old life, and felt stripped in the cold as her hands throbbed. She watched the other women sucking their fingers and tucking them into armpits, enthralled and disgusted, before Karolina took her fingers, almost grey now, and folded them into the fabric of her coat. She curled herself into her sister's side.

'Papa,' Alicia whispered into Karolina's ribs. 'My painting.'

Later the clamour of the crowd, its rhythmic calls and cries of distress, faded as exhaustion set in. The trundle of wheels around them slowed, and crouching figures, resting on haunches or even stretched out by the side of the road, sat grey in the fading light like boulders. Karolina murmured stories about them to her sister, how they were enchanted, like the rocks outside Aladdin's cave. Janina, pinned in place by the squeeze of people on her cart bench, hadn't moved her legs for several hours, and the blood pooled there, into her feet and ankles. Anna had put her head into Janina's lap, not asleep but staring at her daughters.

The other passengers were all women. Janina tried to peer into faces to see if she recognised anyone. She thought she saw a woman who had sold her some shoes, and another, not a Jew but close to the neighbourhood, who was of a higher class and who might have attended a dinner or two. In the corner, two women with identical red, curly hair, sisters, were murmuring to each other over the creak of the cart's wheels, the clop of the horse's hooves on the path. One of them wriggled so that a small sack appeared between her feet, and she pulled out an apple and a plum. They were passed to Alicia, with an instruction, 'Eat these.' Alicia turned the small, bruised fruit over in her hands. The apple was wrinkled and she picked at a brown spot near the stem. The whole cart was watching her now. Even her mother and their old neighbour were staring. She blushed and ate the plum, sucking the fruit juice out so it ran down her chin and onto her wool coat.

'Thank you,' called Karolina, elbowing Alicia as she did so, but the red-headed women were folded in on themselves, one's head on the other's shoulder, readying for sleep.

The cart plodded on through the night. The skies were clear; there were no planes, nor clouds, and Janina could see the faint stars behind stars. Her husband had known so many of their names. He would have known what to do. *But you are doing all right, Janina,* she told herself. *You are getting out of the city, you have found people, you will go to Lwów and this will all be all, all right.* In the gloom the sounds and shifts of the cart, her ark, every throat clearing, every swallow and tooth click, were a comfort. She burrowed down into her coat a little, feeling the heaviness of Anna's head in her lap.

18

Dawn was sluggish and grey, showing up the blur of hedgerow and the sleepy sack-like shapes of the people on the cart. Alicia briefly held the eye of her neighbour, Mrs Kardas. Her lip puckered at the bottom and Alicia wondered if she was missing teeth. She started to drift into a story about her, breaking her teeth on a step, or perhaps she'd met the man who had attacked Papa on the night of Alicia's birthday. She lost her threads of thought and memory, too tired, and saw that Mrs Kardas's eyes had closed again. When Alicia tried to find sleep, she drifted back to the soldiers who had surrounded their car. They became giant insects, tapping at the windows with long, spidery legs, so she forced her eyes open again, tried to find some game in the cart.

Alicia had counted everything – buttons, fingernails, boots, her own teeth, by the time the cart jolted to a stop. People opened their mouths as though to cry out, but little sound came from cold throats, only a collective croak, and a shift, a clutch at each other. With a low grunt the horse buckled to its knees, and the man was pulling back on the reins, leaning in with his weight.

There was a sound like wind on wheat, the whisper-rasp pleas of the cart. 'No, keep going, make it move, you mustn't stop.' People raised their hands, as though to push the horse on. Alicia watched her mother and Mrs Kardas begin to rise from their places on the bench, her Mama's hair falling out of its bun, her lipstick bitten away. Alicia had always thought she might like a horse. She'd seen beautiful chestnut mares being ridden around the parks near the Wawel and along the river, girls like her in smart, tailored coats, their hair in low plaits. This horse was thin and looked patched together, like a poor child's toy.

The driver jumped down and tugged gently at the reins, the crowd on the cart craning and shuffling to see if the beast would move. In the minds of the grown women there was a collective flash of bloodied horse flesh, the bit cutting into the soft mouth, the red stripes and sweat on the flanks. *Panic makes us cruel*, Anna thought, *but it's true, it's true, I would flay that horse alive to get away.* The man moved in front of the animal, bearing it up with his weight, and he touched his cheek to the horse's nose, whispered something.

'There are children here,' Anna called, her breath making wisps in the cool dawn air. She felt a wash of hatred for the dirty, grasping man in his warm clothes and good gloves, stolen from some fleeing husband, she thought, and her pearls, strung in a boutique in Rome, shipped in scented paper, rattling in his pockets like pretty stones plucked from a beach.

'Horse needs to rest,' the man said, unyoking the cart, and holding up his hands to the flood of protesting voices, still low and dampened by shock and cold, but forceful yet, carrying each other, *I paid you to take me to Lwów, not the side of a road. Yes, yes, so did I, we said Lwów, I'll have my coins back.* The driver, himself stooped with fatigue and grim-faced, waved them off the cart. For a moment they didn't move, and Janina even wound her arms around the wooden slats that had been digging in to her back. Then the red-haired women who had given Alicia the fruit jumped down, landing heavily in the mud. The driver held out an arm swaddled in his heavy coat, and when it was refused, he shrugged, pulled out and lit a cigarette. In the early birdsong, the red-haired sisters gathered their lumpy packs on their backs, and set off walking along the track without looking back. The cart emptied after that, some remonstrating with the driver as they went. One older woman, older than Janina, toothless, spat at the man's feet. He spoke in a low rumble to them, held up his hands, smoked, looked at his feet, gestured to the horse, which had moved to the side of the road and was nibbling at the hedgerow. 'In a few hours, only,' he kept saying. 'My horse must rest first.' He didn't return any of the money or jewellery. 'It's your choice to go. I took you this far, you get off early, fine, your choice.'

Anna watched all this from her gaggle with her daughters, holding onto them with a slipping gloved grip on their shoulders. She was vaguely aware of the strangeness of the old woman's place with them, instead of Adam. Her girls were staring dully ahead, and she gripped harder as though to feel the still warm flesh and blood beneath the layers. She hadn't touched her children so often in her life; Janie and earlier nursemaids and governesses had dealt with lost teeth and spit and dribbled food, the realities of their bodies as babies and little children, their smell, the texture of their skins. Anna had kissed them lightly on cheeks, perhaps patted a head now and again. Now she felt an urge to somehow pin them to her, hide them inside her coat, feel their hearts beating against her skin.

'Just us women then,' a woman's sharp voice said. Anna turned to look at her, gave a tight nod, a sign she didn't want to talk. The woman looked poor, a servant or a governess, a shop worker. Anna hadn't noticed her on the cart.

'I left my husband back in Kraków,' the woman said. She was pretty, with small features like a porcelain doll. 'Stupid man,' she spat. Janina had turned now too, from where she had been watching the driver fuss over his horse, cooing at it like a beloved firstborn. She shifted from foot to foot, chafing, a blister on a toe screaming at her. She mustered her most disgusted look.

'You left him deliberately?' she said. She and Anna exchanged a glance.

'Was he injured?' Anna snapped.

The woman rolled her eyes. As she turned away Anna saw that she was pregnant. A small boy sat at her feet, wrapped in a shawl, his face dirty with what looked like berries, probably picked from the road.

'Shameless,' hissed Janina, scenting a chance to connect with Anna in their disapproval, bind them together. 'Imagine.'

Anna nodded. Adam tugged at her somewhere beneath her ribs, but she knew, too, there must be something else, something to do with the children. She placed a hand, gently, on Alicia's bare head, who leaned into her at her touch, too exhausted to resist. If it had come to it she would have thrown Adam into the dirt herself, she knew, and he would have done the same.

The woman had taken on the particular stillness of one discussed by others within earshot. She placed a hand on her belly, then began rooting in her pockets for her papers, smoothed them out and licked her finger to leaf through them as though counting money. Janina watched her, shifting from foot to foot.

'She should be more careful with those,' she hissed at Anna.

'Do you have yours?'

'Of course!' Janina patted her coat pocket.

Anna felt, absurdly, a memory of girlhood panic, from school: *Everyone has brought the correct things, and you are to be in trouble.* She disentangled Alicia from where she had threaded her hands around her mother's waist, using her as a leaning post to sleep against, and pushed her towards her sister.

'I don't have ours,' she confessed in a whisper.

Janina's mouth fell open. Anna waited for her to crow, or smother her in false, delighted concern, but she only looked at the girls and worked her mouth as though preparing and rejecting things to say.

'They were in the car with everything else,' Anna said, struggling to keep her voice low and calm. 'Surely if we explain—'

'I don't know,' Janina said, without any malice.

'But lots of people must be in that position,' Anna said.

'Yes, yes,' Janina said, concentrating a hate-filled gaze at the back of the pregnant woman's head, who had slowly put her papers back in her pocket, and stood with her hands clasped around her son.

'I must ask for the pearls back,' Anna said, almost whispering, mostly to herself. She had unconsciously turned to face her children as she did so, and they stared at her, seeming very young, even Karolina with her woman's hair and figure. Her eldest daughter's eyes were wide. Anna knew her own face must be ashen, unable to falsely brighten it in the quiet panic of the moment. Alicia was regarding her with a detachment Anna found in equal parts chilling and admirable.

'Are we just going to stand here in the road?' Janina said to the man. Around them, the other women were dispersing, setting off in one direction or another, some trudging back towards Kraków, others along the path. The pregnant woman with her papers was trundling away, looking capable and steady. Anna wanted to run after her, beg her to mother them all, get them somewhere safe. *I'm not capable,* she'd explain. *I've never been capable of taking care of them at all.*

'Stand, go, wait, it's your choice,' the man said.

He drifted over to his horse, the smoke from his cigarette and the steam from the horse's breath mingling together. Anna listened for the low rumble of other carts, other horses, other people, the crowd from Kraków that had streamed out of the city. There was only the birdsong and the snorting of the horse.

'We'll find a house,' Anna said, imagining Adam's low, soothing voice, saying the same words, how simple he would make it. 'We'll find a house and they'll see we have children and they'll help. I would, if it were my house . . . wouldn't you, Mrs Kardas, Janina? I'd take people in, people are good, they will let us rest, we can eat and rest, and then when the horse is rested, we can go, or we'll find another route.'

An urgent hunger came upon her, and she swallowed heavily, ashamed of the flood of saliva that had filled her mouth as she imagined a family taking them in and sharing fresh morning bread, the yeasty dough burning the roof of her mouth. The sky had lightened even more now, the streaks of colour and mist becoming washed out by a cool grey.

'Mama, shall we go?' Karolina was gently insistent. 'It's cold.'

'Sir?' Anna called. The driver touched the horse's nose, whispered something in the beast's ear. Its sides swelled and fell like billows.

'I'll let her rest, then leave again for Lwów at sunset,' he called. 'Better to travel at night.'

The road had made it seem they were stranded in the middle of nowhere, but when they pushed through the hedgerow, farms dotted the fields. The field was freshly harvested, hay packed in clumps. Alicia stamped and broke the stalks, enjoying the popping sensation through her thin shoes, satisfied at their clean collapse. Their colour was a muddy yellow that would work well for canvas skin, mixed with a pearly white. For a moment Jozef's fingers blending paint came to her. He rubbed his forefinger and thumb together, held them against the sunlight stream that poured through the front rooms of the apartment. Then he frowned at the palette again, turned to study her bare arm like a mathematical problem. He'd been pleased with how the skin had turned out, though it was more golden and rosier than her real paleness.

'Mama,' she started to say, though she had no plan of what to say. She was desperate to urinate. Her mother was waddling inelegantly ahead, lifting her coat and raising her feet high like a stork, trying to avoid the swampy puddles beneath. Anna turned with difficulty, Janina clinging to her arm, the two older women locked in an awkward dance. Karolina was also unsteady, gripping Alicia's shoulders.

'I'm ill,' Alicia tried.

'We're all cold and tired,' snapped her Mama.

'I shall faint!'

'Then we'll leave you here in the corn!' Anna said, before lurching around again.

'Come on,' Karolina said, as they set off across the field again. 'There is a bed and food waiting for us nearby.'

A gunshot cracked across the sky and burst a startled flock of pigeons into their path. The fog they were in was scattered, and all four darted forwards, reaching for each other, struggling towards the nearest farmhouse in a bumbling quartet of trips and heavy breaths. None of them spoke, but Janina heard again the Kraków tempo: *They are here, they are here, we must go, we must go. Germans on the road, Germans shooting horses, Germans shooting people.*

The farm was awake: smoke ghosted from the chimney. Small, surrounded by simple wire fencing, Anna thought, these are the places children escape to in fairy tales, inhabited by kindly woodcutters and wives with dirty aprons who cook soup. They vaulted the fence with all the ease of the terrified, even Janina, who launched at the door and pounded it like a betrayed wife.

On the other side: not the fairy tale of Anna's imaginings, but a group of young men. Farmhands, streaked with dirt and finger-thick grime on their aprons. They sat and leaned, arranged around the meagre furniture, murmuring to each other in rusty early morning voices, cigarettes dangling from their mouths. The room was dark and thick with smoke, an earthy, sweaty smell. One of the men, dark bearded and with an angular face, was at the stove, where some kind of salted meat fried in a pan. The men did not immediately react to the women and girls on the other side of the door, but looked in open curiosity.

Janina took charge. 'We need to speak to your master or mistress please, the farmer. It is rather urgent.'

'You've come from one of the cities,' the bearded man said. One of his friends held out his burning cigarette to Anna.

'Water please,' she said to him, and he went to a jug by the sink.

'Come on, come in,' the bearded man said.

'Jews, are you?' the man with the water jug said, passing a cup to Anna, who sank into a chair. The question hung in the air, heavy with pity. The fumes from the meat and the cigarette were heady and made her hunger spark back into life. Her daughters and Janina had shuffled in and stood against the stained walls. Their silence answered the man's question, though Anna wanted to add, *It's so unfair, we don't even*

*practise, my grandfather would be so unhappy with me, and here
we are anyway.*

Janina said, 'What does it matter, we've come from Kraków,
where the Germans have—'

'Yes, yes, all right, fine,' one of the other men said.

'No master farmer here, we're all working on bringing the
last of the harvest in,' another chimed in.

'Why aren't you fighting? Don't you know Kraków has
just been invaded?' Janina said. *Where are your mothers?* she
thought. *Don't you know my boy is fighting?*

'Even if the world is going to hell, we still need to bring the
harvest in,' one of the men said, after a long pause.

'What was the gunshot?' Karolina asked. Her voice was
raspy from misuse and the cold. The men gave a collective
shrug.

The bearded man said his name was Peter. He took them
to a barn building at the back of the farmhouse, full of rolled
bales of fresh hay, sweet smelling. A low window showed a
view of more fields and a smaller box-like building. 'You can
go to the toilet out there,' he said. 'We need to work but we'll
bring food over.'

Anna kissed his hand and he blushed, nodded and left.

They went to urinate in turn, keeping watch for each other
at the barn window, but it was soon clear that the men were
no threat, even seemed to be avoiding the area around the
barn to give them some privacy. Then they slept for most of
the morning, woke to eat bread dipped in dripping and some
puckered plums that were left for them at the door. Karolina
caught her mother's eye as Anna licked fat from her fingers,
and was astonished when her Mama smiled, carried on. The
barn became sticky as the day heated, and the smell rose from
of their dresses and skin, doused in fear.

'Sunset, the driver said,' Janina murmured, her voice almost lost to the rafters as she lay on her back in the hay.

'Yes,' Anna replied.

'But is it safer here? Maybe we should wait, we don't know what's out in the fields.'

'Nothing, just the farmers,' Anna said. 'Adam knows we were heading for Lwów, so we must get there, to meet him.'

'What if Papa is stuck back in Kraków? Maybe we should go home,' Karolina said. 'And Jozef —'

'No one asked for your opinion, child,' Janina said, and felt an instant shudder. She mustn't make Anna angry, mustn't be cast out. 'I'm sorry, dear,' she said, sitting up and studying Karolina, who looked unruffled. 'It's only that—'

'Yes, of course, we can't go back,' said Karolina. 'I know.'

'What about all our things and my painting?'

It was Anna's turn to flare up. 'Your Papa is missing and Robert and Janie and Jozef, Stefan, everyone we know is back there but it's Jozef's painting you miss?'

Alicia bit her cheek. She had never been able to explain what it meant to her, the image Jozef had made, that they had made together.

'Mama, if we get it, I mean if we hadn't lost it, they'd know we are important people, we are rich. They'd see. Now we just look like peasants and they can kill us.'

'*Kill* us? Are we soldiers? They don't kill girls and women.' Anna's shock at her daughter's calm heavy words made her voice rise.

'Then why don't we go back and look for it? And for Papa, and Jozef, I mean, of course,' Alicia said, half to her sister, whose face was closing in a way that meant she was becoming angry.

'My God, you were sent to try my patience!' Anna found

her mother's sayings came too easily at times. 'Because as I have just explained, your father is to meet us in Lwów.'

'But—'

'Stop it, Alicia,' Karolina said.

'But he is with those Germans. He won't be able to—'

Anna got up and began to walk in circles, kicking up hay-dust. 'He will explain – have you forgotten that your Papa is a businessman? They wanted the car, he'll give it to them, probably make a deal of some kind. Then he'll make his way to Lwów—'

'Do you think he got the painting from the ground? Maybe he used it to make a deal,' Janina said, trying to soothe Alicia and her own nerves at having offended them all.

'Yes,' Alicia almost whispered. 'Perhaps he'll bring it to Lwów.'

This seemed to bring an end to the discussion. Anna went to the small window, looked out. For a few minutes, the only sound was the soughing of the men bringing in the harvest, and the thuds as they dropped it outside the barn.

'How can they keep working when we are under attack?' murmured Janina to herself, for something to say. In truth it made her inexpressibly glad, calmer, not only that these men surrounded them, but that they were working as though nothing had happened.

When the thumping stopped, an hour or so later, one of the men came back with a jug of milk. He placed it on the ground and scuttled out again. 'Like we are wild animals,' Janina sniffed, but she gulped the milk straight from the jug along with the others, cream coating her mouth.

The afternoon settled into an unreal calm.

'I wish we had a radio,' Anna and Janina kept echoing to each other. 'If only we had a radio, the radio will be telling people what to do and where to go, and what is happening at home. Do they have one at the farmhouse, do you think? I think we should go and ask them. Why don't you go and see if they have a radio?' These phrases they cycled around and around in between gulps of milk and watching the sky, looking for the signs of sunset, neither making any move towards the house in search of a radio. Finally, Alicia, from a spot she'd taken up by the window, said, 'The light is changing.'

'You and light, my God,' Anna muttered. 'Is the sun setting?'

'It's beginning to.' This was painting time. Every line edged with the softest light.

They all looked at one another. None of them wanted to leave the warm, dry barn with its veneer of safety, its quiet. Anna and Janina both toyed with similar words in their mouths. *Perhaps we should, maybe it's safer to?* But when neither of them spoke, Karolina and Alicia finishing the last of the milk, they began to layer up again in their double coats and re-lace their shoes, and left the barn.

The sky was full of nothing but birds swarming like bees, flying from tree to tree, practising for their long flight. The day had cooled. Anna inwardly cursed again for not thinking to wear her beautiful watch, still sitting on her dresser. It was worth something, but it was also disorienting not to know how many hours it had been since they left the house that morning, which already felt an impossible age ago, saying goodbye to the servants and packing up the cars, arguing over the curtains. Except it wasn't that morning, but the day before, that they had left. All those hours Adam had been alone. Her apartment empty. The Germans swarming in the streets she knew like flies, smashing windows, beating people in the street, killing them, if the newspapers were to be believed.

They were halfway across the field, its expansive flatness feeling too big and open, before they realised they hadn't thanked the farmers.

'It doesn't matter,' Anna said when Alicia complained. 'We can't miss the horse and cart, and I'm sure they know we're grateful.'

'How can you be so rude, Mama? They even gave us milk, that was probably for their coffee, and they didn't have to help us, we could have been sleeping in the field all this time.'

'For God's sake! Do you think thanking people is important today?'

'You always said that manners—'

'Alicia, stop,' Karolina warned.

Alicia didn't care about thanking the farmers, but she knew that pushing her mother, bickering about something as at home, a point of etiquette, soothed for a moment her racing mind. 'I think we should go back and—'

Her mother stopped, and shook her hard by the shoulders. 'No,' Anna said. 'You don't. You're just afraid. We keep going.' They eyed each other. Alicia was still short and slight, not much grown since the days Jozef had painted her, but her face was sharper, growing more like Anna's. She nodded.

It was a fruitless argument in the end. The man with the horse and cart was long gone, back along the road to Kraków to pick up more fleeing people with their coins and jewellery, their heirlooms of medals from the last war. They waited until the sun was past set, and no trace of light marked the sky, watching the odd gaggle left from the flood of people out of Kraków, all on foot, scanning for any faces they knew, before stumbling back through the fields in the dark towards the farm.

19

ALICIA QUICKLY CAME to love the sweet hay smell of the barn. For years afterwards she'd enjoy buildings like this: sun-filled, warm wood, beams, piles of hay stacked around the walls. It was a time of strange peace, before Lwów, and while she was still healthy enough to not notice her body any more than usual.

Janina made them all beds from the old hay, even covered patties of it with some of the layers she and Karolina had worn, to make pillows. Alicia liked to take handfuls of it and hold it next to her nose as she rested (they were always tired, in the barn, though none of them could explain why, when they did nothing, walked nowhere, except outside to urinate). It masked the rising smell of her stale clothes. After a while, it distracted her from the nagging discomfort in her abdomen. The farmhands mostly left them alone, except to bring food and sometimes news. It turned out they didn't have a radio, but the farm across the fields did; when they went to collect their orders of eggs and milk they would also get a bulletin.

'It's true about Kraków,' was the first of these, from Peter. ('God's sake, did he think we were running away for fun?' Janina said, after he'd left.)

'What does it say to do? Where does it tell the refugees to go?' Anna asked.

He shrugged. 'Not many left of these,' he said, handing out apples. 'Don't worry,' he added, prompted by the look of panic that had fleeted across Janina's and Anna's faces. 'No advice on the radio. It just reports lots of people heading east, out of Poland altogether.'

'So we shouldn't go back to the city, for certain?' Anna said.

'Did they bomb the whole city?' Janina asked, thinking of her house, how little she had packed, just a photograph of Aleks, in his new soldier's uniform, and her identity papers, snatched from the dresser when she finally succumbed to her fear; she had left everything else.

'The radio says it was bloodless.' He shrugged. 'They just surrendered.' He shook his head, tutted a little. 'You should go east, with the others. The radio and newspapers say that Lwów will be occupied by the Soviets soon. It will be better for you.'

But the prospect of the road, walking all the way to Lwów, was impossible. Better to wait it out here, where it felt quiet and safe. Adam would be in Lwów by now, Anna told them all, and they just needed to wait for things to calm down a little, and then join him.

They stayed and stayed, even as the farm went more and more quiet, until only Peter visited them. After a week, he came with hard-boiled eggs wrapped in a towel.

'It's getting colder,' he said. 'Do you need more blankets?'

'Why can't we just sleep at the farmhouse?' Anna said. 'All of your friends are gone, aren't they? There must be lots of spare beds.'

'You can't stay there.'

'But—'

'They're here, in the village. They're visiting all of the farms.'

They all fell silent. Karolina began peeling the eggs. Peter crouched down, picked up some of the hay from a bale, rubbed it between his fingers. 'I have to take this out to sell,' he said.

'Oh,' Anna said, after a while. 'Can we stay here, still, in the barn?'

'I think you should go east, I said before. Lots of people are going to Lwów. Safer there.'

'We should walk over to the next farm, what do you think? They might have a cart,' Janina said.

'So, have all your friends gone? It's gone so quiet,' Alicia added, pulling her legs beneath her.

'Yes,' he said.

'Well, what will you do?' she said.

'The next farm, that's a good idea, isn't it? What do you think?' Janina pressed.

'I'm sorry, they wouldn't help you.'

'But why not?' Alicia said, as the others sighed and sat back.

'They just wouldn't,' Peter said, flushing a little. 'They don't like Jews.'

'We're not Jewish,' Anna said, too quickly, with too much a pitch of fear, and he only looked at her in response, without any sneer or satisfaction.

'I think you are.'

'On what grounds?' Janina said, reaching for the language of the law, or Laurie's way of speaking, to steady herself.

Peter only looked at them. The barn seemed to shrink to Anna then. She liked Peter, his steady way of speaking, his country accent. He was between them and the door.

'Please,' she said, as he stood.

'I'll take you myself,' he said, seeming to just think of it.

'You have a car?' Anna almost gasped.

He laughed, and it was the strangest sound in the world to her just then. 'No, of course not. We borrow horses when we take the harvest in, and I can get a cart.'

Peter remained silent as the cart approached the outskirts of Lwów. He'd been taciturn on the journey, and stared straight ahead as the crowds thickened, choking the narrow roads. He'd spoken only to calm Janina, who yelped as the crowds grew, hissing at him not to stop.

'We'll be overturned and the cart stolen,' she said.

'I don't think so,' he'd returned mildly. The people on the road, those not lucky enough to be on horseback or similar carts from the farmland close by, were moving in the weaving lumber of the deeply exhausted, their faces turned to the ground, watching their own feet.

Now, after hours on the road, Anna felt only guilty relief at the crowds. So they weren't the last, weren't alone. They were headed the same way as everyone else. She'd been imagining closed gates, walls, a huge wooden door, as on a castle, just closing, as a Soviet official shook his head, *too late*. There were few cars, and Anna wondered if they'd been stolen, imagined thousands of Adams left in the dirt, the Germans cavorting around the cities in their new cars like children with new toys. Her daughters were asleep, Alicia's head on Karolina's shoulder. Karolina's hair was down, and blowing over her sister's face in the blessedly mild wind. Alicia kept scrunching her nose in her sleep and pawing at her cheek where Karolina's hair tickled it. The skin of her face could be wax in the afternoon light. Anna eyed the horse, willed it on: *Don't stop, don't get tired, for God's sake please don't leave us stranded with the rest.*

'How much further?' Anna called to Peter.

'Yes, God, why do you go so slowly?' Janina cried. Anna pressed her foot onto Janina's: *Shut up*.

Peter's steady, calm face furrowed a little as he twisted, his hands pulling at the reins as he did so. *No, no, that will tell the animal to stop*, Anna thought. Peter looked puzzled.

'We're here,' he said, gently. 'Lwów is a few miles' walk.'

'We're here, girls,' Janina said to them warmly, taking Karolina's hands and rubbing them. She felt stupid. No gates, none of the high walls she'd been picturing, like a fairy-tale city. Just the road stretching forwards, some low, flimsy-looking buildings, and the crowds from Kraków and everywhere else. How could this keep them safe?

Peter pulled up the reins. He rubbed his hands together and blew into them, then took a sharp breath in. He blew out his words on the outbreath, 'Good luck. I'll have to go back now.'

'Take us a bit further,' Janina said, her body vibrating with fear. 'Or wait in case you have to take us back, what if there's a problem?' Her voice sounded loud in the subdued crowds, carrying over the sounds of trundle and trudge.

Peter gave a helpless shrug. 'Even if . . . I can't take you back. I told you, they'd find you. I have to' – he bowed his head, ducked as though Janina would strike him – 'I have to, you know, take care of myself, too.' He twisted around, took in Anna and her daughters, their closed faces. 'Good luck,' he said again, and gestured for them to get down. 'Take some bread,' he added, uncovering a loaf and flapping out the cloth like a housewife. 'I baked it yesterday, still fresh,' he smiled. Anna could have kissed him, but Janina made a tiny sound of panic as Anna took the loaf, beginning to move off the cart.

'Who knows when we'll eat again?' she worried, jostling at Alicia's arm, who shook her off and jumped down herself. She landed awkwardly and her face twisted in pain for a moment, but then shook off her sister's hand on her shoulder as well.

Anna spoke to Janina. 'In a few hours, I imagine, let's not be hysterical.' The older woman fell silent. They were all on the ground now, looking up at Peter. Anna wanted to cling to him, beg him to stay. She breathed and swallowed, took Alicia's cold hand in hers. 'Thank you, Peter. If you write to us in Kraków, when all of this is over, my husband will thank you properly.' She gave the name of Adam's business and its address, feeling the familiar pride swell in her at the respectable district, hoped it offset her dirty dress and wild hair and the sour smell of them all. Peter looked at her blankly, then gave a tight smile and a nod. He steered the horse back and the cart crawled away. The women watched as he made slow progress away from them, stopping to speak to people as he went, as they tugged at the pony's bridle or called up to him, opening his arms, the gesture of *I don't know.*

The line was mostly polite and quiet, nothing like the panicked crowd that had left the city. It snaked in a thick coil back to the road, and people shuffled, shared food and stories. They were all similar: farmhouses, abandoned houses, the kind generosity of families. Some had slept in hedgerows. The Oderfeldts and Janina only listened and ate their sweet-smelling bread. Anna felt she swallowed Peter's kindness, warm in her belly. The girls had eaten theirs quickly, and now seemed ready to sleep again, Karolina swaying on her feet, gently pulling on Alicia, her hands on her shoulders. They followed the shambling crowd.

Lwów, 1939–1940

20

HER UNCLE'S HOUSE in Lwów was smaller than Alicia had imagined, and smelled of damp.

'Isaac and your Aunt Margo are in bed,' the servant said, ushering them inside. They were stiff with cold, exhaustion and the remnants of shock that had lodged in them like shrapnel. The servant had small, kind eyes in a moon-shaped face, a short beard, and a belly that seemed hard and perfectly spherical, a ball for the beach kept under his shirt. Though he seemed to be dressed for the office rather than woken in the middle of the night, he carried sleep with him in the crumpled state of his thick dark hair and deep creases around his eyes, their purple, bruise-like shadows. His ample cheeks seemed to sag, and he shrank against the wall as they came in, nodding apologies as they were forced to brush against his stomach. As they staggered in, their feet burning, he looked behind them, then stood for a while at the door, looking out into the street, where a trickle of refugees was still coming into the city, more sacks and carts and suitcases, more exhausted and stooping backs. He stood watching for a while before the door clicked shut.

In the main room men sat around a fire with newspapers stacked up on a table. The room hummed with their worry. They got up as the women came in, unhurried but polite. Karolina and Janina propped Anna up between them, though their ankles and backs were also screaming. Alicia hung back, her mind tugged to the spot by the road, miles away, where all their life lay scattered in the mud, her own face left there for anyone to take; the red, softer than blood, bright among all the drab earthy colours of dirt and rags.

'Please, tell my husband we've arrived,' Anna said.

The collective shift of heads downwards, hands clasped, told them all he wasn't there.

'But it's been weeks,' Anna whispered. 'It's been weeks,' she repeated, louder; she might be complaining about slow service in a restaurant.

'Is it right the Soviets have put up a border?' one of the men asked. 'The newspaper says it's a rumour, but the radio and people coming in are saying it's true.'

'Did you see German troops out there?' someone else asked.

It's all right, Alicia thought. *Somewhere Papa is walking, or getting into another car, or riding a horse.*

'You haven't heard from,' Anna began, then faltered, picked up the stranger's question instead. 'I don't think so, no . . .'

'Maybe there are border checks we missed,' Janina said.

'Come, come,' the man who had opened the door called from the kitchen. 'Please, sit, get warm. Coffee, I think, and we have soup.'

'But it's been weeks,' Anna said again to Janina, as they sank into low armchairs. Janina only nodded, holding her claw-like hands up to the fire, unfurling her fingers one by one. Karolina had already fallen into a chair, her skirt drawn up around her so her legs showed to the thigh. The men who had stood up for them began to file out, shaking hands with the servant as they went, sometimes gripping his shoulders and planting kisses on his cheeks.

Alicia's mouth was dry. Her bladder's dull ache, her companion for so many hours on the road, became again a throb.

'Soup, please,' she said to the servant. 'And,' she added, glancing at her mother in inspiration, 'tell my uncle we are here.'

The man laughed sadly. 'Ah! Little Ala doesn't recognise me.' He began to dance slowly, comical with his large belly. 'You remember? Ignacy's wedding? But you were very little.' She shook her head.

'Your Papa and I danced all night!' He was whispering now, as Janina began to softly snore, though Anna's eyes remained open, staring into the flames.

Her Uncle Schmuel's face fell, as though pulled out of this memory. 'So, your Papa, he's still in Kraków?'

Anna spoke in a soft monotone. 'Sammy, it was so awful,' she said, and she burst into tears.

His cheeks seemed to fall further, his long girlish eyelashes fluttered.

'Perhaps I should get Margo up. We've been waiting up every night, since . . . I'll wake her?'

'No, Uncle Schmuel,' called Karolina in a low voice, turning, her face rosy in the fire glow. 'We should all rest as we can.' He blinked at her calm assurance; she looked so young in her simple dress and messy hair. On impulse, Sammy went to check the front door again, ran his fingers along the rusty, fragile bolts.

'Have someone make us some soup, can't you?' Alicia called, and was surprised when her uncle gave a gentle laugh as he returned to the room.

'Well, I'll fetch it myself,' Sammy said.

She trailed after him, resisting the fire with the heaviness of the three women there, who she knew would pull her to them, cry against her coat, kiss her fingers. After the long hours of the journey, she craved air around her, to be untouched, let the air touch her skin, in spite of the cold. The thought of any weight pressing on her swelling pain was unbearable.

The kitchen was also tiny, a shrunken, dirty version of the basement room at home, which Alicia only visited to retrieve the dogs now to play, and as a younger child had used for dares – touch Dorothea's bread yeast, steal a sugar mouse from the pantry. This room was gloomy, with newspapers pasted over the dusty windows and a stickiness to the floor. Alicia's senses snagged on the pot on the stove, with its simple, potato smell. She no longer felt the hunger in her stomach. It was in her limbs' ache and the tremble of her hands as she watched, vaguely aware of the strange wrongness of it, her uncle taking a ladle and spooning out a bowl.

'We've made extra for you since the invasion,' Sammy continued. 'Adam sent a telegram, and somehow, God's will, it got through. We've been waiting. Not that we would have ever turned you away. My friends had a lot; we eat a lot when times are bad, may as well feel some comfort in the bones.'

Alicia was hardly listening. She drank the soup right from the bowl, dripping some onto her coat. She didn't care what her poor uncle in his tiny house would think of her. He wiped her chin for her with a dirty cloth.

'Poor Ala,' he said. 'Here, take more for your Mama and sister and friend.'

Something from the drips of her uncle's words squeezed through.

'Papa telegrammed?'

'Yes, to my office.'

'When? After we left? So he went back to Kraków?'

He scraped a finger around the edge of the pan of soup, licked a yellowed paw as Alicia watched in fascinated impatience.

'No,' he said. 'Well, I don't know,' he added as she slumped. 'He sent me many telegrams, as he was preparing to leave, to get everything ready. I mean the last one was the morning you left, it was sent, but I didn't get it until – everything has been chaotic, you know, here, there has been nothing but rumours and soldiers and is it the Germans or the Soviets—' He stopped himself, scraped out soup from under a fingernail. 'You should sleep, rest with the others. We can all talk in the morning.' Alicia felt a slow well of homesickness build as this not-quite Papa spoke to her, the same restless hands and brown eyes, but squat and plump as though Papa had been swollen and flattened.

They slept in chairs by the fire that night, in the small front room, without even taking off their coats. The empty soup bowls, licked clean, lay at their feet, as though they were in a dog kennel, but if anyone cared it wasn't spoken. Floorboards creaked above them as weight shifted around the house, and shouts and the rattle of movement outside was constant until morning. Through the night Alicia heard knocking at the door, saw figures and shadows at the windows, and sat in an agony of indecision while the others slept, wondering if it was her Papa come to his brother's house, and shouldn't she let him in? Once the knocking was so loud it woke Karolina too, who took Alicia's hand into hers.

'Sleep,' she whispered. 'You must sleep.'

'But it could be Papa,' Alicia whispered back.

Karolina slowly shook her head. 'It isn't.'

'If we had my painting—'

'Forget the painting, it's just a thing.' Karolina spoke in a rush, as she always did when anything touching Jozef was mentioned, unfocusing her eyes as she spoke.

'You know that isn't true.' Alicia groped for the right words, how to explain. 'It's those days with us somehow. Those days making the painting. You and me and Jozef—'

'It's *just a thing*. Jozef is a person with breath, and sight, and a beating heart, and warm skin, flesh and blood, not colours on a piece of canvas.' Karolina spoke mildly, but her hands gripped, and Alicia felt heat rising through her sister's skin.

'I only mean, I mean that – I don't mean it's him, I mean it's—' Alicia wrenched her hand back, dug at a nailbed in frustration. 'I mean, if we had it—'

'Where do you think he is?' Karolina cut across her.

'He'll come.'

'Jozef, not Papa.'

Alicia reached for her sister again. 'That's who I meant,' she lied.

Hearing the lie and the fear in it, Karolina dropped her voice to a lulling whisper.

'Close your eyes. Where shall we go? Out to sea? A forest . . . it's late summer, and the light is golden through the branches—'

'Let's go home.'

So they whispered a route through their house in Kraków, describing everything they could see and touch, from the floorboards under their feet to the weight of the doors, to the sunlight, fractured by the Wawel, pouring through the windows, and the soothing sounds of the trams. Alicia had just reached the top of the staircase, heading for her room, when she fell asleep. Karolina felt her sister's heaviness, noted her silence, and peeled her imaginary self from Alicia's side. She slipped out of the house, flew across the river, landed silently on the rooftops of Jozef's building. She glanced back at the family apartment as it glinted from across the water and crossed gratefully into a dream.

21

THE MORNING CAME cold and damp, so that despite the sharp scent of Janina's skin, its sweat and old-woman mustiness, Alicia was grateful for her arm around her, and buried herself deeper under the old neighbour's coat. Janina gave a deep snort and Alicia caught the sour edge of her breath, curdled by the slightly rotten teeth of a woman who lived on cakes, pastries and treacly coffee. There were sounds from the kitchen: the careful opening and moving of things, her mother and sister attempting to navigate in silence, in a strange place, without servants. The floorboards continued to creak and sag, shadows now visible through the slats. Perhaps her uncle had paced all night.

More knocking at the front door, and both the kitchen and upstairs stopped, sound and movement suspended for long seconds before starting up again. Then another knock, not of a tentative stranger but insistent, one who belonged.

Alicia sprang up to get her Papa in from the cold, making Janina gasp as she threw off the coat that she'd spread over them, like plunging into icy water. Anna and Karolina came from the kitchen, and footsteps came heavy on the stairs.

'Sammy! Sammy!' it was a woman's voice, harsh like a cough. The name creaked in her mouth like a rusty see-saw. The wrong voice, but they all crowded into the tiny hallway anyway, Anna struggling with the old latch on the door.

Behind them the footsteps had stopped, and a deep, creaking elephant sound indicated that Sammy had sat down on a step.

'It's Margo,' he said.

'Sam-*my*! I will—'

Anna flung the door open, and there was the Papa-less sight of a short, strong woman on the step, dark hair pulled into a rough ponytail like a servant's, holding a basket. Anna and Margo eyed each other.

'I suppose it is too much to ask to be allowed into *my own house*?' the woman's voice escalated from icy whisper to shriek, pitched behind them and towards Sammy.

Stunned, the women stepped aside. Margo tutted her way towards her husband, who gave her a weak, confused smile.

'What are you doing?' he asked. 'When did you leave? I told you not to go to the market today.'

'And so you locked me out. What a husband! What a lucky woman I am! What a gentleman!' she spat. He nodded slowly along, opened his hands.

'We can't leave the door open in times like this—'

'Don't tell me about doors and strangers and the safety of my house! Making your wife go out in the streets to look for food! Well, lucky you to have me to find some bread, the last in Lwów, I'm sure.'

'But how much did it cost? You said you would make bread yourself. We have some soup to keep us going—'

'Oh! There's my thanks!'

Margo wheeled around to face the invaders, who moved together a little for protection.

'Thank you very much, Margo,' Anna said. 'Can I help you prepare a lunch?'

'You see,' Margo said in a low voice to her husband. 'Manners, Sammy, better from strangers than from my own kin.'

'We're not strangers,' said Anna, with a small, tinkling laugh that told Janina and her daughters her disgust, but that Margo greeted with a face of pure confusion. 'We're Adam's wife and daughters—'

'I know who you are, my God, am I an idiot now?'

'Then we are family,' Anna said, 'and we must stay, at least until my husband, your brother-in-law, arrives.'

'Oh! Now I am the wicked woman who throws destitute refugees out onto the streets! I didn't buy you bread, I didn't have a fire ready for you all these nights, I didn't make you soup! How you will be safe in such a place of evil I don't know! Worse than German-occupied Kraków, I'm sure!'

Margo threw the bread at her husband for him to catch, and squeezed her way past him, stomping up every step and calling for her son. As she clopped up the stairs she called back, 'The Soviets are here.'

'Ah,' Sammy said, nodding, his brow furrowed, as though thinking through an interesting problem. The visitors stared at him.

Sammy opened his mouth, taking in breaths to speak, but then only breathed out, seeming to choose and then discard many replies. He looked around at them all, then spoke to Anna.

'They've been saying either the Soviets or the Germans will come, for weeks. The Germans were camped out in the suburbs.' He moved to the small cheap radio that sat on the mantelpiece as Janina sagged against the wall. He added, almost cheerfully, 'Better the Soviets, they say.' The radio blurred between voices, before settling on a calm, emotionless man's voice, speaking in Polish, announcing the end of the Battle of Lwów. The Soviets now occupied the city. Sammy nodded, a little pale.

'There you are.' He turned to them, offered a smile. 'At least we know where we are.'

'In Russia now?' Anna snapped, but he didn't catch her tone, and gave her a tired laugh. He peeled one of the papers from the table, right where they had slept in exhausted ignorance. 'See?' he added, gently. He passed one to Anna, who glanced at the screaming letters, *War*. She responded with irritation.

'Yes, yes, this is all we've been hearing for months: war, war, war . . .' There was something hideous in the endless expectation, a hunger for it, obsessing over the newspapers and the newsreels, ruining a day at the cinema with chanting and ugliness.

'But it's real now,' Sammy said. Anna heard the faintest tinge of the excitement that so disgusted her. She turned away, to find her daughters watching her: Alicia with her narrowed, inscrutable eyes, Karolina with the far-seeing stare that told she was elsewhere in her mind, wherever Jozef might be, caught up in this war that had been coming, coming and now dropped on them all like a hunting net. Anna went to sit down again, ignoring the offered newspaper and its smug hysteria.

'But it's safe here?' Janina said.

'Well, certainly safer than Kraków,' came the reassuring, calm reply, so like her husband's voice, that Janina felt anchored where she stood, could have kissed Sammy's face.

'All right.' Anna smoothed her skirt. 'Is there some kind of centre, we should register, I don't know? A place for the refugees?'

'Anna, you aren't refugees! You are—'

'Just visiting until things calm down, yes,' she said, while at the edge of her sight Janina was nodding, rejecting the word *refugee*.

Sammy seemed about to say something else, but a gasp from Karolina stopped him. She had picked up another newspaper, begun turning the pages. It was from a week after they'd left the city. There was a photograph of the Wawel castle, taken from the other side of the river, so that to Karolina it seemed backwards. She searched the edges of it for the apartment, but it was blurred, and this distracted her from the image while her uncle had been talking, but then she looked properly, and the air burst into her lungs. She held it up for her mother to see. The shine of the sun on a black Cadillac, the sea of grainy flags, that they all coloured, in their minds' eyes, in red. The sleek car was pulling right into the courtyard of the Wawel. Anna came closer, stared hard at the page.

'No,' she said, firmly, in answer to Karolina's unvoiced question: *Isn't that our car?*

'It is, it is,' Karolina said, flipping the page around with a rustle to look again.

'Well we can't see the plates to be certain,' her mother argued.

'If this' – Karolina scanned the page – 'this new "King of Kraków"—'

'*King of Kraków?*' Janina and Anna parroted back, their voices matched in eager outrage. 'These people,' Janina muttered, and Anna joined her, 'Have you ever heard anything so *ridiculous*—'

'—So vulgar!'

'I suppose his wife will call herself *Queen of Kraków*, my God!' Anna cried.

Janina hurried to Anna's side. 'What will the silly bitch do, parade around Glowny with a crown?' she asked.

This was better, this was safer, the old ways of bitching

and gossiping in scandalised delight; Anna found herself casting around for the others: Marta Hartmann, Hannah Friel, even Janie and Dorothea, even Stefan, who loved a gossip and delighted in the ridiculous, but glancing around the cold little room she found only Janina, and her daughters and brother-in-law, watching her.

'Mama, if Papa has given his car to this, king—'

'I'm sure this pretender-king has his own car, Karolcia,' Anna said.

'Hans Frank,' Sammy said. 'And, he isn't really calling himself that, but the papers – it's Governor, I think.'

This earned a sniff and a haughty, 'Nonsense,' from Janina, but Anna had been pulled into the newspaper, where Alicia and Karolina were already absorbed. Karolina kept turning the pages; photograph after photograph of their world was there. There was a photograph of the Glowny, seeming unchanged, but full of the same foreign soldiers and the same flags, as though they had simply dressed their city in a silly costume.

'They say they'll rename it *Adolf Hitler Platz*,' said Sammy, softly.

'He's like a schoolboy writing his name all over everything,' Janina said, making the others laugh, except Alicia, who was stone-faced. In truth, though she knew it was the fashionable thing, Janina didn't hate Hitler in the way she ought to. He didn't seem a real person at all, but a figure in a fairy tale, made of smoke and a disembodied, tantrumming voice. She felt it wasn't Hitler who had dislodged her from her apartment at all, stolen her son and her life. It was her own fault: stumbling, afraid and slow, she should have read more, listened more, to the radio and to her own heart's terror, which knew months, years before, and prodded her and prodded her until she was walking out into the streets on the day of the invasion, towards the Oderfeldts and their steadier, richer lives, in the hope they might save her.

Karolina turned a page: there was the Wawel and its mock coronation ceremony. Another page: lines of Polish soldiers, their heads bowed. There were images of the strange world of the journey, too, already seeming like another life, carts and streams of people, carrying everything they could piled on their backs and in bulging coats. Anna felt a jolt, as when she caught her own tired, un-made face in a mirror, on waking. Had she too looked like that, like a broken, small, frightened victim in a newspaper photograph, to be tutted at over breakfast across Europe?

22

THE KRAKÓW REFUGEES had imagined Isaac as a young boy, a precious child to be kept safe. Anna had sent cards and presents when he was born, then every year, prompted by the calendar on the desk in the study, filled in every new year with her best pen, her mother's habit. She'd seen an old photograph of him from a visit Adam had made to Lwów on business: a skinny, happy child, with a ball under his arm. She was surprised by the sullen young man who came down the stairs, stretching to touch the beams of the ceiling in the little room.

He was all Margo, thin and sharp all over. His eyes were quick too, darting and taking in the four newcomers, and giving staccato polite nods to each as a kind of welcome. It seemed there was none of Sammy's bumbling bear-like gentleness about him.

'Your mother bought bread. Are you hungry?' Sammy asked.

'Give it to my aunt and cousins,' came the reply, and his voice was like his father's, low and lilting. He spoke such a gentle expression of kind, good manners that all four from Kraków felt a leap of warmth for him. Janina and Anna gave the boy approving smiles, but both waved away the offer of bread.

'Is she coming down?' Sammy called after Isaac as he went to the kitchen. In answer the boy came in with a plate of newly sliced bread, brow furrowed and shaking his head.

'She's very proud,' Sammy said to Anna, by way of apology, as he buttoned his coat. Seeing he was about to leave for the office, Anna stood, smiling a refusal as Isaac offered her a slice.

'I'll come with you.'

Sammy seemed stricken by this idea, first gabbling about safety and *let's see how the land lies*, which Anna prepared to ignore, rising to button her coat, but then she caught Sammy glancing over her unmade hair and dirty dress, her torn stockings, and flushing. Anna realised she would embarrass him. She sat down, smoothed her skirt.

'When you make the calls, telephone to Bernardyńska, you have the number?' Anna asked. 'Robert might be there, he might have gone back to check on the apartment, so he can take a message for you, or he might already know where Adam is.'

'Yes, yes, so the factory, the—'

'The factory, the office, the apartment building, and Stefan's office at the Jagiellonian,' Anna said, counting off on her fingers. 'And the message is—'

'Anna, I know, I will tell him his family are here with us and safe—'

'And that he must come to us,' Alicia added.

'Yes, Ala.'

The rest of the day was spent in more suspended strangeness; the same bubble of held breath Alicia felt they had lived in since they left home. The streets too had quietened, as though the city held its breath with them. Margo stayed upstairs, her sulk seeping through the floorboards, making the visitors tense, but her son seemed at ease, if a little shy. He sat with the visitors, his legs sprawled over a chair like a sunbathing cat, brewed endless carafes of weak tea. Alicia drank tepid water that tasted different from home, chalky and sweet.

Isaac gently asked about Kraków, the journey, Adam.

'Why did you decide to leave, Aunt Anna? Lots have stayed. Lots of Mother's friends.'

'It was your uncle's decision. It was a matter of safety for the children.'

'Did you see any bombs or dead bodies?' He asked this with such artless simplicity that Anna felt she couldn't reprimand him for ghoulishness.

'No.'

'No, I think there aren't any bombs there. There are lots everywhere else.'

'Here?'

'No, but lots of fighting just outside the city. Did you see any arrests and beatings and murders?'

Janina and Anna gave each other a helpless look. 'We thought it would be safer here,' Janina said.

'It is safer. The Soviets will protect the population. We don't want the Germans here.' Isaac saw his aunt's face had a small smile of surprise. 'Father says,' he added, with a small embarrassed shrug. 'Did they arrest people there? Father says—'

'Yes, I am sure there have been arrests, but we left just before the Germans came into the city,' Janina said. 'Of course, Adam . . .' She trailed off as the Oderfeldts stiffened.

Soon visitors began to arrive, neighbours, full of news: *And so Kraków is in Germany now . . . They say that Russia and Germany will take over the world between them now and carve it up like a pie . . . They are putting up notices in the Kraków streets . . . The shuls there are closed and the markets . . . And here? We're all Russian now. Is it better? Hitler won't last, but Stalin*

might. Are you going into work? No, no, not yet. Let's see how the
land lies.

The visitors offered kind smiles and shaking heads in sympathy, muttering, *terrible, terrible.* They brought blankets and clothes from their wives and daughters, extra food. Isaac offered them coffee, explained his mother was unwell upstairs.

Anna longed for women, to discuss things properly.

'Where do you live?' she asked a respectable-looking man, his beard well trimmed and smelling of good cologne. He smiled at her with kind grey eyes.

'We're just two doors down.'

'Oh.' This was a poorer neighbourhood; she had hoped for better. She held out her hand. 'Anna Oderfeldt.'

'Theo Skliar,' he said, taking it gently. She was conscious of the state of her nails, the un-moisturised skin. 'You're the sister-in-law then?'

She nodded. 'What do you do?' she asked, and they both laughed a little, and she grimaced at the stupidity of making small talk as though at a dinner party.

'I'm a doctor. I was researching childhood diseases. Measles mostly.'

'Your research will stop?'

'I honestly don't know. Now that the siege is over, and the Soviets are here, we will have to reapply for funding perhaps.'

'Will your wife visit? What's her name? Sorry,' she continued, blushing as he blinked at her, 'I was just hoping—'

'She's been very active, she's very busy organising help for the refugees, donations, that kind of thing, through her work at the university and so on.'

'I can help, we'd love to help,' Anna said. To be one of those busy, capable women, to make lists and pack boxes, to be occupied . . .

'What would you like? Sophia keeps sending me with these blankets, that's what everyone seems to be sending, but it's rather warm in here by the fire anyway. She thought books – you must be bored? Some games for the youngest? Cards? It's hard to know what refugees need, you see.'

'But where is Mrs Skliar—'

'Sophia, please—'

'Where is Sophia active with the donations and so on? Is there somewhere we should go?'

Janina, sitting in perplexed boredom trying to follow a conversation about the Battle of Lwów on the other side of Anna, turned her head. 'Anna really, you must correct people when they call us that. We aren't refugees, really,' Janina directed this over Anna's lap to Theo. 'I have a beautiful apartment in Kraków,' she added, 'and I have plenty of money, I should be able to access my account here, I have my identification papers – and you too, Anna.' She turned to Theo again, 'We aren't homeless, you know, just as soon as everything is calmer we'll go home again.'

'My apologies,' Theo smiled at them both, rising.

'Please have Sophia visit,' Anna called after him. 'I'm sure Margo won't mind. Or we'll come to her, please have her leave a card . . .'

From her spot curled up in a chair by the window, taking peeks through the curtains, which Sammy insisted stay drawn, just in case, Alicia watched her mother flicking dirt from her skirt, patting her hair, noticing the stains and holes on her stockings and crossing her ankles to try to hide them.

As the afternoon died, the visitors left and Margo came to stand in the doorway of the main room with her hands on her hips. She let out a sharp breath from her nose, like an angry horse, Alicia thought, and began drumming her fingernails on the doorframe.

'Are you going to stick to my furniture like honey all day?' she said.

Anna glared at her, then softened her face. 'Can we help?' She and Janina slowly sat up straighter. Isaac turned a page of his book. His mother tutted and cast her head back, rolling her eyes as though appealing to God himself, muttered something under her breath.

'I'm talking to my son,' she said.

'You said I wasn't to go to school—' Isaac started to protest.

'Anna,' Margo said, her voice blade-sharp. Alicia's heart gave a rare lurch as her mother turned, and she caught her face, bleak with misery. Margo paused as she looked at her too, and seemed to forget what she was going to say. When she spoke, her voice was softer, more hesitant. 'Would – would you and the girls like to wash?' she asked. 'Clean clothes, Isaac, why didn't you offer before?'

'Father said they should rest.'

'My God, poor things, sitting in your own filth! Anna? You'll go first,' Margo said, taking her by the elbow and drawing her gently to her feet. She placed her hands either side of Anna's face, and Anna let her. 'Come on,' she said, almost a whisper. She stroked Anna's hair and kissed her forehead, radiating kindness until she'd cracked Anna open like a nut. Alicia turned away as her mother crumpled into Margo's birdlike arms and sobbed, not in the pretty way she had cried on the road, not gentle streams of tears, but in a guttural wail, from the belly. Alicia took the chance to open the curtains a crack, look at the street, as footsteps told her that her mother was being led away. The crying continued to come through the ceiling, and the slosh and hush of water as Margo, sitting on a little stool by the tub and shushing, poured water over Anna's back from a small jug, smoothing soap through her hair. Later, that would be Alicia's memory of Margo's house in Lwów: the sound of crying through the floorboards, magnified in the bathtub's echoing tin.

23

THE NEXT MORNING Margo buttoned her coat, tutted as she noticed one missing, its threads trailing.

'You're not going out?' Anna asked.

'Yes, for bread and news. What? You don't want to eat?' She crossed the small room where the visitors had slept, swept open the curtains as Anna whispered, 'Wait!' The others were still asleep, or pretending to be, taking refuge in closed eyes. Margo stood by the open curtains, eyebrows raised in a triumphant question. Anna didn't know what she'd been expecting.

'Aren't you afraid?' she said. 'What if they arrest you?'

'What for?'

'I don't know,' Anna admitted lamely. 'They arrested Adam for, well, I suppose they didn't arrest him, just took the car.' She faded back into the chair as she trailed off, speaking more to herself.

'This isn't *them*. The Germans aren't here, we're lucky,' Margo said, adjusting her scarf. That gentleness had crept back into her voice, at the mention of Adam. 'Do you want to come?'

'I don't have any good clothes—'

'It's just to the market!'

'But my hair—'

'Suit yourself.'

Anna glanced back at her still-sleeping children and neighbour, tasted the sour, caged breath in the air. She nodded.

The familiar sky made Anna relax a little. Early winter sun brought people out, coats unbuttoned, walking and talking in clusters. When they were travelling from Kraków, Anna had thought she would never want to be outside again, would always want walls and a roof and a fire, but now she turned her face up to the sky and breathed deeply, rolled up the sleeves of the ugly cheap coat that smelled of cigarettes, a donation from the Skliars, to feel the sun and air on her arms. When they reached the main road, the morning birdsong and low rumble of cars and buses reminded her of Kraków. As they turned down a steep road Anna recognised it as the one they had come in through, when her panic was still raging, and she'd counted cobbles to distract her, watching her own feet and feeling how her weight pressed on Janina and Karolina; shameful, but she had reached her limit, and they were so much stronger than she was. It had been dark then, and she'd been sick and hungry and feverish with pain and relief that they'd got here, away from the Germans, to where Adam would be waiting.

Margo gripped her arm, gave it a small shake as a car roared around a corner and they rushed to the pavement. Margo took a breath, and Anna prepared for sharpness, to be spoken to like an errant child, dragging her feet. Instead Margo patted her hand and they walked on. *So I'm to be treated like a fragile hysteric then*, Anna thought. *I'd rather be snapped at like before; I'd rather go to war with her.*

This steep road led to broader ones that were like the streets at home. There were the same high stone buildings and shops: flowers, bakeries, a bookshop. Anna recognised too the adverts painted on the sides of buildings: the same smiling women, their heads thrown back, the same families with happy children, under large red letters. Even the shape of the street signs was the same, the rectangles with white writing. Margo saw her looking at them and pointed, said, 'They're going to replace them with Russian names, they're saying.'

'Will you learn?'

'I already speak it,' Margo said proudly, and Anna could have rolled her eyes back into her head for how her sister-in-law had laid the soil for that little fact to be sown.

'How very helpful for you.'

'For all of us! I'll teach you and the girls and Janka.'

'Janina – she won't like it if you shorten it.'

Margo stiffened. 'Oh! I think I may take some liberties since I give her houseroom, and she a stranger to us!'

Anna dropped Margo's hand. 'Just don't throw her out, please, please. I know she's annoying—'

Margo stared at her. 'My God, what do you think of me, that I'd throw an old refugee out into the streets?'

'And *don't* call her a refugee, she can't bear it. And—' Anna broke into a laugh, 'certainly don't call her an *old* refugee, or she'll burn the house down.'

Anna turned and walked in the direction she thought they were headed. Margo caught up with her and they walked in silence until they turned a corner, 'It isn't far,' Margo said, and the street opened into a small market square, stalls opening up for the day. It was nothing like the Glowny, its grand Cloth Hall and clock tower and the beautiful marble buildings. Anna liked it anyway, felt with every busy seller unpacking wares from boxes, or every snatch of laughter or conversation – mostly in Polish, she thought – how her breathing was getting deeper, how the state of fear she'd been in – mouse-like, a headachy heightened awareness of sound and movement – was unknotting.

'See? It's all right,' Margo said.

'I know. Look, this fabric is cheap. Could we get some to make new dresses?' Anna held it up, thin and of dubious quality, but a pretty print of green leaves and yellow flowers.

'Food first,' Margo replied, eyeing a snaking line towards the food halls.

'And I need hat pins and some rouge. Look at this fabric. Alicia would like it, and we could make a headscarf for Karolina with it, perhaps for me too, for when visitors come, since you don't have a servant to do our hair,' Anna chattered. She glanced at the seller, ready to barter, a little excited to try her rusty skills; she had been sent to market every week for years, until she was married and too rich to ever set foot in one. The seller was an older woman, grim-faced and with huge arms she crossed against her breasts. She was glaring at Anna, who offered the woman her most charming smile.

'How much?' she asked in Polish. The woman only stared at her. Margo fixed her with a look and said something sharp in Ukrainian, repeating the question, and the woman looked over Margo's head.

Margo began to steer Anna by the shoulders. 'The war,' she said, shrugging, 'makes people crazy.' She spun abruptly and spat on the ground as they walked away, narrowly missing Anna's shoe.

'Margo!' Anna hissed, but feeling a smile erupt, seeing Margo's fierceness on her behalf. 'Do you ever get problems here?'

'Some people are just nasty,' Margo said in reply.

'Yes, anyway there's no way to tell, is there? I don't think you can tell at all, we don't dress like the conservatives do;

I don't even go to *shul*, do you?' Anna knew she was gabbling, tried to stop. 'Anyway, are you, even? Didn't you convert to marry Schmuel? Though you know his father probably didn't care, but their mother was such a stickler—'

'There, look.' Margo pointed.

There they were, in their uniforms, just walking around the market. People ignored them, moved around them like apparitions. There were four of them, looking relaxed, wearing heavy coats and boots, probably too warm. One of them was laughing, the other picking up fruit.

'It's all right, don't be frightened,' Margo said.

Anna watched them meander through the market like tourists. She glanced back at the woman, who was now smirking at her.

'Can we go home?'

'I just need flour. Forget about your hat pins and rouge. And we have plenty of dresses from donations. Besides, you can wear mine.'

'Margo?' A woman was walking towards them. Plump and graceful, she steered her way through the lines of people. Anna noted her ugly dress with a garish striped pattern, and as she got closer, the extraordinary beauty of her face: huge blue eyes, glowing skin and the gently curling, thick blonde hair of a film star. As she approached, Anna stiffened in surprise as the woman threw her arms around Margo's neck, and was stunned when Margo hugged her tightly back.

'This is Sophia Skliar,' Margo said, laughing as Sophia planted a kiss on Margo's cheek, leaving lipstick there.

This grinning doll was Theo Skliar's wife? Anna had been expecting a no-nonsense, professional woman, perhaps kind but stern, like the women she knew at home. Hadn't Theo said his wife worked at the university?

Anna held out her hand. 'I met your husband, Theo—' she began, and Sophia spoke over her, breaking her wide, welcoming smile, 'My husband told me all about you, and I've been meaning to visit, since yesterday, and I have so much to say – can you understand me? Margo, does she speak Ukrainian – let's talk in Polish.' She switched, 'There, hello!' and she pulled Anna into a hug so tight that Anna felt her ribs complain. 'Are you going back?' She turned her smile on Margo.

'Just some flour—'

'Oh, we have plenty, come and take mine, come, come.'

Sophia's presence made Margo younger somehow, more relaxed, and the three walked back together linking arms like students, Sophia talking incessantly as though she and Anna had been friends since childhood. 'Aren't you proud to have a sister-in-law like this? We're taking in refugees too, just for days at a time. Oh! I've been so busy!'

'There are others in our street? Are they from Kraków?'

'Some, others from Warsaw I think. Some from Germany, even—'

'But we might know them!'

'Perhaps,' Sophia smiled at her. 'So many strange things! So many coincidences! Just yesterday I saw God reunite a husband and wife. He was coming from Berlin. Imagine! And she from out near Kielce! And they just so happened to both register on the same day! They saw each other in the line. Oh! I could have danced! God brought them back together.'

'I wonder why he didn't do the same for all of the separated husbands and wives? Why must your God play favourites?' Margo asked, and Anna heard the rhythms of a long-held debate, an argument between friends that had stretched on for years. Sophia was nodding patiently, using her free hand to stroke a tiny gold cross at her neck. Anna too had a thousand angry questions, ready to batter Sophia's smiling face with the stupidity of what she had said, but Sophia gasped and reached for Anna again.

'Oh, my stupid mouth, and Theo told me your husband isn't here. Ach,' Sophia said, smiling her beautiful smile. 'It will happen for you too – Margo, don't tut at me; there's always hope. Are you praying, Anna?'

'I don't practise,' Anna said.

'Well, come to church with us tomorrow.'

Anna usually hated women like this, younger and beautiful, sunny and sweet. But Sophia's shiny surface, gleaming like a polished car, and her earnest, warm face, they were irresistible to Anna now; a light switched on in the bedroom of a child waking from a nightmare. She reached and squeezed Sophia's arm, feeling herself to be playing a role very well, as a shiny person too.

'God loves everyone,' Sophia added.

Anna took a few seconds to parse this out, but then remained silent when Margo shot her a quelling look.

'So, your church is being used as a refugee centre? Is that where we should go?' This was what Anna needed: official papers, to find out what they should do, how they would access the money.

'Yes, yes, come to the church. Everything is going to be fine.'

Sophia lifted her face to the sunlight as they walked, closed her eyes briefly. She wasn't so much older than Karolina, Anna suspected. She must have married very young. They stepped off the kerb and Sophia came to herself, gave Anna's arm a squeeze. 'The world is still so beautiful,' she said. 'Look at the sky and the sunlight falling between those buildings there.'

'Be miserable if you like, Anna,' Margo said, lightly. 'Sophia, don't preach at her. We're at war now.'

'All the more reason to appreciate the sunshine and the sky and all the things the Soviets and the Germans can't fight over like dogs over sticks,' Sophia said.

The day was ripening. Anna tilted her head towards the sunlight and felt its soft early winter light on her face. She had come to think of the sky as belonging to Alicia somehow, so obsessed with light was her youngest. The full white clouds had drifted now, revealing the depth of the sky. With all the remnants of her parents' prayers, her grandparents' voices, what she could dredge up from memory, Anna sent up something like a prayer; harder and angrier than Sophia's, but with the force of all the love she had.

The Oderfeldts and Janina began to fill their time with tasks Margo set them: sewing and planting and peeling, or writing letters which would be sent into the unknown, to everyone they could think of, asking for information, help, reassurance that their world was still there. Anna wrote to the Bernardyńska apartment, hoping one of the servants might pick it up; she wrote to every neighbour and acquaintance she could think of, walking the streets in her mind, checking off half-remembered dinner party lists; she wrote to Stefan, to Janie's parents. She copied out her letters to Adam four times, thinking of old stories and the four corners of the earth; her daughters copied out their own, so Anna could tuck them in next to her letters. She felt in doing this she was making some pantomime of family for their hosts, felt the old hollowness in her, but when she licked the seal and Alicia insisted on scrawling little sketches on the envelopes of her Papa's face, and a tiny perfect one of the apartment and its tree-lined street, Anna's heart caught and she didn't feel so much of a fraud.

Karolina stayed up late writing to Jozef, piled the papers up on the little table waiting for Sammy to bring more envelopes from the office. Later, both Anna and Alicia made sure to leaf through the letters, in the rare seconds the room was cleared of the others. Anna scanned through the detritus of her daughter's heart, looking for evidence of plots to run away back to Kraków alone; she wanted to smile at the youthful, stormy passion she might find, too, but instead found calm, quiet sorrow: *When I think I may never see your face again, I wish I could draw as you and Alicia can; I write of, to, and for you, but my words lumber and fall short.* Anna placed the letter down as Janina came in, caught her eye.

'Of course you must look. What if she's in trouble?' Janina said.

'Oh, she isn't,' Anna said, lightly, knowing there had been blood on the journey, which even in her state of panic Anna had noted with relief. When Karolina was close to her again, coming in from planting in the garden, it was all she could do not to hold her in a fierce grip, cling to her and cry for the child who disappeared and left a young woman in her place without her mother even seeing the changeling switch.

When Alicia looked it wasn't even to read the words, but just to run her eyes, fascinated, over the scrawl, so rushed and intimate, none of the careful lettering and prim lining up of lines in how they had been taught to write. There were doodles in the margins: flowers and a sketch of the fields outside the barn from the journey. This gave Alicia a jolt of unexpected envy; Karolina was not to draw, or sketch, or paint, not to cross the invisible border that Alicia had drawn around Jozef and herself.

*

Sophia brought them out from the little world of Margo's front room, its tinny sounds of the cheap clock and cheaper radio, and the smell of tea and soup. The Skliars' house had a bright blue door and was never locked, and they all took the short walk to visit at all hours. The layout of the house was the same as Margo's but full of bright furniture and rugs, books lining every wall, and a beautiful, huge writing desk that seemed to belong to a Bernardyńska apartment. Theo was always out at the university, campaigning for his research grant, or protesting at government buildings against the restrictions on refugees. Sophia would join him with handmade banners she painted in the living room, asking Alicia to decorate them with stars and flowers. There was a carousel of refugees at their house, changing day to day, using the Skliars as a first port before they could find more permanent rooms through the church or Theo's contacts at the university. Sometimes Sophia patrolled the bus stations and outskirts, gathering up gaggles of lost people with their hastily stuffed suitcases and bringing them to the house.

'You're so lucky you have family here,' they said, with the same dazed faces Anna recognised from the road. 'So lucky.'

Anna sent her daughters away, back to Margo's house, before she asked, 'What news? Tell us everything,' and the newcomers poured out stories like bile onto the beautiful rugs, poisoning the room. It was all stories they had heard before: *I heard they've passed a law that all Jewish businesses are to be closed. I read they've stolen people's homes, and where have the people gone? There are rumours they sent them into awful, cheap houses, or even out of the city. They say they are shooting people in the street.* Now they became: *They closed my business. They stole our home. We ran before they forced us out to God knows where. They shot my friend in the street. Right in the street. In front of his wife.*

Anna and Janina could only gape and offer their hands, and think of their lost husband and son, look to the calm street outside, rain washing the brickwork. 'It's all going to be all right,' Janina whispered to the newcomers.

One day a man from this sea of passers-through tugged at the threads of their old life. He sat at the beautiful desk, running his hands over the smooth walnut surface, and opened one of the lids, took out a pen, looking for all the world like he was an entranced child playing at grown-up life with a beloved new toy that he could pretend was just like his papa's. Janina was helping Sophia prepare a lice wash for one of the women in the kitchen, and Theo was in earnest conversation with a small group of volunteers, making notes and getting ink all over his hands. Anna was free to stare at the man at the desk, fascinated by his slow, enchanted movements. There was something in his face that caught her. She went to him and introduced herself.

'We've met,' he said, distracted, glimpsing at her then placing his hands back on the desk. 'Doesn't Adam have a desk just like this?'

Anna's heart quickened. 'You know my husband?'

'I worked with his oldest friend, at the university. I've been to your house several times, Mrs Oderfeldt.'

Anna laughed, elated and terrified at this chance. 'Well, I hope you won't reprimand me for my terrible manners, forgetting you,' she said, drawing up a chair, 'only the last few months have rather dulled my social graces.'

'Hmm.' He used to wear glasses, Anna saw, as she came close to him. He had that mole-look of one who was missing them.

'Do you know anything of my husband? I haven't heard from him since—'

He was already shaking his head, and Anna turned to look

out of the window, gave herself a few breaths to let go of her stupid fantasy, embedded in seconds: *Of course, he gave me this letter for you! He's on his way to follow it, and with all your money too!*

'Only Stefan and the others.'

'Stefan! We've been writing to him, but—'

'No, you wouldn't be getting any replies.'

Anna held the edge of the desk. She could see Stefan, as though perched on this desk, his arms folded, a small smile on his face that told he was about to make a great argument, ready to dismiss the soldiers with jokes, quotations, sheer intelligent good will. She felt, briefly, his thin arms wrapped around her as he said goodbye on that last day, heading for a lover's house, clutching a bottle of Adam's best cognac. He had told her not to worry, kissed her on the cheek.

'Adam will be devastated,' she whispered.

The man turned to face her. 'I don't know that he's dead,' he said. 'They arrested all of the professors at the Jagiellonian.'

'What? All?'

'Tricked them. Said they were to meet in a conference room at the university, not long after the invasion. They were all there, ready to discuss. And they just arrested them all.'

'Not you?'

'I was just an assistant.'

'And?'

'And what?'

'And! What happened to them all? Where did they take them?'

The man gave an exhausted shrug. 'We protested the next day, wrote letters . . .' he shrugged again. 'How long will they let me stay here? Is it safe here?'

*

Anna planned to tell Karolina the news lightly, simply, without preamble or decoration. Her daughter was in the tiny, frozen garden at the back of Margo's house, digging holes in the hard soil, her hair spilling around her. When she looked up, the cold had given her cheeks and nose a rosy glow and her dark eyes were full of tears from the wind.

'Mama?'

'Has Jozef replied to any of your letters?'

Karolina sat back on her heels. She bit her lip. 'No, but—'

'Karolcia—'

'Please don't make a speech about him forgetting me, or I him. I don't complain about it or lie around crying or even write about it anymore. Just let my heart be,' Karolina said.

Anna hugged herself, the cold lashing at her ribcage. 'Was he still going in to work, do you know?'

'What?'

'Did he still have a class running, when we left?'

Karolina wiped her face, blinked at her mother. Anna gave herself up as a coward.

'Go to Sophia's, there's a man there you need to speak to.'

'We should take in more people,' Isaac urged his parents later that night. He fiddled with the radio dial in Margo's front room, trying to find music, but there were only voices drifting through the static.

'Nonsense,' Margo said, pulling a stitch taut by the fire.

'There are sixteen at the Skliars now.'

'Sophia doesn't have any children.'

'And? There's only one of me, I don't take up so much room,' Isaac replied with a smile, stretching to touch the ceiling.

'Sixteen? Too many,' Margo said. 'She's got no sense, that girl. What?' she said, to Anna's raised eyebrows.

'I thought you loved Sophia.'

'I do! Stupid child that she is! Sixteen in one house!'

Sammy cleared his throat. 'Maybe we should ask Theo if there's anyone who needs—'

'Where would we put them?'

'We can sleep on the floor and they'll sleep in our beds upstairs,' Isaac ventured.

Margo sniffed. 'How many did you take in Kraków? Anna? Janina?'

'We left just as everything was starting,' Anna said.

'But the refugees from Germany?' Margo pressed.

There was a short silence. 'You threw a party after Kristall-nacht, Anna. I remember the Germans there. We made them very welcome,' Janina said, looking around, returning a smile from Isaac.

'I don't want any more people,' Alicia said simply.

Everyone looked at Anna. She sighed and said, 'That's not very kind, Alicia—'

'Alicia's right. We can barely afford to keep you all here,' Margo said.

Janina and Anna exchanged a frightened look which Sammy caught, and he gave them a reassuring glance, a slight shake of the head, to say, *No, no, she doesn't mean it, don't worry.*

Margo tore off a thread in her teeth. 'More people. Are you crazy? We shouldn't draw attention to ourselves.'

'There's no law against it,' Sammy said, but he crossed to the window, pinched the edges of the closed curtains together.

Upstairs, Karolina lay on Margo's bed, springs digging into her back, listening to the ebb and flow of the argument.

New letters to Jozef were spilled across the bedspread, never to be posted; she didn't know where to send them, and anyway they were only full of empty phrases and imagining a different turn, that day of the invasion, where she had kissed her family goodbye and walked through the tense city that was still their own, straight to Jozef's house.

24

THE LIGHT STARTED to weaken and the last of the winter sun drained away. Sophia had found French tutoring work for Anna. Anna was a terrible teacher and spent most of her time sighing or laughing at the terrible slow progress of the children of Sophia's friends and church congregation, but was given food to take back to Margo's house with her in payment. Every week she went to Margo's bank in the city and tried to explain about her account in Kraków, took letters signed by Theo and Sammy attesting to her identity, and every week she left penniless, imagining their money mouldering away in infested Kraków.

Janina and Margo took in laundry and filled the house with the smell of soap and starch. Janina's hands began to crack and swell, but she liked to stay in the house behind Margo's walls, and to listen to Margo gossip about the neighbours, providing laughter or a shocked face as required, and earning Margo's friendship with her receptive audience. Even Alicia helped, steaming sheets in the kitchen, folding their canvas-like whiteness, laying them next to each other to notice the different shades, how they glowed in different ways when held up to this or that corner of the room.

Sophia worked hardest to find something for the heartbroken Karolina. She took her to her church, where Karolina, uncomplaining, washed pots and arranged donations; she found her pupils to tutor, and Karolina would teach them in a dull monotone, tears sometimes filling her eyes until she would put her head on the desk in Sophia's house and close them.

Anna had limited patience with it. 'For God's sake, I wish there were more books here to distract her; it's the only thing she really loves,' she said one day to Sophia.

'But that's perfect! I'll find her something at the library! I'm in charge of the archive – oh! We should have her look after the Polish books! There are so many and she can categorise them – we'll work together!'

So Karolina and Sophia left every morning for the library, Sophia chattering happily, as though there were no war at all, Karolina in a carapace of worry. Sophia brought her home every evening with paper and pens for Alicia's sketches, and gossip about people the others had never met: *Veronica is going to get married, Ria has disappeared, they say the whole family has gone.* Alicia listened in envy, wishing she could work outside the house too, but kept on sewing and darning and mending what Margo gave to her every day, and at night, sketched the house and the swollen family: Janina's wrinkled hands, the edge of the window frame, the view from the top of the street.

Isaac went back to school to finish his final year, came home with stories of new German and Polish boys, new drills between Latin and French.

Sammy looked more and more harassed; his gelatinous cheeks hung in sadness more often than they stretched to show his usual beam. He sat in silence while the family and Janina made small talk over simple meals, was slow to rise to Margo's prodding to chime in with someone's name ('Who is it, Sammy, that awful woman with the eyebrows and she wears those ugly rings? She has lots of children Anna could tutor . . .'), and if Isaac – it was always Isaac – asked about his day, and the others would hush, in case there was news of Adam, he would only shake his head.

At night, Sammy lay next to his wife, whispering to her in her sleep.

'Things are getting worse,' he would whisper, watching her face to see if she was hearing him in a dream. 'The cases are piling up, but I can't help anyone.'

He moved onto his back, staring at the ceiling. Imagined the sky beyond it, the ceiling dissolving to leave them all exposed to the cold air. He felt the weight of them all: his wife and son, his sister-in-law and nieces, the old woman, dragging on him somewhere in his stomach, and released a violent sigh of anger at Adam for disappearing, for being arrested, for running, for dying in the street, whatever he had done, for leaving him with this, for weeks and who knew how much longer, when it was only meant to be for a few days. Then he apologised to Adam's spirit, if it had come to that, and the spirits of their parents, and got up to pace around the upper floor of the house and bite the inside of his cheeks until they bled, waking up the women downstairs, who took turns watching the shadows moving through the floorboards and hear the weight pressing down from above, Margo's gentle snoring in the background.

Even through his fug of anxiety Sammy left for work every morning and returned every evening. Every day he answered the same question from Anna, 'Any news?' with the same response, 'No change.' Over the weeks it became such a habit that the words lost their meaning and became like the other inane politenesses of *good mornings* and *how are yous* and *will you have some tea*. Routine soothed and lulled them all, even Sammy, even Karolina.

25

IT TOOK A LONG TIME for Margo's doubts to blossom into anxiety, and then fear. It was normal for Sammy to be late, in these strange days, to be swamped at the office with case after case and to come home stuffed with stories he wouldn't tell until they were curled up together alone in their bed, her head on his huge barrel chest, feeling the false safety of his arms around her. She'd close her eyes and deepen her breathing, taking in the scent of him, which to her was the smell of home. Thinking she was asleep, he'd whisper of whole families disappeared, and only their servants left to report them missing, and tale after tale of arrests for the wrong papers, the wrong tone of voice, the wrong set of the jaw or wrongly pitched look in the eye. 'What can I do?' he'd whisper into the dark. 'I go, I follow all the procedures, I file the paperwork. I don't even know if it's the police or the army who has them. I can't help any of them. And . . . they arrest so many Jews. They say at the office it's, of course, the refugees are mostly Jews, so it stands to reason . . .'

That night Margo lay in bed alone, counting the hours. It wasn't unheard of for Sammy to sleep at the office when things were so busy. Perhaps he had made a bed on the little sofa in his office where years ago she had caught him with a secretary. So when she woke to an empty bed, Margo let her worries be.

By the following night, Sammy had still not come home. Margo went to his office, the lights of one corner still on. When the clerk, working late, told her Sammy hadn't been in at all that day, she thanked him. She buttoned her coat, then put her gloves on carefully, tugging the seams straight over each finger. She walked out of the office and down the stone steps, deaf to the horns and belching smoke of the traffic below, a muffling in her ears. Tucking her coat under her, she settled on the lowest step, and wept.

A hand on her shoulder, like Sammy's heavy but gentle weight, made her leap up, certain it would be her husband as though summoned by sheer will, but it was the clerk again. He looked rather disgusted as he handed her a handkerchief; this incensed her, when she could have torn out her hair, screamed at the passing carts, and still even tears for her missing husband was too much! She took pleasure in filling his handkerchief with a satisfying stream of snot. The clerk cleared his throat.

'Mrs Oderfeldt, there's a telegram for Schmuel.'

'What? So? Nothing from Sammy himself?'

'It's from his brother.'

The line was terrible, full of static, making his voice drift in and out of focus as though he was talking to her from different rooms, whispering from far away, then suddenly speaking with his breath in her ear. Anna pressed the receiver to her head, its heat and its dusty, tinny hardness; with her other hand she gripped the edge of Sammy's desk.

'What are you talking about, what house?' she said.

'The money . . . I can sell it—'

'You want us to go to France? Are you crazy?'

'. . . I tried to . . . France. Edie will send . . .'

She blinked around the office. It was like the edge of the table Sammy was permitted in Margo's house, writ into a whole room: papers everywhere, spilling out of files, stacked in tottering piles, like little falling cities, and propped up with pieces of engineering: rulers, larger files, boxes. Static roared in her ears.

'Anna?'

'You aren't in prison?'

'I'm staying . . . say where in case . . . Stefan's case.'

Anna felt her whole insides shrivel with rage, her lungs almost convulse as she drew breath to shout, but it came out as a strangled whisper.

'I've been here all this time, the girls, and you stayed in Kraków and not dead or arrested or even hurt or anything else and you could have left at any time?'

There was a long crackle down the line. '. . . don't understand . . . safe.'

'And now you're leaving but to go to *France*?'

His voice had gone and the line sang a dead tone. Anna stared at the phone, unsure for a horrible moment if she had pressed the button, unconsciously, before saying what she needed to say to him, before evoking their daughters for him, before exploding in righteous fury, abandoned for that young girl and her son, after everything, after all her years of patient friendship under this one understanding, that when the world was falling apart he would be at her side. She was his wife.

'*Kurwa!*' She smashed the phone against the desk. A man ran in, face slack with outrage, and wrenched it from her hands, listened to the dial tone and gave her a raised eyebrow look that told her she was lucky it was still working. She sat in a hot fug of shame and anger that she bathed in for a moment like summer sun, before smoothing her ugly borrowed brown dress in her lap, adjusting her hat (her own, expensive) and gathering up the bag Margo had lent to her with nothing in it.

She opened the door of Sammy's office as Margo's voice battered at one of her husband's colleagues.

'Don't give me that. There must be a way to—'

'Mrs Oderfeldt, please.' (*Perhaps I'll start using my old name*, Anna thought, *I always liked it, Kotowski, and that little whore can take his name if she wants, why not?*) 'There's no need to panic,' the same man who had taken the phone from Anna's hands said, dismissing the first man with a nod.

'Who's panicking? I'm just asking where my husband is. Do I sound like I'm in a panic? Am I running around screaming? It's been over a week.'

'Well, that isn't unusual, for a difficult case, he will be staying at the police station with the client—'

'Oh! Thank you, thank you, thank God I have you to explain to me, a lawyer's wife and with a degree in law myself,' – Anna looked up, this was extraordinary news to her – 'how these things work,' Margo spat. 'Except he isn't at the police station, because I have called there, and it is unusual not to telephone to the office, isn't it?' She opened her hands. *Et voilà, and what do you have to say for yourself now?* The man stood in his thin suit, badly made tie, and shrugged, blushing. Anna took a wildly childish pleasure in his humiliation and smirked at him. Margo noticed Anna then.

'What news from Kraków?' she asked in a gentle tone. 'Is it bad? Is he coming?'

'No, he isn't coming.'

'Does he have a lawyer? In Kraków they're arresting everyone, without even charging them—'

'I know that,' Anna snapped.

'No, there are procedures,' the young lawyer interrupted her, before stopping at Margo's glare.

'But if he has access to a telephone it can't be so bad,' Margo said.

'Yes, I suppose so,' Anna smiled at her.

'Well then,' Margo gave her a weak smile, then folded her lips, and Anna felt the force of what lay beneath her face: *So now your husband is safe, but mine is not.*

They left the office and stepped into the quiet street; it was Sunday, so few people were about, and the cold kept the majority inside, along with the new bite of disappearances in the air. The young lawyer came with them, locking up the office he had opened only at Margo's insistence, after the telegram from Adam gave a time he could get back to a telephone.

Now, Anna and Margo picked their way through the freezing slush, Anna in a daze of confusion and regret, imagining all the things she should have said, and wondering how to frame this story to her daughters. As she watched her shoes, faithful and strong since Kraków, muddied and bitten by the journey, carry her over patches of pavement, she toyed with the idea of saying it wasn't Adam at all that called, but a friend: Stefan, Jozef? Telling them he was dead. She indulged in the grim daydream for a moment before discarding it. Margo walked beside her with her usual heavy step, a slight limp.

'Do you really have a law degree?'

'Of course. It's where I met Sammy.'

'Why don't you go back to work, since we need the money?'

But Margo wasn't listening. She looked back at the office, then down the street, as though lost. 'We didn't have classes together, but then a professor we shared threw a dinner at the end of the first year.' She spoke over Anna's head, watching the memory play out on the grey street, as though a film of it was projected onto the side of that office building.

Anna took her hand. 'Margo, it's all right, he'll be all right.' Anna was struck by a familiar fear, that she was empty, that she had got lost somehow, and didn't love or feel like other people did, that she was always only pretending. Perhaps that was why Adam had left her, finally, for Edie, not because of the girl's younger body, but because she had a working heart. In the private abyss of her mind she found now how little she had ever cared about Sammy. Now she felt how they were more tethered together than ever, that Sammy's plight was hers, and her children's too. She studied Margo's pinched little face, the pointed nose, the dark eyes. She saw the cleverness in them and the kindnesses she'd shown her, the times she'd ignored Alicia's insolence and smiled at Karolina's sweetness and given them all clothes and her food without complaint. And there was no blood between them, not real blood that bound by memory and ancestors whispering the same thoughts into dreams; there were only the long-ago promises they had made to brothers. Margo's blood was Isaac, and she shared his roof and his food, his protection, with Anna and her children. Shame submerged her from her toes in a rush through her body and poured out of her mouth. 'I'm sorry,' she said, and would have embraced her, had a car with a beeping horn not made them jump out of the road where they'd been walking for the clearer path.

'Stupid Polish bitch!' a man yelled from the window as he sped away. Anna's mouth dropped open, more from the hatred in the words than their meaning, which she took a few more seconds to unscramble.

'That idiot boy,' Margo said absently, pulling her towards home. It took a few more steps for Anna to realise the man in the car had been the young clerk from Sammy's office.

26

'WHEN IS PAPA COMING?' Alicia said, twisting around to look at her mother, who gave her a blank look that Alicia couldn't decipher. 'Isaac, Aunt Margo, aren't you excited to see Papa? When did you last see him?' Alicia went on. 'Karolcia, can you believe it?'

Karolina only smiled at her.

'I'm sorry there was no time to ask about Jozef,' Anna said.

'Adam might have news of some of the neighbourhood,' Janina said.

'He'll drive us home. We'll find Jozef, and my painting,' Alicia said, brutally cheerful in the face of Margo's pale and tear-stained cheeks, Isaac's silence. It was the latter that pierced her, after a few seconds, and she went to her cousin's side, curled up next to him. 'Sorry,' she whispered, 'but Uncle Sammy is only working somewhere.' Isaac clasped his hands together and gave her a vague, dismissing smile.

And so it went on and on and on, while Anna sat fixed in place unable to speak. Time after time the words rose in her throat and crowded behind her teeth. *He isn't coming. He's on his way to France, to be with his other, newer family. His lover and son.* The last word pulled the others back with it, clawing back down her throat to sit in her stomach. She fell into a bitter daydream of a sunlit room, full of Provençal lavender, the very lavender he brought back for her wrapped in silk bundles, that Janie put into all of the drawers and hung in the wardrobes, the girl in a rocking chair, wearing a simple white sundress, showing a miraculously tiny waist, fresh-faced with long, un-styled hair falling across her face, cradling the boy, turning to Adam as he crossed the room with his quick, loping stride—

'Anna!' Janina repeated, having resorted to shaking her arm. 'Could you ask Sammy's office to telegram back to Adam, arrange a new telephone call? When it isn't such a shock, and you are calmer, you can ask more questions about what's happening.'

'But Papa won't be there any more, he's travelling to us now,' Alicia said.

'I just thought maybe, my son, you know,' Janina trailed off, before finding her breath again. 'The newspapers here don't cover the Polish troops so much, perhaps if he could pick up *The Herald* or even one of the cheaper dailies, there might be an address to write to.'

In the small front room where the Oderfeldts and Janina slept, the dead of night knock at the door was absorbed at first into the soundscape of Alicia's dream; she heard only the normal coming and going of what life had been in Kraków: Uncle Stefan, carrying books, or a neighbour coming to drink coffee and trade gossip with Mama. Janina and Karolina, already awake, sat up and gasped at the sound, some new threat, as Anna crossed the room to the door.

The knocking continued, a *rap rap rap*, a pause, *rap rap rap*. Growing fainter. Margo came down the stairs, followed by her son. Isaac was alert and anxious, holding something hidden in his hand. As he came to stand by his mother's side, Alicia saw it was a brick.

Margo looked around at the others with a tutting sound.

'What?' Anna whispered. 'You open it, then.'

But the door handle was being tried, and this made them all freeze in place, frightened rabbits listening to their own heartbeats. At long last Isaac leapt forward, the brick still in his hand; Margo caught sight of it and snatched it from him just as he opened the door.

'God, God,' Isaac said. He moved as though he would close the door again, gripping the side of it, and this sent a current through them all, a quick rifle through the mind and where to run, hide, a fight-or-flight work of milliseconds, but then Isaac stepped back, and as he turned, pale and looking younger than before, Sammy shuffled in behind him.

He was still wearing the same suit from the day he'd left, but it had been ripped off at the knees, exposing his thick shins, and the jacket was torn at the elbows; the effect was like seeing a grown man in a schoolboy uniform, humiliating. There was dried blood on his shirt, and he cradled one arm with the other. His left eye was swollen and purple, and pulled his cheek towards it, making his whole face a permanent wince. He held out his hands, impotently filling the room with an *I don't know, I don't understand it* before any questions could be asked. Margo darted to her husband, about to put her arms around him, but stopped when they were face to face, her hands hovering in the air between them, moving first towards his eye, then his arm, then curling back on themselves as she folded her arms, hugging herself. Isaac began pacing back and forth, chewing on a thumb and throwing glances at his parents.

Margo led Sammy to a chair. His throat was working, swallowing. Alicia thought of a summer with strep throat, every swallow a task. She reached for and found Karolina's hand. Her sister began to steer Alicia out of the room, but she resisted.

'Schmuel?' Margo prompted.

'They . . .' Sammy began, faltering. He swallowed again, and they all felt a wave of collective, reflected humiliation. *Weak*, Alicia thought savagely, before a horrified sob threatened to erupt. She swallowed it away, looked at the floor with its thin carpet and faded colours.

Anna caught Margo's eye. She mouthed, 'Shall we leave?' but Margo waved a hand in dismissal of the idea.

'Why is your suit torn?' Isaac asked, in his gentle, open way. 'Why would they . . .'

'They made me wear a sign.'

'A sign?' Margo echoed.

'Around my neck,' he gestured, circling with the fingers of his good hand. 'I left it in the street outside.'

'What did it say?' Margo pressed.

'It doesn't matter,' Karolina said quickly, squeezing her sister's hand.

Margo cleaned and dressed Sammy's wounds, used a mirror to look in his mouth.

'You've lost three teeth at the back,' she said matter-of-factly, wiping her hand on her dress.

'Oh,' Alicia let out a tiny sound. That explained the strange way his mouth looked, and how his voice was different.

'No, it was many more,' he mumbled. 'I remember swallowing them.' He looked around at them all. 'I was walking along swallowing my own teeth and blood, I remember the feel of it trickling down my throat,' he said, his voice rising. 'They were slapping me around the head like a child—'

'All right, all right,' Margo said.

'They beat me,' Sammy said in a tiny voice. 'There are

procedures, they can't do that, I was asking for the paperwork, insisting, they have to, there are laws. They made me wear a sign,' he mumbled, as Margo lifted his legs and he curled up, his huge frame stuffed onto the small chair, his face on an armrest. 'I swallowed my teeth . . .'

Margo cupped her husband's face with her hands, whispered something and kissed his nose, shrinking the world to the two of them, and they all looked away. As she broke away from him, Sammy seemed to relax.

'You have to leave,' he said.

Margo's mouth opened as though to argue, then closed again, and she joined the others in just staring at him.

Anna was the first to react, picking up her rage where she had let it trail at the sight of Margo's tenderness and Sammy's bowed head.

'I hope Adam is dead,' she began, satisfied to hear them all draw sharp breaths and to see Sammy's head snap up in surprise. 'Yes, so he never has to hear how you have treated us. It would break his heart straight in two, cracked—' Anna sliced the air, and Sammy jumped, 'right in two!'

Sammy stood in open-mouthed horror, but Anna found she was only flaying the skin of her rage and there were still layers and layers of disgust beneath; she almost laughed with the release of her temper after days, weeks, longer, of sniping frustration. She filled her lungs and let her voice hit Sammy full force.

'How can you be so useless, so immoral? Have you forgotten Adam? What would your parents say? Throwing his wife and daughters into the streets! You're a hypocrite! This ludicrous act you put on, to impress your friends, oh! What a good man! So charitable! So kind! *Welcome*, oh!'

She went to strike him, now, hit his shoulder as he stood

staring at his shoes, Margo's arms around him, though her face was grimly inscrutable as she heard Anna's abuse. *'Stay as long as you like!'* She said, hitting him again, then pulled back, elated and horrified at how her whole body had willed her to fall on him and rip him to pieces. 'But when it's really time to act, to help, it's *you have to leave!* You weak, pathetic man! I hope your brother is dead so he never knows how you've failed him!'

The room quietened; the only sound was Anna's hard breaths and the rustle of Sammy's sleeve where Margo was stroking it.

Isaac went to his aunt, put his arm around her shoulders.

'They're your brother's wife and children,' Margo said, gently.

Sammy wouldn't look at any of them as he left the room without a word, closing the door softly behind him.

Anna went to the Skliars', banging on their bright blue door. The house stayed dark and quiet. She knocked on the window, cupping her hands around her face to see inside. There was the beautiful furniture and the piles of books, half-drunk cups and piles of papers and half-written protest signs and banners rolled up and leaned against the wall.

She stepped back, her skin only now feeling the freeze of the street in the early hours. How mad she must look, having run out without coat or shoes. Hugging Margo's housecoat around her, she turned and watched the wind blowing leaves across the cobbles, heard barking dogs. She picked her way back to Margo's house, her toes stabbed by the cold and sharp cobbles. Blowing in the wind just outside their front door was a placard, made of thick white paper and tied with a string. The same message was written on both sides, one in Polish, one in Ukrainian. *Jew. I will be quiet.*

27

THE POUNDING at the door became a rash of knocks around the window. Fumbling with the locks, Anna found Sophia panting and red.

'Come . . .' Sophia faltered, catching her breath. 'No, listen,' she added, as Anna waved her in.

'Well, what is it? Come in!'

Sophia darted into the front room. It was the afternoon; Isaac was at school, Sammy and Karolina at work. As Sophia spoke, Janina gave little cries, shushed by the other women, who moved together, Margo holding Anna by the waist. Alicia came in from the kitchen, where she'd been secretly painting sheets with beetroot juice, and stared at the spectacle.

'They're, they're arresting Poles street by street. Theo got a message to me. They've started at the university and they're going through the whole city.'

'Karolcia?' Anna said.

'I – she's still at work . . .' Sophia quietened at Anna's face. 'She's safe there,' she added. 'I'm sure it's fine—'

'Did you tell her about Theo's message, will she know what to—'

'I don't know, I'm sorry, I came to warn the family at my house, I had to run. Theo and I, we're all, trying to – we have a basement at ours, you can hide there with the others. You don't have one, do you?'

'But we're here legally,' Janina tried again. She went to her little box under the chair by the fireplace. 'We're just waiting for the bank accounts to be accessed.'

'Forget about that, do you want to risk it? Something's changed,' Sophia said.

'Yes, that doesn't matter now,' Margo said, as Janina produced her papers, holding them out for Margo as though she were a guard.

'You have to go,' Margo added, and it wasn't clear if they were being dismissed from the house, or urged to flee.

'Come on, then,' Sophia said.

'We'll wait for Karolcia,' Alicia said.

Margo hesitated, looking from Anna to Sophia. 'Wait, wait. Let's think about this,' she said.

'I'm telling you, come on,' Sophia said.

'But surely they'll search the basements,' Margo said. 'They'll find them.'

Sophia paced, all eyes following her stunted march to and fro across the tiny room. She pressed a hand against the far wall and turned like a swimmer, plunged back to the window, back again. 'The church?' she offered.

'Your church is the first place they'll go, all that noise you've been making,' Margo muttered.

Sophia gripped her hands together and whispered a prayer into them. 'All right,' she said. 'I know where I can take you. But the others – oh, Margo, do you think they'll really search – of course they will, so stupid, Sophia. All right.' She rushed out again, leaving the family staring after her.

'Come on, Janina,' Anna snapped, fear making her spiteful, 'you'll slow us down on the way there as it is, so don't make it any worse by fumbling around for your coat. They were at the university,' Anna went on, gabbling as Janina buttoned her coat and handed gloves to Alicia, who was watching Margo, watching the window. 'How far away do you think they are? Oh God, but what about Karolina?'

'We're going to her,' Sophia said from the door. 'Come on. The refugees at my house won't move,' she called to Margo. 'Keep an eye out, won't you? I'm going to take your family myself.'

'Are you sure, Sophia? If they find them – I'm sorry, Anna, don't look at me that way, but there are risks—'

'I know.' Gone was all Sophia's girlish excitement. She was a little pale, kept touching the tiny cross at her neck. Anna wanted to shove her child at Sophia, say, *Take her, take her, look after her for the rest of all of this.* Margo squeezed Anna's hand in apology and she gave her a small smile in return.

'Are you bringing the car to the front here?' Anna asked, checking the window again.

'Theo has it. He's picking up souls all over the city to hide at the university. We won't get the message to him in time. We'll have to walk.'

They walked at the edge of flight, just at the point of breaking into a run. Sophia went ahead, scouting for soldiers, waving them forwards. She held up a palm for them to stop, and like well-trained dancers they all turned at this cue to look in a shop window. Anna saw reflected in the glass first a truck full of Soviets roar past, her own blank face, Alicia's closed one, Janina's almost-gibbering terror. She took Janina's hand. 'Come on, we've got this far,' she said. 'Even if they do arrest us,' she spoke to Janina's reflection, and then broadened her gaze to Alicia, 'so what? They aren't the Germans. Your Papa is coming, Alicia, and he'll explain everything, and so we spend a night on a prison bench instead of on a chair.' Anna had closed her eyes now, and had taken Janina's other hand. Alicia nodded along to her mother's words, rose up on the balls of her feet at *Papa*, as though he was before them and she was rising for a kiss or to be swept up into his arms.

In the hush and cool of the library lobby Anna felt soothed, as though the wooden doors were a magical barrier, as though decency and decorum would protect them here, among readers and scholars and people preparing for legal cases, researching papers. The rustle of pages and scratch of pens, the clunk and echo of heavy bags full of books placed on the gleaming floors, the musty scent mixed with beeswax, all of it made Anna feel stupidly safe.

The front desk was manned by two women, Dora and Paulina, bickering cousins who spent their days completing word puzzles and rating the men they could see from the front desk in a complicated system of ranks of face, body, voice and manners. They threw up their arms in unison at the sight of Sophia, and Paulina theatrically looked at the giant clock that hung on the wall behind the desk. The others hung back awkwardly as Sophia approached. She still had Anna by the hand, pulled her with her. The cousins, sensing drama, leaned in, and began to whisper furiously:

'Where did you go?'

'We thought you'd, you know . . . *dis-a-ppeare-d*,' Dora said, her bright lipstick bleeding onto her teeth as she spoke the syllables with relish. 'Are you in trouble?' She directed this last question to Anna.

'This is Karolina's mother,' Sophia said, and the girls gave her polite nods.

'Karolina's down in the stacks,' Dora said, as Anna almost bit through her own tongue not to cry out in relief.

'They say that they're arresting Poles street by street,' Sophia said.

'What? No! That's awful!' the cousins whispered, in the same tones they used for an errant husband, or a ruined party.

'Have they been here?' Sophia breathed, not even a whisper.

The women, wide-eyed, shook their heads.

The Polish books were kept in the stacks on the ground floor. The cool and silence of upstairs was deeper, richer here; all of them relaxed, feeling the floors above them as a shield, as though the room were a secret.

Karolina sat cross-legged against a shelf, surrounded by piles of books, writing on a spine, her hair spilling around her shoulders. She started as Alicia flew to her.

'Oh! Hello . . . what's this? Look, Alicia, this is an art book, I was going to bring it back for you . . .' She trailed off as Sophia shushed her.

Anna leaned her forehead against the cool painted wall that ran in a circle around the stacks, while Janina scurried around the edges of the room like a trapped mouse, whispering to herself. Sophia and Karolina took Alicia to see how the wheels at the ends of the shelves could be turned to make the stacks move.

'But you could crush someone in there.'

'No, silly, you can see if someone is looking at the books! Besides, the shelves aren't so heavy.'

'I don't like it.' And it was true that as she peered into the dark tunnels of books Alicia felt the opposite of the rooting, calming feeling her sister had described to her in this place; instead she felt this was another frightening maze to navigate, like unfamiliar streets, new fields, all the dark and shadowy places outside Kraków. She didn't like how loud their voices were here, how their footsteps seemed to

247

bounce around the walls. She didn't like the colourless room, the bright, white walls, the books all in pale green or brown leather.

'Look, they're Polish,' Sophia said, taking one from the shelf. Alicia recognised a series from the bookshelf at home, the same font and cover, poetry perhaps. Then she recognised her sister's handwriting on the sticker in the spine, her looping, sloped hand categorising it. 'You're home now,' Sophia said. 'You're in Poland, we're surrounded by Polish words. You'll be safe here,' she said, kissing the book she was holding. Karolina smiled at her.

When after an hour, two hours, there were no soldiers, and no one came down into the stacks, Alicia began daring herself deeper and deeper into the dark book tunnels, whistling so Sophia would remember not to crush her. Soon the murmur of the others was absorbed and dulled by the reams of pages. She looked for the large hardbacks from Papa's shelves and Stefan's office, the art books with prints in rich colours, double pages with close-ups of details from the masters, the ones Jozef had been teaching her. She should have asked Karolina to bring her these things before, but the library had seemed like an imaginary place. Her hand snared on a familiar book, the *Odyssey* Karolina had been translating for years. She could see it splayed open in various spine-broken places around the apartment, always on chairs or windowsills or on the floor. She pulled it down; it was the same edition, the same green cover with its vaguely Greek design around the edges.

'Karolcia, look,' she said, her voice carrying louder than she'd intended, as she walked back towards the others, holding up the book for her mother to see just as the lift roared open, and there was a confusion of sound: one of the women from earlier, her sister's friends, was talking in a manic rapid language Alicia couldn't follow, there were two other footsteps, and men's voices.

They couldn't be seen from the lift, here on the other side of the book stacks. Anna held a finger to her lips and Janina clamped a hand over her own mouth, not trusting herself. Paulina was chatting determinedly in Russian, the edge of flirtation in her voice. She was leading the soldiers in the other direction, but they would loop around and see them soon. They scuttled into the stacks, into the dimness, the centre of the book maze, wincing as their shoes hit the floors, hoping the books would muffle it. As they reached the middle Sophia gestured with her hands flat and they all understood but Janina, who watched with a grim face as the others clambered on the shelves, undignified, hiding like robbers in a fairy tale, like rats in sewers. At least the books were clean. The others burrowed back deep into the stacks, lying on rows of files and boxes behind the books, the whites of their eyes showing in the gloom. Janina felt the whisper of the monsters at their back and took Sophia's hand to pull her up; awkwardly she lay among them, her legs wrapped around a steel joint. *It's all right, it's all right, it's all going to be all, all right*, she pulsed through her mind and body, imagining her spine throbbing with it, *all right, all right, all—*

Anna's hand gripped her shoulder. Had she begun whispering it aloud? She bit the inside of her cheek. The receptionist's chatter was faltering, now becoming shrill. Janina willed her on. *Come on, you stupid little tart! Lead them away. Sophia and Karolina are your friends, aren't they?* The others echoed the message, in varying degrees of temper: Anna was ready to murder the stupid girl herself, bash out her brains on this shining floor. Sophia felt only warmth for her, hearing how much she was trying.

'Translate for us, I can't follow,' Janina whispered to her, but Anna's *shush* was so savage she hardly dared breathe after that.

Sophia's breathing quickened, and that told them enough. They were coming into the stacks. Their boots sounded like gunshots on the floor. Wordlessly, they all reached out to hold something: a hand, a knee, even hair, and gripped. Karolina and Alicia held hands, something they'd become used to since they left Kraków, when they'd barely touched before, but now they knew the smoothness of each other's young palms by heart, the calloused, cracked fingers and thumbs, the flaking nails. Sophia felt sick at the thought of her husband and parents, and regretted, suddenly, coming here; in this last moment, she couldn't remember what loyalty she'd felt to these people at all, and felt like a stupid child. This passed after a heartbeat, and Sophia added this failure to the others she must list in her prayers.

Shadows moved across the floor, though all but Alicia had closed their eyes; she stared up, at the books above them, trying to count what pages she could see in the dim light. The air changed as they held breaths, feeling the pressure build in lungs and stomachs; like a train passing and leaving a violent, manufactured wind behind it, the guards seemed to push all the air back towards the hiding family. Nails dug into skin then, gripped fabric, unfeeling and inflicting no pain, until later when they would find the bruises and broken skin.

They passed by. The sound of the boots grew quieter and quieter. Soon the men were laughing, the receptionist echoing laughter back to them, and the lift sang its dull song as it was called back to the stacks basement.

Janina schooled herself in breathing again, so afraid of the traitor sound of the air in her nostrils, the rise and fall of her tightened chest, that she sipped instead through a pursed mouth. It failed to work; the air wouldn't reach her lungs. She thought, I will drown here, and I will never see Aleks again—

It's all right, it's all right, it's all going to be all, all right, everything is—

A grip on Janina's arm tightened. She remembered Aleks after a nightmare. *It's all right*, she soothed him. *It's all right, it's all right* . . . She thought of Laurie, his spirit worrying for her, watching. *Laurie, tell me it's all right.*

Janina opened her eyes to the panicked white orbs of Anna's, the gleam of her teeth as her mouth fell open. Around her, like owls, the wide eyes of Anna, Karolina, Sophia. Karolina let go of Alicia and began to move towards Janina, brushing away her mother's hands, as the footsteps' echo still bounced around the walls. Janina tried to whisper, *Karolina, stay still*, and it was only then she connected the panicked, clouded part of her brain to her moving tongue and throat. She clamped a hand over her own babbling mouth just before Karolina did.

Paulina had begun chattering wildly, but was silenced by a harder word from one of the soldiers. The shadows grew again. Karolina was at the edge of the shelf now, her hand over Janina's weeping face. She glanced back at the others. Alicia's eyes were open and staring at her, always so intense and unblinking. Her mother's face was alive with panic, her hands reaching for Karolina, mouthing, *No, no, no, don't.*

Karolina slipped out of the shelf, hearing the family scuttle further back, a whimper that could be any of them. When the soldiers came she was standing as far from the others as she could, hoping the soldiers wouldn't sweep through the stacks with a torch. She picked up Janina's lines and told the soldiers in Polish it would *all, all be all right*, as though they had come to her for comfort.

28

THE LOBBY WAS EMPTY when they passed back through, and the library closed; Sophia took a key from behind the desk to let them out of a side door, into an alleyway. She slipped her arm around Anna's waist and steered her out. She talked in clipped, determined tones as they picked their way through the rubbish-strewn street.

'Sammy is a lawyer. That will make a difference. I know others, if, if it turns out we need a more prestigious one. Theo has contacts. We can mobilise a whole army of volunteers at the church, to write letters, to protest, we're already organising one for this Sunday, we can bring it forwards, we'll picket the main barracks, the government buildings . . . Oh, I wish I'd jumped out and protested there and then! May God forgive me; I'll never forgive myself for such cowardice!'

'We should have stayed at the house,' Janina fretted, as they moved into the wider main street. Her voice was cracked, her throat dry with mortified sobbing. Anna closed her eyes as the older woman spoke; it had seemed wisest, until she was sure her other daughter was safe, to pretend Janina did not exist. Alicia had no such qualms, and met Janina's voice, her first spoken words since Karolina had been taken, by launching herself at her old neighbour, hitting her arms and stomach, aiming for her face. Janina wheeled back.

'Alicia!'

'Stop, Alicia, we have to be quiet,' her mother said. She met Janina's eyes for a moment and let Janina see the ice in them. When they walked on again, Janina stayed behind, an invisible, terrifying barrier now drawn between her and the others. She tried to calm herself but found only a deep well of panic she dared not look at; instead she spoke to Aleks and Laurie in her head, biting her lip hard so she was sure not to speak: *You understand, don't you, my darlings? You forgive me?*

'Why didn't we just stay in the stacks?' Alicia said, feeling the electricity of her rage at Janina still crackling through her fingers. 'Karolina sacrificed herself for us and we just—'

'Don't be so dramatic,' Anna snapped. 'We'll go back to Margo's and discuss what to do. What, are we going to hide with the books forever?'

Yes, yes, yes, they couldn't see us, why not? Janina thought. *Why not?*

The streets of Lwów were quiet again, but this time with a feeling of something hollowed out, no longer hold-ing its breath but not breathing at all. Curtains were drawn, offices shuttered, the lights in front windows were unlit, families having retreated to back rooms or even cellars, until the rumours changed and the knock-knock on doors and questions stopped and the reliable gossips began singing a different tune. They passed one defiantly open bar, clusters of men sitting around small tables, playing board games, smoking, reading the papers. All locals, no soldiers. They walked past unnoticed. *Or perhaps,* Anna thought as one of the men pulled his coat around him, determinedly fixed his gaze on a chess piece, *they feel a chill as we pass, as though we're ghosts.*

*

It was Margo they saw first, standing at the window. She was making sharp motions with her wrists, as though flicking something from the back of her hands, the same she used for *stop talking* or *tell me* or *where is that thing* or even *you know I love you.* She looked over her shoulder into the room behind her, to Isaac or Sammy or both, back to where the three women stood fixed in place. Margo placed a palm on the window. Anna wanted to raise hers in return, but found she couldn't let go of Alicia's hand. Her body was flooded with heat; she felt sweat forming on her back, but Alicia's hand was bloodless and cold in hers. Sophia wasn't even looking at Margo, but instead staring at the line of refugees kneeling in the road, hands behind heads, looking at the cobbles. They made a line like a breadcrumb trail up to Sophia's front door. At the end of the line was Theo, standing, his face against the outside wall of their house, hands behind his back.

Sophia lunged towards him and a soldier caught her gracefully, in one arm, and manoeuvred her like a dancer to Theo's side, her heels ringing out across the cobblestones. The soldier murmured something to Sophia and she put her face to the wall like her husband, reaching for his hand. The soldier noticed and gave an uncertain smile to another man in uniform, shrugged towards them, *How sweet.*

For a wild moment, Anna considered diving towards Margo's house, a children's game in which if she could get across the threshold, they would be safe. At the window, there was now only the lining of Margo's drawn curtains. When the soldier approached them she started to assemble some lines in Ukrainian, briefly wondered if she should pretend they were French, but the man's small, knowing smile, his quick glance back at Sophia and Theo, made everything fade to grey. She began babbling, 'We have all our papers in order, we have family here, that is my brother-in-law's house, he's a lawyer, we have money in Kraków, my husband—' and suddenly around her were Margo and Isaac, taking up her pleas, the same facts, the same arguments, counting them off on their fingers, *papers, family, money*, and Isaac kept calling *Father, Father, come and explain*, but Sammy's shape behind the curtain was still. Janina was silent, nodding along, afraid if she tried to speak she would start to cry in fear, while Alicia didn't trust herself to speak, knowing she couldn't beg or plead like the others, that only the worst curses would come out, the most unimaginable hatred and bile, and damn them all, so instead she clung to her mother's side, as though she were a tiny child, and buried her face in her coat, breathed her in as she wished she had done more with Papa, while her mother and Margo and Isaac bleated the same hopeless charm that never worked.

One of the men held out his hand to Anna. She took a breath, steadied herself, and gently disentangled Alicia. At least she would not be manhandled across the street like poor Sophia. The soldier's hand was limp in hers.

He laughed, looking down at her hand in his. It spread to his colleague, who said something in Russian and shook his head. The laughter rang around the silences of the kneeling refugees and jarred against the walls of the watching houses.

'Papers,' the soldier said in Polish.

Margo ran inside, and Anna put her hands together. The sounds of an argument from Margo's house: Sammy's voice rising and being cut off by Margo's sharp exclamation. She came back with Janina's papers. 'Here,' she said, as she handed them to Anna with anxious questions in her eyes.

The man flicked through them like he was counting bank notes. 'Hmm. Only one here. You all should have registered.'

'Yes, sorry, we will,' Anna said.

'We need to know who is here. It's important to register.'

'Yes,' said Anna. She paused for a beat. 'My elder daughter – she was taken by some . . . colleagues of yours, this afternoon.'

'Hmm. Don't worry, they'll process her then she can contact you.'

The huge knot in Anna's chest unfurled one tiny fibre.

'Contact us how?'

'Okay, go, collect your things.' He gestured for them to go inside.

Anna stared at him.

'But—' she said.

'Go, go.'

Anna's legs wouldn't move. The man from the Jagiellonian who had told her of Stefan was kneeling at her feet, swaying a little. His hands were splayed either side of his knees and she saw that one of his fingers was broken.

The soldier followed her gaze and his face softened a fraction. 'You're to be sent home to Kraków today. There are trains taking you all.'

Janina gasped. 'But the Germans—'

'It's all right, it's all right there,' the soldier waved her away.

'My daughter will be sent there too? Is that where they're taking the arrested people?' Anna asked.

'Yes, yes, all the Poles are being sent that way. Come on, get your things, quickly, quickly.' He glanced at Margo, who had moved to put her arms around Alicia.

'Polish?' he called to her.

'No, no, we live here,' she said.

The soldier glanced at the house.

'Hiding illegals like your neighbour?' He nodded at two

256

colleagues, who headed towards Margo's house. She shook her head.

'Jew?' he asked, moving towards her. She hesitated, then nodded. Everyone and everything seemed still. The two soldiers returned, smooth-faced.

'Poles are to leave,' the man called. 'Jews here stay where you are.' He didn't add *for now*.

They stood facing each other like country dancers in the little front room: Margo opposite Anna, Sammy across from Alicia, Isaac from Janina.

Sammy patted Alicia's head. 'Say hello to your Papa, when you see him. Say we'll keep doing all we can for Karolina this end, though it will be easier for you there, better contacts . . .' He trailed off as Alicia regarded him coolly. 'Glad we could help, little one,' he added, offering her a smile. She gave him a tight nod. When he held out his arms she put out her hand to shake. He laughed, showing his missing teeth, and kissed it.

Janina was holding Isaac tightly. 'My lovely boy,' she said. 'My lovely, lovely boy.'

'Good luck, Mrs Kardas,' he replied, pulling himself free. 'I hope you find Aleks.'

Anna and Margo were both fumbling with Anna's coat.

'This thing!' Margo cried. 'I bought it for a wedding and the buttons have never been right—' Her voice caught and she pulled Anna into an embrace. 'I've sewn cash into all of the linings,' she whispered. As she pulled back she shook her head, so that Anna wouldn't give this away to Sammy.

'How can I ever,' Anna began, but Margo was shaking her head, tears in her eyes mirroring Anna's own, and Anna could only kiss her sister-in-law's cheek. 'Should we go?' Anna burst out. 'What if it's—'

'You don't have a choice,' Sammy said. 'They'll drag you out.'

'The stories from the others,' Anna said.

'Maybe it really is safer to go home now,' Margo said, her eyes full. 'Look what happened to Schmuel.'

Margo kissed them all as they went through the door, then turned away, unable to watch them make the short walk to the waiting truck. It was Isaac who watched them from the window, smiling and holding up a hand to Alicia when she looked back.

29

JUST AS ON the journey from Kraków, now many months before, the number of people was a comfort. Janina scanned over the lines and groups, all chattering in Polish, Kraków accents seeming to rise above the others, and felt the ground firmer beneath her feet. Their little group, even smaller without Karolina, stood on the edge, and the three of them felt a pull to the middle of the crowd, to be invisible, swallowed up, to hear stories and share theirs, to talk of home. The small front room of the house in Lwów was already dissolving. Janina looked up to a cloudy sky, flecked with blue, cold air on her cheeks. It was all going to be all, all right. Her boy would be able to find her in Kraków more easily. She should never have left.

Janina looked at the child. Girl, little woman, whatever she was now. Her unnerving stillness, her thin face. Anna had dressed her in layers again, dress under dress with the coat she'd fled in, so, as on the way from Kraków, she looked like a fat swaddled baby, until you saw her face, the sharp eyes and set of her jaw which showed she was gritting her teeth hard together. Janina didn't know if Alicia was angry or afraid. How she missed Karolina now, who could read the child as easily as any book. Still she felt a warmth for her, her calm so like Anna's. Being with them in times like this, the nervous times, was like a cold flannel pressed to the forehead in a fever. She reached for Anna's cool hand, but Anna wrenched her hand away with such force that Janina almost lost her footing.

'Sorry,' she said, for the thousandth time. Anna only stared over her head. It was better than being screamed at, called a stupid old woman. Still Janina's loneliness hollowed her out. She clasped her hands together, stroked her own thumbs against the back of her fingers. It was something she did for Aleks when he was afraid, something Laurie had done for her.

Soldiers leaned against the railings and walls of the station, smoking, smiling to each other, talking in low voices that erupted into punchlines and laughter. The drivers of the peasant carts that had brought them this far had been the same: relaxed and friendly, talking to them in accented Polish, like overfamiliar cab drivers of their life before: *Ah! You're going home! How nice for you, you must be so happy! We're happy too, fewer people to worry about! Ha ha ha!*

This along with a thousand other scraps of luck and bounty – the genteel fellow passengers, one of them from their very own neighbourhood, and he'd been living right on their street; the flecks of blue sky; the reassurance, from Sammy to the driver to the people on the cart, that Karolina would be released: *It's happening to everyone, a full pardon, an amnesty, whatever you want to call it, she'll probably be there on the train with you* – all made Janina feel the world had righted itself, and here was a day to balance out that first, terribly wrong, topsy-turvy day when they had left Kraków behind.

Anna was scanning the crowd. 'I can't see her, can you see her?' she called back to Alicia. 'Should I ask, perhaps a guard, or at the ticket office? They must have lists somewhere.' She went back to looking, pressing down on Alicia's shoulders as she rose on her heels, rotating like a lighthouse beam to find her elder daughter.

'It would be so lucky to meet her here, Anna,' Janina tried. She had to strain her voice above the crowd. 'She'll be on a different train, perhaps, they'll have sent all the arrested ones separately. There were so many. We'll meet up with her in Kraków.' The two women shared a look, the inability to imagine being home again. Who else would be back? What would life look like there now?

'I don't want to get on the train without Karolcia,' Alicia said.

'We might have to, Ala,' her mother said, a shiver in her voice.

'Without knowing where she is,' Alicia bargained.

'No, of course not,' Anna said.

But when she tried to speak to the leaning, laughing guards, they repelled her with benign force, *Oh, it's fine, it's fine, everyone, yes, everyone is returning. There's no need to check, everyone, everyone will be on the trains. Please don't worry. It's all over for you, you're going home now. Please, back over there.*

'But I can't go without knowing my daughter is safely on her way,' Anna argued. 'Please, just check the list, or tell me where to go and check.'

They took up their song of soothing cheerfulness again, but when she didn't move, one of them beckoned her, putting out his cigarette on a railing.

'What's her name?'

'Karolina Oderfeldt. She worked at the library but then she was arrested for no reason at all—'

'All right, that's all over now,' he said. He mouthed Karolina's name to himself, memorising it, and strode off to a building next to the tracks. His comrades smiled, a little shyly, at Anna, and then at each other. She'd interrupted their easy chatter. They were all too young, she judged, to have any children.

The first soldier came back quickly, a newly lit cigarette bobbing in his mouth. 'Yes, she's on the list,' he said. The others gave her wider smiles, one of them said, 'Hey, there you are!' as though she'd found a lost earring.

'Can I see the list?'

'Please, madam, just go back to your people. It's all right now. You're going home.'

The Polish crowd chattered away to itself, just as it had on the way here, different voices but finding the same old rhythm, an incessant chatter of stories – mostly between women, there were few men there – soothing and lightly self-mocking: *I would never behave so rashly, usually, but wasn't it an extraordinary week? Remember how the radio whipped everyone up – my sister is in Warsaw, she said it's practically as normal, except for, you know, perhaps the Jews, she's still going to work, I mean people will always need shoes . . .* Janina joined this hive conversation: *My son is with the army in France, he wrote to ask me to leave, of course I should have gone there to him, but then it was all so chaotic, you remember, and it will be easier to get to him from Kraków, where I know everyone, I know where to go . . .* while Anna and Alicia were part of a larger, silent group, exchanging glances and nervous smiles, those who felt worry welling inside them, those whose family or friends had disappeared. Some were simply exhausted.

Janina found herself next to a sharp-eyed woman with a pinched look that told Janina she was trying not to cry. Janina touched her arm. 'Polish?'

The woman nodded. 'Warsaw.'

'Beautiful city.'

'Yes.' She sniffed. 'You?'

'Kraków.'

'Lovely.'

Janina smiled at her, feeling more at ease every moment; they might be in line at the bakery, or younger, walking prams in the park.

'Have you . . . much news?' Janina ventured.

'The letters are so slow—'

'Oh! I know. What are they doing? Do they read them all?'

'It's a shambles. Remember how quick the post used to be?'

'When my husband was away I had a letter every week, without fail.'

'My sister writes, she's still in Warsaw, she thought I was crazy to leave.'

'And?'

'They've been moved to a new house, I'll— oh!'

Whether chattering or silent, the crowds were such that the trains weren't clearly visible until they were up close. Janina heard Anna's unmistakeable 'My God,' and realised she and Alicia were just behind her. She turned, and she and Anna shared an appalled glance.

'Oh, oh dear,' the woman from Warsaw said.

'Well, this is no good,' Janina echoed her new friend's tone. 'We should speak to someone.'

Anna put her arms around Alicia's shoulders again. She closed her eyes against the lurch of realignment, reimagining. When she opened them, saw again the dirty, rickety cattle carts, she laughed. A few around her did too.

'Now I feel foolish,' the woman from Warsaw confided to no one in particular. 'I thought it would be a proper train, like to Berlin or the French coast.'

'I was planning to order breakfast—' Anna stuttered, shocked laughter still clogging her words.

'Well, I'm not going in there,' the woman announced, and turned her heel. She gave Janina a polite nod as she left, her hat bobbing above the crowd. Alone again, Janina moved back to Anna's side.

Alicia looked up at her mother. 'We'll go back to Margo's house then?' The thought depressed her, keeping them stuck in Lwów like insects pinned to card, but there would be Isaac, and Margo to protect them from Sammy's fear. They would have to write to Papa, explain he must come to Lwów after all, and bring the dogs and her painting with him.

'But Karolina . . .' Anna felt a helpless, dull panic. What else wasn't true, in her ridiculous fantasy?

People started to step up into the cars, arrange themselves around the edges, spread blankets. The three of them were jostled and pushed.

'We'll be left behind,' Janina said. 'I'll . . . I'll see what it's like.' She held out a hand to a man in the closest car, and he pulled her up with difficulty, her long skirt catching on the edge. The floor was uneven and wooden. She could see the tracks through the slats. She dusted off her skirt and looked down at Anna and Alicia, then around the car, like a box on its side. It was filling quickly, and she pushed back to the front.

'It's . . . just wood, but . . .' she said, 'I don't know.' She looked beyond them, to the crowd surging behind. 'Well, you come up or I'll get down! We'll be separated!' she called.

Anna gave her a complicated look, both eager to be rid of her and bound to her by their months together, the simple need for the familiar in the world of strangeness. She gave one more frantic glare behind her, towards where the guards had reassured her about Karolina, then pushed Alicia towards Janina's waiting hand. With help from others in the car they pulled both of them up. People were taking off their shoes, and lining them up along the back of the car. 'We'll have this section,' a woman was saying, drawing an invisible line on the floor with her finger, and a man was folding his arms, preparing to argue with her.

Janina was aware her breath was laboured and tried to slow it, counting so that her lungs would fill more deeply. She looked up. The roof was made of the same slats as the floor, with a small square of glassless window covered with iron bars. Other gaps at the top of the walls were covered with the same bars. Janina tried to reach one and felt sick with claustrophobia when she realised she couldn't. But the front of the car, where they had come in, was completely open.

'Won't it be terribly cold?' she murmured. She moved towards the edge again, where soldiers were now leading lines of people along the tracks, towards emptier cars. She sat with her legs hanging over the edge, her ears tuning in to Anna and Alicia's low conversation.

'Why did you let her come in here with us?'

'Shush.'

'She's the reason Karolcia was taken.'

'Karolina did that to herself, too,' Anna said, shocking herself.

'Because the stupid old woman made so much noise!'

'Be quiet. You don't know everything.'

'You hate her too. You don't speak to her anymore.'

Janina tried to ignore her churning stomach. She pointed and flexed her toes, her faithful boots placed with the others. She watched the line of stragglers, unsure if she should feel superior to any who couldn't fit into the cars. She noticed the woman from Warsaw among them, red-cheeked, clutching her bag, a soldier's hand on her shoulder.

Anna copied the woman drawing invisible lines, found a space near the edge, where there would be air. 'My daughter and I will have this part,' she said, ignoring Janina as she swung her legs back, moved to the other side of the car.

It went dark.

Alicia felt it as a painting covered in black cloth. Anna, panicking, tried to picture Karolina's face, but in a nightmarish way couldn't find it for a few seconds, in the new darkness. Janina felt only cold, and a second's wild relief that perhaps it was all over at last: she waited for Laurie to come and find her. The darkness plunged them all into a silent individual confusion, locked in their own heads, unsure if their eyes were open, and then they reached out to touch each other, strangers and family alike. Then came the screeching sound of the locks, a clunk of metal and wood, and people began to cry out. Someone started to scream. Janina pitied her, and then checked her own mouth and throat with her fingers.

When they began to move, the light adjusted again, or their eyes did. The square on the roof let in some air and light, and as the train of cattle cars moved strips of sun and gloom began to ripple across their faces, calming them. They lifted their faces to it, wanting the cooler air and the slice of sky the windows promised.

Anna couldn't speak. She was frightened that someone would agree this had been a terrible mistake, a poor move in a game that couldn't be taken back, a catastrophe. But she looked around at the strangers, thought of the others, in car after car. They had all made the same choice, this was what everyone had chosen, it wasn't just her stupidity. She stretched out her legs, accidentally nudging another woman with her hip.

'How long is the journey home?' Alicia whispered, for the people in the car hadn't yet started speaking, only descended into a shocked kind of calm, now that the screams had stopped. Whispers had begun to rise in small groups, wind through a forest.

Anna found her daughter's hand. 'Maybe a week?' she whispered back.

'So we'll stop for food and walks in the air.'

'Yes,' Anna said, arching her back to breathe the fresh air that floated above their heads.

'Papa will meet us at the station.'

'Perhaps.'

'Or at the house?'

'I don't know, Alicia.'

'And Karolina too.'

'Alicia, please.' Anna felt the tiny vibrations in her chest and throat, the pain around her jaw that threatened rare tears. She hadn't cried since the night they had arrived in Lwów, in Margo's arms. She pushed the homesick thought of Margo away, how desperately she missed her. Sophia too was gone: all her helpers and protectors. They would have known what to say.

Alicia found her mother's hand. 'They'll both be there.' It could have been a statement or a question. Anna squeezed.

A rhythm of movement and sound was quick to establish itself in the car. Rattles and clinks ran through it like a talentless child practising a musical scale. The group shared shy smiles and nods, adjusted themselves. Voices from other cars were carried on the wind, wordless shouts and sometimes what sounded like names. Those who had prepared them brought out canisters of water and offered them around. Conversations sprouted, discussing the heart of their fears like small talk.

'Do you think it was a mistake?'

'I wasn't expecting them to lock the doors.'

'I thought it would be a proper train.'

One of the women stood, tall and graceful, and hooked a foot on a metal rivet, pulling herself up to look out of the window. She looked like a tourist taking in the view, relaxed, holding her blonde hair out of her face as the breeze played with it. Everyone watched her, hoping she would report what she could see, but she only laid her head on the cushion of her arm, and watched. Just as Anna was beginning to despise her, the woman curled herself back down to the floor and said, in a low voice, 'We're moving north. We aren't going to Poland.'

30

SOME PEOPLE IN the car were like saturated ground, full of too much change and shock already. The fact they were not going back to Poland after all simply sat on the surface like more heavy rain.

'My garden will be so neglected,' a woman said. 'I've been away for months now, and you can be certain none of my selfish neighbours have bothered with it, even though they promised they would.' She was the one who had drawn lines on the floor, in a family of young women. They all had the same beautiful thick black hair, and nodded along to the woman's words, murmuring about her garden: *I remember your lawn, Aunt Riane; don't you have an apple tree?*

'Didn't you hear what she said?' a man called out to them. 'Blathering on about lawns! North, she said! Didn't you hear?'

'And?' someone else snapped. 'There's a war on, in case you hadn't noticed! Don't you think there are broken rails, bombed bridges, detours?'

'I'm sorry,' said the woman who had stood up to look at the sky.

The currents of argument died down quickly and everyone returned to their little whispering groups, reassuring themselves, or sat in silence, if alone, like Janina and the man who had shouted at Riane. Soon they knocked on the adjoining walls, called through the windows to the other cars, listened to the voices in return. *Hey, what are you doing about a toilet? Hey, what did they say to you? Yes, Russia, it has to be Russia. Do you have a pipe at the back of the car? It goes directly onto the tracks . . .* They found it, erected sheets around it which they tucked into the wooden slats. Riane hung more blankets around her little set, their bare feet sticking out.

The sun was setting. Alicia watched the roof-square, the size of a sketch, turn twilight blue, then there was the warmth of that rosy light she so loved to paint in. Amid the whispering of the car, Jozef's voice came to her, to her younger self standing at the window in the apartment at home, the Wawel behind her, yesterday and a lifetime before.

'It's best at dawn, a cleaner light. Paintings made in twilight skew the colours too much,' Jozef said, but smiling, and mixing up the touches of gold for her hair or the bright red for her dress and the roses. Karolina said something in reply, something about writing in the early hours, 'Yes, clean is how I think of morning work too, the evening is for reading and editing . . .' That was probably too much, Alicia realised, but she liked to extend the sound of her sister's voice in her head.

'But we need the warmth,' Alicia had insisted. 'Dawn light is too cold,' and Jozef stopped and looked out of the window at the fading day, murmured to Karolina, 'Yes, I see what she means,' before Alicia lost him for a while as he gazed between Karolina's face, the fading light and her painting.

'Papa's waiting for us there,' she said now to her mother. 'He's in the apartment, with Janie . . . we have to get to him and to Karolcia. We'll get my painting back and then—'

'I know, darling.'

'Papa won't know where we are.'

'Yes, but he's very patient, he's waited this long, and you

mustn't worry,' Anna said, guilt squeezing her insides until she felt her stomach would disappear.

'I wish I had a sketchbook and some paints.'

The angry man, the one who had shouted, raised his voice once more. 'Paints?' he cried. 'You want to worry about food and water! Or lights, it will be dark soon! Didn't you know? Paints! Or men with guns and a noose—'

'It will be a long journey if you keep that up,' Anna said. 'Why don't you have a good yell out of the window, get it out of your system so we don't have to smother you in your sleep?'

'Mama!' Alicia said, delighted.

'As for light, it's a clear night,' came the voice of the woman who had told them they were moving north, smoothly cutting through the row. 'The moon is almost full, and will be free to shine. Look,' and her outstretched arm blocked some of Alicia's view of the sunset, 'soon it will be silvering the sky.'

Alicia stayed quiet, waiting for more.

'I'm Leo,' the woman's voice came again, nudging Alicia a little. Anna leaned over to shake her hand. 'Sorry for causing drama, only it's true. At least there's a good full moon.'

'You don't seem so worried,' Anna said.

'How do you know it's full if you can't see it?' Alicia said.

Leo shrugged to Anna's words. 'There's no point panicking. It's important,' she dropped her voice to barely a whisper, 'to accept the truth.' She nodded to where Riane and the black-haired young women were still talking feverishly about some Polish garden, its rot and trampled leaves.

'But what truth? Where are we going?' Anna said.

'Russia, you stupid bitch,' replied the shouting man. 'Didn't you know?'

A thousand old curses rose to Anna's mouth, from the days before she was married. In Kraków she would have used every ounce of influence she had to remove this man, discredit him, complain to his bosses, even destroy him. All lost to her now. She ignored him, floored by her powerlessness. Alicia imagined a giant hand ripping off the roof of the car, plucking the man out and bashing him against rocks. She mouthed along the words, *Dashed their heads against the floor as though they were puppies.*

'Be quiet, Frank,' Leo said.

'He's with you?' Anna asked.

'Not really.'

'Not really?' The car creaked as Frank came over to them, picking his way through sitting figures. He towered over Leo. 'We hid together in Lwów! We hid – unbelievable! Now you're denying you know me?'

'Don't be ridiculous, Frank. Sit down,' Leo said, in the tone of a parent on their last nerve. Frank sat.

'We hid together, we're friends,' he said. 'Didn't you know? We hid behind an oven,' he said, taking Anna's arm in confidence; she slapped him away, and he continued, in the same newly friendly tone, 'a couple from a church hid us there – so clever, they'd hollowed it out – did you know they were hanging people, taking them away and hanging them in the square? So we hid, didn't we, Leo, for weeks—'

'Frank, stop it,' Leo snapped. The car had fallen silent, only the music of the train and the voices carrying on the evening air.

'That isn't true,' Anna said, the car swaying around her, and Alicia's breaths seeming very loud next to her. 'Why did you say that? That isn't true. No one was taken to be killed.'

'Didn't you know?'

Alicia tried to stand up, but Anna held her tight. She could hear Janina whimpering. 'It isn't true – shut up, Janina! – we stayed with family and there was never *any* – they took people to police stations,' she said, looking around, but in the faded light there were only the silhouettes of faces. She leaned over to Leo. 'Make him say it isn't true,' she hissed.

'No, I won't,' the man said, in childish defiance.

'So we imagined our dead father then?' one of the dark-haired young women said to Anna, her voice stretched thin and sharp to a needlepoint.

'I – they told me the arrested ones would be on the same trains as us,' Anna said.

'Didn't you know?' Frank echoed.

'Frank,' Leo said. 'It's time for silence now. You're upsetting people and I know you don't like to.'

'But—'

'Was that silence?'

He shook his head.

'Come here and I'll talk to you about the sky.'

'But,' Alicia said. Her mother's face was stone as she looked towards Janina. 'Mama,' pleaded Alicia, feeling if she didn't have arms around her she would fly apart, out of the tiny square windows, through the bars. Anna was completely still, so Alicia went to the old woman, who flinched as she approached. 'Alicia, I—' she began. 'Oh, there, there,' she continued, as Alicia curled up next to her, under her arm. 'She's all right, I'm sure Karolina's all right.'

'I hate you,' Alicia whispered, burrowing further under her arm, wrapping herself around Janina's thick waist. 'It's your fault.'

'It's all right,' Janina said, stroking her hair. 'It's all, all right.'

Leo beckoned Frank closer to her. He sat with his legs crossed as she began, 'That star there is the North Star . . .'

A banging on the wall of the car stopped her, silenced them all, even Alicia's tears. Anna jumped out of her stillness.

'We're slowing down,' a voice called, from above.

They stood and tried to jump up to the windows, but none could reach. Leo lifted herself up again. 'Hello? Oh!' She looked down at them all. 'We're pulling into a station.' She leaned further out, and her words were carried away by the cool dusk air.

'Let my husband up to look,' a woman said, pulling at Leo's dress. She jumped down so that a heavy man could balance on the rivet, heave himself up. Their two children watched with her: they were a miracle, a complete set, like a pack of Russian dolls with none missing.

'Well?' his wife called. 'Gregor, are you going to just stare?' She hit him on the leg.

'Get off me, woman!'

'Oh get down, you great lump, let me look!'

He shook her off his leg, as hands came through the slats holding canisters. Gregor said thank you in Russian, handed them down to Leo, still standing beneath him; she opened and sniffed one. 'Soup,' she announced, to a chorus of *Oh thank God, they aren't starving us to death*, while Frank spoke through them, 'It's poison, that's how they'll do it, didn't you know?'

After the shocked quiet and false calm of the clanking train, the clamour was deafening. There were roars of anger, plaintive cries, and bangs along the cars as though they were being struck from within or without. Frank caught the idea and began kicking at the car. 'Let us out! You didn't say you would lock us in!'

'Gregor, ask them when they're opening up the car again,' his wife said.

'Is there water too?' Riane called up.

'Ask them about the arrested people,' Anna said. 'A man at the station said there was a list. Ask about the list!'

Up at the window, Gregor was asking someone, 'We were told Poland, where are we going? You said we were going home—' before he fell back, pushed by one of the bodiless hands, stumbled over Janina. A rising voice, speaking Polish, carried above the din outside the car. 'Where's your thanks? Stalin is saving your lives!'

Anna pulled herself up onto the rivet, looked out to see a twilit station, soldiers ambling down the platform, shooing small crowds that had formed around the cattle cars. She tried to twist her neck one way then another, but couldn't see far beyond the metal bars. A figure stood to one side, wearing a greatcoat, gazing across the tracks. 'Sir,' she called, 'my daughter was arrested in Lwów, and I was told she'd be on the train with us, or sent the same way, there was a list, please can I . . . sir? Hello?' Laughter was rippling down the platform, and anger chafed her. 'I just want to know where she is, my God – sir, I *know* you can hear me—'

'Careful,' Janina called up to her. 'They'll push you back down.'

A woman approached, all headscarf and yellow teeth in the near dark. Her laughter was quelled by Anna's face. She handed Anna a package.

'Don't worry, I'm sure he's taken care of your daughter too.' She nodded to the figure. Anna craned her neck again, saw the glint of the dying light against the statue she had been harassing. The ringing laughter of the passing boys in uniform made sense. She nodded a thank you to the woman and jumped down.

'Well, I made friends with Stalin,' she said, showing the package to Alicia. 'We're sure to get anything now.' Leo laughed long and deep, and the mood shifted. They had food. Anna felt she would fall to the floor and howl and then kick at the doors until they let her out to walk back along the tracks to Lwów, back to Karolina, but she sat on the floor with the others, cradling the woman's package in her lap like a baby, waiting for the canister to be passed her way. *I'm a failure*, she thought. *I have failed Karolcia every day since the moment I first held her in my arms, and I felt nothing but relief the pain was over, and now her father is in France with his lover and son, and she has only me, and here I am being pulled away from her and she's in a cell somewhere and—*

'What's inside?' Leo asked, gently prising the package from Anna's grip. She had torn the paper a little, and Leo tugged at it. Inside was a pack of cards and some cigarettes. Some pamphlets in Russian, which Leo threw to the side. They had no matches, so the car took turns smelling the tobacco.

'We could chew it, like Americans,' Janina said.

'And spit out black bile all over the sheets and blankets?' Anna snapped, and Janina was quiet, went back to sniffing the cigarette, rolling it around in her fingers.

'We could ask for a match, at the next station,' Frank said. 'And set a fire!'

'No, Frank,' Leo warned.

'What, it's wood, isn't it?' He tapped the floor. 'Then they'll let us out, for air, they'll have to!'

'Or let us burn and suffocate,' Janina said. 'Sorry,' she added, for this had prompted a chorus of *Mamas* from two young boys, and the woman in charge of them had begun singing to distract them. 'I always say the wrong thing.'

Janina sipped the lukewarm soup. It was like in Lwów, endless watery baby food, pap and grey vegetables. Still, she thought, eyeing the lumps in the broth, someone had chopped these, and warmed them for the strangers in the cars, even if only under orders, checked and stirred and poured for them. That gave her comfort; she sent up a silent thanks to the stars beyond the barred windows.

By the middle of the next day they had realised no one was coming to open up the car, and their faces turned inward, categorising each other, making mental notes of names and groups. They were made up of three families and three strays: Janina (whom Anna enjoyed savagely cutting out of her own family group in her mind), Leo and Frank, whose early anger Anna quickly realised was from a terror more profound than the rest of them put together. He was a tall, timid creature, jumping at unexpected bangs from down the cars, and the only one to refuse to stand up to the windows at stations: 'You'll see, they'll shoot us through those, that's what they do with cattle, didn't you know, that's what the windows are for . . .' This was his verbal tic: didn't you know? *Didn't you know they'll execute everyone, this is for the newsreels, this part, didn't you know? Didn't you know that Stalin and Hitler had an agreement, and we're all being drafted into the Russian army as soon as we arrive? Yes, even the children! Didn't you know?* Every few hours he would start weeping, using up precious rags to blow his nose. The only person who could calm Frank down was Leo, who sat with him sometimes, talking in soothing tones about what constellations might be out that night, or the phases of the moon. She whispered to the car when Frank was asleep or behind the sheets in the corner of the car, 'He's different, I'm sure you've noticed, he's like a child, a frightened child, please be patient with him, if he shouts . . .'

Leo was everyone's favourite. A German astronomer, at night she talked about the stars they could sometimes see glinting through the high windows. If there were no stars, she would talk about the importance of things that could not be seen, the forces high beyond the stars, the vast expanse of the whole of what was to be found if you kept on going up and up. She had a beautiful voice and spoke in the gentle, lazy way of one completely relaxed, which Anna liked about her. She warmed to her still more when she discovered that Leo, belying her smooth skin and thin waist and the pert breasts that showed under her thin cotton dress, was forty-five. She loved to hear about the huge open spaces beyond the wooden roof of the car, beyond the sky.

31

WITHIN A WEEK, stomachs cramped and skin sweated and fevers flared up and died down, passing from car to car, creeping in through the windows or in the food passed through the bars at stations. Soon the faces of the car became as familiar as a neighbourhood they had all lived in for years. While the Bernardyńska set, and even the street in Lwów became faded and hazy around the edges, so that Anna had to work hard to recall the names of people she had dined with, whose daughter married whom, or even the exact pitch of Margo's voice, the world shrank to these fifteen: the curves of their faces, the shape of their hands, the exact shape of this one's nose, that one's crooked teeth. She vomited through the pipe and onto the tracks while Riane held her hair. Anna tipped water onto Frank's lips, when he was so dehydrated he became disorientated and weak. Janina crouched in a corner, her head on her knees, like a dying animal, and Leo dabbed her face with the bottom of her dress, smoothed her hair. They fell into a comradeship of near silent nursing and wiping and gentle sounds of comforting each other.

As the first wave of sickness died down, Alicia lay with her head in Anna's lap. Anna stroked her daughter's hair, her nails scratching the scalp a little too hard, Alicia's neck bent too far around. The ache in her back was so sharp, the skin so hot, she only vaguely registered the pain in her neck. Her bladder throbbed in sickening pulses and where she had begun distracting herself by counting them, now she could only breathe and swallow, trying not to vomit. Her view of the truck was distorted into patterns of light and shade, shocks of harsh colours when the pain peaked. At first she had sat on the pipe, cold air on her thighs, and wept as the burning came. ('Oh, I know!' Frank called. 'Like pissing knives, I know! Don't tell me, stop whimpering, girl, it's the same for all of us!') Within hours, she was shaking in Janina's lap, her whole abdomen aflame, until her mother had reclaimed her, pulled her to her side of the car and their awkward embrace.

She fell into a fever dream of her painting. That dress, clean and thick, the velvet against her skin; she could still remember the way, if she ducked her head to rub her chin on her shoulder, it would feel soft and rich against her skin. In her mind's eye she returned again and again to the way the painting glowed red and gold, how Uncle Stefan had told her it would hang in a gallery some day, her name on a bronze plaque. She remembered how she'd wanted her Papa's attacker to see it and be afraid. Somehow, he'd become the first chink in the smooth wall of their old life, pried it open with his dirty, angry hands, let the others – the soldiers, the guards, the men in uniforms, it was always men in uniforms – pour through, erasing Papa and Karolina as they swept through their lives, wrecking and trampling everything. But the painting was still intact somewhere; her younger, richer, happier, smoother, cleaner, well-fed, spoiled face was hanging on a wall, or propped against a bookcase, or laid flat, wrapped in tissue paper, ready to be unwrapped again by careful hands; somewhere, those men in uniforms were looking at Alicia-in-paint, thinking, *These are important people, these are famous people, save those ones, and save the painter too, he's an artist* . . . and someone would go to Jozef's cell, and apologise, release him, and Stefan too, once Jozef intervened. This was the reverse-dominoes she imagined hour after hour, a reversal of the collapse, all because of the painting, finally fulfilling its role, as Uncle Stefan had promised.

'She needs water,' Anna said.

And so the small rations of water were passed, uncomplaining, towards them. Even the little boys in the miracle family. Anna passed those back. The water was warm and metallic, dripping down the back of Alicia's throat. It joined the pulsing in her stomach, rising and falling until she vomited it up again, coloured spots dancing across her vision.

Anna called to the next car. 'A doctor, we need a doctor for my daughter, pass along.'

'We all need doctors, woman,' came a gruff reply.

'She has an infection and she's really sick, please.'

Anna could have imagined the call being taken up, passing down the cars; it could have been only the rush of air and her own panic.

As they pulled into a new station, Leo and Janina took turns to stand up at the rivet, calling for help. Leo bellowed in Russian, 'There's a sick child, a sick girl in our car,' but it got lost in the other voices, other calls of sickness and wounds and *give us more water* and *how long will it be now?* She stepped down, and Janina got up to beat at the bars with a canister, but it was a tiny tinkling chime in a whole orchestra. She looked down at Alicia, small and curled up in her mother's lap, her face blank, her eyes open but seeing elsewhere, lost in a world of a fever that wouldn't break. Anna caught her eye, and there was none of the rage of the days since Karolina had gone. There was appeal, and terror, and something of the days they had reached for each other in the street in Kraków, trying to speak of real things among shoes and gossip, and of the day they fled, holding each other in the sea of people. Janina turned again and screamed into the night, straight from her belly, her lungs full: 'Help! Help! Help!' She abandoned every-thing but her raised voice, shooting straight through the bars, cutting through the other voices, the rhythms of queries and complaints. A soldier came towards them. He tapped his rifle on the bars.

'Hey. Quiet now, old woman,' a voice came in Russian, and Janina heard only the sense of his words, a dismissal. She reached out of the bars, grasped and found cloth. A shocked cry came out as she tugged and screamed again, 'Help us! Help! Help!' A crack as he dropped the rifle and his head con-nected with the bars. Her hand was wrested away, a painful grip on her wrist.

'Stupid old bitch!' More men came. Janina's courage drained. She stepped down, backed away. The men's eyes were wide through the bars, looking down at the people below. One of the little boys started crying, the other watching him in wide-eyed toddler disdain as he chewed on his mother's hand.

Janina began gibbering, 'I was trying to help. I was trying to help.'

Voices called down. 'Hey. Hey! Who was that just attacked me? Where is she?' A collective gasp came up from the car as a shock of flashlight beamed in, whipped around them.

'Please,' Anna whispered. Then tried again, found her voice, though she spoke to the floor. 'My daughter is sick.'

'Quiet, quiet!' Frank said. 'They'll kill us all, didn't you know?' Leo shushed him, reached for Janina's hand. Anna did too, gently lying Alicia's hot one in her lap, so they held Janina between them. She felt the bucking pulse of Janina's wrist, and her own heart quickened still more. The flashlight dis-appeared, and in the gloom Anna took Janina's hand, kissed it. Janina kissed Anna's cheek. 'It's all right,' they whispered to each other.

The screech of metal and wood was a shockwave through the car: they cried out, and huddled together, as the doors were wrenched open. There was the world: a station platform, a rush of cool air, floodlights beyond the station showing the tips of woodland. Leo took a long gulping look at the sky, but the lights were too bright to trace the stars. A boy in soldier's uniform stood with his arms crossed in petulant fury, while three others shone torches into the car. A small crowd of sol-diers and civilians milled up and down the platform, large Alsatian dogs on chains barking into the night. The air was full of smoke and petrol.

'Is that child dead? That one, dead?' one of the men called, shining his beam on Alicia's limp form.

'Oh my God, is she?' shrieked one of Riane's girls, and there was a scramble away from the car, a collective recoil, but the soldiers held up their hands, and everyone stopped.

'What . . . what did he say?' Anna said.

'No, she's sick,' Leo called, in answering Russian. 'We've been asking for a doctor.'

'Where's that old woman that attacked me?' the boy called. He pointed theatrically to his head, a small stream of blood. He drew a finger across his temple, held it up in indictment, the red inky stain. 'Come on out, you old bitch!'

'I'm sorry, I'm sorry,' Anna whispered. Her breath, on Janina's face, was somehow still sweet. 'I – Janina, I'm so, so sorry, oh my God, I'm sorry—'

'Thank you for trying to help me, for bringing me with you,' Janina whispered, as she unknotted Anna's fingers from her own, one by one, as she had used to do when Aleks gripped the railings outside school, frightened of bullies.

'I'm so sorry about Karolina,' she added. She once more held the smooth cool skin before laying Anna's hand back on Alicia's form. As she stood, Anna called, 'Wait,' and others stood, blocking her way, trying to explain, but the torchlight was on her face, and the boy she had hurt stood grim-faced, triumphant. 'It was an accident, it was an accident,' Anna cried, with all the authority of her old self. 'She was trying to get help for my daughter!' The men broke their stare, spoke to each other, and it seemed for a moment that the nightmare months had fallen away, that Anna could save her by sheer will, by the force of her outrage, as though they were simply young, offensive boys in Kraków; their mothers would be furious, *That's a dear friend of the Oderfeldts you were rude to, do you want your father to lose his business deal?* But then the boy beckoned Janina again, and all the fantasy protection fell away. Anna faded from her as she picked her way through the figures in the car.

So, it's to be a Russian prison, Janina thought, as the boy led her away from the platform, Anna's cries still carrying across the air. *I can write to Aleks from there*, she thought, the boy's rifle in the small of her back, small shouts from the other cars, as they noticed her, calls of *what are you doing?* As they stepped further away from the floodlights of the station, the expanse of air and sky above her, she thought, *It might be better, I'll be alone, but I won't be in that damned car full of vomit and stench . . .* As she was pushed to her knees, she thought, *Perhaps they'll send me back to Kraków after all.* As they told her to look ahead, cold steel against the back of her neck, Janina's last thought was of her own apartment, the little chair by the window, Aleks's photographs, her china set with hot bubbling coffee, Laurie working at his desk, turning to smile at Aleks playing with his toy soldiers on the floor, and she almost sobbed with relief and contentment, as though waking from the worst of dreams.

Chelyabinsk, 1940

32

THE GUNSHOT didn't sound right, dull and quick as a dropped brick. Anna replayed it anyway, over the next days and weeks of the journey, as the car doors were relocked and the train trundled on, leaving Janina behind. To the gunshot memory-sound Anna added the thundery echoing she had always imagined, and soon expanded into deeper daydreams, in which she and Janina had a longer goodbye, more time to explain, then still wilder ones, in which the car door opened and they all rushed out, crushing the guards and running away into the woods. Had she really sat motionless on the floor, while Janina was taken away?

At the next station, she traded her shoes for some apples. 'If you want fruit, I just showed you how to get some yourselves,' she snapped, when hands stretched out towards her in the car. The air was warming, and the apples were cold and sharp. She chewed off chunks to give to Alicia, who sucked on them like sweets.

Over the days and weeks Alicia's eyes refocused, her swollen abdomen and poker-hot skin receded back into pale, thinner flesh. When Alicia's eyes scanned the car for Janina in the dim light, her mother only shook her head, and Alicia said, 'I thought I dreamed it.'

'No.'

Alicia took another sip of water, let savage thoughts run through her: *Karolcia was her fault, so it's right.* But Janina's familiar old face, her puckered, frightened eyes, the way she had looked up at them from the mud outside Kraków, her quiet sewing, her silent language of looks with her mother, even her cold apartment at home, the hot chocolate and pastries . . . she had been one of them and now she was lying dead somewhere.

'Mother.'

'Do you need more water?'

'Are they going to shoot us?'

Frank inevitably fell into a track of *didn't you knows*, shouted down by the others, while Anna stared at her daughter. The commotion died down again as they strained to listen to a message being passed from truck to truck. A new station was approaching.

Leo spoke Anna's lines, 'Janina was trying to help you, but she accidentally hurt one of the soldiers, and they had to take her away, probably only to prison for a little while, or to send her home or back to Lwów, you know? But we are all co-operative and there's no reason for them to hurt any of us, why go to all this expense of the trains and so on, why feed us and give us water? Think, child.' She shushed Frank as he muttered, 'It's for the newsreels, didn't you see the photographers and the cameras?'

Alicia only looked at her mother. Anna could make out her sharp face made still sharper by her weight loss, her deflated cheeks that Adam had so doted on and loved to pinch and kiss. Her recent illness had turned the whites of her eyes more sallow, almost yellow, and her hair was scraped back from her face, from the worst of the fever, held in a strip of fabric torn from Janina's dress. Under her clothes, Anna knew, under her thin and flaking skin, the wasting muscles, Alicia's bones were sore and her organs as old and sluggish as an old woman's. She felt seized with the layers of loss she tried so often not to look at, this one buried so deep under the obvious absences, spaces where the others should be. Who Alicia would have been was gone, and here was this creature in her place, hard and angry and confused. 'I don't know,' she finally replied, and Alicia met her honesty with a tiny nod, before curling up again to rest.

They arrived in midsummer. The shock of the opened car doors, air rushing in and bathing them all in what felt like cool water, kept them all static for a moment, before the blinking and squirming against the fierce light began, the turning away of faces, the pressing shut of eyes. All around was the sound of the doors opening, and the rising smells of bodies long packed in boxes and sent on rails across countries through a hot season. New guards beckoned them down, held out arms for them to jump. They were in different uniforms again, with gentle hands. There were few voices. People clustered together, holding hands, eyeing the strangers from the other trucks, whom they knew only by voice.

The beauty of the landscape was a shock. Alicia readjusted her mental image, the Russia she'd seen in her mind's eye, populated by the conversations on the journey, was from fairy tales: snowy, with palaces and bare forests, bears and frozen streams. Instead, here was a wheat field, whispering under the sun, a forest beyond, green and lush. Tall grasses rippled like a lake. They'd all assumed they would know when arrival was near by the cold. Instead the sky, still and high, was the richest blue, and so clear that a crescent moon sat in the exact shape Leo had described only the night before. Alicia let her eyes bathe in the blue of the huge dome of sky, noticed the deepening of it towards the horizon, the way the white speckles of cloud, almost invisible, seemed to dissolve into the sapphire and lighten it, as though really paint. All this she didn't think in words but saw as a composition: the flecks and smudges of paint. Karolina would have found the right words.

'Is this Russia?' Alicia found the courage to ask her mother, once she had torn her eyes from the sky.

'It must be,' Anna said. 'It doesn't seem so bad.'

'It's a trick,' Frank said. 'Didn't you know?'

'Like Circe's island,' Leo said to Alicia, smiling, but she ignored this; they needed to stay alert. She rifled through her mind for any helpful lies. Who should they ask about Karolina and Papa, and what story might send a thread back into Europe to find them?

'Is there water?' Anna asked a passing guard. She shifted her weight from bare foot to bare foot.

The guard looked surprised, smiled vaguely. Leo repeated the question in Russian, and added, 'It's hot, and we're thirsty,' as she stroked her throat, arching her neck a little. Her blonde curls, stunning even unwashed and unbrushed, fell down her back. The guard gawped at her, and Anna caught Leo's eye, suppressing a smile. Once she'd have done the same, but the journey had made her feel detached from her body, which, besides, was a thin, old, broken and sour-smelling thing now. One of her powers, maybe her only power, was gone. The guard started to answer Leo in a stutter, but then they were all caught in a current of voices and movement, guards herding the refugees through the long grass, calling to them in Russian, *This way, this way.* The grasses waved over their heads, soughed in the breeze, and it was blessedly cool in their shade. The refugees still held on to each other, making chains that flattened paths through the grass. Alicia let her eyes drink in the shifting shades of green. She'd been starved of colour for so many weeks. Through the grass came disembodied calls, always from the guards. Alicia understood the word *Moscow*.

She touched Leo's arm. 'What are they saying?'

She imagined stumbling out of the grass into one of the huge Moscow squares, ten times bigger than Glowny, or turrets of Russian fairy-tale palaces glinting in the sun over the crest of a hill.

Leo turned back to her, breaking her hand away from Frank's in front of her, and using it to wipe at her underarms. Alicia noticed that they were soaked in sweat. She cocked her head to catch the calls, floating across the grass like strange birdsong.

'This is where you are going to live now,' Leo translated. 'We're building a new, second Moscow.'

They came out of the long grass first, emerging like woodland sprites, holding hands. A set of simple barracks. Wildflower meadows stretching behind, towards more forests. There was a low hum, a bees' nest somewhere nearby. The sun seemed swollen and close, throbbed against the white walls of the barracks and their own hatless heads. The others from the cattle cars stayed in their clusters, at the edge of the long grass, beginning to talk to each other, relaxing a little since it was quiet, and the guards weren't shouting, and they didn't have guns. They began fanning themselves, stripping off layers. People began asking for water and shade.

There were still more guards, different uniforms again, more men, more papers, more arms held stiffly behind backs, shoulders pushed back, saluting each other, nodding to each other, talking to each other in a secret language, relaxing and taking out a cigarette when they heard some magic password. How ridiculous they all are, wherever you go, Anna thought, here are more boys dressing up in costumes, playing at a game, thousands, millions of them everywhere, all playing a long stupid game, and here we are again trying to find out the rules and the magic words. Some secret dance was happening between the ones who took them from the trucks and the new guards, a reporting, a deference from one set to another. The refugees watched, trying to decipher it. Eventually another secret signal happened, like chemicals passed between bees in a hive, and the new guards all snapped to attention, began marching around in their stupid way. The first set scurried to stand with the refugees, and they gestured for them to line up outside the large, central barracks building. This was a dance they all knew by now, almost comforting in its familiarity; everyone had survived at least one of these dances, and those with papers dug them out, those with stories to rehearse began running through the details of the narrative in their heads.

Frank was in full flow. 'They're going to line us all up and shoot us, didn't you know? I know, I know,' he said, lurching towards one of the guards, and striking his own temple with a forefinger. 'I know, I always knew! We should never have left Lwów, I knew you were all liars! Hmm? Hmm?' His thin body was curled down towards the face of the guard, who was laughing at him. Leo's hands pulling him back made no difference.

'That man,' Anna muttered, but her traitor heart had quickened all the same; the blood rushing to her head made her dizzy. Leo looked around to her in appeal, and both Anna and Alicia helped drag Frank back. Leo began walking him up and down the line like an agitated horse. The laughing guard stepped towards Anna, another man following him.

'He's crazy,' he said, in patched-together, heavily accented Polish. 'Why'd they bring you all this way to shoot you?'

'There are lots of Poles here, and Jews,' his friend added, in smoother Polish. 'You'll feel at home.'

'This is best time to arrive,' the first man said, and his colleague added, 'Yes, yes, the summer. We came in the winter—'

'The winter!' his colleague rejoined.

'Oh my God!' and they laughed. It was a well-oiled conversation, and they let it run, while Alicia and Anna stood stupefied:

'Oh, just you wait!'

'You won't believe it—'

'You think Poland is cold—'

'But we survived it—'

'It won't kill you.'

'It isn't so bad.'

'Don't look so frightened.'

Leo and Frank returned. Frank had subsided into a mumbling, agreeing conversation with himself.

The laughing man placed a hand on Frank's shoulder, making them all jump.

'Really, friend. They won't hurt you. Look, they don't care about the papers here, or anything. When I was deported I had just the clothes on my back. They don't care here, they just want you to work.'

Lots of the refugees had made the same mistake, and realised around the same time. Some bilinguists on both sides helped, but most understood from watching how the new guards moved along the lines, and how the men who had brought them from the train tracks lowered their eyes, sometimes, or nodded in recognition: whether defiant or deferential, both told the story of a long relationship of prisoner and guard.

'You came through Belarus? That's where I'm from,' the laughing man said, falling into easy conversation, though none of them were replying. 'It's beautiful, no? Did you see the landscape, all the wildflowers?' He directed the last question to Alicia, who shook her head, her stomach still too tight to speak.

'Well, was it Belarus, or not?'

Alicia was saved by the line moving forward again, just as Anna snapped, 'We don't know, we were locked in a cattle truck.' She added, after Leo shot her a warning glare, 'Thank you for speaking in Polish. I can understand some Russian, but—' but the men were drifting away, to talk to other, more interesting newcomers, to ask to trade, sweets or cigarettes or the playing cards they had been given at this station or other, and to ask, urgent in their homesickness, the bewildered new arrivals about the wildflowers of Belarus, the exact shade of the poppies.

33

ALICIA HAD TRIED TO keep up her nightly ritual, reaching for Karolina's mind across countries, passing over fields and towns and marching men, to find her and scoop her up and take her to the apartment on Bernardyńska, but once in Russia she lost the habit. Even in the cattle car, before the infection seized her, it had felt possible to create an invisible barrier between herself and the other bodies, root into the wooden floor, close her eyes and begin travelling through her mind. Here, adults and children slept together in one long bunk. She was sandwiched between Leo and her mother. Every time someone moved, which was often – scratching, slapping at insects, rolling over, kicking each other – everyone would wake, a collective moan rising, until uneasy, restless quiet returned, all of them staring into the gloom and the long hours of thinking, wishing for morning to come.

They lost the first day and night to the confusion of ringing bells, the queue for the breakfast ration, small feuds over soup bowls, soap, registration. There were fresh papers, stamped and with neat writing in capitals, that declared who was to work and where; soon the days were carved up into labour shifts.

'I haven't been given anything,' Alicia said one early morning, watching the others wrap cloth around their hands. 'What are you doing?'

'They haven't given us any gloves for building this new Moscow,' Leo said, smiling. 'It won't take long for the skin to crack.'

Anna reddened a little as she pulled on her own gloves, brought from Lwów. 'We can share these,' she offered, when Leo looked at her. 'Alicia, you'll be going to school.'

'Oh! Nice for her,' Frank said. 'Sit in a room all day, easy! But, it will be to teach you to be a soldier for Stalin's army, didn't you know? They'll probably give you a gun to train with, you should—'

He was cut off by Leo's hand on his arm, as the others in the barracks had started to turn and look at him, to shift glances to the guards standing by the door. 'Any patterns this morning?' she asked Frank, taking his hands in hers and tying the fabric into a knot over his knuckles. He twisted to look at his leg. 'Hmm. Maybe . . . maybe that one could be a bit of Orion . . .'

She looked. 'Oh! Yes, look there's his belt . . . what do you have, Anna?'

'See for yourself,' Anna said, holding out her arms, covered in the same red lumps.

'Hmm, if I trace this one I can see a gibbous moon.'

Alicia began to scratch at her own bites, but her mother slapped her hand. 'Do you want an infection?'

'Will they give me a gun?' *Frank's right*, Alicia thought. *I should, I should, I should. I'll hold a gun to a man's head and make him drive a train all the way back home.*

Anna tutted. 'They'll probably teach you some Russian.' Anna inspected her own arm. 'God, can't we ask the guards for something acidic, some lemon, to wash the sheets in?'

All of them, even Alicia, laughed at her, and Anna felt small, as though she'd opened a door in her old apartment, talking with Dotty or Janie, and walked through into this camp, still wearing her satin dress and holding her silver cigarette holder, continuing the conversation.

A bell rang and the adults stood.

'Where do I go?' Alicia asked. 'Where do we go?' she called to a boy around her age, on the next bunk. He glared at her and Anna turned Alicia by the shoulder.

'He'll be working too,' she whispered. 'I told them you were younger. You can pass for it,' she stumbled a little, struck afresh by Alicia's drab little body, young and old all at once. 'If they ask you're eight.'

'*Eight?*'

'Hush!'

'Tonight we'll try putting the legs of the bed in cups of water,' Leo said, as they filed out.

'They'll just climb on the ceiling and parachute onto the bed,' Frank replied.

Leo seemed animated by the idea of an experiment. 'We'll test it, see if it works, then we'll compare bites tomorrow.'

In the yard, guards strolled about in the sunshine, directing workers into groups. There had been a new train of arrivals that morning and they were queuing, huddled together and confused, to be processed. Alicia thought they seemed to be pulled from a different painting using darker, murkier paints; their clothes were dull against the bright day, the white of the processing office.

Anna impulsively gathered Alicia back to her, clutched at her shoulders, watching the same queue. She'd felt so clever making sure Alicia was saved from whatever terrible labour was in store for them, but now – seeing the line of people fresh from the miserable train, all the security of the last days: *We have arrived, so we are here, the worst is perhaps over, and so we'll*

*work but it could be worse and we have roofs over our heads and
they give us soup* – it all fell away and she felt yet again like a
lumbering idiot who threw her children into harm again and
again. Who was to say the school, the labour, any of it, was
even real? Who was to say they wouldn't just take them into
the woods and shoot them, like Janina? She caught Frank's
eye, but he was waving and smiling at the new arrivals, seeming for once to have lost his anxieties. Alicia twisted to look
up at her.

'What is it?'

'I just . . . I'm just not sure if . . .' She was winded by
an unexpected and savage certainty that Karolina and Adam
were dead. She gripped Alicia's shoulders tightly as a guard
approached. 'I think you should stay with us after all,' she
said. The guard was inspecting a clipboard, calling out names.
Leo and Frank, Riane and the others from the car fell into line
as the man spoke in Russian and Leo murmured translations
under her breath. 'We're going to chop trees, build more barracks, more people are coming . . .'

'Mama, you're going to chop trees?' Alicia felt she might
laugh, but her mother's face stopped her, closed and afraid.

'At least the sun is shining,' Leo said.

Alicia's name was being called by a tiny woman with hair
cut short like a boy's, wearing trousers and a jacket covered
in badges. She looked out of place among the guards, but
marched around with a whistle just the same, calling out
names, each name followed by a whistle blast, a strange dis-
cordant song across the yard.

'I think you should stay with us,' Anna said again, as Alicia
moved towards her.

'I don't want to chop down trees,' Alicia said. The guard
noticed her then.

'Are you with us? Name?' he barked in Polish. 'Go, go, over there,' he added, as the tiny woman approached. Leo took Anna's arm as they were led away, whispered, 'It's all right, best she doesn't come with us, it isn't going to be easy.' Anna stared hard at the short, stern woman who was corralling Alicia into a small crowd of children, holding up her hand for silence. Leo pulled her away, reading her thoughts. 'She's just a young girl,' she soothed.

The school was a warm wooden hall, with rows of low desks with a hole in the corner for inkpots; there were no inkpots or pens, so instead they sat and listened and tried to remember things.

The tiny woman from the yard who had led the new children to join a class of twenty or so stood at the front. She spoke in Russian, but slowly, and with a gentle smile, with a hand raised towards the newcomers, as though to say, *Don't panic, you will understand soon.* As she spoke she made elaborate, slow gestures, to herself ('Ursula'), pointing down to the floor, meaning here ('Chelyabinsk . . .'), and raising her hands she cocked her head for her new pupils to repeat the name of the place they found themselves cast out to, pulled away from home by an unexpected riptide. The other pupils sat low in their seats, hands under their bottoms, as though afraid they would be led away somewhere. The youngest tottered about and held onto the desks, pulled books from the sparse shelves. Ursula ignored them, and soon they were asleep on a thin rug placed at the back of the room.

Alicia sat in silence, soaking this in, wondering how soon she could ask for painting supplies and sketchbooks. There was one painting on the wall, of Stalin. His eyes had been lightened by a good speckle of white paint, a technique

Jozef could do better. It was easy to make eyes in paint sparkle like that.

In her portrait, Jozef had changed her eyes, made the dark brown parts almost fill her whole eye, just small dots of white in the corners, and again in the centre. He'd shown her, one of those last days of the summer, before Papa came back from France, the smell of paint and sweetened ice tea in the air, and Mama's perfume, and roses, wilting and dying in the heat. Jozef's hands had been steady on her shoulders, steered her this way, then that. 'See how your paint-eyes follow you?'

'They don't look like mine.'

'Too much brown, you think.' He was biting the inside of his cheek a little. He seemed pleased; the conversation was taking the direction he hoped for. This usually meant he was going to teach her a technique, and she smiled.

'Yes, too much brown.'

'Karolina thought so too.'

'They don't look like my real – like any real eyes.'

'No, but look at the whole. Here, step back.' She did, and saw how the darkness in her paint-eyes picked up the brown of the chair and the depth of the colour in the answering corner.

The deep pools of brown there made the light on the skin and hair sing. The eyes were two globes of light. And always there was the red of the dress, everything else in the painting polishing it to make it bright.

'It isn't a photograph,' Jozef reminded her. 'It's an image that uses illusion to be more real. Do you understand?'

She shook her head; she was always honest with Jozef when she didn't understand. He tried again. 'So your eyes don't look like this in real life, fine. But . . .'

'It makes the red and the light look better.'

'Yes, yes . . .' he smiled down at her, pleased she was following that far. 'But it's more than that too. Look at her. The extra colour in the eyes, there. That's how I show the depth. That's where the cleverness is.'

Ursula spotted Alicia looking into Stalin's eyes, wondering who painted him, wondering if that painter had the same idea, to tell the truth through a fiction. She marched to Alicia's desk and Alicia stiffened, prepared to be castigated for half-listening, and ready to adopt the sweet, dull persona that had been useful with some governesses in the past. But Ursula was smiling, and came to stand with her hands on Alicia's shoulders. She spoke in fluent Polish, addressing the whole class.

'The eyes of this young lady have found the most important person in the room. Your hero, father and the man who has brought you here to save you and care for you, as he saves and cares for all of us.' She moved back to the front of the class, under the portrait, which Alicia saw now was in poorly mixed colours, a dullness to the skin, a waxiness that suggested cheap paint. Ursula continued, beaming, looking like those in the grip of religious fever, keen to pass on the good news, who would call from house to house and street to street sometimes (Robert had indulged them on the doorstep in Bernardyńska, but Janie would close the door in their faces.), 'Dear Stalin will take care of you and send you gifts. When you need something, pray to Stalin. Try praying to God: you'll see you get nothing. Then pray to Stalin and see what happens!' She wrung her hands together in joy. 'You are so very, very lucky. So, let's begin! I will switch to Russian, but don't be frightened.' And she went back to the slow, calm rhythm of the Russian, writing some words on the board in chalk, which they couldn't copy, but traced on the wooden desks with their fingers.

There were no other children from the school in her barracks and the others weren't yet back from work duty: Alicia had a dizzying few minutes of being alone for the first time in many months. She lay on her bunk, feeling the crawling sheets beneath her and watching the weakening light move across the ceiling. Her arms were pinned to her sides by habit and she felt cold, missing a hand on her from Karolina or her mother or Janina. Papa. He felt far away and vague, the edges of him blurring.

Ursula had given them all sweets as they left, 'from Stalin.' Alicia ran her tongue along her teeth to taste the sugar. Papa's face came back, and the thousand things that made him real and living for her as she lay alone: the tickle of his beard, his way of throwing out his hands when he spoke, how she could catch him gazing in admiration at her mother when he thought no one was looking, the feel of his fingers inside mittens clasped around her own. Hope swam through her limbs and she felt strong for the first time since the train. This was fine. Sitting in a warm room every day and pretending to love Stalin: she could do that, that was easy. They'd wait out the war here at the edge of the world, and then they would gather up all their lost people and lost things and carry them home.

Frank shook her awake. 'They're feasting on you!' he mumbled. He seemed drunk, stumbling towards the bed. Alicia brushed lice from her bare legs and sat up. Frank still loomed over her, but behind him men and women were shuffling in, some bent almost double.

'Where's my mother?'

Frank collapsed next to her on the bunk, held an arm over his face. Alicia spitefully poked a sunburned cheek and he slapped her away, grunted and turned over.

More weight on the bunk made Alicia turn to see her mother and Leo. They'd both sat down on its edge, hanging their heads as though they had been given terrible news. Leo was breathing smoothly but Anna's breaths were ragged and she was murmuring.

'Mama,' Alicia said, and went to kneel so she could look into her face. A vivid bruise was just beginning to find its colours along her mother's cheek. Anna's eyes were closed and it seemed she would sleep where she sat, she and Leo leaning into each other. The others were the same, dropping onto bunks or some simply curling up on the floor. 'God,' they were muttering. 'God, God.'

'Mama,' Alicia repeated, and took her mother's hand to shake her awake; she jumped as her mother yelped. 'Sorry!' she cried, seeing the raw flesh she'd touched.

'Ach, oh it stings,' Anna murmured. 'Oh Alicia, get some water, so I can bathe them . . .'

'No,' Leo murmured. 'Let's just sleep, sleep and they'll heal. Don't send her out.'

Anna's eyes focused on Alicia's face. 'Were they kind to you at the school?'

Alicia shrugged. Her mother's face crumpled and she pitched forwards, her face in her hands. She whispered through snot and tears, 'Oh God, what did they do? What happened?'

Alicia spoke over her in a tumble of words, 'Nothing, nothing, it was only strange and boring, they gave us sweets. Who hit you?'

'Bed,' Leo said, but Anna had already tipped backwards so she lay with her head cradled on Frank's legs, as soon as she had absorbed Alicia's words, her face still wet.

'Tomorrow she must wear these all day,' Leo muttered, peeling the gloves, wincing, from her own hands as she curled up too.

'Then they'll get stuck to the flesh and we'll have to rip them off,' Alicia said, feeling she had stolen Frank's voice and should add *didn't you know?* But Leo was already asleep, the whole room but Alicia lost in dreamless exhaustion within minutes.

Anna could not believe she had been so undone, after everything, by broken skin. The sting and chafe were so relentless the first weeks that she would stop to check her palms, expecting to see the white glint of bone. She dwelled on the other pains to distract herself, as she pushed the wheelbarrow of soil or rocks: the ache in her back, the sun burning her scalp and nose, the blisters on her feet. But her hands screamed and screamed at her and she would put down whatever she carried and cradle them or hold the flesh against the cool skin on her arm until a guard came. On lucky days, she sat in circles with the others, sorting broken bricks into useable piles or ones to be broken still more to make dash for fortifying walls, and after a string of lucky days her hands began to heal, and then harden. She and Leo took silly pride in their new workman's hands.

'Look at that callus. I'm proud of that one.'

'Feel mine,' Anna said, holding her palm up to Leo's cheek.

'Like a wooden puppet!'

'Like marble!'

'Ask your friend Stalin where *your* statue is.'

And so they found again the world that had fallen away beneath their feet rearranged itself again, and what had seemed impossible, day after day of that work, became somehow normal and they could even laugh again.

Soon Anna turned brown in the sun, and put aside the hat that Alicia made for her from plaited-together long grass. She felt her muscles getting stronger, despite the poor quality food and the lack of sleep. The loss of Karolina and Adam gnawed somewhere beneath her ribs, and on the lucky days when they could sit sorting rubble and stones, she kept up a silent one-sided interrogation of her elder daughter: *Where are you? Do they feed you? Has Margo found you, and come to visit you? Is it safe? Has your father come for you? But he must have come for you, he's sure to have come for you, or Margo will have found you, one of them is with you now.* Other voices answered her: Janina, Adam, Margo. Karolina's voice was silent.

34

THE TURN OF THE SEASONS in Kraków could be sudden. A September morning could see the Oderfeldts dressed in cotton, Anna ordering ices for after dinner, the rooms to be aired; by the afternoon a drizzle, and the fires to be lit, by evening, a cold fog might descend, and the boots brought from the winter wardrobes, the furs unwrapped from their layers of mothballed paper, Janie sent to put hot water bottles between the sheets. None of that prepared them for the savagery of the winter that came overnight in Chelyabinsk.

Alicia was half-awake, trying to lure herself into sleep by drifting through an imaginary home, trying to fall into grief-stricken dreams. She was walking down the stairs, Mimi or Cece licking at her heels, when a deep throbbing ache in her legs made her stumble and open her eyes. The room seemed darker than usual, and a chill in the air brought a brutal homesickness. Alicia pulled the thin covers, only used so far as a useless bed bug barrier, up under her chin, but a shiver ran across her ribs anyway, and she turned into Anna's back, moved her feet to rest on Leo's legs behind her. She waited for sleep to come, but her fingers were cold, and holding them in her armpits made little difference; her throat, too, was sore. She sat up, causing the whole bed to stir. Clouds of breath rose as people exclaimed and pulled blankets closer, huddled together. Someone got up in the darkness to pull the door closed, and stood for a moment silhouetted in the frame, absolutely still. As she turned back Alicia saw it was Frank. Her young joints clicking, Alicia struggled out of bed, making everyone sigh and turn over and punch the thin mattresses, but she ignored them, went to him anyway. He grinned at her as she approached, the frozen floor like needle-pricks on her toes.

'Alicia, see?'

'Oh!'

Thick snowflakes were falling. Here was a familiar muffling of the world, a piece of home, where there would be skating once the river froze, and hot chocolate ready on their return. Alicia looked into Frank's face, his childish smile; she could see he was imagining snowball fights, perhaps a day or two of suspended work.

'I'm still sunburned from yesterday,' he said. 'But it's winter now, didn't you know?'

His arms were still bare and peppered with gooseflesh. Alicia's mind went to her coat, handed in on their arrival. Had they given her mother a receipt, a ticket, to get it back? It was a good coat, thick and lined; Alicia could sleep under it.

Alicia didn't say, *But Frank, think*. She didn't say, *But Frank, now it is a frozen world, don't you see how much harder everything will be?* She studied his face. He was so old, as old as Papa and Uncle Stefan, but he was younger than she was in his mind. He seemed to think the snow would melt like sugar. Alicia felt the ground shift beneath her yet again; the brief summer, the stolen season was over.

Alicia said, 'It will kill the bed bugs.'

Frank let out a guffaw that bent him at the waist. 'Come, come!' he said, beckoning her out into the snow.

'Frank, no! It's freezing! Come back in.'

He was running in his socks and thin trousers, only the

filthy jacket from the cattle car over his shoulders. He bounded in circles and pointed his footprints out to her.

'Yes, I know, come inside!' she called. Behind her, other voices rose, *Close the door, are you crazy? Alicia, is that you? Is that Frank? Get him inside!*

A floodlight illuminated the snow. For a moment Alicia was stunned into a child's wonder: the flakes were fat and thick, falling in that gleeful way, riding on the wind. In the floodlight they looked like the sparks of a vast bonfire drifting down from the sky. She pointed upwards so Frank would notice: she knew he'd like to see it, but he was holding out his arm, the dark sleeve there, to catch the flakes, exclaiming over the intricate patterns. Neither of them saw the guards coming.

In the classroom, Ursula wore thick, padded gloves that she removed with her teeth when she needed to write something down. Alicia sat with her hands in her armpits, working her toes inside her boots, trying to make clouds into shapes; on the walk over, some of the guards were making smoke rings with their breath and laughing.

While Ursula turned to the board, writing the Russian for *snow* and *ice*, Alicia told the children of Frank's beating under her breath. She expected a reflection of the sickened lurches her stomach had taken as the sounds of fist on flesh, breaking and splitting and shattering bones, crashed across the yard. She wanted to pass on that feeling so that she didn't have to sit with it there in the cold schoolroom.

Instead the other children looked at her with blank expressions, and one of them, a boy with missing teeth, said, 'Did they stamp on his head?'

'What?'

'That's what they did to my grandfather,' he said.

'Here?'

'No, at home.'

He had taken his daily boiled sweet from Stalin out of his mouth so he could speak through his toothless gums, and now he put it back and turned back to the front, where Ursula was glaring.

She came to Alicia's desk.

'Alicia, pay attention,' Ursula said.

'Yes, Miss Ursula.'

'What's the matter? You'll have to get used to the cold.' Ursula spoke in Polish, although she knew there was to be Russian in school only, or how would they learn, how would they know the language of their new country, and all its music; despite this, Ursula could not shake out of herself a core of kindness that responded to a sad, a bewildered, a lost face of a youngster in her care with the sound if its mother tongue.

'Yes,' was Alicia's simple reply, in Russian. She preferred to keep quiet with this one. It seemed nothing good would come, here, of seeming anything other than docile and pliable. She looked up into Ursula's elfin face, the tip of her sharp nose red, raw and flaking. She affected a sad little girl voice, despite not feeling like a little girl, perhaps, since the day she lay in her bed in Bernardyńska and thought of ways for that man to die.

She mimed drawing in the air, tried to think of the Russian word for it, only managed, 'Please . . .' and the mime. She gave up and asked in Polish, 'Please can we have art supplies?'

'Oh! Yes, ask Stalin and he'll provide for you.' Ursula beamed at her, and walked on.

When she arrived back at the barracks, Frank was alone on one of the bunks. Alicia was annoyed: her five minutes before the adults came back was the joy of her day, a slice of stolen time when the guards who escorted them back from school went to their own buildings and the workers had not yet arrived. One of the kinder guards had brought them boiled water and poured it into canisters which they placed around the room like little heaters; Alicia took one and hugged it.

'Leo?'

She ignored Frank's mumbling as she went to sit on her frozen hands on another bunk.

'Leo, Leo, did you see they sent me back early?'

'Leo's not here,' Alicia said.

'Who's that? Sarah?'

'Who's Sarah?'

'My sister, didn't you know? We hid behind the oven, so clever . . .'

Alicia snuggled under the thin blanket with the make-shift hot water bottle, rubbing her feet together. The sheets smelled sour.

'They sent me back early.'

'Good for you.'

'I couldn't keep my balance.'

'It's icy.'

'No, it's . . . I can't see properly, somehow . . . I can't . . . there's something wrong with my eye or my . . . I kept falling.'

Alicia sat up, the blanket still wrapped around her. She folded her swaddled legs under her to look at Frank. His face didn't look so badly beaten as all that. Not as though a guard had stamped on his head. His lip was split, and there was a small bruise at the top of his nose. They'd mostly hit his back and sides as he curled up in the snow, cracking ribs, Alicia and Leo trying to pull him away, screaming at them to stop.

'You just need to sleep. It was nice of them to let you come back early.'

'Yes, yes, little Ruski, they're teaching you well, ha? *Stalin loves me, Stalin will take care of me!*' he sang tunelessly, waving his arms as though conducting an invisible orchestra.

'You know back in Poland they are stamping on people's heads?'

Frank stopped waving. 'What, didn't you know?' he echoed.

Leo and the others came in, bickering about the temperature in a herd of companionable irritation.

'Must be fifty below, I'm telling you . . . look at my fingers!' Leo said.

Anna snapped, 'We'd all be dead, you stupid woman.'

'Oh God, shut up you two . . . why don't you just look at the thermometer by the well?' someone called over.

'They've taken it away! They *want* you think it can't possibly be fifty below, but I'm *telling* you . . . Frank, how are you, sweetheart?' Leo leaned over him and he tried to sit up. 'No, no, you rest.'

Anna pulled Alicia into an embrace for warmth, took her daughter's hands between hers and began to rub them. Together they watched Leo press the back of her hand to Frank's forehead.

'Shall we try to tape up his ribs somehow? We could cut a sheet into strips,' Anna said.

'I think he just needs to rest,' Leo said.

As they sank into their fitful frozen sleep, Frank resurfaced, reached for Leo. 'So dizzy,' he said.

'Shall I tell you about the sky to help you sleep?' she whispered.

'Oh yes.'

They all listened as Leo talked of the Pleiades, and the trail of stars falling to the horizon, and the moon, which was almost full now, about to wanc again into a sliver.

'Thank you, Leo,' Frank breathed, as they all sank again, snow drifting in through the slats.

Anna said a very quick prayer, half-remembered from a long-ago home, and tried to close Frank's eyes. They stayed open. How had she forgotten that? Her mother's eyes had done the same. She stroked Leo's hair until she woke.

'What? Come on, it can't be, it's still pitch black,' her friend mumbled.

'Frank is dead.'

Even Anna, who barely tolerated Frank, had felt the heaviness of it when she woke to see him staring glassy-eyed at her, unbreathing. To have run and hidden and made it all this way, then to die at the edge of the world, for no one who loved him to ever know. She'd touched her fingers to his face and tried to remember the right prayer. So she was prepared for Leo's grief to swamp them all, perhaps even to have to manage Leo's untrammelled rage at the guard who had beaten her friend. Instead Leo seemed to shrink and diminish; she hugged herself, said only, 'Oh, but I promised his sister, oh I *promised* her,' bowed her head for several seconds, as Anna took her hand.

'Do you think he was suffering very much, but didn't say?' Leo whispered.

'No, I think he just slipped away. They must have hit his head, and . . .' Anna shrugged. She added, 'Should we wake a guard?'

But Leo shook her head and Anna was glad. Instead they sat with Frank as the others slept until dawn, holding hands over his still chest, letting their thoughts drift to other lives and losses. When Alicia woke, she surprised both of them by crying over Frank and kissing his icy forehead. It was she who went to alert a guard. It was the same one who had beaten Frank. It gave her a little satisfaction when he furrowed his brow and bit his lips. It was unclear if it was guilt, irritation, or both. *I hope you get into lots of trouble*, Alicia thought. *I hope Stalin shoots you in the head himself.*

'Well, he'll have to be buried,' he said, as another guard came in, the kind one who brought them hot water.

'Who?' the kind guard asked. He was short and slight, always seeming too small for his uniform.

'That soft in the head one. He'll have to be buried,' he repeated, looking around. 'Who speaks Russian? Come on. Out by the woods,' he added.

There was a pause.

'You want us to do it?' the small guard asked, and laughed, loud but short. The small crowd that had gathered around Frank's bunk, where Leo and Anna still sat either side of him holding hands, took a collective breath. Some of them glanced at the canisters of hot water and the extra blankets the kind guard had brought.

'Won't . . . won't you help?' Leo asked.

'I'm busy, we're busy! Come on, it's not so bad. Go and ask at the mess for shovels.'

'But it's completely frozen!' Anna said. She felt a shock of laughter threaten and swallowed it down.

'Better get started then.'

Anna and Leo went. On the way, Anna took Leo's arm and said, 'I don't understand, he has been so helpful.'

'I see it,' Leo said, shaking. 'He sees us like pets, perhaps, Anna. Don't be cruel while they're alive, fling them in the ground when they die.'

35

Soon after her mother and Leo buried Frank in the woods, coming back hours later with fresh blisters and bruises from driving shovels into the icy ground, Alicia came to her desk to find pencils, paintbrushes, little pots of paint, paper. She looked up to see Ursula wiping tears away, overcome by her own generosity, the kindness of her dear Stalin, her country, towards this little waif. Alicia blew on her fingers, warming them slightly, so she could feel the slick wood of the paint-brush, undo the lid of the paint, take in the smell of those days with Jozef, her lessons. She went to Ursula and hugged her around the waist, burrowed her face into Ursula's small, soft belly for a moment. Ursula touched her hair, and told her to thank Stalin, and Alicia did, curtseying to the portrait for added effect.

While the others copied out a Russian poem with the new pencils, Alicia held on to the moment of seeing her mother carry out Frank's dead body, the shock of its white flesh and open eyes. She saw Frank's feet go last, thinking of how, soon, they would be covered with the frozen earth. So she began a sketch of poor Frank, who couldn't know what a clean death luck granted him, taken by a quick beating and an unlucky fall onto ice.

As winter deepened and hardened, everything was hunched and clawed; backs and knees and fingers curled up. Soon the snow was too thick to work properly and people huddled under blankets all day; if they were clever, they kept moving in a slow, steady walk from barracks to barracks, around in a loop, not too much, or they would need too many calories, but enough to make the cold chase them a little.

School became a place to stay warm. Ursula got ill, listless and pale, coughing and feverish, so for weeks she curled up at her large desk at the front, told them to read or play quietly, remember to thank Stalin for all their gifts. Alicia planned to sketch and then paint Papa and Karolina, bring their faces to her, hang them up in the barracks like Stalin's face in the class-room, so they could pray to them like family gods. Instead, as she sat at her little desk, she found that when her own pencil touched the page, it was details of her own painting that kept finding their way onto the paper. Sometimes it was her fingers wrapped around the back of a chair. Sometimes the dress, the folds of it, or the eyes. She knew she was getting it all wrong, knew it was misshapen and the perspective was out and the light points were the wrong shade. Without Jozef she couldn't find the painting again, and had to think hard to remember how her face in paint had looked; when she thought hard, she could only find the feeling of richness, fullness, pleasure in helping to make something beautiful, something that would make her Papa happy, and show that man what an error he had made in attacking them. She flipped page after page and brought Papa and Karolina into the frame, Janie and Leo, Margo, Frank, Janina, her mother; they stood like ghosts behind the girl's figure. She put Stefan's face in the walls behind her, added Isaac's in the folds of a curtain. When she tried to add colour the whole thing looked childish, and she ripped it up.

Somewhere the real painting was waiting to be found again and reclaimed. Alicia hoped whoever had it took care of Jozef's canvas, didn't put the girl in direct sun, or let her go damp and cold, let mould creep across her painted skin. Alicia was going to need her, when they all went home. They would start there, build a world again around her: a wall, floors, furniture, and everyone back in their place. The weeks and months since the day they left Kraków would be rolled back like a long carpet, and everything as it should be again.

Kraków, 1939–1940

36

His friend's face was so changed that Adam looked behind him for a moment, thinking they had called out the wrong prisoner. His eyes were unsmiling as he shuffled to sit at the small table in the police station.

'They tricked us, gathered us all for a meeting,' Stefan said, looking at the table, pressing it with his fingers until the tips turned white. 'They booked one of the largest conference rooms. We'd all agreed our points. We even invited press, but do they care? They'll do anything in front of anyone!'

'I came as soon as I heard,' Adam said. 'I've been trying and trying to—'

'Then they just arrested us, for nothing, nothing!' Stefan said. 'They were laughing at us—'

He seemed to only then notice who was sitting in front of him. 'Adam, you child. What are you still doing in the city? You said you were going that morning!'

'Anna and the girls have gone, but I—'

'Well, go after them, go, go.'

'I will, I will, only—'

'There's no only. Where are you staying? Don't tell me you're so stupid to stay in the apartment?' He glanced at Adam's arm. 'Have they made you register? You haven't registered yet, have you?'

'No,' Adam said, following Stefan's glance and rubbing at his arm, as though there really was a star there that could be smoothed away. 'I'll be gone soon.'

'They'll make you if you stop to talk to any of them. Don't stop for anyone, just walk straight out of the city if you have to.'

'Walk? To Lwów? I still have two cars at home, I – Stefan, I'm here to help *you*, not—'

'Well, you can't go back there. Where are you staying?'

Adam shone a smile, a sliver of their old life. 'I'm camping out at your dirty room behind the university.' He longed to tell of his escape from the Bernardyńska apartment, down the back stairs and crawling through a window like their boyhood games come true; already it was an adventure in his memory, while on the night he had been so fixed by fear that he had vomited into the trees in the courtyard until he thought his stomach would disappear. Looking at Stefan now, he swallowed his story. His eyes had seemed empty before, but were now hollowed out.

'See?' Adam tried. 'You're wishing you'd thought of that.' He wagged a finger at Stefan, eager to make him smile. The room was a long-running joke between them, Stefan's dirty hideaway for girlfriends, boyfriends, lost weekends with various students.

'I did,' Stefan said, his voice so small Adam had to lean in. 'I was letting lots of students stay there. Jews. Must be over a dozen. They're . . . they're all gone?' He held out his hands and looked into his palms. Adam took them into his own.

'I – maybe they decided to leave, like me and Anna.'

'The rooms are so near the Jagiellonian. They were swarming all over there. You're crazy, you can't stay there. They'll move you over the river. Adam, you have to go.'

'And leave you here?'

His friend's face changed again. 'Oh! This. It's nothing. They treat us well enough. At least here they bring us books sometimes. You can go, you can go, please, please.'

37

THE CARETAKER WAS exhausted, his stinging eyes struggling to stay open, his head heavy. He sat in his usual leather chair in the factory reception, where three well-spoken, serious young women used to answer telephones and march to take messages upstairs. On day shift, he liked to try to flirt with the two pretty ones, dark-haired and with pert bottoms in tight pencil skirts; at night, he was alone, a torch and a paper bag with something sweet from the bakery, picked up by his mother that morning. Now, it was just past what his mother called witching hour, and the night was bitter. Ice streaked the pavements outside, where he was supposed to patrol. The new bosses had told him he must patrol carefully.

He stretched and snuggled further down into his chair, looking again at the three empty chairs behind the reception desk. Martha, that was the name of the prettiest. She never smiled at him, rolled her eyes when he tried to talk to her, which made him wild for her. All three of the girls had been gone for two weeks now. Martha had left her little woollen shrug behind, still draped over the back of her chair. The workers, too, were depleted. The Jews were all gone. Some had left weeks before, presumably of their own accord, and the others bitched about them, dropping their team in the shit, with the boss gone too, and what was to happen? Others showed up for work one morning but had disappeared by first break, their work permits in a neat pile on the reception desk. The receptionists among them. It made sense perhaps, keep everything in its own place, a different factory where all the Jews could work together, over the river. But he had liked Martha, the way she punched numbers on the telephone with a sharply polished nail, *tap tap tap*.

He closed his eyes again. It wasn't just the chill, the late hour. The panic that had risen in him like bile was receding. For weeks, the tension humming across the river and through the streets, in the crackle of radio static, the flick and crack of newspapers on the tram, had made everyone alert, unable to sleep; voices came out off-key, conversations were smothered around children. Then the Polish troops streamed out of Kraków, heads bowed, leaving behind mothers, lovers, school friends. The new flags went up, parades, new names for the squares were announced and ignored. His friends stopped meeting in their usual bar and went home early, straight after their shifts. The sound of marching troops, shouting German voices, the thud of boots on the pavement, was monstrous, terrifying, unbearable, until it became as normal as traffic. Then new faces, new names of new bosses to learn, new procedures, new papers, a new receptionist, a crone with bitten fingernails and a barking voice. The anxiety that had gripped them all was beginning to lessen, leaving exhaustion behind.

The caretaker jumped as his torch rattled to the floor, dropped from his almost-sleeping fingers. He yelled out, a childish cry of a boy seeing a monster-shadow on the wall: a figure stood at the door.

The figure raised a hand and came closer. A face became visible through the glass panels. 'Lucaz? My keys don't work,' a voice called.

The caretaker felt a moment's embarrassed relief. 'Sir,' he said, rising, for in the fug of his doze he had forgotten everything, falling into the old pattern. As he stood, the new reality gripped him and he stopped. 'Sir? Mr Oderfeldt?'

'Open the door.'

'They . . . they changed the locks, sir.'

The figure was unmoving. Lucaz fumbled with his keys, his torch glinting on the edge of filing cabinets and the telephone's gleam. As he opened the door, he began a speech without knowing what he was to say, only prompted by a nervous anger that his old boss had forgotten the new rules, was naïve, senseless, stupid.

'Sir, you shouldn't be here, I – we thought you'd already gone—'

'I've just come to collect some things. From my office.'

Lucaz found the words of his speech fading away, as Adam strode past him.

'Put the lights on,' he said.

'They said I wasn't to . . . just to patrol.'

Adam stopped at the door that led onto the factory floor.

'Just for a moment.'

Lucaz shook his head. He had an idea that his new bosses were testing him, watching from a nearby building. 'You shouldn't have come,' he said. 'I don't think it's . . . safe, you should leave. Most of the others, the Jews have left.'

Adam came back towards him. In the gloom Lucaz saw his face was thinner, his eyes bloodshot. He towered over Lucaz without threat, putting his hands in and out of the pockets of his good coat. He seemed to begin and dismiss several words before answering.

'I am leaving. I am not causing any trouble, Lucaz. I only wish to go to my office. Just for a moment, you see. Then I will leave.' When he marched to the door again, Lucaz trotted behind him.

Adam dug the sharp nails of his thumbs into the soft palms, an old childhood trick to stop him from the horror of crying in front of Lucaz. Opening the door of his office, he had been prepared for chaos, a stripped and broken room, all his pride lying in tatters on the floor. Instead it was the cruelty of the perfect room, just as he left it, already feeling like a relic, and he was clutched with a strange grief over this little piece of the world that had been his, that he had carved out for himself. It felt absurd, in that moment, that he would not settle into his chair, do some paperwork, tell Lucaz to fetch him a coffee, share a late-night doughnut and even a little gossip, before calling Robert to pick him up in the car, and crawling into bed next to Anna.

The young man was near sobbing, 'Sir, please, they said I had to call, if – sir, Mr Oderfeldt, you don't understand, this office will be cleared, you have to leave.'

He had been so proud of this room. When his father ran the business he had a different building outside the city, a tiny office at the back of the factory floor, down some stairs. Adam could still remember the uneven walls under his fingers as he tried to hold on, unbalanced by the depth of each step. He had insisted on a larger, lighter office when he grew the business and moved closer to the city, where he could stand and watch the workers, hear the hum of the machines running off sheet after sheet. Their textiles were in every bedroom in Kraków, he was sure. These new bosses probably slept in sheets and on pillowcases made on those machines they had stolen from him.

He went to his desk. The lock and key on the drawer was still his own. He shot a questioning look at Lucaz.

'It's all to be cleared, they said. Soon, I think,' he shrugged. 'I – you can't take those,' the caretaker added, jangling his keys in his hands, his torch wobbling over the papers and cash that Adam had taken from the drawer, feeling the steady, calming weight of them in his hands.

'What? They're mine.'

'Don't you read the newspapers? It's all to be seized.'

'Did you think I asked you to open up so I could have a farewell tour?'

Lucaz looked between Adam and the door, as though his new bosses were already standing there.

'Are you going to keep working here?' Adam continued. 'For them?'

'This is no time to be giving up work, sir. They say we have to keep everything routine. Except the factory space will be used to make other things and the change of . . . of management.'

Adam took a long look, to the window down onto the factory floor, the wooden desk, a thin layer of dust dulling its shine; the pictures of Alicia, framed and arranged so she grew up across the walls. In the low light he couldn't see her face clearly.

'I see,' Adam said, putting the papers and the wad of notes, thick, heavy and comforting, wrapped in a band, into a briefcase. On impulse, he also snatched up some loose, unframed photographs in the drawer, ones he had brought from home and had meant to frame one day. The caretaker made a small sound carried on a sigh. He was a large man, the bulk of him blocking the door. Adam turned and clicked the briefcase shut, clenched his hands into brief fists, but when he turned, as straight-backed and authoritative as he could muster, Lucaz gave way, only mumbling, 'They'll ask me, they'll ask me where everything is, they'll think *I* stole it . . . Sir?'

Adam almost galloped down the stairs, back across the silent factory floor, and into reception. 'Thank you, Lucaz, good luck,' he called over his shoulder, as the young man called, 'Wait, sir, I'm supposed to . . . I'll have to tell them you came . . .'

Adam turned. 'Could you arrange a telegram for me?' He pinched out a wad of notes, held them out.

Lucaz eyed the notes. It was more than six months' wages. Just sitting in the office all this time. Just spare cash. 'I'll have to tell them you came,' he repeated, taking on the tone he used for the boys who tried to jump the fences in the summer, bored and looking for trouble. He rubbed his chin in an imitation of deep thought.

Adam's breathing quickened. He offered more notes. 'Lucaz, it's just a telegram.'

'Have you registered?'

'What?'

'You're supposed to register,' Lucaz said, feeling his stomach seethe at the strange thrill of reprimanding the boss. 'So they can move you to the . . . the new place for all the Jews.'

'Well I'm not going there. I'm going out of the country.' Adam's hand was still proffering the notes and he let his arm fall. Lucaz crossed his arms again as Adam took another wedge, folded it in half.

'Lucaz, I just need you to—'

'I'll need all of it.' Lucaz swallowed down his shame. The man had made it so easy, holding out money like that, coming alone in the middle of the night. He could do so much worse and no one would say anything. He'd even get pats on the back.

Adam stared at him. A series of tiny pulses seemed to go through his body, like little electric shocks. Lucaz counted on his fingers. 'Opening up for you. Against orders. Covering up you were here. Unregistered, that's, that's extra. Sending a telegram extra again.'

'I'll give you half. That's generous,' Adam said, as Lucaz sucked air between his teeth like a market seller. Adam's heart was racing. He'd spent all of the cash in his coat lining already. This was all he had to get out of Kraków and to Anna. 'I need some,' he offered honestly. 'I have nothing but this.'

Immediately he realised his mistake. All residual deference ebbed out of his old employee. He simply took the notes from Adam's hands.

'Wait, please,' Adam tried, but Lucaz only shrugged.

Adam's scrambled mind struggled to make a decision. *Forget the telegram*, Stefan's voice whispered. *Get out*. But if he could reach Sammy, find out they were safe, he could change course, after explaining to Anna, and get to France, sell the house, Edie would understand, recoup their losses, use the money for visas . . . he could still get out of this if he could get to France.

'The telegram?'

'I said so, didn't I? I'm not a cheat,' Lucaz mumbled, looking at the floor as he folded the cash into his pocket.

'And I'll need to come back here once more, to use the telephone.'

38

ADAM FELT THE familiar sting of betrayal and guilt, even as he told himself, yet again, that this was the best way to help, a clever plan, and Anna would soon understand once he could explain everything. He took the photographs, the ones from his office drawer, from his inside pocket. On the top, Anna's smile was wide, a rare full-toothed childish grin, and he brought the image closer to see the wrinkles at the side of her eyes, his favourite detail of her face.

Years before, in bed, he'd been telling her a story of him and Stefan as boys, a stupid prank on Stefan's older brothers, and he glanced at her as she lay on her side, the sheet pulled up over her nose in the cool room. He so desperately wanted to make her laugh, made his voices ever sillier and higher, his gestures more elaborate, almost knocking over the jug of flowers next to the bed, but his new wife's breathing was steady, her face still. He stopped, embarrassed, and lay next to her again. Her eyes narrowed to almonds, and spidery lines creased at the edges, ran right to the edges of her face.

'Ah, you *are* laughing!' He was elated, not just by the relief that he was not such a dull disappointment after all, but by the expressiveness of her eyes, how he could read her whole face by them.

'I'm smiling, silly boy.'

'That was a laugh.'

'Come on, what did Oskar say?'

'You don't care,' he teased, turning to light a cigarette.

Anna really did laugh then. 'All right, I don't I suppose. Tell me a different one.'

And then he'd lit the cigarette, or had she taken it from him and thrown it, pulled him to her? Was it even so early, perhaps after Karolina was born . . . ? He glanced up from the photograph, young Anna's smiling eyes, to think, then let the memory go. In the picture her eyes were closed, so she hated it, 'It makes me look ridiculous, like one of those fussy old grandmothers in a long black dress, like I don't know how a camera works!' but he had kept it in his desk at work, because of her smiling eyes. In the image she held Karolina in her arms and stood on the front step of the apartment. Just behind them was a ghostly figure – Janie perhaps, or Anna's mother, ducking out of frame. Adam searched Anna's arms then, saw only the bundle, a tiny blurred suggestion of baby fingers poking out. He kissed the photograph, looked out of the window at the city, dull under grey soggy skies. The telephone sat shining on Stefan's desk, waiting for its moment. He'd been too spooked to go back to the factory, too afraid of Lucaz's greed and slowly dawning awareness of his power, which he'd soon start playing with like a glorious and frightening new toy. He'd taken a chance instead and hoped that Lucaz had sent the telegram as planned, and taken yet another one in trying Stefan's office, a little ransacked but with the phone line still working, on a Sunday. Waiting for the time he'd asked for, he ran a finger along the huge globe that still sat next to Stefan's desk, a terrible sickness settling on him at the thought of his friend still sitting in the prison, left behind if Adam's plan came together.

He dialled for the operator, held for long minutes, was patched through across the broken and smoking land between him and where Anna sat in his brother's office. When her voice came through the static his heart lurched for her. *Where are you? Are you coming?*

He talked through her, realising she would only hear his voice as he heard hers, as though carried on the high winds of a storm. *Listen, I'm going to get to France to sell the house there. Edie can move back in with her mother. She'll understand. Then we'll have money for visas out of Europe, if it comes to that . . . I don't have any other money.*

The line went dead as he was trying to explain. Even through the stormy line he could hear her spiralling anger at the old incendiary words: *France, Edie.* And something with poor Karolina, heartbroken over Jozef. She hadn't mentioned Alicia at all. He sat back in Stefan's chair, feeling a fool for risking so much for a conversation that had achieved nothing but to know his wife and daughters were safely in Lwów, which perhaps was enough, though he felt sure he had known it anyway, that if any of them had come to harm he would have felt it in his cells, in the marrow of his skeleton.

Adam cast around his friend's office. He should bring him something, before he left, before he found a way to France. He started to open drawers, but they had already been cleared out. He turned to look on the shelves, see if there was a beloved book he could bring, and became so lost in the titles, their gold lettering, that he didn't hear the men coming down the corridor, Lucaz's tip-off fresh in their ears.

Kraków, 1945

39

IN MOSCOW, Alicia walked up and down the platform of a huge station with elaborate mosaics on the walls, gleaming with rich jewel colours that made her think of Stalin's boiled sweets. Her legs ached and the old weakness in her bladder stung.

It took a long time for the trains to be organised, but Alicia was well-trained in waiting. She had a sketchbook full of figures, a pencil, even a small mix of paints and brushes that she had carefully arranged in a towel, wrapped like an artist's set. She looked away from the tiled walls and out across the street, into the city. It could be Kraków, or Kraków as it was in her memories, which might be now more cobbled together memories of other people. She was nineteen now, and already that distant childhood was slipping into an imagined landscape, a half-remembered conversation, an unfinished sketch. She started to draw the lines of the platform and the shapes beyond it, trying to feel her way into the focus point. Colours started to rise: a glint of those mosaics against the grey, but they had to hold off until the shapes were there.

Somewhere across the cities and fields was the barrack room they'd lived in, the hot summers and freezing winters, turning through extremes like a tossed coin. But this felt like a different place. Alicia scribbled in figures and details: porters, a few lost-looking soldiers, but mostly clusters of travellers like her, thin and wearing expressions of shock and relief. Both the perfect, infinite sky of the Russia she'd first met, and its snowscape twin, were gone. Instead the sky was grey, and a misty drizzle washed the streets.

It had been a week since the announcement. People smiled uncertainly at each other, and laughter punctured the air, muffled by the roar of traffic. The station was busy, queues stretching into the street and voices raised at the ticket counter. Many times, sitting on Margo's suitcase, wearing Janina's coat, Alicia fancied she recognised someone; her eye would catch on a face, the particular gait of a hurrying figure, the angle of a head as someone spoke: *You know them*, something would whisper to her, some spark of recognition, *from the journey, from one of the journeys, from Kraków, all that time ago, from Lwów, from Russia, you know them*. She imagined them all as objects bobbing on an ocean. Now the tide had changed again and they were all to be swept back with the receding waves. None of her recognised people ever materialised; they were phantoms and doppelgangers, a Leo there, a Margo, a Jozef, Adam striding towards her, arms open, his coat flying out behind him. The day before, so certain had she been that Karolina was leaning against a wall, laughing with a group of soldiers, her hair grown down to her waist but the set of her jaw, the low cadence of her laugh unmistakeable, that Alicia had started towards her, calling out, 'Karolcia,' her whole body throbbing with joyful relief, before the woman turned again, showing a stranger's face.

On the train, a gaggle of young women were talking excitedly about boyfriends returning home, falling into whispered intimacies as Alicia passed. They were around Alicia's age, but she felt a thousand years younger and older than them, in her dowdy coat, plain face, thin hair and body. She was one of a species of girl, a lucky one, that was everywhere, on trains and by the side of roads, waiting in queues, knocking on the doors of those who knew them in other lives: thin, sallow, body stuck in childhood, mind quick and instinctive as a wild animal. The young women, with different stories to Alicia, let their whispers rise into shrieks and whoops of laughter as she opened the door into the next carriage.

She had a window, the luxury of a passing landscape. She watched the city crawl by, blocks of stone buildings, opening into grand squares, posters and placards everywhere, full of the announcement. She glimpsed buildings with their faces torn off. They were like doll houses with the wallpaper still inside, children playing in the dreamlike giant toy, a shared game played all across Europe. Alicia reopened the sketchbook and began adding a bombed-out house in the background of the station piece, but soon fell into her habit of sketching Jozef's painting of her younger self. The face, especially around the nose and mouth. The eyes she was quite sure of now.

A woman and a small boy came into her carriage. They sat opposite Alicia and the boy stared open-mouthed at Janina's coat, warm and once lined with money.

'Tomas,' the woman hissed at him. 'Stop it.'

But the boy was already burying his head in the woman's shoulder, gasping and afraid. Alicia fingered the buttons on the coat, tortoiseshell. They might be worth something, so she'd always kept them as a tiny last thing to trade for food and pencils.

The mother glanced a half-hearted apology at Alicia, who was now twisting a button in her fingers, ignoring them both. She knew why the boy was crying.

'It's that stupid rumour,' the woman said, echoing Alicia's thoughts in Polish. Not just Polish, but a Kraków accent.

The effect made Alicia soften, and she nodded. 'I know, I've heard that too. It must have been published somewhere,' she said.

'Tomas, now stop it. It's just a button, darling. You can't turn people into buttons!' The woman glanced up again. 'You're Polish,' she said, and smiled.

Alicia nodded.

'Going home? Tomas, *enough*. Could I have some paper, and a pencil, for him to play with?' she asked.

Alicia looked at the precious paper. To get this last batch she'd worked for a month on a portrait of an officer's girl-friend near Chelyabinsk. When the girl didn't like it, saying her painted face wasn't pretty enough, Alicia had to throw in every ounce of hoarded tobacco, carefully stashed inside a mattress for a month and filled out with bark and shredded leaves, to get the sketchbook and pencils. All her cash had gone on the train ticket.

'I'm working, sorry.'

'On what? You're just sketching.'

'I'm an artist.'

The woman glared at her. 'Sorry, my sweet, this little artist girl needs her paper,' she said to the little boy, who now hung limp and tired on her shoulder. The woman changed course.

'You could draw us? I don't even have a photograph of him.'

'I'd be happy to.' Alicia sat up, turned a page. 'What do you have to trade?'

The woman dropped her voice. 'We have some money,' she said. 'I'll buy you lunch at a station stop.'

'Just one lunch? I'm very good,' Alicia said, flicking through the book to find one of her reproductions of the painting of herself, always her best work. She held it up. 'I was taught by Pienta. You know?'

The woman shook her head. 'Hmm. Okay, one meal. You choose when.'

'Two meals. And coffee. Unlimited. And a pack of cigarettes.'

The woman laughed, and Alicia saw she was very young, maybe only Alicia's age, only seemed an adult because she had the child with her. They shook on it. The woman had the calloused hands Alicia recognised.

'Were you in a camp? No, no, don't pose,' Alicia said, as the woman prodded the boy to sit up. 'I'll watch you for a bit and then find a composition.'

'Yes, for a while, then we left for Tashkent.'

Alicia nodded, beginning to sketch. 'My friend Leo did that. She wanted to go south, where it would be warm.'

'It was warm.'

'And . . . friendly?'

The woman smiled. 'Yes. Your friend will have been safe and happy there. You? Tomas, be still.'

'No it's fine, I don't need him to stay still. Yes, I was in a camp.'

'One of the better ones?'

'I don't know. They worked us hard and there was a lot of sickness. Typhoid one year.'

'42.'

Alicia looked up.

'In Tashkent too,' the woman said.

They looked at each other for a moment, seeing loss written on the other's face, before Alicia dropped her gaze back to her sketch, drawing the woman and Tomas, trying out different positions: his head on her shoulder, or lying in her lap.

The train lumbered on. There were days of station stops

and passengers shuffling on and off, passing gossip and newspapers around, clusters of dead-eyed refugees, sinking back
into the hoods of their coats, ghoulish; excited groups of families, nervous single passengers. The same old stories, Alicia
thought, the same people with different faces. At night they
lay down on the benches like bunks, and Alicia tried to see the
stars, to recapture Leo's voice, the curve of her mother's face in
moonlight through the iron bars of that long-ago truck, but
there were only clouds.

'Here,' she said, as they approached the border crossing
into Poland, showing the woman the pencil portrait.

'Oh! It's . . .'

'You like it?'

The boy – the pencilled Tomas – was staring straight out
of the paper as he had at Alicia's buttoned coat, his face fearful. She'd made him younger and his eyes wider, to show the
babyish terror. But the woman's hands clasped at his waist,
her fingers interlocking to keep him safe. He sat in her lap,
dwarfed by her larger shoulders, a solidity and depth in the
pencil marks. Her face was mostly hidden, hair falling over
her face as she looked down to him.

'But that isn't how we—'

'That's how I see you,' Alicia explained, the bread the
woman had bought her sitting in her belly where it could not
be paid back. 'How you protect him. He's safe with you.'

The woman took the picture.

'Look, Tomas, it's us!' Her smile was uneven but pretty.
'Will you sign it?'

'You like it?'

The woman paused. 'Yes, I do.'

'Well, I'll call it *Train Passengers*.'

'Rose. Tomas and Rose. Shake the artist lady's hand, Tomas.'

'Alicia.'

'Alicia,' Rose repeated, smiling. She turned to kiss Tomas's head, then added, 'Are you alone?'

'Yes. I don't know. I have been. My sister is . . . she might be in Kraków. And my father.' She found she could not say *Papa*, nor speak Karolina's name.

'I pray you find them,' Rose said, and Alicia felt terrible hope quickening deep within her.

Someone called out down the carriage, 'We're crossing the border!'

Guards were waving them through, barely looking up from the platform. Some of the passengers cheered, others hugged each other.

'Tomas, this is Poland! We're home!' Rose said softly to him. He pointed at the banners, brightly coloured and fluttering, held up and pinned against walls as they passed.

Alicia put her fingers against the glass. It was so long since she'd read Polish. She blushed at the strangeness of it, feeling she was betraying home, so used to the ersatz Russian she'd learned. This distracted her from what the banner said. She let her eyes absorb the individual letters. Her mind went to Ursula, writing tight letters with short stems on the board, the smell of chalk. Rose followed her gaze and took a sharp breath, looked around the carriage to see if everyone had seen what she had seen. She caught Alicia's eye and Alicia nodded, to show she had. *For every carload of coal we get a carload of Jews.*

Rose put her lips against the nape of Tomas's neck, breathed in. Fear radiated from her. Alicia let it wash around the carriage. She knew she could easily pass, had been doing so since she left the barracks. She'd bought forged papers that pronounced her a Catholic, and she had rehearsed her part well, could recite the Lord's Prayer, a Hail Mary, all of the Beatitudes, just in case.

'Don't worry,' Alicia said. But Rose wasn't listening; she was staring out of the windows as the crowds thickened, holding more banners, shouting, screaming, chanting. 'Welcome home,' someone inside the carriage muttered, and a low rumble of bitter laughter rolled through them. Alicia jumped back as rocks hit the windows, splintering them, and Tomas began to cry.

At the station all was chaos. Alicia knew chaos now, knew how to weave and find a wall for your back, spot an alleyway that led to a quieter place, resist the pull to cluster around those in uniform. Rose and Tomas melted away, her hat bobbing briefly above the bare heads of the crowd, who were pushing each other and chanting spite. Alicia's chest tightened, more in rage than fear. *I'm Polish*, she screamed inside her head, *I was born here, my father is an important man; lost out there somewhere is a portrait of me, and it is going to save me*— a shove knocked her sideways, and she followed the trickle of refugees who had caught the scent of danger in the air and were backing away, out into the city.

She came out onto the grand Ulica that led away from the station. No one had checked her papers, even now: where were the checkpoints, the lines before guards sitting at tables, the endless clipboards and forms? The Ulica was almost clear of people and traffic, only one bus rumbling over a bridge. The tramlines still criss-crossed the road but the lines had lost their hum and nothing was running. Her unease growing, Alicia crossed to the quayside. She could smell the river, even hear its slosh as it lapped the banks. She looked across to the cityscape, wondering if she could see the Wawel and home.

The line of buildings along the river was unblemished. Alicia turned, looking for the demolished houses, the piles of rubble. Something was missing from the air; it took her several paces to realise it was the smoky metallic smell and taste of concrete dust that was absent. She crossed the road and walked up into a side street, trying to get a wider view. She traced her fingers along the perfect smooth brickwork of a closed and shuttered shop. It was as though the city had been emptied and encased in glass, left perfect and barren as a shell.

She turned her back to the shop, hollowed out by loneliness and exhilaration. No one gave orders or hustled her into groups or lines or gave her papers, and no one knew or cared where she went or what she did now. Somewhere in the city might be her Papa and Karolina, searching for her. They might be breathing this clean air, walking these unblemished streets. She might turn a corner and there they would be, walking together, his arm around her, sharing stories. Alicia let her legs fold and she crouched for a moment in the deserted street, shaking.

As she approached Bernardyńska, every step she remonstrated with herself, *They won't be. They might be, they could be. It could be that easy. Why not? You stupid child. They won't be.* She tried to ignore the perfection of the unchanged street, the window frames and thick hanging curtains, the gleaming black paint on the front doors. Passing Janina's building she pulled her old neighbour's coat tightly around her, sent up a tiny prayer of thanks. A wall of posters in German caught her eye. Someone had begun to tear them down, but the words still called out, half-choked orders and rules, soon to be replaced with Russian ones.

Her steps slowed as she approached home, dwelling in the last seconds of uncertainty. The blinds were drawn. A pair of plant pots filled with red flowers had been placed on either side of the door. Someone had filled them with care, watered the flowers enough to yield that full bloom. Alicia imagined a tall, blonde woman, a German officer's wife, patting the soil into place, enjoying her new stolen apartment. In the rush to leave the woman had left them behind. Alicia thought of tearing the flowers out and flinging them across the cobbles, before being struck with the idea that Karolina had planted them.

The door-knocker sounded like a boom in the quiet street. Alicia put her ear to the door. The clang and crunch of an opening sound made her almost cry out with hope that they would be on the other side of the door: she could almost feel the strength of Papa's arms around her, the tickle of Karolina's hair against her cheek.

'Hello?' a woman's voice said. Alicia looked around to see her standing in the next doorway. The Friels had lived there. This was a stranger. She spoke in Polish but she might be a German, left behind after the retreat. Alicia nodded to her, knocked on her own door again.

'They're out,' the woman said. Alicia looked at her more closely. She wore the same patchwork of clothes as other refugees, as Alicia did: an old pair of shoes, a brown dress under a worn housecoat, no stockings, un-styled hair piled up in a headscarf.

'They? Who lives here?'

The woman sniffed, looked Alicia up and down in turn. The close promise of her family made Alicia feel almost drunk. 'Well?' she said, careless of rudeness, wanting to shake the woman.

'Some Germans were in there,' the woman said, lighting a cigarette from her housecoat. Her hair escaping from the scarf was white. Alicia turned her thoughts from wondering what the woman had seen. After a long drag the woman offered the cigarette to Alicia, who took it, grateful for the steadying smoke in her throat.

'And now?' she asked, drawing the smoke deep into her lungs, letting it warm her. She blew out, waiting for the woman to reply, impatient and afraid.

'New people, just arrived.'

'Polish? A man? Woman?'

'If you're looking for people, you should go to the Red Cross offices. They're back over the river.' The woman held out her hand for the return of the cigarette. She eyed Alicia as she sucked on it as hard as a pipe. 'Yes, Polish, I think. And yes, a young woman, I think, pretty . . . an older man.'

'Their names? Did you speak to them?'

'No . . . well,' the woman leaned against her door, 'when they first arrived I spoke to the man a little. What are you doing?'

Alicia settled down on the step, and was running her fingers across the brass shoehorn that still gleamed there. She remembered the feel of its smooth edge against the arch of her feet as she balanced on it, waiting for Janie to take her for a walk.

'I'm waiting for them to come back.'

'People come and go, get sent to different places . . . I wouldn't hold your breath.' She looked down at Alicia for a moment, and glanced at her own front door as though considering inviting her in. Alicia was relieved when instead she shrugged and went back inside.

The cold came on quickly. She watched the light crawl down a turret of the Wawel. No streetlamps came on, and the city remained quiet, so that footsteps and voices travelled. She would hear them coming.

The strange, still quiet of the city was especially unnerving overnight, but Janina's coat was thick and warm. When she woke again, it was to the woman from next door, the not-Mrs-Friel, gently shaking her arm, telling her it was almost dawn. It took Alicia a long time to surface again, and realise she was home.

40

JOZEF HAD BEEN UP all night, trying to work while Hanna was asleep. Distracted for a while by her deep breaths and the memory of her warm skin on his in the narrow, hard bed, he'd soon sunk into the sketch. Hanna was too loud, somehow. Not in her voice, which was low and sweet, but in the space she took up in his vision: her body and hair and the awareness of where she was in the room always distracted him from a piece if she was awake. Trying and failing to sketch in the early weeks of their affair while she wrote in the corner, tiny scrawl in the notebook on her lap, her bare, thick legs stretched across the dirty floor, was the first time he had realised he had fallen in love with her, and his surprise was so great he had stared at the canvas for several minutes, before pacing the room as she watched him, amused and curious. Awake, she drew him too far from the half-awake state he needed to work well. Asleep, he could hold her separate from him for a few hours.

The sun was coming up now over the tenement blocks of the neighbourhood, not far from Jozef's old apartment. A dreary bird cheep, monotone and half-hearted, irritated him. He looked behind him for the first time in hours to see Hanna's bare feet sticking out from the covers, her large toes. He loved how solid she was, her thick waist and her heaviness, as though under her warm flesh were a skeleton made of steel.

He looked back at the sketch, to the spot where a grey smudge showed the space where Karolina's figure had been. He ran a finger over the space, staining his knuckles further with charcoal. Karolina's tiny bird-like limbs and the delicacy of her fingers came to him. The familiar dread soon followed, of how impossible it was that she had not been swallowed up, so young and trusting and loving and open and soft as a ripe peach. He tried to remember the feel of her in his arms, but could only think of the texture of Hanna's body. He let his gaze fall to the others in the sketched room. A crowd scene: figures holding glasses and throwing back their heads in laughter. In the background, a familiar window. One of the faces was sketched in more detail, a terrified grimace forming in the pencil lines. Adam, his suit's sharp lines exaggerated at the shoulder, his fear made raw at the surface. There was Anna, just the suggestion of a dress, a line to show a hand clinking glasses with another. Amid the other, nameless figures stood Alicia, leaning against the wall, watching. Her face was clearest, layered in his memory by months of sketching that long-ago portrait. She stared out at him now in miniature, challenging him to finish. Not for the first time, he felt the heaviness of the truth that he was painting ghosts, and that everyone in the piece was dead.

Karolina had been haunting him more intensely since he had found Hanna like a miraculous blooming fruit on a dead tree. When he and Hanna agreed to marry, start a family and live, he had a felt a rush of terror, something between hope and guilt, and he'd returned to the apartment on Bernardyńska, begun trying to paint Karolina again for the first time in years. She was elusive, escaping into the canvas and hiding behind other figures, or remaining stubbornly two-dimensional, too betrayed and hurt to show herself.

Hanna shifted and gave a low purring sound like a waking cat. Jozef went back to her, clung to her, living and real and half-awake.

'You've been up all night, sleep,' she murmured, laughing as his hands wandered over her body, across her stomach and hips. Like everyone, she'd had days and weeks of no food, months and years of malnutrition, but except for her hips sometimes bruising his own with their edge, she was healthy and strong. Jozef buried his face in her shoulder, breathed deeply, smiled into her neck, held her so tightly she gasped.

'Will you sleep today?' she asked him later, both sweat-slicked and exhausted by sex and guilt-laced happiness.

He cupped her face in his hands and she smiled at him. 'No, I'm going on a sort of pilgrimage.'

Hanna had cut her hair short with a pair of rusty scissors she'd found in the kitchen when they first started squatting in the empty block. She ran her fingers through the jagged spot at the back of her beautiful strong neck. 'Shall I come too?'

'Don't you have work today?'

Hanna nodded, shrugged. She was a volunteer, helping with the administration of lives and bodies flung across Europe and back again. She got a free lunch of grey sandwich and weak coffee, but no money, though they'd been promised they would be taken care of as things settled, and the best workers given good jobs by the new government. 'I don't have to go.'

'But you should.'

'And where is this quest?'

'Here in the city.'

She smiled at him but with her head cocked to one side. It was rare for him not to confide in her, but she kissed him deeply, and silently began to get ready for work. Pulling her skirt over her hips she glanced at him as he watched her from the bed.

'Do you want me to look for her again?' she asked, keeping her voice as level as she could.

He shook his head. 'I know you tried.'

'People are coming back all the time.' Hanna fiddled with the clasp on her skirt, avoiding her lover's eye, but when his silence drew her gaze to him, in spite of herself, he wasn't looking at her at all, but back at the beginnings of his painting.

The Red Cross offices were housed in the Jagiellonian, sprawling over three floors where piles of boxes and documents sat, holding lives: deportations, letters, queries, photographs, all the terrible bureaucracy and chaos of the years since the radio had propelled Janina out of her apartment and towards the Oderfeldts' door. Hanna and the women like her – they were all women – sat behind the heavily marked desks, tracing the grooves of old graffiti with their fingers in rare slow moments. They offered quick, efficient smiles to the queues of returning lost ones, asked them to spell out names, give dates, the snippets of evidence that could lead to the truth, closure, or the dead brought back to life. Every person in the queue held a terrible hope, perhaps in the way they bit their lips or wound their sleeves around their hands. Even the hard-faced ones, the ones with ribs sticking out so far they seemed walking nightmares, had the tiniest flecks of that hope, and left the offices with either something taken from them forever, or with longing gouged open, painful as an open wound.

Ignoring the gathering lines, longer every day, Hanna pulled open a cabinet of box files and began rifling through.

There were the photographs, faces staring out: *find me*. Names and details and dates. She looked under both O and P. Jozef had told Hanna that Karolina might use his name, that in their early letters, when she had been washed away to Lwów before he could get to her, and he had been swept away himself into the army, they had referred to themselves as already married.

Under O, she quickly found the file. There were the five enquiries from the aunt in Lwów: moving from polite, laywerlike language to shrill paragraph after paragraph. Hanna scanned one of the letters, finding familiar phrases. *Can't you help? I have no one left*. Then the letters stopped in 1941, the poor lady caught up in the catastrophe of Lwów. Only yesterday Hanna had confided in Jozef her fear that she was losing her humanity in the sea of misery that washed up at the offices every day. She'd quoted this very phrase at him: *Can't you help? I have no one left*. It's meaningless now, Hanna said, curled in Jozef's arms. I can't hear the sadness of it anymore; perhaps there's something breaking inside me. But reading the aunt's handwriting, scrawling and quick, seeing the careful folds of the paper, imagining this woman, who searched for Jozef's old love, tucking the letter into the envelope, she wished truly for the first time that Karolina could have been found, for this Margo's sake. Then there were her Jozef's own queries, one after the other, week after week at first, then monthly, before dwindling to nothing.

Hanna double-checked. Nothing else. She filled out a new enquiry form for their sister offices, ignoring the tightness of her chest, the rising fear that she could be stitching together a future of her own heartbreak. She typed out copies of the letters and stuffed everything into envelopes, as her colleagues bustled around her carrying out the same paperwork for the people trickling in in their lines, for friends, lovers and themselves. It felt impossible, Hanna thought, that anyone ever found anyone again. Her own lost ones, her parents and brother and nieces, had died with their hands in hers, something she had not realised at the time would come to feel like a luxury.

'There, Jozef,' she said, putting the envelopes into the out tray. Silently, she added, to the spirit of a woman she'd never meet, 'There, Margo.' And somewhere beyond the reach of Hanna's own awareness an inner voice spoke to Karolina: *Please, please, please stay lost.*

When she returned to her desk, Hanna smiled an apology as her colleague slapped her on the arm and asked, 'Can't you do that in your break? Some have been waiting all night—'

'Sorry. Yes, who's next please?' Hanna liked the sound of her voice in this place, comforting and sure. She knew Jozef loved that about her and tried to live up to it, always calm in his presence. The two women she'd addressed glanced at each other, making an invisible agreement. One stepped forward. She was slight and had a sharp, angular face, dark brown eyes. Her hair was cut short, curling around her ears.

'Yes, I'm next,' the woman said. 'What do I need to . . . um . . . I have papers, but . . .' she hesitated, drawing them from the pocket of a surprisingly good old-fashioned coat.

'Are they fakes?' Hanna asked, in a low voice so as not to frighten the woman away. The woman nodded.

'We see that a lot. You can still enquire. Name?'

'Mine, or the people I'm . . . ?'

'Give me the name of the person you're searching for first, then we'll fill out a form.'

'I'm looking for several . . . all Oderfeldt, is the name. And . . . um. Just look for Oderfeldt first please.'

Hanna almost laughed. 'Oderfeldt? But I was just . . .' Hanna gestured behind her. She used the moments of turning her head to take a deep breath, and wipe at her hopelessly stinging eyes. 'I was just looking at that file.'

'Did someone come looking for me?'

'I was just, I was just this second . . . it's . . . right back here, one moment please . . .'

The woman leaned over the desk. 'Who was it?' she called after Hanna, who had moved mechanically, shocked, back to the boxes of files. 'Are they here?' the woman looked around.

'But maybe there are several families with that name,' Hanna gabbled, her hands shaking a little as she brought the file forward. 'It might not be . . .' She looked into the woman's face, alight with that familiar look of terrified yearning. A sudden urge to embrace the woman came over her, at war with the building dread in her throat.

'It's . . . Karolina, isn't it?' Hanna asked. 'I – this is your file.' She found her throat choking the words, 'Jozef is looking for you.'

'Karolina, yes, yes, I'm looking for Karolina and Adam. Oderfeldt. Are they . . . is Karolina here? Sorry, I don't understand, can you? Please, are they here? Are they looking for me?' Alicia stared at the woman behind the desk. 'Are you crying? What did you say about Jozef?'

41

HANNA TOOK ALICIA deep into her mother's old neighbour-hood, over the river and down narrow cobbled streets Alicia had never seen before. It was nothing like Moscow, where the buildings were bursting with people, children spilling out of doorways, people hanging out of windows. Their footsteps echoed on the cobbles. When a child ran across the road in front of them, Alicia jumped. Hanna glanced behind as though worried Alicia would take a wrong turn or disappear, while Alicia trailed her, feeling relief so powerful it was like a teeth-rattling blow to the face: one of the ghosts had come back and was real, flesh, and that meant she wasn't alone; she had a place to begin.

They came to the steps of a tenement block. A line of washing hung from a window and some wide-eyed children in dirty clothes clustered around the door. One of them held out a begging hand to Alicia, who ignored it, opening her hands to show they were empty.

'Come on,' Hanna called.

She led Alicia through the bottom floor, mattresses and blankets scattered, sheets hung between alcoves to make little private spaces, like children's forts, but all empty. A pair of voices drifted from behind a wall.

The light had almost gone. The room was lit by one small

lamp on the floor. Hanna tutted at it, muttered, 'Waste!' and gestured for Alicia to follow her in.

Jozef was standing in a trance by his sketch, his fingers covered in charcoal hovering around Karolina's blurred face. He didn't hear them come in, and didn't move until Hanna went to touch his arm. 'My love,' she said. 'You'll never imagine who came into the office today. Look.'

Alicia stood with her arms folded around herself, unprepared for Jozef's face as he turned. Years and grief told around his eyes and mouth, his thinner cheeks. He smiled at her.

'Taking in waifs?' he asked Hanna, and touched his lover's hair as she wound her arms around him. 'We can share some food with you tonight,' he added to Alicia. 'Then Hanna can help you with where you could go next. She always—'

'Jozef,' Hanna interrupted him.

'Jozef, don't you recognise me?'

Alicia came to the easel. Jozef was still as Hanna moved away to make space. He watched Alicia look at the sketch and then hover her fingers, just as he had done, over the pencil-line people. 'Isn't this . . . ?' she said.

Jozef felt laughter or tears or both build in his throat. 'Alicia, is it you? You look so—'

He broke off, shocked, as she gripped him around the waist in a fierce hug, put her head against his chest. He put his arms gently around her, looked at Hanna, whose tears glinted in the lamplight.

'Are you all right?' He pushed her back softly, held her by the arms. 'But of course it's you. Look at those dark eyes, just the same. Are you . . . where did you go? I know it was Lwów first. Your parents and . . . and Karolina?'

'Jozef, don't ask too many things at once,' Hanna said. 'Let's have a drink. Apparently Greta in the next block found some vodka. I'll – you two stay here a moment.' Her heavy tread echoed all the way out into the street.

Jozef kissed Alicia's hand, his chapped lips a scratching scrap of affection.

'I don't want to ask you too many questions, but your sister—'

'Mama died. I don't know where Karolina and Papa are.'

Alicia paused, remembering the slick of sweat on her mother's face, how she'd brought back the old joke, *Alicia, won't you tell them I'm friends with Stalin, tell them to get me a doctor, Stalin knows me, do you remember?* When she died, it was mid-sentence, talking in delirium, *France, France, I still can't believe it, Margo. With Edie and little Marc* . . .

Jozef was flicking through a kaleidoscope of memories: Adam, gesticulating wildly with his pipe, full of passion about some new project. Anna in an evening gown, smiling at him through red lips as she lit another cigarette. Karolina, still lost, in his arms.

'I'm sorry,' he said, hating the hollow sound of it. 'Your mother was—' I can't do it in words, he thought. I'll have to paint Anna as I remember her.

'She tried hard not to die,' Alicia said. 'She was angry about it.'

'But Karolcia? The last letter I had from her was from Lwów. Then nothing. I tried to find out—'

'You forgot about her. That woman is your new lover.' Alicia was surprised by the shades of a forgotten voice returning: petulant and young. She could have stamped her foot like her old self, glared, thrown things. It might feel good to do those things, like acting in a play, like the way she fell into conversations in her head with Papa, and she was always careful to play the role of the girl he knew. When she looked at Jozef she felt a lurch of grief, as though his horror was flooding the room. He had covered his face with his hands, and the effect was so childlike that she put her arms around his waist again.

'Never,' he said.

'She might still come back,' Alicia said. 'We'll look for her.'

Jozef wiped his face and when his hands came down again he had smoothed his features over, recomposed himself.

'I went to your old apartment today.'

Alicia laughed in surprise. 'But I was just there.'

'Did you go inside?' Jozef asked.

'No, there was a neighbour I spoke to . . . there are people staying there.'

'Not today,' he shrugged. 'There's a window you can get through in the back.' He blushed. 'I've been a few times, when I'm working on paintings from that time. It helps.' He rubbed his face again. 'Have some tea, it's awful but – you just arrived, you must be starving—'

'I ate a little on the journey,' Alicia said as Jozef moved to the tiny kitchen, a line of hot plates along a wall. 'I sold some sketches,' she added, trying to suppress the pride in her voice.

He stopped bustling around a stove and looked at her, a cigarette held between his teeth. His haggard face was transformed for a moment. 'You still draw?'

'Yes, I'm good.'

He laughed. 'Alicia, that's wonderful. Show me, show me,' he said, holding up a finger to wait a moment while he made the tea.

'You were lucky,' he said, lighting the stove. 'I hope you know you were lucky that Anna got you out. Show me, come on!'

'Come outside, the light is no good in here.'

So they sat on the step under a glowing sky as they sipped the weak tea. Hanna stayed away, chatting with neighbours and letting them be. Alicia showed him the sketches of Tomas and Rose, feeling safer with strangers to start with. Jozef was silent for a while, and she began to feel hopeless, until he began nodding and moving his fingers over the points that mattered: the clasped hands and the boy's eyes.

'How was the final drawing?'

'Good,' she said.

'Show me more,' he said, glancing up at the sky. 'We have a few minutes.'

So she showed him the barn, the way she had tried to capture the warm sweetness of the hay in pencil lines. She showed him Margo's house and the little room and fireplace, the chairs they had slept in, Janina's hands around a clutch of sewing. She showed him Margo in a cramped kitchen, the ceiling brushing her bent back, and then Margo-in-layers: a piece she'd only finished a few weeks before, Margo's faces lifting off one after the other, the beautiful sweetness of Margo's true face left while her hands held the others. She hesitated and then showed him her mother's face in profile, looking from a window in a thunderstorm, then again lying next to Leo with the light split by the barred windows, and the sketches of Anna's broken and splitting hands. She showed him her older ghosts: Papa's face and figure, often in motion, walking towards the frame, purposeful, his arms already open for an embrace. And finally Karolina, curled up like a sleeping seed inside flowers and vegetables, the back of her hair as she leaned over a book, her figure standing on the stairs in the Bernardyńska apartment. Alicia looked away as Jozef looked at these, his breath shallow. She kept looking away as he closed the sketchbook and wiped his face with the back of his sleeve. It was cold now that the sun had disappeared behind the pristine buildings and they sat shivering in the dusk.

'They're good.'

'I know.'

'You have lots of our painting in there.'

'Yes – wait, I didn't show you those.'

'You're a little off on the lines, but the details are almost perfect.'

Alicia felt herself flush.

'Where are all your pieces from before?' she asked.

Jozef shrugged. 'All the unsold ones from my studio are just . . . gone. Some of them from good families like yours were seized. It was chaos.'

'Where do you think my portrait is?'

'I have no idea.'

'We took it with us to Lwów.'

'You kept it? I'm pleased.' The thought of that portrait, that summer distilled in paint, travelling with his Karolcia, made him warm. 'So it's in Lwów, with your family? But that's wonderful! You should sell it, Alicia, I don't mean to brag but I think it will fetch—'

'No, we lost it on the way. The same moment we lost Papa.' Alicia remembered how she had cried out for her painting, how important it had seemed. As though they could hold it out like a talisman or a weapon, a symbol of who they were. Reaching further back, her memory offered up a glimpse of the monster in Glowny Square who had so frightened her on her birthday years before. She couldn't remember or imagine how the two, the painting and that very first attack, were connected in her mind. Instead she thought of Papa sprawled helpless on the ice, with an answering squirm in her guts, still, after everything. She felt pinpricks of gladness that this and the moment in the mud outside Kraków were the worst she had seen of her Papa in the new world that had avalanched over them.

Jozef offered another useless *I'm sorry* and they drew together as the sky gave up the last of its light. The glow of the odd lamp in the windows of buildings made it seem like people were camping in the heart of the city.

'What will you do?' Jozef asked.

'I need money.'

'Yes, we all need that.'

'I'd hoped . . . somehow the portrait of me had come back to you. Or you'd know where to look,' she said.

'Someone might have picked it up,' he offered, opening his hands in a gesture of hope, 'and . . . it's on a wall somewhere, or . . .'

'Or more likely it just got smashed and buried in the mud where we left it.'

'I loved the painting too, Alicia. It meant a lot to me.' He found her hand, gave it a squeeze.

Alicia looked at him. She could only see his profile now, looking down at his shoes, or into his hands. She gripped her sketchbook, smothered laughter at how he had misunderstood her. The painting could still save her.

42

HANNA STILL HAD the Oderfeldt file. Gripped between her fingers in the initial daze as she walked Alicia home that day, she'd transferred it to the inner pocket of her home-sewn jacket, carrying Jozef's letters and Karolina's name next to her heart. Every day for a week, while Jozef and Alicia worked, she carried it back and forth across the river, still so elated by the miracle of Alicia – a real, flesh and blood ghost come to life, and not the ghost that could shred all her happiness to pieces – that for those days she forgot the file, its portraits of desperate searching in paper and ink.

One night, sharing stone-like bread and what Hanna termed 'mystery soup', Jozef and Alicia wearing the same slightly haunted, exhausted expression, lost in the world they were rebuilding across the city, Alicia blinked and asked, 'Hanna, is there no news?'

Hanna licked soup from the back of her hand where it had dripped from a mangled spoon. 'Plenty! Today there was another miracle. A woman and her husband – he'd walked, *walked* all the way from Kazakhstan! And she had been hiding in the city. There's so many,' she added, abandoning the spoon and lifting the bowl to her lips to drink, 'like fairy-tale people coming out of the forests and from under the floors!'

Jozef rubbed the back of his neck while Alicia stared at

Hanna. Hanna drained her soup. 'Of course, you mean about Karolina—'

'Or my Papa,' Alicia said.

'You have been enquiring?' Jozef prompted.

'Of course.'

Satisfied, Alicia and Jozef sat back and fell into low conversation again about their project. It was a feeling akin to the worst of dreams: a prickling horror that spread through Hanna's limbs and stomach. She felt the file, heavy and sharp against her breast, wondered if she was evil or mad or both. The next day she slid the file back into place, feeling like a thief. She looked around as she did so, distracted as though about to be caught out in a terrible crime, and so she did not notice the slip of paper that had been placed where the file had been, a query that had come in for Oderfeldt that morning, from a thin young woman with wild brown hair.

Across the city, Jozef and Alicia were standing in the Oderfeldt apartment, catching the light between their fingers as it filtered through the Wawel and the magically unshattered window glass of the drawing room. Muffled footsteps from next door's flat and the small scratch of paper as it ruffled in the draught were the only sounds. Both artists barely breathed, trying to find something.

The apartment was a shell. The first morning they'd come, Alicia had sped from room to room like a little girl, exclaiming over the missing furniture and the spaces on the walls where paintings had been. The neighbour she'd met on her first night back in Kraków stood with Jozef on the stairs, listening to Alicia run from room to room. She offered Jozef a cigarette.

'You knew each other before?'

'Yes,' Jozef replied, taking the cigarette with a grateful nod and letting her light it.

'There was a couple here for a while, but they're gone. You may as well stay here for now until you get moved on.'

'Yes!' Alicia called down the stairs, her voice echoing against the wood. 'This is where they'll come first if they come back.'

That night they tried to sleep there, Hanna and Jozef curled up together by a fire in Adam's study, and Alicia on the floor of her parents' bedroom. They'd brought blankets and some other meagre comforts – a kettle, Jozef's art supplies – but the hollowed-out rooms, picked clean of everything from the old life that had been lived there, made the skin on Jozef's back prickle, as though he was trespassing on forbidden ground. He and Hanna quickly moved back to their cramped room across the river, and Alicia ate dinner with them every night before returning home, climbing through an open window into the kitchen.

For Alicia, the furnishings didn't matter. The rooms were hers, how the light fell through each window belonged to her, and the sound of the taps and the settling floors. Here she could pick her fingers along and name the missing books, changing the titles as she liked, depending on who she was missing most. A deep calm descended on her: she had done what she must, and come home, and now if her Papa and Karolina were alive they only needed to find their way back too. She felt her way around her old room, touching the walls, but when she came to her old hiding place, the memory of the day they had left pressing on her, stuffing Karolina's letters and her own sketches there, she stopped. She would wait until Karolina was here, she thought, knowing it was a lie to herself, and she was simply not strong enough, yet, to bruise her heart with relics.

*

Jozef and Alicia stood looking at the beginnings of the new *Portrait of Girl in a Red Dress.*

'That line is wrong.'

'No, that's perfect, it's this part,' Alicia curved a finger around the edge of the shape, 'it's a little too wide.'

'All right. Stand there again.'

She took up position, as she had years before, her hand placed just so, the light hitting the top of her head. Jozef began to sink beneath the surface of the light to find the sketch again, just as Alicia said, 'I'm going to paint her myself, once you've got the sketch in.'

'Oh?' He was surprised how stung he felt by this. 'Then it really will be a forged Pienta.' He gave a small laugh. 'Why not just let me paint her?'

Alicia waited a few seconds, trying to find the answer. 'I want to see if I can.'

'But I've already . . . found the colours again. In my head, I mean.'

'So have I.'

'I'd like to do it. I can't explain,' he said. She looked at him with a cool patience that gave him a shock of grief for Anna. 'It's . . .' he tried. 'I want to say goodbye, with it. Paint it for your mother and Karolina.'

'She might come back yet.'

He dropped his eyes back to the sketch.

They did separate sketches of the face first, Jozef's partly from Alicia's face now, and partly from memory of the lost girl he'd painted in 1938; for Alicia, this was an exercise she'd completed whenever she could get her hands on pencils and paper. They asked Hanna to judge one night back over the river, showing her their books by lamplight.

'Oh, I don't know anything about drawing.'

'But which is better, more interesting?' Jozef pressed. He'd found drawing the young girl again had opened wells of sadness in him, but he was satisfied with the way he'd captured her again: the tiny smile, the slightly knitted brows. Adam's view of her face softened by a father's love and pride.

'This one.'

'Ha!' Alicia threw back her head in delight. Jozef caught her joy as she rocked back and forth with it, the first time he had seen her laugh since her return, and the three of them made a circle of brief delight, emanating from Alicia and wrapping up the lovers.

'Sorry, my love,' Hanna whispered, and Jozef shook his head, smiling. He looked at Alicia's sketch and his happiness was quelled and deepened at once: he looked at Alicia again with a fierce respect. 'Yes, it's better,' he said. Alicia had failed in the exercise: it wasn't the same face at all. The eyes were darker, older, less serene. The small smile was almost untraceable. But it was a better, a truer face. Not a self-portrait exactly, nor a replica of the girl she had been, but something of both: a lost world and new forged one shown in nothing but flakes of lead.

By that time they'd finished the sketch, finding again the shape of the little girl Alicia had been, tracing the fall of her once thick hair around her shoulders as it now hung limp, and imagining the fall of the long-gone dress. The paint was hard to come by, especially the red. People laughed when they heard what the eccentric survivor was looking for, thinking him brain-addled by the war, 'Paint? Are you going to eat it? Are you going to write slogans on the walls? Enough of that!', but he found enough to mix a darker, rustier version of Alicia's red dress.

'We could use some blood,' Alicia said, when Jozef showed her the mix.

'Don't be so dramatic,' Hanna called from her spot under the window. She liked to sit there after work and watch Jozef paint, just as Karolina had once done. Neither Alicia or Jozef spoke of the way their hearts ached when she did that, for Jozef loved her too much and Alicia was too afraid to speak of how with every day without Karolina's arrival, her hope of seeing her sister again was draining.

'It's too dark,' Alicia countered.

'Yes, the original was brighter. But no one will remember that. It just needs to be close enough.'

'Mix it again. More vermilion.'

Over days Jozef focused on the folds of the dress fabric, using Alicia's sketches and their shared memories to recreate them. The darkness between the red seemed deeper than before, and the colour didn't sing in the same way, but it was deep and rich, and in the evening light he found the shine in it with touches of white and gold. While he worked on the dress, Alicia was painting her childhood hair, finding Janie's careful brushing there and the way she would twirl her fingers through it to make it curl. She remembered how Jozef's original had lightened her hair to gold, making the sunlight kiss the top of her head and fall in a gleam across her shoulder. This was the way her Papa had seen her, and so she poured his love into each brushstroke. She painted, too, the skin of her old self's arms, exclaiming over their plumpness and holding out her thin, sallow skin next to the canvas. At first they dripped paint on each other and swore as they got in each other's way, but soon found they worked in silent ease, sometimes stopping to watch and enjoy the other's colours. Finally Alicia worked on her own ghost's face, while Jozef, in the sunset pink light, painted Karolina's roses in the background.

Day after day slipped by in the strange quiet. No news came of their lost ones, and Hanna came every evening and watched them work, bringing stories of hope and questions about dinner. They would then walk to the old neighbourhood to cook and eat. The artists both knew they were in the last days of the work, and began to feel nervous.

'Hanna, do you think it will pass?' Alicia asked, on what would be the last day of this time.

'I don't know, I never saw the first one.'

'But do you think it's good?' Jozef asked.

'My love, all your paintings are magnificent.'

'It's finished,' Alicia said, as Jozef paused with a dripping brush. 'Don't add anything.'

'Just a few spots of—'

'No, it's finished. You should sign it.'

While he did so, she took his other hand and kissed it. 'Thank you.'

'So it's done?' Hanna came over, wrapped her arms around Jozef's waist. He leaned into her. 'Come and stay with us tonight, Alicia. We'll celebrate. Find some liquor somewhere. Bring the painting there, Jozef, so it isn't left alone overnight, in case someone else discovers this place.'

That night Alicia watched them by lamplight, Hanna curled into the crook of Jozef's arm. His face had lost some of its withering, softened by the flamelight and the living love in his arms, and whatever exorcism had been cast by remaking their painting. Laughing along to a joke Hanna had made that she had barely listened to, Alicia changed her mind: she wouldn't go back for the letters, hidden in the skirting board of her room, and she wouldn't find a discreet moment to give them to Jozef. Let them lie there safe in the dark, until Karolina came back, if she ever came back. Let Hanna and Jozef stay entwined in each other's arms like this until then.

'What will you do?' Hanna asked, breaking into Alicia's thoughts.

'Hope the first painting stays lost,' Alicia said.

'I mean if it works. You'll stay in Kraków? You and Jozef could start a forgery business,' Hanna said, laughing. Jozef met Alicia's eyes and smiled a sad smile, knowing already her reply.

'I want to leave Poland, if my family is gone.'

'But we can be your family. Jozef and I love you.' Hanna was surprised by herself, realising it was true. Karolina's sister! Perhaps it was only guilt, at her relief the older girl had never come back, but looking at this small, tense young ghost of Jozef's old life, cross-legged on the floor, Hanna felt real warmth in her chest.

'I want to leave too,' Jozef said. 'We can use the money for visas and travel, if it works,' he added, taking Hanna's hand, 'and get married there.'

'Where?'

Jozef shrugged, smiling. 'I don't know. How's your English? Canada is taking people. America too . . . Britain.'

'Not Britain. I don't want anywhere that was bombed,' Hanna said.

The three passed the rest of the evening making each other laugh with bits of broken English, trying different accents from the radio, imagining the food, the clothes, the houses and railway stations and markets. Somewhere in the currents of their conversation, it was agreed that wherever they went, it would be together.

Kraków, 1946

43

MAURICE SAUNTERED AROUND new pieces for secret sale, brought in from he didn't ask where. He was looking for his own work, to feel the queasy thrill of how it fitted in, to anxiously check it was passing. He'd made a hash of a recent piece, rushed and with the wrong type of canvas, so the whole thing was blasted from the foundations up, everything smeared and the colours bleeding into each other. He came close to getting arrested when he took it to a private collector, so now he preferred the safer, bribery-greased route of the gallery, and to walk first through the gallery rooms, listen to the whispered *hush-hush* conversations (for it was taboo, in this new world, to buy and sell; everything belonged to everyone, in this new Poland). He stood back from his own piece, a Milo Zysk. He knew the original had been burned along with most of Milo's other pieces, and with Milo himself, poor bastard, in a Dresden raid. It hadn't taken him long to start sourcing photographs and sketches from Milo's set, and to get to work. Satisfied, he kept walking, smiling at an officer who was pontificating to his girlfriend about the artist's promising young life cut tragically short. He wanted to impress her, and would pay well, Maurice suspected, if he could only engineer a sale.

Maurice was on his way towards the officer when he caught sight of the painting, looked into the girl's face. He had the same vague recognition as seeing a grown school friend, something in the face that sparks the brain, something that makes the time fall away, and he almost spoke to the girl in the painting, almost opened his mouth, right there in the gallery, almost asked, 'Don't I know you?'

He looked at the girl's almost-smile, her serene face, and memories flickered all around him: parties, artists, those rich, rich families and their beautiful rooms. Maurice leaned forward to find the muddy scrawl of the artist's name. Jozef. Of course.

He stepped close to the painting again, forgetting his officer and his easy money; there would be others.

A party on Bernardyńska. Yes, that was right. He'd been invited to a party with the smart Bernardyńska set and their satellite artists, his friend Ben had arranged it. Just before the war. She'd been hanging in a drawing room full of modern pieces, that little circle that clustered around the university set did good work. He'd forged something for the host, made quite a lot, and gone along to see it on the walls and enjoy the thrill of fooling them all. Maurice felt, for a moment, the heat of that night, how stuffy the room had been, all of them swimming in cigar smoke, until the host – Oderfeldt, Adam Oderfeldt, of course, there was a portrait of him, somewhere, probably here, also good – until Oderfeldt threw open, theatrically, the huge doors, letting in the cooler night air, and they all cooed over the Wawel, its lights glowing against the late pink skies of summer. Had the girl from the painting been there? Must have been, there were always the sons and daughters of the house milling around, to show off their piano playing, singing, French. But he couldn't remember her, or what her real name had been. But here was her painted self. The family were Jews, Maurice remembered with a jolt, and as he did so this wisp of the girl's old world, and her real name, he allowed to evaporate, realising he was looking at a ghost.

He went to his usual contact, a short, sweaty man with frightened eyes. He put Maurice in mind of a mole, all wringing hands and darting looks at the floor: he was altogether wrong for this line of work.

'No nibbles yet, Maurice,' the man said, 'on your piece.'

'Milo's piece, Kristopher. I'm merely passing on what I found. For the good of the nation.'

'Of course.' Kristopher gave a nervous laugh.

'I'm just wondering about another piece,' Maurice murmured. 'Pienta, made quite a splash before the war.'

'Oh! Yes, we're excited for that one. To have it back, I mean, for the people to enjoy. Came in a year ago.'

'But where did you get it? From . . . one of my colleagues?'

'It was found in an attic, right here in the city! Hidden, you know, like so many of them . . . but this one was found and returned.' Kristopher dropped his voice, began walking towards the painting. 'It's to be a very carefully managed sale, very delicate.'

'Who brought her in?' Maurice asked. He was becoming excited, but quelled the movement of his arms, willed his skin to stay pale. Kristopher, though always on edge, had nothing of the guardedness, the nerves, of someone who knew he was sitting on a potential fortune.

'The couple who found her. It was all managed quietly. I paid a significant amount. It's the original, I'm certain.'

'I'll give you five hundred for her. I knew the artist, one of my old friends,' he added, with just enough sorrow to be convincing, a small shake as he rubbed at his eyes. 'He was arrested very early, disappeared. He was engaged to be married, you know . . . terrible. I'd so like to have it.'

'So you can flood the market with copies,' Kristopher whispered, and snorted.

'And devalue the work of a mourned friend?'

Kristopher opened his mouth to retort, fell silent as a group of twittering visitors passed, rubbed at his bald patch. 'It's complicated. The family have made a claim.'

It was Maurice's turn to snort. 'You mean a servant, or a third cousin.'

'Obviously we don't want a scene, or authorities . . .'

'Of course not,' Maurice said, wondering if he could get his work out of there in time, if the gallery with its secret deals was to be investigated.

'So we'll take a cut, enough to cover the original sale, and sell it on for her if she agrees.'

'Sell it to me,' Maurice said. 'What is she asking for it?'

Kristopher gave a wet little sniff. 'We'll need to set up a meeting.'

The painting was taken down, covered again, and carried out by Maurice and Kristopher, after hours, into a new room full of more lost things.

The seller was waiting. She was vastly pregnant, holding her hands over her belly and shifting her weight from foot to foot. Her hair had been wrestled into a bun and wisps escaped around her face. As he set the painting down and approached, Maurice assessed her face. It had the hardened look some carried these days, weary and sad but with an underlayer of steel. The woman's husband patrolled around the room, shooting worried looks at the door.

'Don't worry,' Kristopher said. 'It's just us.'

The man whispered something to his pregnant wife and she waved him away.

'Maurice,' he said, holding out his hand and studying her face. He could see a slight resemblance, but she could still be a crook. He was good at spotting his own kind.

'Karolina,' she said, her grip firm. 'I understand you want to buy my painting.'

'Yes.'

'I'm hoping to take it with me to England.'

'But it's been sold to the nation,' Maurice said, with his full, perfect smile.

'Whoever found it had no *right* to sell it. It belongs to my family. If there's a problem,' she glanced at her husband, who nodded, 'we'll have to report it to the authorities, and—'

'Mrs Garside, please, we've already agreed . . .' Kristopher wheedled.

'I didn't mean to offend you,' Maurice soothed. 'Only the painting means so much to me. Jozef was a dear friend, you see.'

The woman stiffened, and he saw he had mis-stepped. She turned away, then back with a surprising sharpness to her movement, given the heaviness of her body. 'I don't understand,' she said. Her voice had changed, softened to a tremulous, thin sound. Maurice was torn between guilt and elation: he had unwittingly peeled away a layer of armour without even trying, laid her bare, ready for the sale. 'You want it to . . . return to him?' When he didn't respond, she continued, answering herself, 'No, to remember him by, to remember him by, isn't it? It is, it is . . .' Her husband rushed to her side as her voice rose, took her hand.

'Ina,' he said, and Maurice clocked how he stroked her wrist in slow, countable touches, how he pulled her back, almost invisibly, from the brink of a spiral of questions she would answer herself, tears and worse; he'd seen it, everyone, all the survivors, all across Europe and beyond, had seen it, played out a thousand times.

'Well, yes,' Maurice said.

She was breathing heavily. 'Which is it?'

'Oh, I – well he was arrested early on, and—'

She nodded, her face becoming blank and hard again.

'I want,' he pressed gently, 'to have her shown in a proper public gallery . . .'

A peeved voice came, 'This *is* a—'

Maurice shushed Kristopher with a look. 'A place,' he drew nearer, considered taking her hand, thought better of it, 'a respectable gallery where she can be really seen. I have many contacts, friends, supporters of Jozef's work, his legacy.'

'Ina,' her husband said. 'Won't you consider it? It's an awful lot to arrange to take it with us.' He had to call after her as she walked away from all of them, towards the painting. She gazed at her face, and a lost world unfurled around her, lost voices whispered in her head. The girl's hand on the chair was the same hand she knew, resting in her own as they whispered each other to sleep through abandoned rooms. She held the face of the girl's ghost in her mind's hands. Looking into it now she felt somehow a grown Alicia's face looked back at her, a depth to the eyes that hadn't been there before. Her eyes drifted to the roses, and the day she had first kissed Jozef pressed into her body. The years between falling away, all the years in Lwów with its horrors, the beatings and murders in the streets, Isaac and Sammy and Margo disappearing one by one. A squirm from her baby pulled her back into the room. She placed her hands back on her belly, its swimming promise.

Kristopher peeled off his own notes, licked his fingers and counted them with practised speed, before stuffing the rest into Karolina's hand. Maurice's handshake was tight. He rewrapped the painting so quickly the girl's face had disappeared under the sheet in the moments Karolina had turned back to her husband for a steadying forehead kiss. When he carried the painting away, the dealer scurrying behind him like a little rodent, Karolina followed even to his car door, which was closed in her face.

Maurice's apartment brimmed with half-finished forgeries, contraband, piles of cash (some fake, some real), medals stolen from dying men, jewellery stolen from the lost. It all sat in boxes or in piles on the rickety wooden table in the tiny kitchen, where Maurice cooked up pills of flour and sometimes rat poison, to sell to men who sold them to other, more desperate men and women, the ones who wished to forget. He hauled the painting in and set her against that table, which tottered and threatened to spill its piles onto the floor. He steadied it, and unwrapped her.

He lit a cigar to sit and study her, steadied his breathing as he sucked, feeling the burn in his throat. She'll fly, he thought. He had a good sense for what some buyers were looking for: a nostalgia hit laced with poignancy, a long-dead child from a world turned to dust, a painting that was written about and talked about in the magazines just before that velvet, that soft hair, that wallpaper, roses and softness and rich, well-fed, milky skin, found itself swallowed up in gun metal and smoke. Sell them a tiny slice of that old world and they'd pay anything for it. Some of them were still rich. The pregnant woman, some old lover of poor Jozef's (he didn't believe for a second she was truly an Oderfeldt, but it was more trouble than it was worth to contest the claim) could have asked for five times what she did and he'd still make a profit.

He traced a finger along Jozef's signature, remembered a long ago night in a bar, before the war. A serious, sensitive soul he'd been. Talented for sure, and nervous about this piece. It had turned out well. Maurice turned away to tap cigar ash into the sink, a rare sadness settling around his chest. He couldn't think of any of that set who were likely to still be alive.

'Do stop smoking around the food, Maurice.' His boyfriend Pietror swept in, his dressing gown trailing behind him, his hair in a silk scarf that Maurice had traded good quality tobacco for, after some row or other.

'Food?' Maurice echoed, still looking at the girl.

Pietror flung out an arm towards a pile of vegetables next to the sink. 'Do you know what I had to go through to get these? You have to eat properly.'

'I'll take you out! I'm about to make a big sale. Look at her!' He pulled Pietror to his side, gave him a kiss. He smelled of cheap perfume and the heavy, sticky cream he insisted on using on his skin.

'Oh!' Pietror breathed. 'What a horrible old-fashioned painting! My mother would *love* it.'

'It seems old-fashioned because the world has changed,' Maurice said, feeling defensive, wanting to cover the canvas again. 'She's like . . . the days just before the world went mad, there she is, just standing looking out from a dead girl's eyes.'

'Ugh, how morbid you are,' Pietror said, moving to the sink. He heard the sullenness in his lover's silent draw on his cigar, and added, 'We can look at photographs, newsreels for all that, not that I see why you'd ever want to, dreadful business, all of it.' He began rifling through the cupboards.

'What are you looking for? There's a lot of money to be made in looking back,' Maurice said, with a shrug.

'A chopping board. You live like an animal. People want to look to the future, Maurice.'

'Oh, don't be such an old woman.'

He gave Pietror a long, deep kiss, but when Maurice pulled back to hold Pietror's face in his hands, his lover dipped his eyes, fiddled with the sash on his dressing gown. Maurice felt a fracture widen between them. He covered the painting up again. 'Forget I mentioned it,' he said. 'Forget all about it.'

A few days later Maurice was back at the gallery, collecting his money for the fake Milo painting.

'That . . . lodger of yours,' Kristopher said, counting out notes from a wad of banknotes.

'Pietror?'

'He's been talking. Saying the wrong . . .' Kristopher licked his finger as a note stuck, '. . . vague phrases. To the wrong people.'

'What people?'

'We won't be working together again, Maurice.' Kristopher gave him a watery, apologetic smile.

When he got back to the apartment, sweating, Pietror was gone. A swift check of the kitchen showed him the piles of cash untouched, but there was a stale tinge to the air, despite the half-drunk cups of ersatz coffee in the sink, the rumpled, cooled bedsheets, that told him Pietror would not be returning.

In the war, a Romany family had hidden behind a wardrobe in the back room. There was a sliding panel: the landlady had shown him when he moved in. *Imagine*, she said, *how it must have stunk in there*, and she'd laughed. Now Maurice slid that panel over the painting, so it was back in the darkness. With it were golden chains, watches, the knives, the piles of money. Maurice was just looping back to the kitchen to pile up more cash into his arms, along with the bags of fake pills, when banging on the door shook the little flat. The voices of the police outside sent a shake through his body that scattered the cash and pills across the floor.

Kraków, 1977

44

KAROLINA BITTERLY REGRETTED letting the painting go to those crooks, who had buried or lost it, or let it go to some fat red-cheeked private collector who would leave it in a drawing room to be forgotten. She read stories of uncovered lost paintings and objects, stolen from families like hers, and made sure to talk about the painting and its subject every day to the baby, then the boy, then the young man.

She named him George, eager to cement his Englishness. He was pale, tall and thin, with Adam's frame and long, elegant hands, and Anna's sharp tongue and eagerness to be alone. He inherited, too, Alicia's love of colours and shapes of things, her quietness and watchfulness, her capacity for lies and secret-keeping. His mother told George, a thousand times, in a thousand different ways, in her lisping Polish accent, patting his head or kissing his cheek or doing up the buttons on his coat, *That painting is yours, you know, make sure you get it some day. They all but forced me to sell it, I had to, you know, we were trying to get to England. A man who loved me painted it of our little Ala, who died somewhere out in Russia in the snow. But you know things stolen from us are being returned. Make sure you get the painting, you get her some day, she belongs with you. He'd want you to have it, the painter. They'd both want you to have it.* George nodded along and half-listened, just as he did to the other, rare flakes of her old life that floated through her accented chatter like dust in sunlight, always of before the war: Anna's soft skin, when you kissed her cheek goodnight, her perfume, the silk dresses, a gold pen her father had owned, Alicia's curls, their little dogs, the fresh flowers every morning in summer, sugar mice in the kitchen . . . he absorbed it all as he played with toy soldiers on their front lawn, then on walks along the beach, on the way to school, in the car. He grew up with a Sussex accent and a vague sense that his blood ran back to somewhere over the sea.

In the wilderness year after his mother's death, George travelled to Poland for the first time. He was thirty but looked eighteen, awkward and too tall and wearing a florescent backpack full of ugly knitwear, terrified of the legendary Eastern European cold. When he arrived, he realised he had imagined the world his mother had conjured for him in a kind of theatrical display, as though there would be a waving grandmother in an immaculate dress, an official handing the painting over to him at the airport. On the first day he dutifully followed a city map, biting off his thick gloves every time he needed to get it out of his pack, then swearing as his fingers froze, to Bernardyńska. His mother never gave him a number, but he stood outside the most likely address, just opposite the castle building, as she'd said. There was illegible graffiti on the door, behind an iron grate. A woman smiled at him and asked something in Polish as she approached.

'Oh, sorry, English.'

'Tourist?'

'Yes, well. This was my mother's house. My mother lived here.'

'Halby?'

'Um, no, Garside . . . no, sorry, Oderfeldt.'

The woman gave an elaborate shrug and a smile, and opened the door, a delicious warmth curling from the hallway inside.

'What flat?'

'Um, I don't know.'

She shrugged again, and he felt stupid, stepped back into the street as she closed the door.

The National Museum where the painting lived now was outside the city: he had to get a bus, and wandered around, lost, before he came across the pretty building with large stone steps. The woman at the front desk didn't speak English but handed him a leaflet with sections in different colours. He headed for Polish paintings, on the top floor, where he passed frame after frame of faces and family groups and landscapes, fruit and flowers, buildings, dogs. He didn't know anything about art and began to look forward to his hotel room back in the city, a film and room service. There was no girl with blonde hair in a red dress to be found. He went to sit in a window seat, a view down into a courtyard full of trees. Not a bad place to end up, he thought, if he could only find her. A man in a suit was walking through the gallery, a lanyard hanging over his tie, his hands behind his back like a soldier. George approached him.

'I can help?' the man asked.

George blushed. He must look so out of place, he realised.

'My mother always told me about a painting here.'

'Yes?'

'Um, it's called *Girl in a Red Dress*, no, sorry, *Portrait of Girl in a Red Dress*.'

'Ah, yes, Pienta?'

'Oh, um, sorry, I don't know. It was of my aunt, my

mother's younger sister, actually,' George said, blushing again as the man raised his eyebrows, seemingly impressed.

'Ah, please. This way.' He led George to a side room, sofas and plants, a new receptionist. There were paintings stacked against a wall, face down, the whites of their backs exposed and pencil marks scrawled on the bare canvas, serial numbers and arrows George could not decipher.

The man chatted in Polish to the woman behind the desk, then turned back. 'Sorry, please,' he said, and smiled, gesturing to the pile of paintings.

George rocked on his heels, hooked his long fingers under his backpack straps. In moments like these, when he felt like a little boy, he missed his mother with breath-taking fierceness. Besides, she could have spoken to them in Polish. He felt stunned by his own incompetence as a son in not bringing her here before.

'Please,' the man said again. He came over and pointed again at the paintings, smiled, as though inviting a child to play. 'You can look for her.'

'Oh.' So he put down his bag, began gingerly moving the canvases. 'I can just . . .'

'Yes, yes.'

Here were more figures, fields. One striking one of a group on a bus, or a tram: ghostly faces seeming to stare out of the frame.

'No, not this one, you said, *Girl in Red*, no? Hmm,' the man said, picking up another frame and setting it aside with ease. 'No, no, no . . . ah! This is her, yes?'

He flipped the painting around, set it down on the floor. It was frameless, taped to a piece of thick white card. George stood over it and looked into Alicia's face. 'This is her?' he echoed, looking into her face. She wasn't what he was expecting, although she was also exactly as his mother had described: the dress was blood red, billowing at the shoulders, the girl's, his aunt's, young little face was serious and playful all at once, a tiny smile playing at her lips, her dark eyes seeming to hold laughter in them.

'I should have brought her sooner,' George said, to himself.

'You can't take her,' the man said, simply.

'Oh, no, I know, of course,' George laughed. 'She's . . . it's a beautiful . . . why isn't she on display?'

'Ah, now we come to the point,' the man said, smiling. He came to stand at George's side, looking down at *Girl*. 'It seems she's only a copy.'

George looked at him. 'Oh?'

'A forgery. So many from the period, you know. It was a chaotic time!'

'Yes, of course.'

'But you're too young to know,' the man dismissed him with a wave of his hand. 'Anyway, this is a good one, a very good one. We're looking for the records of the original sale.'

'I see.'

'We're doing some tests. This one was found at the back of a wardrobe in the sixties. But it's just a copy! It's an interesting story,' the man said, as he guided George to the door. 'There were rumours that a whole Romany family hid behind the same wardrobe in the war. A space made, you know,' he made a box shape in the air with his hands, 'and then later one of these . . . thieves, bad persons . . . hid all kinds of things in there.'

'All right. Well, thank you, anyway. I'll, um, if I leave a number, would someone call me, if, I don't know, the real one is ever found?'

'Yes, of course, but if she is, she belongs to the museum.'

389

George nodded and smiled, feeling his failure settle on his shoulders. He felt a desert opening behind him, the realisation that he had no family at all, that he was the last of a line, all of his mother's and father's blood stopped up in one body. He made fervent resolutions as he was walked back through the side door, through the gallery rooms, down the steps: he'd hire an investigator, for his dear Mum's sake. He'd ask the press in England to look into it; that kind of thing sometimes ran at weekends. This would give him something to do. But by the time he stepped down from the bus back into the city, his resolve was already weakening.

Back in Kraków, George strolled through Glowny Square, taking pictures of the Cloth Hall, the beautiful church spire. He joined a small crowd to watch the bugler who called in the hour. He drank beer in patio bars, and took a bus to a stadium to watch the football match he really came to see. He hoped his mother's ghost might be satisfied, noticing only a tiny seed of disappointment not to have the money she'd promised he was owed. If he wondered how the painting was forged or by whom, it was fleeting, a vague plucking at the back of his mind.

Kraków, 2009

45

GEORGE AND MARC STEFAN met first in Glowny Square, where they ordered hot cider and grinned at one another, almost overcome by shyness. They both laid out prepared packages of photographs on the tablecloth as a waiter placed the cider in smoking carafes at the edge of the table and brought them blankets for their knees.

'You've been to Kraków before?' Marc asked in French-accented English.

'Yes, just once, years back. My mother always wanted me to come, and find the painting, but it turned out it was a fake! Must have been . . . let's see, my Mum died in '76 . . .' George smiled at him. 'Do you think we look like each other?'

Marc smiled too. 'I don't know! I think maybe you look a little like my granddaughter, you have the same ears.'

They smiled shyly at one another.

'What time is the . . .'

'Two o'clock.'

Marc took out a pen. He sketched out the family tree on the back of a napkin while George filled in gaps as he knew them.

'So Karolina, she's this branch . . . that's my mother. And her sister, Alicia, that's the girl in the painting, and she's your . . . hang on . . . so my aunt and your half-sister.'

'Okay, so, I add my mother here . . . Edie.'

'Yes, that's right.'

'And here I add me, my daughter Natalia, my grand-daughter Sophie . . . so she's the youngest of the line!'

'A little heiress!'

'Bof,' Marc said, making George laugh with the French sound.

George hesitated, then asked, 'Do you know what happened to your father, my grandfather?'

That made them smile at one another, both unused to family connections they hadn't built themselves, but Marc's faded.

'Yes.'

'You do? My Mum never . . .'

'It's easy to find. I asked at a library, I remember, doing a project in high school. My mother always knew or suspected I think but . . .' Marc shrugged.

George took a sip of cider. 'Could you . . .'

'He was arrested in 1940, early. Taken to the ghetto. Then to the camp. Auschwitz. The second one, Birkenau.'

George felt an impulse to reach out, as though his mother had stirred somewhere in him, and wanted to embrace the little brother she never met.

'I'm sorry,' he said lamely.

'I'm sorry too, very sad, but I never met him,' Marc said. 'That I remember, anyway.'

'Do you . . . want to go to Auschwitz, while we're here? You can do a day tour . . .'

'No, I don't think so.'

They sat looking out across the Glowny, pigeons chasing each other across the cobbles. George's mind drifted and imagined, how right until the end, his grandfather couldn't believe it: he still thought there would be a letter, a phone call, a car to pick him up, that Edie or Anna or both would be waiting for him beyond the barbed wire.

'And this side . . . Anna, my grandmother?'

Marc smiled. 'My mother never met her. I think, you know . . .' he brought his hands together and then separated them.

George laughed again. 'Yes, I wonder if they knew about each other.'

'Oh yes, well my mother knew, anyway. She used to find pictures of Anna in his pockets, you know? And pictures of the daughters, said it drove her crazy.'

'And here, Alicia,' George said, underlining her name with his finger. 'My Mum talked about her all the time.'

'What happened to her?'

'I think she must have died in Russia, perhaps. My mother looked for her when she came back to Kraków, but there was never any word of her. She said there were files, for if people had made enquiries, you know? At the Red Cross. And there was nothing for her, our, family at all. She went to her old apartment too but it was empty. She moved to England soon afterwards. Started again.'

The family tree sketched in, warmth brimming between the men, they paid the bill and made their way to the museum. There they wandered through rooms of landscapes and faces until they came to the little girl in the red dress, her hair falling across her shoulder. Next to her was Jozef and Alicia's second painting, retrieved from the back rooms, the twin Jozef had sold to Kristopher and his crooked art gallery. The curators had written a small piece about the excellent quality of the forgery, mounted next to the brass plaque, but it was in Polish, which neither Marc nor George could read.

Adam's son and his grandson stood with their arms folded, glancing at each other, Marc fiddling with his watch.

'Well, there she is,' George said. *There you are, Mum, I found her*, he added silently.

'It's a pretty enough painting.'

They laughed.

'I'm afraid I don't know anything about art,' George said.

'I prefer modern pieces, you know?'

They lapsed into silence.

'Must have been a thrill to find it, though, in the walls like that!' Marc Stefan tried.

'Skirting board, they said. A panel.'

'Skirt?'

George laughed, pointed to the ones in the room.

'Ah! And . . . it's nice, that it was at home all this time.'

George took a step closer to the portrait. The man on the phone had been almost breathless, telling him how a decorator had dropped a tin of paint that rolled across the room and cracked open a secret panel. Out they'd pulled the portrait, rolled up and covered in dust, along with old, flaking letters and books. George drew still closer to Alicia's face. 'My mother said she was terribly spoiled, her little sister.'

'Yes, look at that dress!' Marc gave a small laugh. 'Though she must have been well behaved enough. Can't imagine Sophie ever standing still long enough to be painted like that!'

'Do you have a photograph of her? Do they,' George gestured to the painting, 'look alike?'

'Oh! Not really . . .' Marc fumbled in his bag, pulled out a phone. 'Look. You should meet her! Come to France sometime, you must come in the summer . . .'

They drifted away to a bench and sat looking at photographs of the young Sophie, smiling in a sundress and shades with pink plastic frames.

Absorbed in this way, they almost missed her. She stood back from the portrait for a long time, legs crossed like a ballerina, her arms knotted behind her back. Her stillness was almost audible; people turned to her as though she spoke, and studied her poise, the elegant lines of her face. She seemed unaware of the room, fixed on the painting. Soon she moved closer. Marc and George, now delighting in the broken ice between them, were laughing over a story of Sophie's naughtiness just as the woman passed them, and George glanced up. He watched the woman, admiring her elegant, slow movements and feeling a quietly reflected pride in how absorbed she was by his family's portrait. She studied the plaque Marc and he had been unable to decipher. Marc followed his attention, and when the woman gave a little sound, of surprise or perhaps recognition, Marc stood and ventured, 'Oh, do you speak French? Or English? Could you translate for us?'

'We can't read the Polish,' George added, joining Marc as he approached the woman.

'Of course,' the woman said. 'It's about finding the forgery, this one,' she gestured. 'And then the real one so recently. It theorises,' her face broke into a wide smile, 'that Pienta himself made the forgery, so accurate and good it is.'

'Thank you,' George said, and she nodded. He glanced at Marc and shared a look of embarrassed pride as he began to add, 'That's actually our—'

'They're half right,' the woman interrupted him. She had an accent, American or Canadian, that George couldn't place.

There was something powerfully familiar about her. 'It was Jozef and my mother herself who made it together.'

Marc, translating in his head, took a second longer than George. By the time he had broken into a delighted, astonished laugh, George was already holding out his hand, embarrassed by how his fingers trembled with shock and joy. 'I think we're cousins,' he said.

Kraków, 1939

46

ADAM WAS ALREADY rifling through his pockets for his papers, ready for the arrest procedures, calculating how much cash was in the lining of his coat, enough to bribe these ones or perhaps the next, or at least to get a phone call, to get to Sammy or to Friel, when the soldiers slammed the door of his car, honking the horn like excited teenagers behind their first wheel. They waved him away, starting the engine and beginning to push through the crowd just as he had done. One of them was waving his gun through the windows, laughing at the cowering people who scattered as they saw it, saw them.

Adam stared after the car, becoming aware of the cold as the sun drained away, realising he was gloveless. He put his hands in his pockets, and struggled back towards where Anna had pulled the girls from the car, the piles of carpets and suitcases, paintings, books, jewellery, their life in Kraków scattered through the mud and grass. He stood on tiptoes, called Anna's name, knowing it was trying to catch water in his hands.

The piles of things he tried to gather together into tighter space, waiting for Anna to find her way back to it with the girls. He sat for a while on one of the rolled-up carpets, yelling at people as they kicked over the piles as they walked, and one or two who simply picked up small boxes, even cases, wrapped furs around them and walked on.

'Thieves!' Adam cried, rage coursing through him, but unable to give chase, to take on the wretched criminals; only one he tackled, wrenching Jozef's painting of Alicia from a woman's hands, and pushing her violently back into the stream. He could have struck her face, but instead took the painted Alicia back with him, to sit on his knees and wait for her living figure to come back. Wrapping his hands in one of Anna's scarves, snarling at the thieves, he waited for two hours. By then only the carpet he sat on, two suitcases, and the paintings were left.

He looked into Alicia's painted face. When Jozef had first revealed it to him, back in the apartment, her portrait seemed on the point of laughing, the little smile just curbed; he imagined her biting her tongue behind her lips, so as to appear serious and not get into trouble. How he loved that rare look on her face, how he loved her laugh for its rarity, just as he did her mother's. But now that he looked in the bleak grey light, the people streaming around him, picking at his things like crows at carrion, the painted eyes looked sad, the eyebrows just beginning to knot, as though tears were coming. Stupid, childish: Anna would roll her eyes at him, laugh at him, call him a boy. Still he held the portrait to him as though comforting it, or it him, wrapping his arms around the heavy frame.

'Where have you and your mother and sister gone? Back home?' he asked her. Alicia's painted face stared up at him. He wrapped her up in one of the rugs, patting her in place as though tucking a child into bed. The evening was closing in.

Adam turned to go home. He looked back to see two German soldiers picking through his things. They didn't notice him staring, or feel his fury at them and himself for leaving everything behind. One of them was holding the painting. It was pointless to torture himself and watch them carry it away, but he stood anyway, risking arrest and a beating and the what-else to twist the knife in his own stomach. Instead he watched the soldier lie the painting down against a rolled-up rug, and walk away, disappearing across the field. On impulse, Adam hurried back and flipped the painting over, unhooking the frame, and rolled his painted daughter up in his inner pocket.

When he was twisted by the shoulder to face the wrong way, carried with the current of refugees away from home, he dodged and stepped until he was back on the right path. As he approached Kraków he listened for the wail of sirens and the engine-shudder of planes, watched for drifting smoke, even fire. But there was only the trudge of people and the smell of churned-up ground, sweating bodies, fear. The radio had been so certain, but apart from the boys who had taken his car, there were no soldiers: was it all a trick? Were the boys who took his car even German? Adam felt himself grow hot with humiliation, a welcome distraction from the thought of Anna and his daughters standing in the mud, and what Anna must think of him, how angry she must be at his failure.

It was dusk as he limped back into the centre, his feet screaming in the smart shoes, made for pacing on carpet, in an office. The streets were still clogged with people, late-deciders, scurrying and looking around them like field mice under hunting owls. All eyes looked to the sky in impulsive, cringing expectation, but it remained clear. From streets away, Adam heard shouts, unmistakeably military in their strange sing-song aggression, but couldn't make out words, whether German or Polish. As he turned onto Bernardyńska, like a runaway child slouching home, his insides, which had seemed to crawl upwards, cramming into his chest and throat, began to settle. Anna would be there, and they would make a new plan. He wondered, looking up at the row of shuttered windows, which other neighbours would still be here. Wawel Castle stood benign and calm, and he scanned for a new flag, reflexively, just as he had the last few days and that very morning, neighbours arriving with every new broadcast. He stopped with a withering feeling of horror as he saw, finally, the red and black fluttering on the highest turret. Perhaps until then he had not truly believed it. 'Look, look,' he urged one of the trickling people, who carried a suitcase in each hand. Adam grabbed the man by the arm. 'Look, look, the Wawel. See, they've put up the flag, they're really here.'

The man nodded. 'I know, son,' he said, and gave Adam a weak smile. Adam almost laughed at 'son', for they seemed to be of an age, but perhaps in his wonder Adam seemed younger.

'Yes,' Adam said, feeling a fool even as his fear grew. 'So they're really here.'

'They're really here,' the man echoed kindly. He added, 'Good luck to you,' as he walked on, swinging his cases.

Adam was only yards from the apartment, but felt a thousand eyes, watching from every turret and wall of the castle, as he approached home. Reaching the door, he was already planning to stay sequestered in the back of the flat, away from the huge windows he was so proud of, as he waited for the family to arrive; or perhaps they were already here and waiting for him. He stood for stupid seconds touching the door, waiting in his panic for Robert to open it. Mechanically he felt his empty pockets, praying for the cool weight of brass. He tried the door, the bell, knocked on the window, knowing it was hopeless. When he laughed, an explosion of nervous tension, a woman rushing past, a young child swinging on her arm, spat on the floor. 'What's wrong with you?' she said, before storming on.

Adam cupped his hands to his face and looked through the tiny crack in the downstairs shutters. All was dark. His key was in his car. 'Anna?' he called through.

A narrow alleyway led to the back entrances of the apartment blocks, for deliveries and servant business. Adam trailed his hands along the damp wall, grateful for the glum light that shone from a lamp in the back courtyard. A pocket of quiet sat over the trees and benches of the shared garden, ice glittering on bark and wood. He felt the windows of the Bernardyńska buildings as eyes on him as he took the back steps leading to the kitchen. He knocked and called to silence. Even the dogs had gone. He looked up to see only darkness behind his neighbours' shutters, listened hard for a few seconds, the rustle of his own blood in his ears, before looking for a rock to smash one of the window panes.

He crept through his own house like a burglar, shying at the floorboard that creaked too loudly, the coat hanging in the hallway that looked like a figure standing and waiting to arrest him. He battled with his body as he went, stern with his heart and his lungs, his shamefully shaking fingers as he clasped doorknobs. Dotty and Janie had left everything immaculate, from the swept kitchen floor to the folded newspapers neat in piles and screaming danger, serene next to a vase of chrysanthemums in the dining room. There was no sign of Anna and his daughters. The strange quiet persisted, his steps echoing: the rugs had gone, of course, he realised, and there was no hum of trams and traffic, only the odd stray cry from the street, wordless shouts. Across Kraków, people were vanishing under floorboards, disappearing into attics and cellars, climbing into the sewers, curling up like mice, trying to become dormant until this all passed.

In the room where that morning he had stood with his neighbours watching the Wawel and drinking, Adam paced for a few minutes, feeling his pockets. He drew out his wallet and papers, laid them on the small desk, next to the newspapers and flowers. He took off his coat and felt in the lining for the cash, thumbed it through the fabric where Janie had sewn it in. He would need more once the family arrived and they had to try again; now that the chaos of the first day had waned, it would be harder to slip away. Or they might stay, he thought, glancing around the dark room, stripes of light from the shutters slicing across the paintings on the wall. All seemed well enough. Stefan was staying.

He was still holding the coat, and his left hand strayed to the inner pocket, stroked the roll there for a moment, the smoothness of the canvas almost like marble under his fingers. When he pulled her out she was a little crushed, bent in the middle. He unrolled her on the desk, Alicia's little hand holding the handkerchief, the red of the dress hanging in its folds, the beginning of her hair falling over the shoulder. The clumsy crease he had made cut her in half, across her arm and Jozef's pleats in paint, the darker streams of red. In the low light the colour was warming in the chill room and Adam began to think of lighting a fire in the grate. He'd already turned to look at the fireplace when he heard breaking glass, the sound travelling up the staircase, from where something had smashed the windows around the front door. The apartment shuddered as the door was wrenched open by force of something. Footsteps in the hallway and on the stairs. He strained for Anna's voice, Karolina's unmistakeable measured tread, Alicia's quicker, stomping feet, but it was male voices that called to one another as they came up the stairs, laughter mixed with German.

He snatched the painting, rolled it up again. Some strange panic-pulse in his mind drew him to the fireplace as though he could ignore the crisis and light the fire; he even cast about for a match before crouching down to look up the chimney. He couldn't fit; even so thin, he would be stuck at the waist and his legs would dangle. They'd laugh at him and pull him out and beat him on his own carpet.

He heard them rifling through the lower rooms as he took the stairs up to his daughters' rooms, full of scattered clothes and Karolina's books. He knew where Alicia's hiding place was, the loose panel of the skirting board. It popped out with a tiny satisfying click, and he almost vomited from fear, hearing the sound travel across the room and stop at the door. Voices were carrying from the rooms below, laughter and the turning over of furniture. He thought he heard the clink and glug of wine in glasses.

As he fled down the back stairs, feeling every hair on his body on end, every nerve set alight, Adam couldn't believe his own stupidity; it was just a thing made of canvas and paint. Still, he reasoned as he clambered through the back window: it was for Alicia; his little Alicia loved that painting, and she would want it kept safe until the world could be put right again.

Acknowledgements

Thank you: Ed Wilson, Anna Kelly, Helen Garnons-Williams, Alex Gingell, Naomi Mantin, Franciska Fabriczki, Jo Walker and all the brilliant team at 4th Estate.

Thank you, as ever, to my wonderful family and friends, and especially to my dad for not being annoyed with me for pillaging and mangling his family stories.

I'm grateful to Arts Council England for funding a research trip to Kraków in 2016 to see the real painting on which this work is based: *Portrait of a Girl in a Red Dress (Józefa Oderfeldówna)* by Józef Pankiewicz. Many thanks to Robert Kotowski, director of the Muzeum Narodowe in Kielce, for kindly meeting with me and sharing his vast knowledge of the painting and its subject. Józefa is my great aunt, and I'd like to thank her and my grandfather, Jerzy, for seemingly not minding that I have changed her name and her story as I pleased, since they have not haunted me about it. I'd also like to thank Janka Wasserberg, and Anna and Pietror, for being so generous with their time and stories.

Arts Council England also kindly funded a week at an Arvon writing retreat in Devon in 2016, where I wrote thousands of words, few of which have actually ended up in the book you have just read, but which sparked its story. Many thanks to the lovely writers I met there, and particularly to Laurence Scott and Romesh Gunesekera.

I'm grateful to everyone who read early drafts of this book and helped me batter it into shape, particularly my workshop group: Richard Lambert, Vicky Rangeley, Alex Ivey, Tom Benn, Tim Sykes, Gordon Collins and Birgit Larsson. Thank you also to Georgie Codd, Armando Celayo, Ruth Weyman, Leander Deeny and Kate Deeny for reading early drafts and giving me feedback, and also to my eagle-eyed parents for the same.

Thank you to Kate Muirhead at UEA Live, Martin Figura and Peter Goodrum at Café Writers, and Keith Packer at Future FM for opportunities to do readings of the novel in progress.

I'd like to thank my brilliantly supportive colleagues at Norwich School, and especially Maria Brown for discussing Polish swear words with me over morning break coffee.

The detail of Frank and his sister hiding behind the oven in Lwów is borrowed from the family history of my friend Emma Phillips. Sammy's beating, and the sign he is forced to wear, was inspired by the treatment of Dr Michael Siegel. For many other details and stories, I'm indebted to the Schindler Museum in Kraków, the Steven Spielberg Jewish Film Archive and Slawomir Grünberg's film *Saved by Deportation*.